THE LOST VAN GOGH

THE
LOST
VAN GOGH

A. J. ZERRIES

A TOM DOHERTY ASSOCIATES BOOK NEW YORK

THE LOST VAN GOGH

Copyright © 2006 by Al and Jean Zerries

This book is printed on acid-free paper.

Edited by James Frenkel

A Forge Book
Published by Tom Doherty Associates, LLC
175 Fifth Avenue
New York, NY 10010

www.tor.com

Forge® is a registered trademark of Tom Doherty Associates, LLC.

Library of Congress Cataloging-in-Publication Data

Zerries, A. J.
  The lost Van Gogh / A. J. Zerries.—1st ed.
      p.   cm.
  "A Tom Doherty Associates Book."
  ISBN 0-765-31250-6
  EAN 978-0-765-31250-1
  1. Police—New York (State)—New York—Fiction. 2. Art
thefts—Investigation—Fiction. 3. New York (N.Y.)—Fiction.
I. Title.
  PS3626.E77L67 2006
  813'.54—dc22
                                                        2005032940

First Edition: May 2006

Printed in the United States of America

0 9 8 7 6 5 4 3 2 1

To Celia B., who loved to read, and to Herman

ACKNOWLEDGMENTS

Thanks to Barbara Braun, our unflagging agent, as well as to her partner, John Baker. Among others whose knowledge and advice proved invaluable are Frank and Carol Fischer, Sarah Jackson of *The Art Loss Register,* Robert E. Speil, Michael Jude Jannuzzi, Esq., Dr. Albert Sacknoff, Dr. David J. Weissberg, Dr. James D. Frevola, Dr. Elliot Gerdis, Mike and John of Northport's Snug Harbor Marine, Steven A. Schmitt, Captain Frohnhoefer of Sea-Tow, and The Cushing Historical Society. In a class by himself, special thanks to Jim Frenkel.

THE LOST VAN GOGH

CHAPTER
ONE

Neither of the two men trusted the other, but that, after all, was the nature of the business.

Anxious to get started, uncomfortably close, they faced one another in the semidarkness, each with a shoulder pressed against the exit door to the roof. The tight, airless space at the top of the fire stairs barely concealed them, and they strained to keep apart, to maintain the few inches separating them during the long wait.

When they finally emerged at ten-thirty, the brisk breeze that had whipped up at sundown was gone, smothered by a thick, warm haze. Below them, neighborhood air conditioners coughed into action, many for the first time, even though May was nearly over. Nineteen ninety-nine was one of those years when the only sign of spring had been the steady lengthening of the damp, cool days.

Their black clothes and three-day beards were indistinguishable from the rooftop, a vast tarpaper field interrupted by stray ducts and pipes, mechanical weeds sprouting toward the night sky. The shorter man dropped his gym bag next to a vent and knelt to open it. The bag was packed in exact order: the coiled line that ended in a small, four-pronged grappling hook was right on top.

His partner, a man of average height and build, lifted it out and hoisted himself up onto the flat roof of the shed that topped the stairwell. When he stood, legs slightly apart, he was as close as he would come to the twentieth-floor penthouse across the street, two stories above. Both co-op apartment buildings fronted the west side of Park Avenue, and each was by far the tallest structure on its block. Blurred by the night, the two buildings hunkered like opposing mountain peaks on the northwest and southwest corners, the side street a narrow gorge between them. The man on the shed gathered up the line below the hook until he came to the dull glow of a fluorescent paint stripe, then let the rest slither down the side of the shed.

The trickiest part came next, and the smaller man was convinced his new associate—it was the first time they'd worked together—hadn't practiced enough. After all, this was basically a one-shot deal. The slightest miscalculation, and a window could shatter, a chunk of masonry dislodge—hazards not even all the whirring, croaking air conditioners on Park Avenue could drown out. Besides, the guy's eyes had made him jumpy right from the start: heavy-lidded, they moved slow as two gray garden slugs . . . and they never stopped moving. Bracing himself for his partner's screwup, the little guy grabbed his end of the line, just above where it ended in a loop.

Like an easygoing cowboy, the taller man began to swing the line in a lazy circle over his head. Never looking up, he played it out gradually, simultaneously increasing the energy behind its orbit. His hips swung into the rotation, gyrated along for a while, and then he let it fly. The rope soared, arced, and plummeted.

As soon as he heard the faint, metallic clink, the man with the sleepy eyelids began to reel in through his long fingers. The hook had landed on target, and he nodded approvingly at the first hint of a drag on the line. He imagined it skipping from stone to stone along the penthouse terrace. Then, nothing . . . no resistance at all. His fingers stopped. The terrace was enclosed by a three-and-a-half-foot stone balustrade, with vase-shaped balusters that tapered at the top and bottom. The hook had to be dangling between two of them. Unless one of its barbs caught on the curved stone handrail, it would glide right over the top and nose-dive into his building. If it hit a window and alerted a tenant, they'd be forced to abort the job, with a reduced chance of exiting the building undetected.

His breathing shallow, he resumed. Slow and steady, he spooled in the line. It jerked slightly, then locked. Tentatively, he gave it a light tug, then several more, each progressively harder, hoping every yank was working at least one of the prongs deeper and deeper into the railing. Satisfied, he signaled down to his partner to start walking backward with the loop end; every reverse step would increase the tautness of the line.

After flexing his fingers a few times, the taller man hopped off the shed and went straight to the gym bag. He retrieved the next two items, a circle of chain and a ratchet-lever-hoist. He dropped the chain around a sturdy rooftop pipe and attached it to the hook that was on one side of the hoist. Extending from the other side of the hoist was a five-foot chain with a snap link at the end. His partner stretched the rope to it, and, with a sharp, hungry click, it closed over the loop. Then the man with the droopy eyelids worked the hoist's lever; it creaked as the chain fed through, squeezing the slack out of the line. He cranked until the rope was taut, but not rigid. His part had gone well. Now it was all up to the little spider shit, who was peeling off his sweats and running shoes.

His body, sheathed in a one-piece suit of black stretch fabric, could have belonged to a prepubescent child: a flat, compact tube of a torso, no butt, five feet five, one hundred twenty pounds. His face, however, which had been battered far more frequently than it had been repaired, gave no indication it had ever spent much time looking childlike. He dipped into the gym bag and pulled out lightweight ankle boots. Like the rest of his personal gear, they fastened with Velcro strips. Next were two bands fitted with scabbards: the one holding his knife went around his right leg; the one with the pencil flashlight strapped over the left. A thin nylon belt with a pouch in front circled his waist, and a flat strap looped across his back and chest on a diagonal. Tugging on the balaclava—its eyeholes were no bigger than quarters—loosened his earpiece, and it was difficult forcing it back into place through the snug fabric. Last came the gloves, which he worked over his hands as he strode to the parapet.

The tense line slanted low over the edge. Out of habit, he stood in place, scraping his soles back and forth over the gritty tarpaper. He didn't pray. He turned, leaned back, and slipped under the line. Reaching over his head, he grabbed it with both hands, then hooked his ankles around it. The top of his head was closest to the penthouse, his buttless ass closest to the pavement eighteen—soon to be twenty—stories below. If he was going to fall, better higher than lower. Better to splatter than shatter.

Long ago, he'd learned to put himself above it all, in every sense. Nothing could shake his concentration: not the constant thrum of the city, not thoughts of how he'd spend this job's payoff, not the risk of being sighted, not even fear of falling. Hand over hand, propelling himself up with his feet, he advanced steadily until he sensed the building just above his head. Ankles locked tight, he held on with one hand while the other went exploring. The base of one of the balusters was at his shoulder, and he slid his hand around it, twisted his torso, and scrambled over the railing.

The diagram in the information packet he'd memorized depicted the L-shaped terrace as wide, but it didn't prepare him for the lush country garden that sprawled before him. Even through the balaclava, he could smell the fat pink flowers that spilled over vat-size clay pots, the damp earth, and freshly cut grass. Randall Broyce, the guy he was about to rob, had posed next to an antique mower in the *New York Times* article—also thoughtfully included by his employer. Clearly, it wasn't just a photo prop.

"My horticultural addiction, my summer hobby," Broyce had described his patch of green up in the blue. With Central Park two blocks away, the thief didn't see the point of hauling three tons of earth twenty stories skyward. The only part of the garden he'd consider keeping was the gurgling fountain: a marble boy exactly his size, with a smile (a little shy or a little sly?) difficult to read behind the flute raised to his lips.

No pictures of the apartment's interior appeared in the newspaper story, but Broyce's winter hobby was well known; he was one of the most active art collectors in New York City.

The boss's report had also noted that the elevator vestibule and the fire stairs were protected by an unbreachable security system. These constituted the penthouse's only possible entry points . . . until tonight. The very same night Mr. and Mrs. Randall Broyce were cosponsoring a charity fundraiser at the botanical garden up in the Bronx.

Multiple sets of French doors led into the penthouse, and he entered the closest pair. They led into the master bedroom, where a single lamp spread a faintly rosy glow over embroidered bed linens. The painting on the bedroom wall wasn't high on his shopping list. Confidently, he strode past it, out into a hallway. Bypassing the living room, where Broyce had installed the cornerstones of his collection—two mural-size allegories, far too unwieldy—he slid through the shadows to the climate-controlled room where the more portable master-pieces were housed. To maintain the proper temperature and humidity, the door was supposed to be kept closed at all times, but the thief, wary of cutting himself off from the rest of the vast apartment, left it slightly ajar.

He slipped off the bandolier-style strap and draped it over the top of a wing chair. The section that had spanned his back consisted of a long fabric pouch resembling an umbrella sheath. A flick of his finger undid its Velcro closure, and it fanned out to several times its original width.

Playing his flashlight over the art on the walls, he made matches with the photos locked in his memory. When he came to the primary piece, the one he absolutely would not leave without, he wasted no time. He plucked the El Greco portrait off the wall and laid it facedown on the wide library table in the center of the room. A nudge with his knife in the right places, and the brittle antique gilt frame split with a hollow pop and broke apart. The knife sliced along the rear edge of the backing. Almost tenderly, he laid the canvas on the deeply cushioned seat of the wing chair, then whisked the frame's splintered remnants off the table. Under the balaclava, he was smiling: anything beyond the El Greco was pure gravy.

Number two was a Frans Hals portrait, a Dutch merchant with an alcoholic's spongy nose, decked out in a black suit and wide lace collar. Evidently, the frame had been replaced recently, secured with triple the nails necessary. All of them were tiny, and frustratingly snug. By the time he pried the last one out, at eleven twenty, the burglar had fallen behind his optimum schedule. Maybe not *every* painting . . . maybe one less.

He was finally coaxing frame from canvas when a series of mechanical reverberations began: The hum of the elevator, ascending. The muffled grind as it docked at the penthouse. By the final click-click-click of the parting doors, his flashlight was off and stuffed in its scabbard. His knife was at the ready.

This wasn't supposed to be happening. A third man was down on the street. Even such an overgrown oaf as he should have been able to handle his single, simple duty: to contact him and Sleepy-Eyes if the Broyces returned early. That, of course, had been considered highly unlikely, since the annual affair never even started to wind down until one A.M. He tapped the earpiece through his balaclava; it had worked when they were huddled in the fire stairs and the Broyce limo had pulled away from the building.

Dim light filtered in from the opposite side of the living room, the general direction of the entrance foyer. The staccato click of high heels played across a marble floor. Whoever was wearing them was moaning, gagging. A door banged open and full-pitched vomiting commenced. Frozen, the thief listened for a man's footsteps, strained to hear a husband's commiseration for a wife so violently ill. But nothing was audible except the woman, retching and gasping, spewing and choking.

Despite the dark, he made the decision to go for the second canvas, and edged his blade around the backing. Just past the halfway point, it snagged, making a short, soft ripping sound. His fingers trembled slightly as he worked the knifepoint free. After a quick intake of breath, he fought the urge to increase the cutting pressure, the desire to race through to the end. A long groan tinged with relief sounded just as he completed the circuit. Bending over the seat of the chair, he lined up the two paintings, one on top of the other. The whites of the Dutchman's eyes, boozy but forthright, stared up directly into his. A toilet flushed. Fingers flying, he rolled both canvases lengthwise, into a single scroll. Because there were only two, he didn't have any trouble fitting them into the unfurled fabric holder on the bandolier. When he fastened it across his back, it had the shape of an archer's quiver. Far away, water ran.

Another light snapped on, this time in the living room. He backed up against the wall, sliding toward the door as his mind shuffled his limited options: Back the same way, skirting the living room and out through the bedroom. Or, if she went straight to bed, an exit through the living room's French doors. Either way, there was the risk that she'd see him out on the terrace. And what about the husband? How soon before he showed up? In the split second that he remembered he hadn't closed the library door, light flooded the room.

From behind, he watched a blonde in a long, form-fitting gown enter, her steps shaky. Long legs and high heels put her near six feet. Except for two flimsy crisscrossed strips of gray silk, her square shoulders and broad, well-toned back were completely bare to the waist. The exposure of so much luminous skin, which might have emphasized a smaller woman's vulnerability, made her seem all the more formidable. Slender and shapely as she was, compared to him, she was an NFL fullback.

Her right hand was up, pressing something against her forehead. When the empty space left by the El Greco registered, it hit the floor with a wet smack. She looked to the left, then to the right, and took a step toward where the Hals had hung. One of her shoes rolled over a fragment of the El Greco's broken frame. Just as she stumbled, he rushed her, grabbed her by the hair, and snapped her

head back, arching her throat up to meet his knife. Through his glove, he felt the
hot gush of blood. He kept up the pressure on the blade, driving it deeper and
deeper, until the steel finally struck bone. Her body slumped, incredibly heavy.
He leaped out of the way, and she fell on her smooth, naked back with a thud
that made him thankful he wasn't pinned under it.

Blood was splattered over her face and chest, and it pumped onto the floor
in twin rivulets. Even so, it was impossible to ignore the one piece of jewelry she
was wearing. Her diamond necklace, with its big square stones, would clean up
very nicely. Kneeling down, he used the tip of his knife to lift it away, then tore it
off with one hard wrench . . . his personal reward for a job that could've been a
total disaster. Nearby on the floor was what she'd been holding to her forehead—
a moistened, fringed finger towel with a big *B* for Broyce. He used it to turn off
the library's lights and close the door. Back on the terrace, he wiped down his
knife and gloves with the damp cloth and wrapped it around the necklace. Next,
he removed a large triangular snap link from the pouch at his waist, and dropped
the towel-package in its place—the *B* for Bonus right on top.

After climbing over the balustrade, he clicked the link over the line. Grabbing the triangle's base with both hands, he stretched out his legs and once again
crossed his ankles over the rope. The link lurched forward only a foot or so, just
far enough to leave him stranded between buildings. The only way to get moving again without jerking the line was to concentrate his weight. Eyes clamped
shut, every muscle straining, he lowered his legs as slowly as he could. For a few
seconds he dangled, limp as a rag doll, twenty stories in the air. Suddenly, he
heard a whirring—the link speeding along so fast he barely pulled his legs up in
time to avoid crashing into the opposite roof's ledge.

The man with the hooded eyes reached out to steady him. Using his own
knife, he stretched up to cut the line. It recoiled like a shot. Although it was too
thin to see in the dark, it was easy to picture it, hanging slack against the wall of
Broyce's building. "You're early," he whispered. "Did you get them all?"

"All?" Incredulous, his partner peeled off his balaclava. "I figured something was wrong with my earpiece, but you didn't get a signal either, did you?"

The other man's hand flew to his ear. He jerked his head hard to one side,
then began to tap at his earpiece.

The smaller man's bitter smile was stretched wider by an old scar at one
corner of his mouth. "Just what I thought! That big, worthless lump of shit
downstairs screwed up! What do you bet that idiot's fast asleep?" He picked up
his neatly folded sweatshirt and pulled it over his head. "The wife came home
early. Score two portraits for us, one still life for Broyce."

CHAPTER
T W O

His body had been balking lately, presenting him with the past-due bill for all the old push-to-the-limit shit. Back then, it never occurred to him how pointless it might seem from the perspective of thirty-five. But he wasn't the first young guy who'd been seduced into believing in his own invulnerability.

He broke through the surface, forcing down the sputtering, the gasps for air. His best time underwater was a distant memory; even the diminished goal he pushed for required a feat of will.

"I frankly feel fucking fine, Fred!" he shouted, loud enough for the words to bounce back off the tile walls of the deserted Police Academy pool.

Years ago, after some Navy doctor had figured out that the inability to pronounce two consecutive words beginning with *F* signaled an embolism, a full-throated "I feel fine!" was required of SEALs surfacing from a deep dive. Detective Clay Ryder preferred the enhanced version. Even if he didn't feel fucking fine. Even if he hadn't felt fucking fine for a long fucking time.

That those were often his first spoken words since leaving work the previous evening no longer disturbed him. Dripping his way back to the showers, he avoided eye contact with the small group of early-morning regulars headed in the opposite direction.

He now knew all he had to about the coming day: if he was going to die, Death by Air Bubble wouldn't be the cause.

About forty minutes later, as he settled in at his desk in the big open squad room at Police Plaza, Clay caught sight of Deputy Inspector Hickey striding into his office. Only a few minutes passed before his head reemerged, an oversize periscope scanning the room. Most of the Special Investigation Division detectives weren't in yet, so it was easy for him to zero in on his objective.

"Ryder," Hickey called out, "you know a Lieutenant Malenkov?"

"Yes, Chief. From when I was up in the Nineteenth."

"This Malenkov's still up there—Precinct Squad Commander. They had a murder-burglary last night. Some pricey paintings were lifted. He knows you're the Art Guy, and asked for you to come up and take a look."

"Okay with you?" asked Clay.

"He got the standard galleries-and-museums speech, but I gave it a nod." He held out a scrap of paper. "Here's his contact number." When Clay walked over to take it, Hickey muttered, "I don't want to loan you out every time somebody snatches an Elvis on velvet."

"With all due respect, Inspector, a really mint period Elvis isn't all that easy to come by these days. But even if it were, it would bring only a fraction of the price you'd get for a floating pig's head in Lucite by—"

"A pig's head, a pig's ass," Hickey muttered, as he retracted his head into his office. "Just remember, Ryder, Major Case is your squad, and we're first in line anytime your desk is clear of that art crap."

Not bothering to sit down again, Clay punched in the number. Major Case was one of several squads composing the Special Investigation Division. Kidnappings, bank robberies, extortion, unlawful construction practices, and truck hijackings and commercial burglaries in excess of $100,000 were the business of Major Case. The squad also covered art thefts from—as the DI had pointed out—museums and galleries. Clay had been the Art Guy for just over six months.

The job had opened up when Hank Vandam was transferred. To his credit, Vandam never hid the fact that he lacked any art training whatsoever. Neither did he attempt to conceal that an hour inside a museum triggered his otherwise latent claustrophobia. Vandam's excellent job performance as the Art Guy was based on his finely honed investigative skills, even if the first thing that came to mind when he heard the name Goya was a can of beans.

When news of the transfer filtered through Major Case, Clay waited to be tapped as a replacement. After a week, he knocked on Hickey's door and presented himself as Vandam's qualified successor.

Hickey didn't bother to mask his surprise. "The art thing? You?"

"I have a B.A. in art history. After I left the Navy, I worked at Esterbrook-Grennell."

"No shit? The big auction house?"

"Two years."

Hickey rolled back from his desk and stretched his legs. He had a tall, gangly build, and they extended out like a pair of stilts attached to size-15 shoes. "Art and underwater demolition—you have to admit it's one odd mix, Ryder."

"Like art and being a cop?"

That pairing, even weirder to Hickey, made his bushy black eyebrows meet above his nose.

"I'm proud of my service record, Sir," Clay blurted out, "but it tends to overshadow the art credentials. They're in my personnel file, like bookends around the Navy, but it's like they're printed in invisible ink."

The DI stood, terminating their interview. "No promises. You know how it is when a job like this comes up. I'll look into it . . . do what I can."

Later, Clay discovered that Hickey had been trying to unload the art position the entire week. But all that mattered was that he got the job, the first good thing in his life for a long, long time.

"Ryder. It's been a while."

Lieutenant Malenkov's deep, scratchy voice sounded exactly the way he looked: a husky man with a perpetual five-o'clock shadow. "We have a homicide up here, plus some big-ticket paintings are missing."

"Give me the address, Lieu. I'm out of here in five minutes." The number on Park Avenue in the seventies meant nothing to him, but the name was another story. "Randall Broyce was killed? The big collector?"

"Big everything." Malenkov lowered his voice. "A big pain in the ass, and I only met him a couple of hours ago. No, it's his wife who's been painted out of the picture."

The Crown Vic's brakes screeched at the lightest tap, and its air conditioner blew hot air; the crawl up the FDR Drive was worse than being trapped inside a skirling bagpipe. Exiting at Sixty-first Street, Clay considered the shrinking dimensions of his loner life, a loaner cop in a loaner cop car. To escape, he switched on the radio and caught his old precinct's frequency as he headed toward the Broyce crime scene. A few blocks later, a red light provided another distraction: the oversize arrangement a florist was struggling to fit through a funeral parlor entrance—a heart of red carnations the size of a backboard, with white carnations spelling out "Our Bad Ass" across it.

The radio jolted his attention back with an urgent "Man with Gun!" call. The location was only blocks away, Eighty-first between Park and Lexington. Before the rest came over—the gunman had been spotted inside the open door of a United Parcel Service truck—Clay had the red light jammed on the roof and was flying up the First Avenue fire lane. As he approached from the east on Eighty-first, he watched a squad car charge down Lex, first on the scene. The driver straddled the blue-and-white across the corner, closing off the block to vehicles. Clay angled the Crown Vic to tighten the seal. He could see the big brown van on the north side of the street. It was just beyond the Eighty-first Street entrance of the tall corner building, parked along the yellow-painted curb bordering a fire hydrant. The two uniforms were already out of their car and closing in on it.

Flapping his shield over the breast pocket of his sports jacket, Clay took off after them just as a solid, square-built man a couple of inches under six feet hopped out of the UPS truck's passenger side. The shapeless gray shirt and pants he was wearing gave him the look of a building superintendent, some sort of maintenance man. Long hair straggled out from under what appeared to be a Mets cap. He started toward Park at a steady clip, but not so fast as to call attention to himself. Evidently, he didn't suspect that whatever had happened in the truck had been observed and reported. Clay saw no gun.

The only pedestrians in view were a pair of elderly women cooing over what had to be grandchildren-snapshots. As they strolled toward Lex, the maintenance guy gave their Kodak moment a wide berth—otherwise, they would've walked right into him.

The officers kept up behind him until the old ladies were out of the way. The cop on the right, his hand playing edgily over the butt of his holstered gun, called out, "Hold it right there!" The guy in gray responded by picking up the pace a bit, even though the block's steady uphill grade suddenly became more pronounced. Escalating to a take-no-shit tone, the cop ordered, "You, in the gray uniform, halt!"

As he passed two converted carriage houses, the man glanced over his shoulder for the first time. Droopy mustache, big aviator glasses with deeply tinted lenses. As soon as he saw the police, he broke into a run. So did the cops. Weighted down by his equipment, the heavier of the two officers, who was radioing in the suspect's direction, began to lose ground as the slope steepened. His partner outpaced him, but not enough to narrow the gap between him and the alleged gunman.

For years, Clay had pondered why some cops let themselves get so badly out of shape. In that moment, he realized that they had something there: the masochist who never missed a day at the gym would always beat the beer belly to the barrel of some drugged-out perp's gun. Yelling, "I'm on the job! I'm on the job!" to alert them he was NYPD, he came up behind the cops just as the object of their pursuit rounded the corner onto Park Avenue. The large apartment building that took up the corner extended a good way down Eighty-first, with two separate entrances for doctor's offices.

Suddenly, the man reappeared, a gun in his hand.

Simultaneously, Clay and one of the officers screamed out, "Gun!" and they all scrambled for cover. The more agile of the two catapulted into the gutter between two parked cars; his heavyset partner ducked behind a tree circled by a wrought-iron fence—some arborist's double shield against the dings of parallel parkers and the dung of dogs. Clay pressed himself flat in the scant hollow of the doctor's doorway closest to Park.

In a shooter's stance, the guy in gray fired off a series of *Thwhommmps!* that boomed as if he had a portable cannon in his hand. From the way he was aiming, he'd taken no notice of Clay: he was concentrating solely on the uniforms. Glass and metal erupted everywhere—his attempts to hit the cop concealed between the cars turned into an automotive volcano at full spew. The force of the barrage left a Hyundai literally rocking on its wheels. A large chunk of the stone lintel framing Clay's doorway exploded into a nasty spray of shards before the bullet lobbed to the ground—a ricochet, most likely off the tree guard. It hit so close, he instantly recalled his post-swim cockiness about air bubbles. Now he could add Death Mode #2 to the Never-in-the-Same-Day list: Slug Deflected Off Anti-Dogshit Device.

The firing ended abruptly. Ears ringing, Clay cautiously bent forward, gun drawn. The gunman was gone. "Anyone down?" he called out. Keeping their cover, both cops signaled that they were okay. Clay pointed to himself and then to the corner, to let them know he was going to Park. If he was going to die today, he'd do the world a favor and take Handy Andy along with him.

In a low squat and with gun drawn, the leaner of the two uniforms zigzagged across to the downtown sidewalk, where he began to advance behind the parked cars. Stooped down, his hefty partner abandoned his tree and crept ahead in the roadway, using the cars on the uptown side as a shield. As horns joined in protest against the bottleneck back on Lexington, the light on Park Avenue turned green, and traffic glided quietly uptown. Clay took off, stopping just short of the corner. Hugging the wall, he edged along, ready to round onto Park. As soon as the officers were positioned to give him cover, he took a darting glimpse around the side of the building. No sign of the gunman. He swerved onto the avenue in a firing stance.

No one was on the sidewalk except the tall, slender blonde coming toward him. No headphones, so her hair-tossing played to a beat inside her head. The closer he sprinted, the younger she looked—just a kid, fifteen if she was a day. Judging by her skimpy, expensive clothes and the portfolio tucked under one arm, she was either a model or a hooker; whichever, she should've been in school. The music stopped when she finally registered the gun in his hand.

Pointing to his shield, Clay shouted, "The man who just came around the corner—which way did he go?"

Clearly, that was too much for her to process at once. She looked around, and, as if she suddenly understood, asked back, "You mean the janitor kind of guy?"

"Right," he replied, with a hurry-up wave of his left hand. "Where'd he go?"

"He got into a car." She gestured toward an empty stretch of curb Clay had just run by. "It was parked there. Someone drove him away."

He began to reholster his gun. "What kind of car?"

"A black car."

"Make? Model? Year?"

"The only car I know is yellow. You know, as in cab," she giggled nervously. His scowl made her take a small step backward. This was a major airhead, as well as a minor, and his impatience was getting in the way. But hard as he tried to lower his voice and speak slowly, she contributed no more, not even the smallest detail.

Wary of his mounting frustration, she finally asked, "Are you really a cop? Is this being filmed? Like that TV show?"

Before he could point out that there wasn't a camera in sight, cars converged on the mouth of Eighty-first Street, two from the north, three from the south. Grim-faced cops barreled out, weapons drawn. A wide-shouldered man in a rumpled suit, his beard stubble visible from twenty yards, emerged from a backseat. Clay waited long enough for the preliminary debriefing of the two uniforms, then escorted the teenager back around the corner.

"Ryder, can you believe this shit?" was Lieutenant Malenkov's greeting. "A Park Avenue crime wave! Like Fort Apache's rich uncle, Fort Ritz." He glanced at the blonde. "Why isn't she in school?"

After Clay explained that she was the only witness so far—and not to the actual shooting, either—Malenkov waved over the patrol sergeant, the officer in charge of securing and setting up the crime scene. Taking them aside, Clay confided, "She says she saw the shooter get into a waiting black car. Period."

"It's been that kind of a day since two A.M, hasn't it?" Malenkov rasped over his shoulder to the sergeant as he steered Clay east on Eighty-first. "The only good news is that everyone's alive up here, including, I just heard, the UPS driver. The perp pistol-whipped the piss out of him. The bullets, those he saved for the cops." He stopped and studied the area. "Where were you?"

Clay pointed out his doorway. Close by lay the spent bullet that had chinked the stone frame. Both of them stooped down briefly to examine it. Malenkov glanced around at the bullet-riddled cars that looked like the bull's-eye in an aerial bombing raid. "Son of a bitch!" Malenkov muttered. "The prick was using hollow points."

He called over to a detective who was on his hands and knees where the guy in gray stood when he blitzed them. "Tommy, whatta you got?"

"Looks like he emptied a clip, Lieu. Seven casings—a .45."

Malenkov pointed to the sidewalk. "One right here and six to go." Squinting up at the buildings on both sides of the street, he added, "Make sure every single one is accounted for. The way today's going, number seven hit some old lady sitting on the crapper."

"Mean fucking gun," said Clay. "It sounded like a howitzer." He and Malenkov headed toward the UPS truck. A gurney was being wheeled back to an ambulance waiting at Lex.

"Did you get anything out of him?" Malenkov asked the young officer stationed in front of the van. The day was sunny and turning hot, and her hat was riding low on her forehead, slid forward by perspiration.

"He was pretty groggy, Sir. EMS got his name out of him. They seemed to think that was a good sign."

"What'd the perp get away with?"

"The driver was definitely rolled. No wallet, no watch. I heard UPS is sending another truck to transfer the packages, so I guess they'll figure out what's missing from their manifest. But from what I saw, Sir, except for some blood, everything looks pretty neat back in there."

Malenkov nodded, then turned to Clay. "Did you notice if the guy was carrying anything?"

"He didn't even have his gun in his hand until he came back around the corner. No, not that I saw."

Taking a step back, Malenkov studied the van. "You have a car here?" he asked Clay.

"That Crown Vic by the corner."

"Okay. Drive me back to Broyce's place."

When they reached the car, Clay asked, "Lieu, a getaway car on a nickel-and-dime job like that—wouldn't you call that pretty unusual?"

"Unusual?" Malenkov muttered. "Used to be a Saturday night special and the subway. Now it's a bazooka and a chauffeur. Don't ask me what's unusual anymore."

CHAPTER
THREE

Not one, but two uniforms were posted outside the co-op. The doorman, his supreme authority over comings and goings temporarily suspended, glared at Clay, yet another invader from the proletariat, as he followed Malenkov into the building.

The lieu pressed the elevator button marked PH. Broyce's penthouse took up the entire twentieth floor. Under normal circumstances, Clay noted, the elevator would permit access to the foyer only if unlocked by a cylindrical, notched key. After that, there was the alarm keypad at the side of the elevator door to contend with, a camera, and a motion detector.

As they wended their way through the crime-scene people, he kept upping the ante on how many apartments the size of his own one-bedroom could fit inside Broyce's place. Without seeing the whole spread, he'd gotten up to a dozen when they came to the L-shaped terrace. It made for another dozen, easy, and that wasn't even counting the ivy-covered Italianate tower at the rear. Malenkov ambled over to the railing and lit a cigarette. While he basked in the first sunshine to make an appearance in a week, Clay took in the Victorian glass conservatory, trees, shrubs, gurgling fountain, and emerald lawn.

"Who's up in the tower, Lieu? Rapunzel?"

"Nope. Just a two-story water tower in disguise."

"How many acres?"

"Amazing, huh?" Malenkov took a deep drag on his cigarette. "I think this was the first time I ever had to stop gardeners from mowing the scene. Sure pissed off the land baron." Smiling, he buried the butt in the perfectly balanced soil of a terra-cotta planter. "That got to him. So did the stolen paintings. The missus—wife number four—that grief is more subdued."

Shielding his eyes, Clay squinted up at the sun. "Got a time?"

"The medical examiner says eleven-thirty, midnight. The Broyces were at some society shindig up in the Bronx. She gets sick, barfs in the ladies' room, tries to stick it out, goes to woof again, bolts just before eleven. The chauffeur drops her off here, goes back to wait for Broyce, who had to stay because he was getting some green thumb award." For emphasis, Malenkov held up his middle finger. "According to the chauffeur, she rode home with her head hanging out the window all the way back. Ran out as soon as he pulled up, not a word to the doorman, just sprinted for the elevator. So the time checks out, Broyce was in the Bronx, and she wasn't the only one at the affair who got sick . . . just one of the first."

"What about the alarm system?"

"Apparently she opened it and reset it immediately. Nothing went to the dispatcher. No signs of tampering. There's a radio backup in case anyone fucks with the phone line. They have panic remotes and the only other way in is the firedoor. Equally, if not more, secure."

Clay pointed up at the cloudless sky. "Helicopter?"

"You ever hear the expression, 'by hook or by crook'?" Malenkov beckoned Clay closer to the balustrade that enclosed the rooftop. "This time, the crook used a hook." They stopped in front of a four-pronged grappling hook; two of its barbs were imbedded in the curved limestone handrail. From it, a thin line dangled down the building's exterior.

"You've got to be kidding," Clay whispered in disbelief. Careful not to touch the railing, he angled over the side to gauge the length of the rope. "What did the downstairs neighbors say?"

"Nobody saw, nobody heard."

Clay straightened up. "How the hell can you toss a grappling hook up on a vertical line, anyway?"

"You can't." Malenkov pointed to the apartment house on the corner opposite. "But *that* building—its wall to this wall, sixty feet. We're two prewar stories higher, so add about thirty feet more. Our dangling rope—after being cut—measures eighty-five feet, eight inches."

"Jesus!"

"No, Jesus walked on water. Whoever did this walked on his balls, as in what a set of. We've already got that roof blocked off, and the crime-scene guys'll be fine-combing it for evidence soon as they finish here. The tenants over there are being questioned as we speak." Malenkov, eyes scrunched against the sun, stared across at a low shed. "Plenty of ways to sneak into that building and hang out in the housing at the top of the fire stairs."

"Then come out and launch the hook somehow?"

"Needless to say, we're checking out every store in the Northeast that sells climbing gear." Malenkov raised his eyebrows expectantly. "Ryder, in your experience with art theft . . . any of this look familiar to you?"

"Twenty stories up, no net? No cat burglar I ever heard of. Not even in the movies." From far away, a horn beeped, and Clay looked down at a taxi trying to get around a garbage truck. Both looked no bigger than matchbox toys, and the sheer daring exercised the night before gave his stomach a churn. Even to him, relentlessly government-trained to take risks, the gamble was staggering. "Maybe I'll do better after I see how he worked the inside."

"Sure." Malenkov's arm swept toward half a dozen French doors that opened onto the terrace. "Broyce said they never had reason to lock any of these, so we're guessing the killer entered at the closest point—the master bedroom suite."

Blinking at the Cassat on the wall, Clay wondered how many entire lifetimes of cop-pay it was worth. Something about the bed struck him as odd, until he realized that the embroidered pale peach linens had been ironed—they were that flawlessly smooth.

"You didn't tell me Broyce might be having financial problems, Lieu."

Malenkov's head whipped around. "What'd I miss?"

"No mint on the pillows."

A hallway outside the master suite brought them to a living room the size of a tennis court. Waving a dismissive hand as he breezed by its two panoramic seventeenth-century paintings, the lieu said, "These he didn't touch. The murder—" A few more steps, and he realized Clay was no longer right behind him. "Kid in a candy store, Ryder? Man, you remind me of how I used to hide the latest *Playboy* inside a big art book. I bet you hid your art book inside—"

"Right. And this is like being locked in the bathroom with the centerfold. In the flesh." He sighed. "Go on, I'm right behind you."

"The murder," Malenkov resumed, "took place in what Broyce calls his *salon*. Temperature controlled, like a goddamn wine cellar—if you keep the door closed. Our connoisseur is all bent out of shape because we've had it propped open so long."

Clay saw the chalk outline of the body from the hallway.

"Considering the paintings survived a few pre–air conditioning centuries," Malenkov added, "I don't feel guilty about taking my time."

"Big woman," Clay noted as they walked around the chalk marks.

"Big, but she didn't have much of a chance. The intruder grabbed her from behind, slit her throat. M.E. says she was dead before she hit the floor."

"My God!" Clay was already pacing along the walls. "What the hell did he steal, if he left these? Five, six . . . seven! All world-class paintings!"

Malenkov pulled his notebook out of his breast pocket. "Nine, until around midnight last night. The perp took an El Greco and a Hals. The El Greco was there." He indicated the blank space opposite them, on the far side of an antique cherrywood library table. The Hals had evidently filled the blank on the right wall. "Broyce put all his stuff on one of those photo CDs for his insurance company. He printed out copies for us. Here, take a look, and let me know what's your gut on why he took these paintings in particular."

Clay shuffled through the copies. "The El Greco would be up there, definitely. But the Hals . . ." He did a quick survey of the room. "Off the top of my head, no, I wouldn't necessarily call it the second most valuable in here. What about the frames?"

"Those splinters on the floor are what's left of the El Greco's frame—old wood, real brittle."

Clay nodded. "And that's the Hals frame, leaning against the table?"

"Yup. Apparently intact. Oh, and another thing Broyce is crazed about—he's convinced the burglar destroyed the paintings, cut them up. That stuff." Malenkov pointed to two limp heaps at the end of the table.

"No, that's just what's left of the undercanvas," Clay said after a brief examination. "The paintings are affixed to it. The undercanvas runs under the frame and extends around the backing. In most cases, you can slice along the rear edge of the backing and still leave a safety margin of several inches, with no threat to the painting at all. No, the original canvases—wherever they are—should still be intact." Clay squatted down in front of the Hals frame. "Where are the nails?"

"Pile of them over on the corner of the table."

Clay straightened and examined them. "A relatively new frame, no obvious rusting on these nails. They held the Hals snug and secure. The perp had to pry them out one by one, and they're damned little. That took time." He moved back to the undercanvas. "I assume the tech guys did this room first?"

"Right."

"Let's get one of them in here to spread all this undercanvas out flat."

Five minutes later, Clay was comparing the canvas strips. "This is interesting. See how careful he was, cutting the El Greco? The Hals subcanvas is nowhere near as precise. More ragged. See that snag? I still doubt he damaged the painting, but I'd say he was in a hurry here."

"Okay, that makes sense. Like he was rushing because he heard the wife. That had to be a big surprise. Broyce told me they were the sponsors of that Bronx party. Major annual event, always runs late."

Clay nodded. "And so far it looks like everything happened in this room?"

"Nothing's turned up to indicate otherwise—except for the wife heaving in the powder room off the foyer. Broyce got back just after one-thirty. Figured his missus had gone to bed, didn't feel too great himself, had a drink. By the time he finds out the bed hasn't been slept in, locates her, and calls us, it's after two." Malenkov's eyes strayed back to the chalk mark. "Oh, yeah. With all this art stuff, I nearly forgot. Broyce's wife was wearing a diamond necklace worth half a million. It was ripped right off her throat. He gave us computer printouts of the necklace, too."

"Good luck." Clay didn't even bother to look. They both knew that the thief had wasted no time prying the stones out of their settings. "I can't give you good news, Lieu. In this day and age, stealing paintings of this caliber . . . you'd have to be crazy. Or really naïve. No dealer, museum, or auction house would touch anything like this."

"They check all the pictures out on the Internet, right?"

"Right. You've got a better shot at tracking the killer through the climbing gear than by waiting for one of those paintings to turn up."

"No known fences?"

"For stuff in the thousands, not the millions. We're talking lost in space . . . sucked through a black hole."

Like a retractable tape measure, Clay felt himself begin to coil back up. The last couple of hours—confronting the berserk handyman, concentrating on the paintings, studying the crime scene's debris, even just being around Malenkov (a superior he hadn't known personally, but nevertheless associated with a less troubled time)—had temporarily untwisted him, stretched him out, aired him out. But no matter how much better Unwound felt than Wound, there was no holding onto it.

Malenkov shrugged. "Not the news I wanted to hear, but thanks for coming up."

"I still have some computer searches I can do—you never know what'll turn up."

The lieu nodded, then checked his watch. "Got to meet with my detectives. As far as I know, Broyce is taking a nap. You want to look around?"

"Until you kick me out."

As Malenkov did a careful final visual sweep over the remainder of Broyce's collection, he said, "Hard to forget, Ryder, the way you made detective. Did you know I got to the scene just when they were loading you onto the ambulance? Man, you really cleaned some shit off the street that day!" He shrugged. "Who would've figured you were into paintings and all?"

Et tu, Malenkov. Another cop who thought there were two NYPDs—the one he worked for, and the one Clay worked for. "Hey, art makes me hot. We've already established that. Actually, it had a lot to do with me becoming a cop."

The lieu gave him a raised-eyebrow look without raising an eyebrow.

"You take all these art history courses," Clay explained. "You write papers and take exams that test your understanding of what the artist was attempting to express. Answer questions along the lines of, say, 'Which of the major eighteenth-century themes are manifested in this work?' You're expected to probe and interpret the juxtaposition of objects, symbolism, color, linear composition, religious and historical context . . . and so on. They're your clues. The picture, versus The Big Picture. There's a correlation between that and solving a crime."

"I never saw it that way before," Malenkov conceded.

"Neither did I. I was never very good at it. You can guess the only kind of artist I ever was."

"A bullshit artist?" The lieu's eyes narrowed. "Are you bullshitting me right now, Ryder?"

"Maybe."

"So whoever killed Mrs. Broyce is like . . . the artist?"

"Right. We just have to figure him out."

Malenkov shook Clay's hand and headed for the door. As he walked out, his sandpaper voice grated back, "Ryder, I don't believe for a minute that's the real reason you became a cop."

"No? So what was?"

"You just wanted a better fucking medical plan."

CHAPTER

FOUR

The next day started out with considerably less of a bang: a stop at a Fifty-seventh Street gallery neatly scammed by a con artist dressed head to high heels in Chanel, whose gender was still in question. After grabbing a quick lunch, Clay didn't arrive back at Police Plaza until early afternoon. The phone started to ring before he had a chance to glance through his messages.

"Clay—it's Florene."

Florene Cope was Clay's contact at the Metropolitan Museum of Art. A former NYPD detective herself, she'd taken early retirement and entered the private sector. "Lady, I know at least thirty Florenes. Which one?"

"The smartest and most beautiful of all." Quickly turning all business, she said, "Listen, a situation's come up. Don't ask me to explain over the phone. The director asked me to call in the NYPD."

"The *director's* involved?" Few dared challenge the man's unofficial job description: Ra-God of Culture. If he was not supreme over all the cosmos, then at least he ruled the runner-up, New York City. His voice was literally the Voice of the Met—museumgoers with rented headphones crashed into one another like bumper cars while they listened to his guided tour of the Renaissance, or his take on the Civil War's effect on Winslow Homer.

"It was the first time I heard him on the phone," Florene confided. "He really talks like that." She paused. "He also had me contact the FBI."

"How much backup should I bring?"

"No, it's not like that. Just you. No danger here, just a *very* unusual set of circumstances. Unique, I think. How soon can you leave?"

"I'm gone."

"You're Detective Ryder, aren't you?"

Fist in midair, he was about to knock on Florene's office door. "How do you know I'm not the FBI guy?" he asked the young woman approaching him.

"Because I'm just back from walking him over. The only man in the museum with sunglasses on. Come on—it's lots of turns and at least four city blocks from here, so I'll take you, too."

Somewhere in the middle of their hike, he asked if she knew what was going on. "Me? Not a clue. All I know is that the director's involved."

She left him at the door of a conference room.

Standing in a cluster at the far end were about a dozen people. One of the women glanced over her shoulder and made eye contact with Clay. Florene looked great, at least five years younger than the last time he'd seen her. He quickly concluded that her gold earrings, mascara, and sleek black dress didn't deserve half as much credit as what she *wasn't* wearing: a gun. After a tight smile his way, she announced, "Our NYPD contact is here." She half-waved, half-pointed at Clay. "Detective Ryder."

"Detective, something interesting arrived in our UPS delivery today."

Florene had hit it right about Director Armand Castelblanco's voice. The resonance on the museum tours was not electronically enhanced. No corner was given to contradiction or to challenges—even Clay shifted into Best Behavior Mode.

Once the knot of men and women around him broke apart, Castelblanco—who could've just stepped out of a John Singer Sargent portrait, so exquisitely tailored and amiably unapologetic for his hauteur was he—took a sideways step as well. Doing so, he revealed a small, unframed oil painting on an easel: a portrait of a man, head to midchest. The subject, well into middle age, was hawk-faced, intense, wary. The artist was unmistakable. Clay moved closer, reeled in by an invisible hook attached to an invisible line.

"A Van Gogh . . . in your UPS delivery?"

"Apparently."

"Saint-Rémy?"

"Very good, Detective!" Castelblanco stared at Florene. "Did you tell him, Miss Cope?"

Small flames of indignation rushed into Florene's cheeks. "As agreed, I mentioned nothing over the phone."

"Then do keep going, Detective! Excellent! Excellent!"

The entire situation was making him uneasy—the irresistible magnet resting on the easel, what he assumed to be Castelblanco's uncharacteristically high spirits, the almost giddy, Christmas-morning anticipation of the Met's top brass. If he wasn't the object of some elaborate joke, maybe he was in one of those dreams where everyone else is dressed for work and you're naked. Or really stupid. His mouth, totally dry, croaked out, "It's the head orderly of the asylum."

"It is indeed!" With the ratcheted-up enthusiasm of a game-show host, the director urged him on. "Name him, and you match the curator!"

"The name is unusual . . . starts with a 'T'. . . . No, I'm afraid the rest escapes me." He was still a few feet away. "Is it . . . authentic?"

Instantly, Clay regretted his question. Stupid had crept through, and won. Only the rankest amateur would have asked. An answer would require a battery of tests—X rays and chemical analyses—followed by a poll of international Van Gogh experts.

Nothing could have made him appear more unprofessional.

Nothing, consequently, could have surprised him more than Castelblanco's reply.

"It's fair to say that we are . . . unanimous in our optimism." With an outstretched arm, the director drew Clay closer to the easel. "Detective Ryder, permit me to introduce you to Monsieur Trabuc." Lightly, he exhaled the *ah* of the "Tra" and blew out the extended *boo* like a puckery kiss, ending it with a hard *k*. Sliding into a stage whisper, he confided, "I'm afraid that he is lost."

For a moment, Clay had the queasy feeling that Florene's assistant had led him directly into one of Saint-Rémy's wards for the insane.

A man pushed forward and handed Clay a business card. "First thing we should do is work out the jurisdiction here." The sunglasses visible in the breast pocket of his dark suit, along with his wooden delivery, hardly lessened the madhouse effect. Clay gave the FBI agent a quick, cursory nod and let himself be drawn back to the painting.

Monsieur Trabuc was gaunt-cheeked, balding, mustached. His guarded, flinty stare was the type that hardens over a lifetime spent witnessing deviant behavior at its most extreme. The overall impression was of a man in a state of constant high alert, primed for the worst to strike from any corner and when least expected. His anxiety was accentuated by restless swirls of paint: in the brilliant blue coat, the wattles under the chin, the sunken cheeks. A background of turquoise, rose, and lemon yellow whirled about him in contrarotation, amplifying the tension. The picture was so suffused with motion, it nearly vibrated when Clay squinted at it.

The Van Gogh, Florene was explaining, was shipped via UPS from Buenos Aires. Shaking her head in disbelief, she added, "As an ordinary package."

The previous day's UPS encounter flashed across his mind: *A few more stops on Eighty-first Street, a left and a quick right, and you're at the Met garage, Fifth and Eightieth. What if the Trabuc had been on that very same van? What if . . .* But he was already trying to take in as much as he could, as fast as he could.

"It came in *that*," said the director. His eyebrows arched in disbelief as he pointed at the untidy heap of paper and cardboard on the conference table. "Sandwiched between two sheets of cardboard, like a slice of luncheon meat. I shudder to think what might have befallen it."

Clay and the FBI guy walked over for a closer look. The cardboard had been cut from two different Argentinean wine cartons. One had held Rio de Plata Malbec, and the other, Cafayate Cabernet Sauvignon. The crumpled paper was tan with a shiny finish. For wrapping paper, it was heavy duty: the creases were still sharp edged where it had been shaped to fit around the cardboard. Wide transparent tape had secured the parcel. Someone had smoothed out the part with the mailing label, a neatly printed "Metropolitan Museum, 1000 Fifth Avenue, New York, New York." The return addressee was a Señora Paula Reyes-Martinez, 14 Plaza del Pescador, Buenos Aires.

The director moved next to them and indicated a square, peach-colored envelope. Beneath it was a matching folded note card. "That was also inside. I was the last of five museum people to touch it. Miss Cope has prepared a list of our names and phone numbers. Understandably, everyone involved has been instructed not to discuss this . . . this event."

Using a pencil, the Fed pushed the envelope aside and lifted the top flap of the note. The handwriting was labored and messy, markedly different from that on the label.

"Here's a translation," said Florene, handing out copies. It was brief:

> *Respected Museum,*
>   *Now I am very old and I want to do this while I still have strength. The picture belonged to a person dead many years. The name I knew him by no matter, because not his real name. His family all dead before him. I send you this picture he kept it locked away secret a long time. Maybe he stole it. Yes, I think he stole. Please give back to its true owner. Or keep. I do not give to the government here because of what they did to Argentine people in the 1970 years. My conscience now is clear.*
>
>   *P. Reyes-Martinez.*

"What kind of market value are we talking about?" the Fed asked bluntly. "Assuming it's genuine, of course."

Castelblanco demurred to a man he introduced as the curator for Van Gogh, Jonathan Haybrook. Aside from Haybrook's age—thirty years past adolescence—Clay had never seen anyone who so strongly resembled the comic book Archie: carrot-topped, freckled, even bow-tied. Haybrook looked dazed, like he just woke up naked in a rumpled bed with Veronica. "This is such an unprecedented situation," he mumbled.

Castelblanco simultaneously translated and embroidered: "This is a *discovery*—a painting that is literally new to everyone."

"But how much . . . ?" the agent pressed.

"Over twenty-five million," Haybrook blurted out. "But it's not difficult to imagine twice that." He swallowed and looked to the director for confirmation.

"That's a question better asked of an auction house. However, if Jon's estimate is off, I'd say he errs on the side of caution."

"Excuse me, Mr. Castelblanco," Clay broke in, "but you and Mr. Haybrook keep referring to this as 'unprecedented' . . . as 'a discovery.' This isn't the first time someone's anonymously dropped an artwork in the hands of a museum. Besides that, I've seen this picture before."

"No, that's just it! You've *never* seen it before, Detective! This painting isn't in any of the three Van Gogh *catalogues raisonées*! This painting vanished as soon as Vincent painted it!" Haybrook's initial bewilderment had quickly given way to excitement. "Because Vincent Van Gogh wrote to his brother Theo regularly, and because Theo's widow took the trouble to organize their correspondence, we have firsthand information about what happened.

"Vincent didn't follow his usual procedure, which was to send Theo the original of his latest painting. Instead, he sent his brother his own copy of Monsieur Trabuc, which we refer to as the studio copy. Although his letter doesn't mention what he did with the portrait from life, it is presumed that he made a gift of it to the sitter—the man you correctly identified as the head orderly at Saint-Rémy, where Van Gogh voluntarily committed himself." Haybrook stopped to catch his breath.

"After the ear thing?" the FBI man asked.

"After his self-mutilation," Castelblanco interjected dryly.

Haybrook resumed. "Theo's studio copy is now in Switzerland. The original was never seen again. We'll run this canvas through the gauntlet of tests and fly in a panel of Van Gogh experts, but I'm willing to stake my reputation on it, here and now—the painting on that easel is Vincent's portrait from life!"

All eyes turned to Trabuc, and Trabuc, out of sorts, stared back.

"It's as if the world's been blessed with a virtually new Van Gogh—that's how most of us here at the museum feel," said Haybrook. "It's absolutely electrifying!"

"No other artist approaches his popularity," Castelblanco added in confirmation. "Van Gogh is perceived as a sort of Art Christ—the tortured soul everyone seems to identify with, or to pity, or to revere, in one way or other. And Trabuc was Vincent's keeper during one of the most desperate periods of his short, unhappy life." Returning to the easel, he positioned himself so that he was looking out at the room at exactly the same angle as Trabuc. "You know what I see, when I look at this portrait?"

The conference room fell still. No one dared presuppose a Castelblanconian thought.

"I see the way every man, woman, and child must have looked at Van Gogh." Narrowing his eyes and hunching his shoulders, the meticulously groomed Castelblanco slid into the role of Superstitious Peasant Woman: " 'Here comes that crazy artist—take care! God only knows what that madman will try next!' "

"What a draw!" a man in the group exclaimed. "An absolute blockbuster! My God, can you see the lines?"

A woman, her arms crossed tight across her chest, countered, "And, right on their heels, millions of claimants! Priorities, people, please! Nothing is more important than tracking down the rightful owner of this painting. We don't want to be caught in the middle of a legal tangle with presumptive Holocaust heirs, like MOMA's mess with that Wanda portrait. I shudder at what exhibition of this piece could lead to."

Except for the name—not Wanda, but Wally—she's absolutely right, thought Clay. Disputed ownership had led to a court order, temporarily preventing Egon Schiele's painting of his red-haired mistress from being returned to Vienna after an exhibition at the Museum of Modern Art.

"I couldn't agree more." A take-charge Florene moved to the fore. "Besides contacting you gentlemen at the FBI and the NYPD, I made two other phone calls. Information in Buenos Aires has no listing for Señora Reyes. I also checked the Art Loss Register. No match in their data bank. Nothing even close."

The Art Loss Register, which listed stolen art online, was a service created by insurance companies and the art trade in 1992. It had quickly become a tool powerful enough to prevent artwork listed on its Web site from coming to sale on the open market.

"I can check out the return address in Buenos Aires," the Fed monotoned, "but I think we all know the chances of that being a real street. And the Bureau can get somebody to talk to the staff at the UPS place down there, but to be honest, I'm not sure what kind of crime has been committed." He held up Florene's translation. "We have this letter, ostensibly from an old lady, who says 'maybe' the picture was stolen. But what if it wasn't? And what about Argentina's laws? Is it state property? Is *she* the thief?"

"Argentina," Clay ventured, "that's the kicker." He looked down at his copy of the translation. "Reyes is old. She writes of someone 'dead many years,' who kept the painting 'secret a long time.' It's hard not to think World War II."

"Right," agreed the agent. "Argentina. Nazi heaven." He spoke with the conviction of someone who'd seen it all on The History Channel.

Clay turned to Haybrook. "Did Monsieur Trabuc spend most of his life in the Saint-Rémy area?"

"I believe so. Let me check." After a few minutes consulting a heap of books that had been piled on the seat of a swivel chair, he answered, "Apparently he worked in Marseilles before Saint-Rémy. But it's safe to say he lived his life in the south of France." Straightening his bow tie, Haybrook added, "I don't know if it's of any consequence, but Van Gogh painted Monsieur Trabuc's wife as

well. Her portrait is mentioned in the same letter to Theo—and the same unusual procedure applied, with the studio copy of Madame Trabuc going to
Theo, instead of the original."

"Really?" Clay perked up. "Who owns the original of the wife?"

"Also a blank. I imagine it would've been rude, making a gift to the husband, but not to the wife, agreed?" The curator brought Clay a thick art book,
open to a portrait of a weathered woman dressed in black. Her expression, if
possible, was even more distrustful than her husband's: a face like a prune, with
a mouthful of lemons. "Theo's copy. It's hanging in St. Petersburg."

"And the actual Madame Trabuc—she spent her life in the south of
France, as well?"

"She did," replied Haybrook.

"Okay," said Clay, "the Trabuc portraits aren't exactly . . . flattering. They
never turned up again. Let's assume they were initially stuck away in an attic in
Provence, maybe looted during the war. How was artwork stolen in France reported, once the Germans were kicked out? Didn't the Allies set something up?
Aren't there records?"

"Mr. Weinberger?" The director beckoned a stocky man with a neat salt-
and-pepper beard. After a whispered consultation, Weinberger consulted his
wristwatch, the director his gold pocket watch, and they both shook their heads,
like two commuters who'd just missed the last train to Greenwich. "Records of
wartime losses are at the Museum of the Jeu de Paume in Paris," said Castelblanco. "It's closed by now."

"But aren't the Jeu de Paume's records shared with the Art Loss Register?"
asked Clay.

Weinberger rocked back on his heels. "The French have their own system."
He rocked forward. "A French system. Two thousand paintings that haven't
been claimed postwar are on display in French museums. On the other hand,
countless claims have been filed for paintings stolen in France that have yet to
be"—he rocked back and looked Clay straight in the eye—"reported as found.
One hundred thousand artworks stolen from French Jews, forty-five thousand
returned. The public has no access to the government dossiers. French policy is
to give information only to claimants."

Clay nodded. "I hear you. I'll put in a call when they open tomorrow."

"If the crime took place in Europe half a century ago, whose jurisdiction is
it?" asked the FBI man, clearly exasperated. "And who's taking custody of the
evidence?"

"You mean that?" Clay pointed to the rumpled papers on the table.

"No, I mean *that*." He pointed to the Van Gogh.

"My God!" Castelblanco broke in, "You wouldn't take it to some evidence
room, would you? A fifty-million-dollar painting?"

"You want to keep it here?" asked the Fed, his voice tinged with relief.

"Where else? It's not as if this were a crime scene! There's no safer place for a painting in the city of New York—until we find the rightful owner, naturally."

Castelblanco couldn't see Florene roll her eyes heavenward at his offer. The last thing she wanted was Trabuc setting off motion detectors on her turf. The federal agent saw an international hot potato. Clay was determined to find out who lost Trabuc.

"That's an excellent solution, Mr. Castelblanco," he said, trying not to meet Florene Cope's angry stare. Monsieur Trabuc offered no opinion.

For the next two days, Clay set his alarm at 3 A.M and squeezed information out of the Jeu de Paume. In the interim, the FBI guy called twice, first to confirm that both Señora Paula's name and Fisherman Plaza were as fishy as expected, and then to report that an elderly lady had in fact brought the package to a Buenos Aires UPS drop.

"She asked the service rep to fill out the label for her—her right hand was shaking, like she had Parkinson's or something. The trembling hand, that's how the UPS agent remembered her. She described her as close to seventy, probably medium height—the 'probably' because she was bent over pretty bad. Anyway, she was wearing big, thick glasses and a black dress. Paid cash."

"Natch. Hair?"

"Scarf over it, but the UPS gal thinks it was gray. Oh, and she also told our person down there that old Paula talked like she wasn't local."

"Meaning . . . not from Argentina?"

"Well, not from Buenos Aires. You know, from out in the sticks." He cleared his throat. "What's your take on this, Ryder?"

"Remember how she wrote, 'now my conscience is clear'? I see a servant or a nurse who lifted the painting when the old guy died, spiteful because she was stiffed for her last days or weeks of work. A petty theft—petty in her estimation—but the kind that would gnaw at a basically law-abiding person. As time passed, she felt compelled to make amends. Didn't give her real name, because it had bothered her long enough, and she was finally setting things right anyway. Any sane person with the slightest inkling of the portrait's worth never would have shipped it like that."

And God, you don't know how close—he stopped himself from telling the agent about Eighty-first Street, not wanting to get into a lengthy explanation. The UPS tracking number on the package had confirmed Trabuc had indeed been on that same truck. By the time the UPS people dispatched to the scene were permitted access and had determined everything on the manifest was accounted for, delivery had to be postponed until the following morning.

"That was where I came out, Ryder. Still waiting on Paris?"

"That French connection—I'm not really counting on it," said Clay.

"It's a slim thread, for sure." The agent took a deep breath. "Well, we're really up to our necks over here with all this Internet crap. Mail fraud, wire fraud, transport of stolen property across state lines . . ." Another deep breath. "So this Trabuc deal . . . my supervisor keeps asking me, *'Where's the crime?'*"

"No problem if you want out," Clay replied, "just put it in writing. Hey, no go in Paris, I've got my next step all planned out."

"What's that?"

"Put Trabuc on a milk carton. 'Have you seen this painting? Last seen outside a Burger King in a blue coat and sneakers in 1889.'"

The Jeu de Paume actually came through.

Someone in Paris had made a hurried, condensed translation for him, and that was what chugged out of the squad room fax machine first, followed by the original French version. A second language had been an asset in the military, and Clay had worked at hanging on to his shaky college French. Shakier than ever, it nevertheless helped fill in some of the translation's gaps. What he read made him contact Florene immediately. "Is anything on the back of the Trabuc?" he asked. "Any marking at all?"

In less than fifteen minutes, she called back. "An extremely faint 'Leonore' is on the back, in brownish ink. My guess is it was black, before it faded."

Goosebumps raced down Clay's spine.

"Come on! Say something!" Florene demanded. "What's it mean?"

"Both Trabucs, Monsieur and Madame, were reported stolen in November '44 by a Madame Annette Bergère. Her description matches your Monsieur exactly—color, dimensions, et cetera. It all fits."

"So this Annette person, is she still—?"

"Hold on, Florene—listen to this. In her claim, Madame Bergère states that she and her daughters—they were about eight and ten at the time—left Paris in late May '44. Her husband Paul was a stage designer. He stayed behind. Because he worked long hours, the Bergères brought the two paintings to their upstairs neighbor for safekeeping. Half a year later, Madame Bergère makes it back—the war's still raging in Europe, but Paris is liberated.

"She walks into an apartment that's been torn apart: mattresses slashed, floorboards ripped up, the furniture destroyed. She runs up to the neighbor, a Madame Delamarche, who tells her that on July eighteenth a German officer pushed his way into her flat. Didn't do any damage, but he was able to sniff out the paintings and confiscate them. Delamarche tried to contact the husband, but no one answered the phone or the door at the Bergère apartment. She figured he'd left town to join his family. That wasn't the case. Annette finds out he was arrested by a German officer in the theater where he was working, while a dress rehearsal was going on. He was never seen again. The arrest took place on July sixteenth."

"Two days before the paintings were stolen from the neighbor," Florene said softly.

"In her deposition, Madame Bergère keeps referring to a list with the names and addresses of the cast and crew who were present in the theater that day. She insists that all of them and Madame Delamarche are describing the same officer, an SS captain. The French don't accept her story at face value. They insist that Madame Delamarche, who was eighty-two, has to appear in person to corroborate. She obviously showed up the next day, but neither her actual statement nor any documentation by the theater people was included in my fax. The authorities also made Annette Bergère duplicate a photograph she used as proof, since she wasn't willing to hand over her original. They didn't go out of their way to make it easy."

"Did they fax over the picture, at least?"

"Yeah." Clay's eyes were locked on the fuzzy image propped up against a pile of case folders. He'd already memorized every detail: A pretty woman in an old-fashioned quilted satin bed jacket, a floppy bow at the throat. She was sitting up in bed, a sleeping newborn cradled in her arms. The mother's face was a perfect oval, framed by thick hair that Clay was ready to swear—even though the image was black and white—was auburn. Curled up at her side was a little girl of two or three, the proud big sister. A white-haired lady (doubtless neighbor Delamarche) sat straight as a duchess in a chair next to the bed. All smiled at the camera—except for the infant, of course. On the wall behind them were the two Trabuc portraits. *"Mes amies Bergère, 1936,"* was written in the lower right hand border.

"Whatever French bureaucrat wrote this all down noted that the claimant presented neither a bill of sale nor a provenance, but attested that her husband had purchased the Trabucs in Provence in 1932. At the bottom of the form was a space for special identifying marks. Paul Bergère had written 'Cécilie' on the back of the woman's portrait, 'Léonore' on the back of the man's. Both in black ink. Those were the names of their daughters."

"Those bastards . . ." Whatever words followed strangled in Florene's throat. After a brief silence, she began again. "They treated her just like a rape victim, didn't they?" Florene no longer sounded like the chic lady at the Met, but the running-on-empty cop who used to blow off steam in the middle of the squad room, both hands on her hips. "Like it was her fault! Her husband's dead—we don't even want to think what happened to him in those two days—she's left with two kids to take care of, her home is demolished, and they hold her over the coals—your typical prove-this-prove-that cocksuckers!"

"Pretty much the same deal," Clay agreed. Dead air hung between them for the better part of a minute. "Well, at least I have a place to start. I'll be in touch."

"I hear they're flying in Van Gogh people to see the painting."

"Isn't that a little premature?"

"No one directs the director."

Once the phone was back on its receiver, Clay realized he'd neglected to tell Florene one detail near the end of Annette Bergère's statement. The name of the officer accused of theft and murder.

Taking his time, Clay walked to the water cooler. Without looking, he filled a paper cup, releasing the spigot when cold water poured over his fingers. Long ago, a grainy clip of an old wartime newsreel had stuck in his head, a scene of block after block of rubble in a bombed-out European city. Only one building stood in the ruins, its facade blasted away. Several floors of undisturbed, cozily furnished flats were exposed—intimate places unexpectedly on public view. Pots still sat on stoves, tables were set for dinner. On an overstuffed armchair, an evening paper waited to be read. Nothing missing, nothing out of place . . . save the building's exterior wall. The Bergère apartment was the other side of the same coin: from the street, no one would have suspected how it had been laid waste, the contents reduced to feathers, plaster dust, splinters, shards of glass. Clay kept seeing the lady in the bed jacket coming home, exhausted but happy, calling out her husband's name as she turned her key in the lock . . . her last moment before she discovered how brutally her life had changed forever.

Eyes closed, he drank the water. He saw her walk into the Jeu de Paume, determined to get her paintings back. Wrenched by sorrow, desperation, anger, and revenge, she'd resolved to nail that SS bastard.

November 1944.

She was probably dead by now. If they were alive, her little girls were old ladies in their sixties.

Back at his desk, he glanced at the small calendar next to his phone. Not only was it almost noon on a Friday, it was the Friday before Memorial Day weekend. He'd be lucky to get anything on either of them before Tuesday afternoon.

Annette Bergère.

And SS Hauptsturmführer Udo Luscher.

CHAPTER
FIVE

Most of the Big Building employees condemned to a full workday before the holiday weekend were working through lunch so they could sneak out early. The only other midday returnee to join Clay on the up elevator was Penny Bloomberger.

Even without the ruffled apron, Bloomie was a dead ringer for a Norman Rockwell granny. Glancing at her little gold wristwatch, she jabbed at the button for their floor until the doors closed. Like a mantra, her feathered lips kept repeating, "So damned slow!"

Everyone knew Bloomie, and Bloomie knew everyone, nickname and all. The year she started working for the NYPD as a civilian clerk-typist was lost in the mists of time, but the consensus was that she'd already qualified for her pension before Teddy Roosevelt joined the force. Time, it seemed, had given her the ability to keep at psychic bay the endless succession of crimes and transgressions the detectives dragged in, like dogs skulking in with dug-up bones, nasty prizes they delighted in gnawing and growling over. Clay stood behind her, gazing down at her white-haired head, wondering how many thousands of tales this *True Detective* Scheherazade had filed away inside it.

With a department store ding—*Lingerie, Hosiery, Detectives*—the elevator opened, and Bloomie motored out toward her command-center of a desk. Snatching up a report, she tilted it, squinted at it, and brought it close to her glasses. Scoping the room until she had the shorter of the two African-American Major Case detectives named Richard in her sights, she scolded, "How the hell am I supposed to read this? Your penmanship stinks, Little Black Dick!"

Clay's path to his desk was blocked by Marcello Martino, a Special Investigation detective who'd taught Clay the ropes when he was new to Police Plaza. Cello was a little over forty, and a lot over forty pounds too heavy. Even though he was going soft in the gut, no one dared call him Jello to his face. He didn't so much walk as roll along, swinging his arms like that "Keep on Truckin'" guy from the Seventies.

"Yo, Rembrandt! Just the man I wanted to see!" Cello held up a thick file. "Your name is on one of these reports—that UPS truck deal up on Eighty-first."

"Isn't that the Nineteenth's?" asked Clay.

"It was, until we sniffed out this pattern—three attacks on overnight delivery trucks, all with the same MO. More than one precinct. And now, this mutt is shooting a motherfucking cannon at cops! What's with that neighborhood and you, Ryder? What's it gonna take to convince you never to go north of Fifty-seventh Street again?"

"You're right, Cello. I'll be like the cabbies who refuse to go to Brooklyn. From this moment on, no more uptown cases. What've you got?"

Two detectives, both obsessively double-and-triple-patting their pockets and holsters to be sure they hadn't left anything behind, rushed by on their way to the elevators. "Hey, Cello," one mumbled as they passed, while the other's salutation was an even briefer "Cello." Threading their way through the desks, they made a point of ignoring Clay, even though they both passed so close, they had to turn sideways to avoid body contact.

"Am I with the Invisible Man, here, or what?" Cello griped at their backs.

"It's a clean job," Clay shrugged, "but someone's got to do it."

A lone, anonymous snicker acknowledged, but it was obvious the Art Guy's fan club had no members in the Big Room.

Dumping his file on an empty chair, Cello directed the slightest tilt of his head at Clay. Then, with all the finesse of a small tank, he pivoted and advanced on the men's room. When Clay followed him in, he was methodically kicking open the stall doors to make sure they were alone. "For a guy who's so fucking smart, Ryder, you don't know shit!" Martino's round man-in-the-moon face appeared oddly pinched as he wheeled back from the last stall. "You think that"— he gestured toward the squad room—"is all about your jerkoff art assignment?"

"Walking into the Guggenheim at high noon doesn't exactly put your life on the line, Cello."

Martino's head launched into no-no-no shakes of denial, but Clay's defense only picked up speed: "Every detective out there resents that I get the same pay as a cop who puts his hands in the shit barrel every day. While I'm doing something I live for, they're peeling the homeless off subway grates and sifting through the drug trade's garbage for evidence. As we speak, they're out there getting worked up over how much I save on dry cleaning."

"Hank Vandam never had that problem," Cello quickly countered, "and he was the Art Guy for over two years to your six months. No detective in this squad would've thought twice about working with Hank when he wasn't on an art case."

"Cello, that just filters down from Hickey—his notion that anyone who was in Special Services should be itching to out-Rambo Rambo. The DI wants to see me report in, collect my daily list of perps, get into a wet suit, swim through the sewers, and put them out of action, one by one. But if I'm the Art

Guy, all that training goes to waste, leaving Hickey to conclude that I'm spending my days goofing off. Or that I'm some kind of prima donna."

Cello ripped a paper towel from the dispenser and wiped it across a forehead beaded with perspiration. "You're so far off the mark, you're pathetic. But first, let me set you straight: Hank was a marine, so don't flatter yourself with the SEAL stuff. And nobody thinks you're gay, either, if that's the next lame excuse you're about to pull out of your hat. No, in case you haven't noticed, there's a wall that's gone up, a wall that keeps getting higher and higher, with you all alone on the outside—and guess what? You're the jerkoff who keeps piling on the bricks! You think this is about *paintings*? Look around, Ryder—you are standing in a crapper inside a bigger crapper inside a crapper of a city. You think you're the only crapee with problems? If you're a cop, you have problems. Some of them are dead, some of them are alive. I've seen the people outside that door talk to you, and you don't answer—you don't even hear them. I've seen you with a look on your face like you're arguing with people who aren't there. You're about as much fun to be around as a grenade with the pin pulled— people don't want to jostle you. They don't want to come fucking close to you. Get it *now*?"

So it was no longer invisible, that monstrous, leechlike thing that had bloated during its year of trenching deeper and deeper into him. Suddenly exposed, it dug down even more ferociously. Unable to hold Cello's accusatory stare, Clay turned his eyes to the scuffed linoleum floor. "That bad?"

Martino crumpled up his paper towel and scored a basket in the trashcan. "God forbid that I should ever know what it's like to be standing in your shoes, but you had a lot of people here who tried to hold you up after what happened to your wife. Old-timers like Richie Sparks, even that new guy Merriweather from Hawaii." A sigh rumbled up from deep inside his chest. "One by one, you pushed us away. Me, maybe I'm harder to push than the rest." He smoothed back his thinning hair, stuffed his shirt into his waistband. "This job. This has to be the most unforgiving job on the face of the earth. You can't let anything distract you. Not for a second. And the biggest distraction of all is feeling sorry for yourself."

"Bullshit! After the first week, I never missed a day—I was here, I did my job!"

"Sure, you were here. Here like a guy walking around in his own personal nightmare. Here like a guy with his skin on inside out. The truth is, it's just the opposite of what you think, laying the blame on the Art Guy crap. You were so goddamn edgy, most of the people outside were *relieved* when you made Art Guy. Yeah, *relieved* because that made their world a little safer—you working alone most of the time. Because what this job boils down to is this: WHO'S . . . WATCHING . . . YOUR . . . BACK." With each word, Cello jabbed a finger in the air. "To be more exact, who you can COUNT ON to watch your back. It's simple—the more guys you got behind you, the longer you live. When someone is so . . . so out of it, so wrapped up in examining his past or his imagined fuck-ups that he's not even looking out for *himself*, he's dangerous. He's poison. Tell me, Ryder, how many people do you have watching *your* back?"

Abruptly he turned to the mirror above the row of sinks, leaving Clay to face the empty space he'd just occupied. The water was running, splashing, washing away the perspiration that had reappeared on Cello's brow.

"Not counting me, of course."

Clay turned to see Cello's reflection nodding at him from the mirror—solemn, but unmistakably the Cello who drove too fast and ate too much and broke into passionate Italian arias when perps refused to speak English.

The rusty scrape and creak of the men's room door preceded the entry of a City Hall administrator who met with Hickey regularly. Nods were exchanged, and the man headed for the urinals.

"Just do everyone a favor," whispered Cello as he patted his face dry with another towel, "and lighten the fuck up." He strolled out, rubbing at a stain on his tie with the wet brown paper.

Ten minutes later, Cello, file once more in hand, approached Clay's desk. "Okay, this is what we've got," he picked up, as though nothing had interrupted his rundown of the case. "Every time, the driver is on his way back to his truck from a delivery to a big apartment building. He unlocks the cab, starts pulling the stuff for his next stop. Then a man—the first time it was a doorman—comes running up with an overnight letter. 'Hold on! One of the tenants says this letter's gotta go out today!' He's got the right envelope, label all filled out except the zip code—it's for this small town in the Midwest. 'The tenant said you drivers carry a zip code booklet, right?' The driver starts to look it up, and the doorman steps up into the truck, like he's gonna write it down on the overnight letter. Except instead of pulling a pen out of his pocket, he whips out a gun. He forces the driver to the rear of the truck. Makes him stand against the back doors. Whacks him in the head with the gun so bad, it takes twenty stitches to close up the wound. The driver wakes up in the emergency room without his wallet, his watch, whatever he had on him. But nothing's missing from the back of the truck."

"When was the first one?" Clay asked.

"Mid-March, a FedEx truck," replied Cello. "Riverside Drive at Ninety-fourth. About a month later, he shows up in coveralls—Airborne Express, Seventy-sixth off First. The third job, he dressed like a janitor in a gray Dickies uniform. Your turn. East Eighty-first."

"I guess you know what was on truck number three."

"Can you believe it? The same fucking truck! He walks away with less than a hundred bucks, a tapped-out credit card, a beat-up Timex, and there's a fifty-million-dollar picture, right under the bastard's nose!"

"Don't forget the gold chain," Clay reminded him. "But seriously, even if this guy knew what it was, no way he could have unloaded it."

"So I've heard," said Cello. "Anyway, the drivers described the perp as Latino or Italian or Jewish—dark hair, olive skin. Fortyish, moustache, medium-husky build, around five-ten. That mesh with what you saw?"

"Fortyish? That hurts. I thought he looked my age. But that pretty much sounds like him. What about that getaway car? Did he have it on the other jobs?"

"We're thinking that the way they set up the jobs was with a car casing the truck while the driver did his rounds. That's what one witness *thinks* he saw on Riverside." Cello shrugged. "Two guys, a car, shooting at cops—for what? Are they that stupid? Or are *we* that stupid, for not getting what's going on?"

"Like I told the lieu from the Nineteenth—nothing adds up."

"Those express delivery companies . . . to them, security is all about the damn packages. A random driver getting his head bashed—no way that's in the same league as having a package stolen. Just a couple of phone calls to their headquarters, and I already know they're not going to knock themselves out to help us."

Clay pushed back in his chair. "God, where do you start? There must be hundreds of those trucks on the streets every day."

"Hundreds to you, thousands to me. For now, all we can do is keep an eye out for cars tailing them. And pressure the express companies to get the word to their drivers that any one of them could be the next target." Cello flipped his thumb up and down through the bottom corner of the file. "So, this weekend . . . you working?"

"Speaking of targets?" He saw it coming, but he liked Cello too much to lie. Between him and his wife, they had enough unmarried female friends and relatives to fill Yankee Stadium. Besides, after all the knives Cello had hurled at him in the men's room, it was comforting that he still trusted Clay alone with a woman. "On Saturday, a gallery owner I have to question is flying in from Europe. After that, I'm heading east."

"Rhonda and I are having our first big cookout of the season Saturday night. We'll be grilling those steak pinwheels you're so crazy about. How about stopping by on the way out?"

The Marinos lived on the easternmost edge of Queens, and only a hop from the Long Island Expressway. Clay's weekend place was—traffic permitting—nearly two hours farther east, on Long Island's North Fork.

"Whose side—yours or Rhonda's?"

"Actually, it's neither." Cello's eyes flitted around the office. He did his best to lower his boom-box voice. "It's our vet. She's terrific—our dog can't wait to see her."

"Thanks, but despite my symptoms, I'm still not due for my rabies shot." Clay gave his hair a quick run-through with his fingers. He wore it close cropped, a look that was so old it was new every few years, and 1999 was one of them. "Sure, I'll come—but just for the pinwheels."

Martino bent to Clay's ear. "What's it been? A year this month, right?"

Clay didn't answer.

"Okay, forget it. I have a better chance of fixing up the pope. Just show up. Eat and run. You're such a miserable son of a bitch, I don't know why Rhonda always loves to see you." He began to walk away, then called over his shoulder, "Say, what about that thing with Florene? Did you wrap that up?"

"The holiday . . . I'll be lucky to get anything before the middle of next week."

"Ryder, is this one of those Holocaust things?"

"Sort of turning out that way."

"That Nazi stuff depresses me. Hey, what's with the look? I do occasionally read beyond the sports page, Pal. You know, I warned Florene she'd be better off at the bone palace over on the West Side."

"Are you referring to the Museum of Natural History, Martino?"

"Sure. Even the Nazis didn't steal dinosaurs."

Hours later, rubbing his eyes, Clay leaned back from his computer. One big goose egg after another: nothing on the Nazi, nothing on the Bergère woman, nothing on the Broyce case. Nothing new on the UPS job, either, except that after stitching up the driver's head, the hospital had released him the same day.

On the pretext that misery loves company, Clay phoned Malenkov up at the Nineteenth. "I'm coming up empty on every search on the Broyce case, Lieu. The closest match is that Frenchman who took a stroll between the World Trade Center towers. A hell of a lot higher and windier. On the other hand, he wasn't on a slanted line."

Malenkov laughed—gravel shaking around in a tin can. "Great minds, et cetera, Ryder. No, he hasn't been in the country for a while. And even though nobody knows exactly how he pulled that stunt off, the consensus is that he shot a line from tower A to tower B and went up B to secure it. Doesn't fit the Broyce scene."

"Anything on the equipment?"

"Not a hell of lot. The line was eleven-millimeter. Light and thin. The experts can't see the climber weighing a hell of a lot."

"A small man . . . or possibly a woman?"

"Why rule it out? Anyhow, except for traces of Mrs. Broyce's blood near the top, the line was clean. The lower end was cut with a knife—still not known if it was also the murder weapon. We can't find a retailer in the area selling either the line or the grappling hook. It's looking like they're both made outside the States."

"Maybe the perp was an import, too."

"Definite possibility. Oh, something else, Ryder. We found fresh abrasion marks on a pipe not too far from the ledge, probably from a metal chain. That made one of my guys think some kind of ratchet."

"Interesting. That would take all the slack out of the line."

"And dig in the grappling hook at the same time."

"Did your guys test it out? Could a line be thrown up like that? That far?"

"Yeah, they went to the park, and one of them made like Roy Rogers. It landed about the same distance. But distance is one thing—shooting it onto the Broyce terrace and hooking the handrail is another. Practice, practice, practice."

"Maybe two perps? A big Pecos Bill guy to throw the rope, a little Flying Walenda type to climb and plunder?"

"And murder. Yeah, that's a fair assessment of their job skills. Extra credit given for neatness zilch evidence left behind." Clay heard someone reminding Malenkov about a meeting, "Got to go. The follow-up's appreciated. I don't know what Broyce's wife was like, but every time he calls—like every hour on the hour—I wish it was the Lord of the Garden who was pushing up daisies instead. Keep in touch."

Saturday night, Clay slipped out of the opening night of the Feast of San Gennaro East that went on all summer in the Martino backyard. The laughter, the Sinatra music, the aromas—peppers and onions, sausages and pinwheels—were all pretty much the same as at the annual festival in Little Italy. In fact, since the mayor had outlawed games of chance, the only thing missing was the dollar-ringed plaster statue of the saint.

A few turns, and he was back on the highway, not too far from where Lauren had died.

Cello had pegged it exactly. May. Just over a year.

They'd barely been married eighteen months when it happened.

The first time he saw her was in Criminal Court.

He'd showed up right on time to testify, but the judge was letting the trial drag on, and Clay had the sinking feeling that the lunch break would be called before he was. Too restless to stay put, he wandered into the hall and peered in at the next courtroom. It was like walking in at the end of a movie, but the case wasn't what interested him.

From the doorway, the Assistant District Attorney looked way too young for the job, like maybe they'd slipped her a law degree instead of her high school diploma. He slid into an empty seat near the front without disturbing anyone. Close up, the attorney looked less guileless, more intriguing. She had a bony build, but its consolation prize was high, slanting cheekbones. Above them, set off by dark hair severely brushed back and fastened at the nape of her neck, were extraordinary green eyes. They were almost rectangular, like two emerald lozenges. Her face was bare of makeup, her plain suit a dull gray. With all the pains she'd taken to appear tightly wrapped, he was blown away by her summation:

"I love mornings when I wake up to an unplanned day," she'd begun, "when I'm free to do whatever I please." A subtle backward movement of her shoulders made it easy to imagine her lazily stretching in bed, hair flowing loose over her shoulders. The green eyes suddenly narrowed with indignation. "The kind of morning the defendant's wife never knew. How could she, when he controlled her so relentlessly? Controlled her right down to what would have been her very last breath . . . had not help so mercifully intervened. Suffocation, in every sense. Would it ever even occur to a person like him how much a healthy blend of curiosity and happenstance can enrich our lives?" The eyes shut briefly, absolute affirmation. Clay didn't have to listen to the rest—jurors were already nodding in assent. She'd just put the guy away big-time.

Activity in the hall forced Clay from his seat—a long break had been called in his courtroom next door. Stationing himself halfway down the corridor, he waited until the ADA emerged. After a quick detour into the ladies' room, she was walking his way, her lips a glossy red.

"Both of us woke up this morning never expecting that we'd meet," he said, by way of introduction. "I also believe in a healthy blend of curiosity and happenstance, but I was never able to put it quite so eloquently."

She laughed, and they held one another's eyes far too long for a first encounter. With a sudden frown, she glanced down, as if devilish, nimble fingers had undone the buttons of her drab suit from the inside. When she looked up, the green eyes were a genie's, newly escaped from a tightly sealed bottle. They glowed with pent-up schemes, calculation infused with fire. She was that Regnault portrait of a wildly and erotically free gypsy woman—the one that unfailingly hot-glued unsuspecting male visitors to the Met's parquet floor, like they'd just come face-to-face with their dream fuck. Here she was, inches away, breathing in the same musty Criminal Court Building air. Only the barrette binding her hair, the simple spring-release that would free the roiling black curls, held her in check.

In that moment, a connection was forged between them, although it was too early to tell if it had the strength of a filament or a chain.

Right from the start, Lauren was in the habit of jotting down things-to-do-lists . . . but who didn't? Newly married, both busy with challenging positions—detective and ADA—how else to remember to pick up milk or light bulbs or postage stamps? Without comment, he watched her lists gradually evolve in scope and detail. But it was difficult to connect them with the Lauren who'd pleaded with such passion for another woman's right to breathe free.

Lauren painted her toenails red, but always concealed them in sensible legal-lady shoes. Her one luxury was pricey, tarty underwear, which she insisted he unsnap, unlace, or unhook. The genie, the gypsy, the real Lauren, he was sure, was always just beneath the gabardine surface, ready to break out and flout all the conventions . . . anytime, anywhere. Sometimes he wondered if others could see that; sometimes he wondered if he wanted them to. Surprises and secrets swirled between them, and that made the sex—which rarely flagged below the pure lust phase—even more exciting.

But then there was the evening with the surprise that changed everything: the full-blown Five-Year Plan.

"Tell me, Lauren," he asked, as he flipped through pages of his-and-her income projections, variable-versus-fixed mortgage analyses, and suburban school reports, "where did all this come from? Who was your inspiration . . . Joe Stalin? Whatever happened to those 'unplanned days'?" He tossed her meticulous paperwork toward the ceiling, but felt none of the liberation he'd expected as the sheets shuffled and scattered and floated to the floor. "You conned me, Lauren."

"Excuse me, but all the ingredients weren't exactly listed on your label, either, Clay! You left out that ton of toxic waste—all the shit between you and your grandfather! You can't—" She stopped short, alarmed by whatever she saw on his face. In silence, she stooped and gathered up the papers.

Because he hadn't even glanced at her plan, he never found out if her number-crunching included the current market value of The Shack.

He'd bought it cheap, on a sleety winter day during a real estate slump. Although he had no regrets about leaving the Navy, he never anticipated how much he'd miss the sea, and the little house was a quick jog from the beach.

Condition-wise, he was positive the former owner had passed the town building inspector cash under the table not to slap a "Condemned" notice on the door. Architecturally, it looked like a transplant from a Depression-era cabin court. Also, it was a pain in the ass to get to. To the good, it sat in the middle of a one-acre rise ringed by towering pines, two of which were perfectly spaced for a hammock. Being a hovel, its housekeeping needs were scant, limited to sweeping out the sand with a broom. Scrubby and windblown, The Shack wasn't the kind of place to summon up peace and serenity, but its grittiness scoured his senses. Less than an hour there balanced out an entire workweek as a city cop. He was crazy about it.

The down payment took every penny he'd squirreled away in the Navy and condemned him to a year of living like a monk. But for the first time in his life, he owned something more than the gear he could transport around in a few duffel bags. By the time he met Lauren, a pay raise had loosened up the financial straitjacket.

Maybe she honestly enjoyed their first summer out east, but the next year, when they were married, she seemed content to stay in the city every time he broke the news that he had to work a summer weekend shift. The first Saturday of May '98, his day to check out how The Shack had fared through the winter, she surprised him by volunteering to tag along.

Shortly after they arrived, a new Lexus pulled onto the muddy drive behind Lauren's old Toyota. With a cheery wave, a blonde woman in a beige suit slid out. She reached back in, to pull out a large briefcase.

"Wrong house," Clay called out, just before he saw Lauren waving back.

After a few steps, the woman's matching beige high heels sank in a deep rut, but she slogged ahead like a trooper, shifting her briefcase to keep her balance.

Without turning, Lauren whispered, "She's sold more houses than—"

"You called a real estate agent? To come *here*?"

"This land has real value!" the beige lady was exclaiming, as if the decrepit structure squatting on it didn't exist. "This parcel was a wise investment!"

Gripping Lauren's arm, he hissed, "What the hell made you think I'd ever sell?"

"A down payment on that house in Westchester we've been talking about."

"No, that *you've* been talking about, Lauren." The closer the visitor came, the higher he pushed up the volume. "For when we have two kids, spaced exactly twenty-two months apart." His fingers squeezed her thin arm down to the bone. "But you're not even pregnant, Lauren! You just finished your period, and I'm waiting for you to tell me when I can pull down my pants and fuck you!"

From the corner of his eye, he saw the real estate agent's cheeks redden as Lauren's drained. While the older woman beat a retreat through the muck, Lauren ran inside for her purse. Before the Lexus was out of sight, she'd taken off in her Toyota.

After waiting all afternoon for her to return, Clay hitched rides that landed him at the railroad station. By the time he made it home, it was after ten P.M, and a message was blinking on the answering machine. While he called back the number left by a New York State trooper, Clay drew a blank trying to connect the cop to his open cases. Not until the guy stammered something about an accident on the Long Island Expressway did it occur to him that the call might be about Lauren.

In weak moments, he gave in to something base and ugly inside himself and blamed her. Then he'd see the school reports drifting down alongside the careful budgets and hear himself ridiculing her plans without owning up to his own pathetic scrimping. That was enough to qualify him as a full-blown hypocrite, but dishonesty was only a symptom. He'd squandered more opportunities to make their marriage work than he could remember. In the middle of the night, fully aroused, he'd reach for her, then recoil from the cold, smooth, dead side of the bed. Until the alarm went off, he was keelhauled in and out of black dreams, grasping only that he'd never viewed or accepted Lauren as a whole person. If he'd seen only what he wanted, what did that mean about his feelings for her? Did they qualify as love, or could love only be the package deal?

That summer, Clay kept picking up the phone to put The Shack on the market. Selling would be an act of contrition. However, since each subsequent trip out east also provided a fresh opportunity for self-castigation, he never went through with it. For a brief spell, he drank too much. But the possibility of driving back to the city drunk and dying on the same highway, in the same place, was too easy and too cheap.

The Sunday of Memorial Day weekend, Clay woke before six. On autopilot, he dialed Police Plaza, sitting on the edge of his bed in the only place he'd ever owned, and once owned so proudly. Now its greatest value was as a reminder of what he'd lost.

Nothing was in on the Bergères, but a sheet on Udo Luscher had been faxed through during the night.

"Is it too long for you to read it to me?" Clay asked the officer who'd picked up.

"One paragraph, no problem," she replied. "'Udo Luscher, born Munich, Germany, October 9, 1921. University of Munich, September–October 1939.'" She paused. "Quick learner."

"Germany invaded Poland that September—that started World War II."

"Right, I see that." She was reading ahead. "He joined up. 'SS Officers' Training School, Bad Tolz, 1939–40. SS—' German word here—'*SS Kavallerie.*' Could that be, like, cavalry?"

"Good guess," Clay answered.

"'Wounded in Poland, June 1941. Resumed active duty in Poland, wounded in Warsaw, May '43. Awarded Knight's Cross with Diamonds, promoted to . . .'" She spelled out *Hauptsturmführer.* "It says 'SS captain' in parentheses, 'by Heinrich Himmler. Transferred to Paris, November 1943. Aide to General Karl Oberg; supervised interrogations of political prisoners in Gestapo headquarters and city prisons. Known as *Le Découpeur.*' Parentheses: 'The Carver. Name attributed to hundreds of documented prisoner deaths and'"— she drew her breath in hard—"'mutilations.'"

In the background, a phone rang insistently. She rushed through the rest, her words running together, but Clay was sure the speed wasn't so much to answer the other call as to get free of Luscher. "'August 1944, transferred to Berlin, promoted to SS major, attached to General Staff. Promoted to lieutenant colonel in February 1945. Last seen May 1, 1945, departing Berlin en route to Munich on special assignment. Also last sighting for staff car and driver. Tried in absentia at Nuremberg. Found guilty of war crimes.' That's it." A relieved sigh, as if she'd crossed onto safer ground. "I'll leave it on your desk."

The beach was empty, except for two men running with their dogs. For a quarter mile, paw and footprints trailed them in the sand. The incoming tide wasn't high enough for a dive off the decrepit community pier, so Clay eased down into the water, careful not to get a splinter in his butt. After the long, cold spring, Long Island Sound felt like the Bering Sea. To take his mind off the icy water, he concentrated on a young SS lieutenant colonel speeding south through Germany in a staff car. In every World War II movie he could remember, it was always a big, black Mercedes.

More boats than he'd expected were already yawing around in the harbor, so Clay refrained from swimming underwater. Not worth it to take a chance on some brat who was too young to drive a car for another five years coming out of nowhere on a jet ski at fifty miles per hour and turning him into fish chum.

Udo Luscher, born 1921.

When Clay was in the service, instructors still spoke with awe of German military training of more than a half-century earlier. If you came out of the SEAL course feeling like the original mean machine, what about someone like Luscher, who'd bounced back twice after being wounded?

Not even twenty-four back in '45, when he made his exit. Not much more than a kid, but a vicious Nazi kid, resourceful enough to do something big enough to knock Himmler's swastika-embroidered socks off . . . If not Luscher, then who else could be Señora Paula's guy in Argentina?

At last acclimated to the water, Clay moved along at a good clip.

Seventy-seven, if he were alive today . . . about the same age as . . .

He pushed his grandfather's face away, concentrated on filling his mind with Luscher, forced anyone else off the backseat of that Mercedes. He tracked the car as it took the curves around steep hillsides, sped through shafts of sunlight filtered through tall pines.

A wreck? Or a Luger held up to the back of the driver's head when the officer made him stop to take a leak? The solid, heavy black car teetered over a precipice, needing only a nudge to send it into a swan dive.

Luscher had died, all right. But Clay's bet was on his death taking place in Argentina, decades later. Just like the old lady wrote. The dim old lady who'd sent a Van Gogh by ordinary UPS.

CHAPTER

SIX

The post-holiday Tuesday began with further details on Madame Bergère filtering in, patchy and incomplete. By Wednesday, with all available sources double-checked, Clay updated and organized the facts:

Annette Bergère had been dead twenty-five years.

Her only heirs had been her daughters, Cécilie (born 1934) and Léonore (born 1936), with whom she'd emigrated to New York in 1946.

Her older daughter, unmarried and childless, had been a Brooklyn College professor. Cécilie Bergère died of leukemia in 1982.

Léonore, a schoolteacher in the city public school system, married Saul Preminger in 1962. They had two children: Michael, born in 1963, and Rachel, born five years later. Preminger, a Ravensbruck survivor, had died young (age 35) of a heart attack in 1971. When Léonore Preminger retired in 1992, she moved to Miami. Four years later, she was the victim of a fatal hit-and-run. A Cuban gang member, whose priors included theft, assault, and drug trafficking, was doing time for the crime.

Like his father, Michael Preminger had also died young of a heart attack, in 1995. That left Rachel, thirty-one years old, as the only living descendant of Paul and Annette Bergère. There wasn't a single conviction in the entire family tree.

Dr. Rachel Preminger Meredith still lived in her parents' co-op on Ninth Street. Just off Fifth Avenue, it was a stone's throw from the heart of NYU's Washington Square campus, where she'd taught film history since 1996. Married, no kids.

"Lady, you are truly the Last of the Mohicans," Clay muttered, dropping what he had on her so far on top of the stack.

"I know I'm being a pain in the ass," Florene Cope apologized. It was her third call on Wednesday. "You've got to understand that the entire Met power structure is clamoring for The Great Reunion. Trabuc and the heirs, face-to-face."

"It's been authenticated?"

"Fast track. Ninety-five percent."

"Florene, it's been fifty-five years since the painting was reported as stolen. What's the problem if I need another day to be absolutely sure?"

"They're scared it'll leak. They want total press control. You know, so they can make headlines like 'Met Restores Nazi Plunder to Holocaust Heir!' "

Clay didn't reply. Many museums worldwide hadn't been particularly scrupulous about postwar acquisitions with blank spots in their provenances. Returning the Van Gogh to its legitimate owner in a tightly choreographed press conference would crown the Met as Most Righteous Among Museums. An invaluable PR coup had fallen, not so much out of the blue, as off the back of a truck. A big, brown UPS truck.

"If I'm driving *you* crazy," Florene pleaded, "think what they're doing to *me*!" She blew out exasperation in a long sigh. At least throw me a crumb."

"Come on, Florene. You know me better than that."

"Not anymore. You're so hollowed out, you rattle when you walk. Listen, Clay, I've . . ." The edge came off her voice. "I've been there. When Audrey was killed, I went for counseling. It really helps."

But Audrey—never Florene's cop partner, but a cop who was her life partner of many years—died working undercover during a sting. A snitch switched sides, and an arms dealer played executioner with a .357. What guilt could Florene possibly assign herself over Audrey's death? Had she skipped her turn to do the dishes that morning?

"Okay, *okay*! I hear you! Tell them it's narrowed down to one person. That has to make them happy—no embarrassing infighting among the kinfolk. But remember, Florene, there's a fifty-million-dollar jackpot. Until I've checked out every angle, I'm not rushing over to knock on the possible's door like the prize squad from Publishers' Clearing House."

By the next morning, Clay had it just about wrapped. Nothing had turned up to dispute the Meredith woman's standing as a thoroughly solid citizen with no extant blood relatives. One last step remained: checking her out in person. He called, identified himself, and asked if he could stop by. No response—had the phone gone dead? During the long silence, it dawned on him that, like her father and her brother, Rachel Meredith's heart might be too weak for the news to come.

"My husband"—she finally replied, in a voice so thin and reedy, it was nearly inaudible—"is something the matter?"

Worse than the heart thing, she was replaying other calls she'd received from cops. The state trooper breaking the news about Lauren came flooding back, the guy struggling for a way to tell him that his wife had been tentatively identified—but only by the Toyota's mangled license plate.

"No, nothing about your husband at all," he backpedaled. "This is a *nice* call from the police, Dr. Meredith, believe me. It's about a piece of family property that's turned up."

"But I took care of all my mother's affairs here, as well as in Florida. Is it something to do with Michael? My brother?"

"Dr. Meredith, I really have to meet with you before I—"

"I'm afraid I have a class in fifteen minutes—summer session. I'll be back a little after one. Please come by then."

"And good-bye to you, too, bitch," he said to the phone after she clicked off.

Meredith's apartment building was quiet and well maintained, unimposing compared to the palatial Old Guard buildings steps away on Fifth. At one-fifteen, as Clay pulled out his shield, a whining arose from the other side of the apartment door. It sounded like a small dog. Ringing the bell turned up the volume, and the dog suddenly grew bigger. Through the door, he heard a woman scold the animal. Dead bolts clicked, and the door opened about a foot.

His throat locked up. The woman in the narrow V opening permitted by the chain was the grandmother, Annette Bergère—except she looked a hell of a lot closer to thirty than to ninety. And he'd been absolutely right. Her hair was auburn, thick and shiny, pulled back from her oval face at the temples by two big tortoise-shell clips. Instead of the quilted bed jacket, she was wearing a thin black sweater that resembled a T-shirt, except its neckline scooped wider and lower.

At the same time, the dog, frantic, forced its nose out.

"Lulu! Stop it!" the woman snapped. After a quick study of his shield, she closed the door momentarily, to free the chain. "Detective Ryder, I confess! I played detective myself. During the class break, I called Police Plaza, to make sure you're the real deal. You never know these days. Come on in."

As if all four paws were on springs, the silver-gray dog bounced up and down. "Please go on ahead to the living room, while I calm her down. Second archway on your right. Sit wherever."

The apartment was airy and inviting, with chalk white walls. Framed black and-white blowups of old movie star photos lined the hallway. The first archway opened on the kitchen, too small for a table, but when Clay reached the spacious living room, he saw that both rooms adjoined a dining area big enough to seat eight. The furniture, clean modern with a homage to Deco, was sand and white and tan. Lowering himself onto the closer of two love seats separated by a low table, he watched as the dog, not calm at all, eyeballs bulging from her owner's neck-lock, was marched to a dog bed in the corner. The way she barely rested on her haunches while her mistress backed away indicated how miserably she'd failed obedience school. He could now see that Rachel Meredith's sweater was tucked into a charcoal skirt that draped from a slender waist to mid-calf. Right down to her clunky black sandals, it was a look favored by no-nonsense New York women who wanted to stay cool on a hot summer day.

The moment she sat down on the opposite love seat, the dog bolted, running straight for Clay. He'd had a dog for three days when he was a kid, a friendly brown and white stray that had followed him home. This creature, madly sniffing his slacks and emitting frantic, high-pitched whines, was a pure-bred Manhattan Fruitcake.

"Ah, Lulu—we meet again!" he managed to croon, sorely tempted to knock her back with a swift, hard kick. Meredith jumped up, jabbing her finger toward the corner.

"Buddy of my mine in the Navy—his folks bred Weimaraners. Funny, but I remember them being bigger."

"They are," she replied, as the dog retreated. "Lulu has to be the world's smallest Weimaraner—sort of the runt of the breed. But she has lots of spunk. Often, far too much."

You call it spunk, lady, but I call it a death wish.

Turning back to Clay, she asked, "Would you like a Coke, or some iced tea?"

"Thanks, no. I only have a few questions. But first, may I see *your* ID?"

Her eyebrows arched up in annoyance, but she walked off into the adjacent dining room. "Do I win a prize if I'm not an imposter?" she called back.

"Yes, as a matter of fact, you do."

She returned with a wallet, and produced her driver's license and NYU ID card.

"Would you have any documents—certificates of birth or marriage, for example—belonging to your mother, or possibly even your maternal grandmother?"

She looked at him suspiciously. "That's all put away."

"In a bank?"

"No. Here. But there's not much. My grandmother lived in Paris during the war. Her apartment was destroyed. All I have is her French passport . . . and my mother's and my aunt's." She hesitated, and he could tell an outright refusal was undergoing serious consideration. Something made her swing the other way. "Just a minute."

As soon as the slap of her sandals receded, Lulu raced back, a rubber hamburger squeaking in her mouth. Showing his teeth, Clay snarled at her. She dropped the toy and backed off. In another part of the apartment, he heard doors opening and closing and the scrape of a chair dragging across a floor. He booted the hamburger under the love seat just as Meredith reappeared, arms around a colorful cardboard container shaped like an old-fashioned hatbox.

When she placed it on the coffee table, he saw that hundreds of small photos of movie stars, cut from magazines, had been pasted all over it, then sealed in a shiny glaze.

The urge to match names with the faces was irresistible. "Jane Fonda . . . Faye Dunaway . . . Brando the Godfather . . . De Niro in his taxi . . . all from the Seventies, right?"

"Right. I made it for my mother when I was ten. Mother's Day. It was a big hit. I actually thought I invented découpage."

Découpage. Le Découpeur. *Both from the verb* découper—*to cut out.*

After lifting off the top, she carefully removed a sheaf of papers, then several more, placing them in small piles on the coffee table. "Reverse chronological order . . . time strata . . . what you asked for is buried way down . . . here!" She riffled through the last stack, and pulled out three little booklets. "Their passports—my grandmother's, mother's, and aunt's."

"Any photographs from France?"

"Only one. I was told my grandfather snapped it and gave it to a neighbor. That's the only reason it survived." The picture she handed him was a glossy print, the original of *mes amies Bergères, 1936.* "The elderly lady is the neighbor."

"You look exactly like your grandmother here."

"Thank you." Averting her eyes, she returned to the final batch. "Here are their U.S. citizenship papers, my mother's and my aunt's high school diplomas—"

He cut her off. "Thanks, Dr. Meredith—I don't need to see any more."

She looked up at him, perplexed.

"What else do you know about this photograph?"

"My mother was the baby, my aunt was about two. But I don't see what—"

"Excuse me, but may I use the phone?"

A tense Florene Cope picked up on the first ring. "Is it a go?"

"Absolutely." After he hung up, he said, "I apologize for the mysterious behavior, but I had to establish if you were really . . . you."

"Am I?"

"Very much so. And now I can take you to claim your property." He pointed to the phone. "You want your husband to come along? We can pick him up at his studio on the way uptown."

"You know he's a photographer? Where he works?" She made a mock swipe at her forehead. "Oh, of course—*Detective* Ryder!"

She kept her eyes on Clay while she telephoned her husband. After a brief conversation, she shook her head, then shrugged—he couldn't break away. "Now for my mysterious prize," she said, grabbing her purse and a cardigan mate to her T-shirt. "With my luck, it's the deed to a Florida swamp, and I owe years of unpaid back taxes."

Afternoon traffic hadn't built up yet, so they moved uptown at a good clip. She asked where they were headed.

"Fifth Avenue. Low Eighties."

"Right by the Met." She turned to face the passenger window. The huddled withdrawal convinced him she was absorbed by thoughts of her mother and brother.

When he at last turned west on Eighty-first—instinctively looking for a UPS van—she sat up straight and glanced at her watch. "I wonder if it'll be worth it to spend an hour at the museum before they close—after we're done?"

"The Met? Always worth it. As a matter of fact, I might do the same myself." He swung onto Fifth, maneuvered into the extreme right lane, entered the museum garage, parked, and came around to open her door.

"This is a joke, right?"

Without answering, he pointed to the elevator. Her eyebrows shot up when they switched to a staff elevator on the lobby floor. It deposited them a few yards from where he'd met with Castelblanco a week before. At the far end of the corridor, a small but animated media throng was setting up equipment near a decoy elevator. Clay quickly steered Rachel Meredith into the conference room.

The second the door closed behind them, scattered applause broke out. Compared to the last time, the room was packed. A camera flashed.

"Dr. Meredith? Dr. Rachel *Preminger* Meredith?" Thus spake Castelblanco, as he bounded toward her. "As Director, I bid you a most heartfelt welcome to the Metropolitan Museum of Art."

With a sidelong look at Clay, she whispered, "Is this what happens to people who sneak in without paying?"

Castelblanco took her hand in both of his. "We wanted to give you a little preview first—before the press." The Headphone Voice, pure silk. "And don't blame Detective Ryder for his secrecy—he was under oath not to reveal a thing." He nodded at a man with a camcorder, and it began to whir. The Voice became even richer, impossibly sonorous:

"Dr. Preminger-Meredith, fifty-five years ago, a terrible injustice was done to your family, a repetition of the same injustice perpetrated millions of times over throughout Europe. All across the continent, people were stripped of their rights, their homes, their livelihoods, their belongings . . . their very lives." While he spoke—as much to the camera as to Rachel—he steadily walked her across the room. Despite the air-conditioning, a warm flush deepened on her cheeks and throat.

"Today, at last, through the combined efforts of the Metropolitan Museum, the Police Department of the City of New York, and the Federal Bureau of Investigation, the treasure that was ripped from your grandparents in Paris all those years ago is being returned to you, their rightful, legitimate heir." Taking a step back, the director pulled a cord attached to a dark blue velvet drape. The heavy folds of fabric drew apart to reveal a painting centered on an easel.

Monsieur Trabuc was dressed in a handsome gilt frame. Not only did it enhance the physical size of his portrait, but it elevated his social status, as well: instead of a mere asylum attendant, he now resembled a *bourgeois* of substance. The distrustful scowl aimed at the artist might even be mistaken for smug class snobbery. Castelbanco's *ta-da!* moment was unexpectedly husky: "Van Gogh's portrait of Monsieur Trabuc."

"The photograph!" Rachel murmured. "My grandmother's bedroom! I had no idea . . . !" The face in the frame had to be blurred by the tears streaming down her cheeks. The crowded room fell silent; even the camcorder clicked off.

Once again, Clay imagined Annette Bergère striding into the Jeu de Paume, a woman in mourning for all the sweet, small moments of her life. By then, she knew that they were lost forever, those mornings and nights in the bedroom . . . dressing, undressing, sleeping, dreaming, making love, waking to the giggles of little girls in nightgowns as they raced in and out, the sunshine streaming in . . . all under the scrutiny of Monsieur and Madame Trabuc.

Surely she understood that her quest for the paintings, even if successful, would be like searching for a book, and finding nothing more than its bookmark.

Nevertheless, she was determined to give her testimony, file her claim.

Now, over half a century later, her granddaughter's face was inches away from Trabuc's portrait. When she dared raise an index finger to touch it, Clay was sure he saw a ripple pass across her shoulders, a surge of kinetic energy powerful enough to connect, if only for a moment, past and present.

CHAPTER
SEVEN

As Clay walked to his desk, a voice sang off-key:

> *Mona Lisa, Mona Lisa, I have found you,*
> *La da da-da, la da da-da, la da daaa . . .*

Cello waved his copy of the *Daily News* over his head like a victory flag. Monsieur Trabuc, annoyed by the commotion, was smack in the middle of the front page. A smiling-through-tears but very fetching Rachel Meredith was on his right, and Armand Castelblanco guarded his left. More than half of Clay was cropped out, to accommodate the rookie heiress in her entirety. The Met's PR mission was a fait accompli. The front-page headline proclaimed:

REUNITED AT THE MET!
$50 MILLION HOLOCAUST THEFT RETURNED

The bubble-gum voice of the detective known to all as Miss Vanilla, who sometimes worked undercover in a platinum blonde wig, purred, "Ryder, did she offer you a nonmonetary reward?"

Clay's head snapped around to locate her, a scornful lucky-for-you-you're-a-woman all over his face. The worst part was, up to that moment, the women at work seemed so much more understanding . . . or maybe they were just better at faking it.

Cello cleared his throat, dismissing both her barb and Clay's thin skin. He turned to page three of the tabloid, and scanned down. "'Met director Castelblanco described the lost painting as . . .' Blah, blah—hold on, here's the good part: 'Castelblanco said that the Van Gogh could not have been traced to Dr. Meredith without the help of the FBI'"—he arched one you've-got-to-be-kidding eyebrow—"'*and* the NYPD Major Case Squad.'" Cello rolled up the newspaper and lightly bopped Clay on the head with it. "Way to go!"

His enthusiasm was not joined by the whistles, hoots, handshakes, or back-slaps that usually acknowledged such a splashy front page. Every cop in the room was either bent low over paperwork, or absorbed in a phone conversation.

Cello swept the room with a withering, bunch-of-assholes look, but left it right there. Pointing at Rachel Meredith's front-page photo, he grumbled, "Very nice. I do my damndest to fix you up, and you've got this hot little millionairess socked away."

"All I see is the painting," Clay countered.

"Yeah, well, it wasn't Vinny Van Gogh who called about two seconds before you walked in."

"Shit! She's got her painting—what the hell does she want from me?"

Clay got the Meredith answering machine. In between leaving his name and number, Rachel picked up. "Don't hang up, Detective Ryder! Sorry—that's flaky, screening like that, but the phone hasn't stopped ringing. We had to disconnect it last night, or we wouldn't have gotten any sleep."

"What are you saying? You've had phone threats?"

"No, no, nothing like that, Detective. This is all going so fast—I still don't understand what happened to my grandparents during the war. My mother was a child then, and when she grew up . . . well, my grandmother refused to discuss those years. Mr. Castelblanco and I have been in touch, but he keeps switching the subject to creating an exhibition around the Trabuc."

"And you've agreed?"

"Not yet, but the painting's at the museum for now, and I'm leaning that way. Anyway, he made the point that since you were the one responsible for tracing the picture to me, you were best qualified to explain how . . . how the painting vanished."

Castelblanco, artful in every sense, had passed the buck—the terrible revelation that her grandfather died during a Gestapo interrogation—while he chatted up a new exhibition.

"We'll never know everything, Dr. Meredith, but I—"

"Oh, thank you, Detective Ryder," she said softly. "My husband will be finished at the studio at four. Can you come by around five?"

She'd totally outmaneuvered his intention to tell her then and there, right over the phone. It would've been heartless, but swift. "That's not really in the rule book, Dr. Meredith."

"What if we come to Police Plaza? Is that okay?" she gently persisted.

"The point isn't *where,* Dr. Meredith. As of yesterday, it's a closed case."

Her silence only underlined how cold he must have sounded. And the truth was, he could get it over with and still do it by the book by leaving Hickey a DD5. The Detective Division 5 form would put him on record as wrapping things up with the Merediths at their apartment. A courtesy call of sorts. "Look, I guess I can work it out. If nothing else comes up, I'll be in your neighborhood around five." That was the truth; he lived only a few blocks away.

"You have no idea how much—"

"Got to go now," he cut her off, clicking to another line that wasn't ringing.

Before Rachel Meredith had the door halfway open, Lulu's nose was twitching up and down Clay's slacks. As soon as she made the olfactory ID, she beat a hasty retreat.

Her owner was too busy thanking Clay to notice.

"Dr. Meredith," he said firmly, "I was only doing my job."

"You're much too modest." A tall man with blue eyes set off by a tan—the other half of a good-looking couple—strode up to them, hand extended. "Hi, I'm Wil. Glad to meet you."

Meredith's grip was strong and confident, and he projected the kind of top-of-the-world enthusiasm that could only come from being married to a smart, beautiful woman who'd just landed on the receiving end of an incredible fortune.

The whole comfortable scene—the apartment, the creative lives, the marriage—it was like hearing that someone had beaten all the odds to win a multimillion-dollar Lotto prize . . . for the second time. Enough to make the masses who'd bought all those losing tickets feel not just shit-out-of-luck, but doubly so.

As they made their way to the living room, Clay declined the Merediths' offer of a cold drink. Both of them sat together on the love seat opposite his, leaning forward expectantly. As much as he wanted to make a quick escape, Clay couldn't exactly jump-start the meeting with the tragic convergence of Paul Bergère and Udo Luscher; even he wasn't that callous. Instead, he inquired about the special Met exhibition.

"The museum came up with quite a unique concept," Wil Meredith replied. With a nod, he deferred to his wife.

"First they considered a collection of paintings from Van Gogh's stay at Saint-Rémy," she explained, "but Mr. Castelblanco was concerned it was too similar to a show they put on a while back. Then someone suggested an exhibit of paintings that vanished in the Holocaust—a memorial to all that was lost."

Confused, Clay looked from one to the other. "How exactly do they plan to do that—if they all vanished?"

"They'll use old photographs of paintings as they appeared in catalogues or actual collections before the war . . . before they were looted," she continued. "They'll be displayed next to similar paintings. For example, a prewar photo of a lost Degas would be displayed next to a Degas canvas of the same period. Optimum would be same year, same subject. You see? All the variations, all the nuances between the two, the record of the artist's development—whatever continued to obsess him, whatever he strove to achieve or to perfect—gone."

"Yes," Clay agreed, "the ongoing self-examination."

"Exactly." Even her quick reply couldn't conceal her *a cop said that?* look. "And because the Nazis carted off absolutely everything, the Met can probably find enough matches in its own collections to fill a gallery—anything from the Middle Ages to Matisse is fair game."

"That gives them a shot at putting it together within a year or so," said Clay. "Not having to deal with other museums or private collectors."

"Actually," her husband joined in, "they've surprised us all. They're aiming for November, in time for the big holiday crowds—warp speed for a monolith."

"The museum is building it around my grandfather's painting," Dr. Meredith resumed, "but the idea itself—the great loss—is the real focal point. As it should be." Tears welled up in her eyes. "I could hardly refuse to participate." She stood up abruptly. "Excuse me—I'll be right back."

Concern gathered in a knot in the middle of her husband's forehead as she hurried away down the hall. "You saw Rachel the other day," he whispered. "Tell me if you don't see a difference!"

"Mr. Meredith, I had no idea that bringing up the exhibit would get her so . . ." He could hardly say *so totally wacked out.*

"Agitated?" Meredith volunteered. "How could you know? I'm her husband, and *I* was unprepared for this reaction! Well, imagine—over the years, she's literally lost her entire family. And now, thanks to your investigation, this painting, this amazing legacy, suddenly finds its way to her! I expected she'd be thrilled, happy, ready to celebrate! But it's just the opposite—she seems to have taken all the weight of the Holocaust on her shoulders."

Clay, contemplating whether he and Lauren had ever been where the Merediths were in their relationship, ever had what they had—with or without a fifty-million-dollar painting—made no reply.

Dr. Meredith returned, eyes and nose red. "Detective Ryder . . . about my grandparents?"

As she sat down next to her husband, he gently took her hand in his, and murmured, "Rachel, maybe this isn't the best time."

"Yes, I'm upset. Yes, I never felt the Holocaust touch my life before. But not to hear about what happened in Paris . . ." Looking up, she locked eyes with Clay. "Don't take this personally, Detective, but that would be like putting off root canal."

He'd come prepared with a short discourse focused on Annette Bergère's determination to retrieve the Van Goghs, ending with her accusations at the Jeu de Paume. He carefully avoided any reference to the SS officer's reputation for brutality. "I doubt anything could have pleased her more than having one of the paintings returned to her granddaughter" was how the script ended.

That was it. He waited a beat or two, then stood, more than ready to go.

Wil Meredith, his mouth compressed into a thin, angry line, broke the strained silence. "Unless that damned Nazi died a long, painful death, there's not a trace of justice in your story, is there?"

"Justice?" Clay repeated.

"I mean, it's no more than chance that Rachel got the painting back, is it? Sheer chance."

The guy had it nailed. Chance had indeed taken the place of justice.

"No, not chance," Dr. Meredith mused, "but maybe something I never believed in before."

Neither man spoke. Clay didn't believe in fate. Her husband's silence was a good indication that he didn't, either.

A little after the evening rush hour, Clay was on his way east, to the North Fork.

He'd never gone back to visit Lauren's grave after the funeral. Far more punishing than a trip to the cemetery was the stretch of highway where she'd switched lanes, unaware of the SUV in the Toyota's blind spot.

As always, he turned off the radio as he approached—less out of respect than to channel in on the monumental anger issuing from that particular strip of road—rage still powerful enough to activate some weird, on-the-spot frequency beamed right at him. Lauren's purse, thrown so far it hadn't been found for two days, was recovered in a thicket high above the roadside. Many things-to-do were on the list tucked inside, but dying hadn't been one of them. It must have really pissed her off.

You couldn't have thought of a more sexist thing to say in front of that realtor!

My intention wasn't to be sexist—just to embarrass you and get rid of her.

How well you succeeded! I turned red with embarrassment. The trooper didn't tell you he threw up when he saw me, did he? And don't whine to me about sorrow and self-reproach—not if you're heading to the Pigsty in the Pines!

I swear, not a day passes that I don't regret everything I said, and how right you were about—

Dead right, that's me. Oh, and if we miss our tête-à-tête on the way back, do send my regards to your grandfather. In retrospect—and that's all I've got, sweetheart—I suspect that you've confused the one who fucked your brains out— hello! that's me!—with the one who totally fucked up your head in the first place.

The remainder of the long ride was rarely enough to get his mind off Lauren, who wasn't exactly the woman he thought he'd married, but who in so many ways was the woman he needed.

That night, second-guessing what Rachel Meredith would do with the Trabuc after the close of the Met exhibit provided some distraction. Evidently, the bidding had already started, or she and her husband wouldn't be disconnecting their phone. Clay wasn't a betting man, but he had every reason to believe that the most persistent of the callers was his pre-NYPD employer, Esterbrook-Grennell.

Earlier in the week, he had to drive by their Upper East Side headquarters, a place he usually went out of his way to avoid. The scaffolding that had surrounded the building for months was gone, and a sleek, expanded edifice was exposed, all black sheathing and tinted glass, like a huge Mafia Lincoln. Living testimony to how the soft art market of the early Nineties had followed the stock market straight up into the stratosphere. The firm's name was affixed to the facade in minuscule chrome letters, legible from the street only if you already knew what they spelled out. Curbside arrogance. The old if you're-one-of-us-you'll-find-us snobbery, starting before anyone even walked through the door. Discretion was one of the auction house's greatest draws: sellers who sought anonymity, whose lots were listed in the slick catalogues as "the property of a gentleman" or "from the collection of a lady," ate it up.

New facade or no, it was still the same Esterbrook-Grennell he'd left in 1993, the place he once regarded as his big chance to use the art history that sat on his brain's back burner while he was in the military.

The Navy was never supposed to be more than a brief holding pattern between graduation and the rest of his life. Reporting for duty the day after he received his college diploma had become a family tradition of sorts: Clay's father had done it as an act of defiance against his father, and Clay followed right in his footsteps, defying the very same man—his grandfather, Jonas Ryder.

Clay's dad, who'd died in Vietnam, had been an Army Ranger; for Clay, the Navy versus the Army had come down to a flip of the coin—a *que sera, sera* moment that would've driven old Jonas nuts. The reason he wasn't witness to it was that he'd already booted Clay out of the house.

(Thanks to his mother's careful subversion of university mail, three semesters went by before his grandfather discovered that Clay had switched his major from business to art history—a clear message that he had no intention of joining the family firm. When an all-art syllabus finally slipped by her, the old man promptly disowned him; only his attempts to obtain a court order that would ban Clay from visiting his mother failed.)

Paying his own way to get his degree stretched senior year to two years of odd jobs. Following up with the SEALs, and then Desert Storm, he was the property of the Navy until August '91.

It wasn't the best time for job-hunting. The art world was on a respirator:

galleries were going out of business, museums were closing off entire wings, and only one of the three big auction houses had an opening.

From the way the Esterbrook-Grennell personnel director kept looking at her desk clock, she had no intention of making room for Clay on the job lifeboat, so he hit her with everything the Navy had taught him about mounting an all-out attack.

"You may have other people up for this job who appear to be better qualified," he said, as she prepared to show him the door, "but how many share my unique experience?"

Puzzled, she took a second look at his résumé.

"Years of independently continuing my studies on sea and on land, in peace and . . ." In a respectful whisper, he added, "in war. A museum in every port." Shameless, but he was having too much fun to give a damn. "My art books saw duty on destroyers, aircraft carriers, submarines. Some were washed overboard—but I dived right in and rescued them."

That'd been thrown in to lighten the mood, but the lady was out there, riding the waves.

"What I'm asking is . . ." Clay had to bite down hard on his lip to keep from grinning. "Ma'am, will you give a veteran a break?"

"Yes," she said nervously, not kicking him out at all. "Yes, I will."

His impulse was to stand and salute her, but he feared that would be a giveaway. His only guess was that military service was so alien, so outré to the art crowd, hiring him would make her look ultracool, a daring innovator.

Except for grunt research, his job had nothing to do with art.

He fielded phone calls, arranged for insurance and photography, fetched coffee and theater tickets. In the course of his duties, he met several very attractive women. His military background intrigued them as it had the personnel director, but they kept him otherwise employed.

The first one was pretty, but so pale—porcelain skin, light blue eyes, hair the color of champagne—she looked half erased. On and off, the two of them had eyed one another around the office for weeks.

Working late one night, he found her at the copying machine. Her back was to him as he leaned against the wall, waiting for her to finish. "Aren't you the one who used to be"—she half-turned, and her eyes crinkled, as if no word could be more amusing—"a sailor?"

"That's me."

"A SEAL." She punched some buttons on the big Xerox, leaving it to spit out copies on its own. A few steps, and she entered the private space that strangers usually respect, with the exception of rush-hour subways and crowded elevators. The music hadn't even started, and their bodies were already dancing together. "Aren't SEALs supposed to have the toughest training in the world? Only a fraction of each class qualifies?"

"Some classes perform better than others."

"Isn't it all about endurance? You just keep going, like a machine?"

"Unlike machines, you're expected to keep pushing past your limits."

"Oooo. That's good." One perfectly manicured index finger tapped his shirtfront. "You haven't lost it yet, have you? That extra push?"

Their closeness made an answer unnecessary.

"What was the longest time you ever spent—"

"A little over ten hours."

"—swimming?"

"Oh. I thought you meant something else."

Her name was Alison, and she was engaged to a guy in his last year at Stanford Law, but didn't wear his ring to work. "You try typing with a Ping-Pong ball on your finger" was all she had to say about the stone size. Banging Clay wasn't her idea of a moral predicament, but in bed one night she confided that she was uneasy about what was going on in the Esterbrook-Grennell salesrooms.

"Like what?" he asked.

"For starters, I think they use shills."

"Sounds like a sale in an upstate cowbarn. Toothless guys in overalls."

"Right. Hayseeds in Armanis. Seriously, I keep seeing at least three of them—they never buy, always bid up. The bank of telephones for phone bids? They ring like mad, but not all of them have dial tones. Oh, and the auctioneers, too. Rat-tat-tat, mid-Atlantic machine guns. I'm absolutely positive they call more bid-ups than paddles up."

"Bidding on the chandelier?"

"If that's what it's called. Really cheesy stuff."

"Alison, they've been in business forever. Why—?"

"Maybe that's the secret of their longevity."

Esterbrook-Grennell, like its two major competitors, dated back to eighteenth-century London. In fact, all three auction houses were considerably older than most of the pieces they hammered down. People trusted them— especially rich, powerful people. Combined, the triumvirate controlled 95 percent of world auction sales.

Alison rose on one elbow, even paler than the moonlight filtering into the room. "There's more. I went to boarding school with Deirdre Sands's personal assistant."

Sands was the president of Esterbrook-Grennell North America, a former financial analyst whose art background ended with Crayolas. Her real art was the way she'd kept E-G from going under when the bottom fell out of the art market.

"My friend saw a handwritten list on Sands's desk. Fifty names. Your typical 'Hugely Wealthy Americans Who Spend Big Bucks on Art.' The deal is, Esterbrook isn't going to bill them a dime in commissions!"

"Alison, that doesn't make any sense."

"Oh, they plan to make up for it! They're about to raise the commission rates *everyone else* pays, buyers and sellers alike. And if that's not tacky enough, the competition's agreed to do the same, and to charge the exact same rates. They're even sharing the list. Isn't that illegal?"

"From all that I know, yes. You and your friend—are you going to do anything about it?"

"Absolutely. My friend is about to leave to run a gallery in Big Sur. In a few months, I'm going to quit and get married. You don't think either of us is about to jump in the path of a 250-year-old steamroller, do you?"

Alison's account of dirty sales practices bothered Clay, but he kept clinging to the belief that Esterbrook-Grennell's art integrity remained separate and unsullied. However, as his eye grew more experienced, he observed that several pieces of dubious value and at least one forgery were regularly included in the big fall and spring sales. Of course, just as the house's expert restorers could do wonders with torn canvas, the gaps in a provenance could be just as deftly patched—thanks to centuries of sales records available for mending.

Esterbrook-Grennell employees who chose to overlook such trickery—or, even better, add a few new dodges to the slate—were assured a steady rise in the company. Clay knew his aversion to fraud would keep him where he was, a miserable half-notch above entry level. He wanted to get out, and to get out clean, but he had no idea where to go.

One morning, his boss buzzed him to say that the call Clay had just put through from Estate Exploration was actually for him. He'd heard of the department, but was fuzzy about what it actually did. Puzzled, he picked up. "Mr. Ryder, do you remember a client named Browning Macpherson? Purchased a Monet last spring?"

"You mean Admiral Macpherson? Sure."

Macpherson had served in the prewar white-shoe Navy; his wife's maiden name was on half of America's cereal boxes. Without warning, the octogenarian couple had appeared at a preview of the big May sale, minutes before Clay's boss was due to meet another major client. After a hurried apology, Clay was introduced as a qualified substitute. That didn't sit well at all with the admiral, who sulked in his wheelchair until Clay identified himself as a former Navy man. Macpherson perked up at that. Before long, he was wheeling through the showroom at a leisurely pace, discussing art, life at sea, ports of call, and the collection he and his wife began on their honeymoon.

Matter of factly, Estate Exploration stated, "Browning Macpherson died a few days ago."

"I'm really sorry to hear that. A very engaging gentleman."

"It seems the feeling was mutual, Mr. Ryder. I was on the phone with Mrs. Macpherson just a little while ago. She said if she spoke to anyone from Esterbrook-Grennell, it would be you."

"About what?"

"Maybe you'd better come upstairs."

The work of Estate Exploration, Clay learned, was based on a list compiled daily by an independent service. The people on the list had two things in common: all of them were very rich, and all of them were newly dead. Besides the estimated value of their estates and contact numbers for relatives and executors, the service also noted the time of interment.

Clay tried to keep his voice level. "You said the admiral died a few days ago. You've already been in touch with his widow—I bet the phone was ringing when she walked in the door from the cemetery. And now you expect me to turn on the old Esterbrook-Grennell charm and convince her to consign you the collection she and her husband built over fifty years?"

Without waiting for an answer, he slammed the door of Estate Exploration, stormed out of the building, and walked the short distance to the East River.

The wind was chopping the water pretty hard, and an ancient green tugboat plowing upriver looked stalwart as any schooner Antonio Jacobson ever painted. Clay kept it in sight until it shrank to the size of a pea.

He'd never make it in the art world and didn't care, because making it had nothing to do with art.

Standing on the embankment, he was aware that if he kept on walking, he'd rip nearly two years out of his life—self-surgery, without benefit of anesthesia. Nevertheless, his feet started putting distance between him and Esterbrook-Grennell. He was no angel, but he'd never felt so dirty in his life.

By chance or not, when he was finally working his way crosstown toward his apartment, he found himself on a street lined on both sides by blue-and-white patrol cars. The reason for the extraordinary police presence soon became clear: the block housed the Police Academy.

Briefly, he weighed whether he was about to make yet another career move to spite his grandfather, or do something solely for himself. All he could be sure of was that filling out an NYPD application was definitely not something he'd foreseen when he woke up that morning.

The highway ended, and he started along the long, snaking back roads that led to The Shack. His thoughts shifted back to Rachel and Wil Meredith, two attractive and surprisingly likable people. But neither of them had any idea how deep and dangerous were the waters into which they sailed. By the time the exhibit at the Met closed, the most ferocious of the world's art sharks would have them surrounded, harrying them to sell or consign the Trabuc. And among the Great Whites leading the charge would be Esterbrook-Grennell, the hoariest and whoriest of all.

Unfortunately, there was nothing he could do. Trabuc was no longer lost, and the case was officially closed.

CHAPTER
EIGHT

The following week, summer came on full blast. In the morning, Clay would work out at the Academy pool, only to be drawn back again in the evening to cool down. The relief didn't last long. By the time he reached his home block on West Tenth Street, he was drenched. His one outward concession to the heat was a loosened tie and an unbuttoned collar; a sports jacket was necessary to conceal the Glock in his shoulder holster. Only the promise of the beer chilling in his refrigerator kept him moving along.

His apartment was the rent-stabilized one-bedroom he'd occupied since he started at Esterbrook-Grennell. B-2 (Basement Rear) might be semi-subterranean and sunless, but it was nestled in the middle of two long facing rows of well-kept brownstones, and he had exclusive use of the tiny garden. Although real estate was never to be common ground between them, Lauren had moved in without complaint—cramped as they were, the savings and the neighborhood made it acceptable.

The streetlights sizzled on, illuminating the elderly lady across the street. She was watering the rose bushes she coaxed into bloom every year in her five-by-eight front yard. Clay watched three little kids wearing nothing but shorts and sandals run up and beg her to spray them. Their father called something from two stoops down, and the old girl smiled and let them have it, unleashing screams of delight.

Turning back to his side of the street, Clay noticed a man in a dark suit and shirt lounging on a stoop, his face blurred by the lacy shadows of the block's tallest tree. He leaned back with his elbows on the steps, his long legs extended to the sidewalk. As he came closer, Clay realized the man was lolling on his next-door neighbor's steps. To get to his own basement entrance, he'd have to give the guy's feet some leeway. Clay also picked out a car parked in front of the fire hydrant across from his building. A plain, dark sedan, it was only three or four brownstones past the kids' leaps in and out of the arcing stream of water. The windows were tinted, but with the overhead street lamps on, there was a hint of someone in the driver's seat. A little farther down, partially concealed by a tree on the opposite side, was a third man. The slight but constant movement of his head indicated he was a lookout, an east-to-west and west-to-east metronome scanning the block.

Clay slowed, glancing from him to the man blocking his path, the car, the kids getting sprayed.

"Hello, Ryder, and not so tense—it's your old friend, Aaron," said the man on the stoop in a slurry accent.

"Those other guys—across the street—are they on your team?"

"Sure, the Tel Aviv Dreidels—fastest dribblers in the East." Aaron got to his feet, keeping clear of the streetlight's glare.

The kids across the street cried out in protest. Their father was telling them they'd had enough, to say thanks to the lady, and come inside. The splatter of the hose against the sidewalk stopped, and a fresh, rainlike aroma drifted over the packed rows of cars.

"Ryder, are you all right?" Aaron asked after they shook hands. "You look exhausted."

"The humidity." Clay hadn't seen Aaron for two years, but he was unchanged: a tall, loose-limbed Jewish guy with curly dark hair, the kind who can pass for a college basketball player until he's pushing forty. Although he didn't dislike Aaron, all he wanted was to sit down and drink his beer. Alone.

"So," Aaron probed, "you're not inviting me in?"

"I didn't know the Mossad made house calls." He dug for his keys, walked down the three steps, and unlocked the gate and the door behind it. "Come on in." Aaron was on his heels as he walked to the end of the hall and opened his apartment door. Clay knew that he'd been the unofficial Mossad-NYPD liaison for a long time.

The two organizations had a quiet, friendly relationship based on their unfriendly view of terrorists. Like kids with baseball cards, they traded information on the rookies and veterans of various fanatic groups. Tips attributed to "concerned neighbors" who suspected explosives were being mixed in the bathtub next door often came from the Mossad. Thanks to them, travelers on circuitous routes originating in Beirut or Teheran were expected at JFK long before their connecting flights took off from Amsterdam or Paris. The Israelis didn't celebrate Christmas, but they still exchanged gifts.

"Neat place, Ryder, except for the boat in the corner."

"It's a ship."

Although she hadn't planned to stay a day longer than it took to accumulate their suburban down payment, Lauren had nevertheless done her best to fix up B-2. She wouldn't have been happy with the clutter of the steamship-in-progress that spread over a card table, an old sheet serving as a drop cloth on the floor beneath it. More than a whiff of freshly sanded wood and glue and paint greeted them at the door.

After peeling of his jacket, Clay flipped on the ceiling fan and opened the room's single window. The lazy breeze that stole in past the window bars was transformed into a small whirlwind by the fan's spinning blades.

Meanwhile, Aaron strolled toward the plans taped to the wall above the ship, which Clay had tracked down at a maritime library. He went on to peer into the coat closet and the kitchen alcove, then pointed to a door at the rear. "What's back there?"

"The bedroom. The bathroom. The garden."

"Mind if I take a look?"

"What are you trying to do, Aaron? Sublet the place out from under me?"

The Mossad agent was already in the back, and Clay heard the distinctive creak of the bathroom door. From the living room, Clay watched as his visitor looked through the barred bedroom windows facing the garden and tested the garden door. It was steel, had three locks, and didn't jiggle in its frame. "You missed the ayatollah hiding behind the shower curtain," Clay called to him.

"I'm impressed. Guys living alone usually don't make their beds."

"It's a Navy thing."

Satisfied that Clay wasn't harboring anyone wielding a scimitar, Aaron returned to the living room. Clay offered him a beer. "Thank you very much, no." Aaron's eyes returned to the steamship. "Is that . . . like a hobby?"

"A hobby? I don't know. It's the first one I've ever worked on. I started it about a year ago."

Aaron had it figured out in no time. "About your wife . . . my sympathy."

"Okay, you've run an investigation on me . . . now tell me what the hell is going on!"

"Someone from our organization wants to ask you a few questions. Possible?"

"He must be important, if he has *you* sweeping my apartment."

"Important?" Aaron's dark eyes narrowed. "I would die for him." His tone challenged the depth of all Clay's loyalties, past, present, and future.

Five minutes and more went by, a long time to cross the street. Just inside the gate, a *thump-thump* sounded, followed by something heavy dragging over the scratchy indoor-outdoor hall carpet. After a pause, the thumping and dragging were repeated. A longer pause. An undertone of human effort became discernible under the next surge of forward motion. Aaron swung the door in, and Clay's visitor entered. Murmuring a phrase in Hebrew, Aaron, who remained out in the hall, shut the door after him, like an ordinary bodyguard.

Clay was shocked that a man so severely crippled managed to walk at all—

if such movement could be called walking. A pair of stout, three-footed metal canes fitted to wide wristcuffs helped propel him forward: the thumps came from the manner in which he had to throw them into his own path. Braces thick and heavy enough to bear his weight were strapped around limp legs, nearly up to the hips. It seemed improbable that his upper body could be powerful enough to haul the rest of him along; his right shoulder was several inches higher than the left, and his neck raked back at an angle, so that he had to see as much of the ceiling as the room before him.

Clay thought his guest's face was permanently locked into a rictus of pain and effort, but after he stopped and breathed deeply for a while, it recomposed itself into regular features. He looked like a man in his late fifties, but Clay assumed whatever affliction he'd been born with had aged him beyond his years. His hair was thick, white, and well barbered, like the president's. "Detective Ryder, thanks for inviting me in. My name isn't important—just call me Eli." Clay knew Aaron was a *sabra*; Eli's English had the same random British-American mix.

"Okay, Eli. I'm Clay. How about a beer? And where would you like to sit?"

From his tilted-back viewpoint, his guest zeroed in on the small dining table with its two straight-backed chairs. "Over there, please. A beer sounds fine, thank you. And Clay—if I need help, I ask."

Only then, as he paused to rest a moment longer, did Clay notice how impeccably dressed the man was. Unquestionably, his tan summerweight suit and cream-colored shirt had been custom-tailored to his unfortunate shape. Inside the braces, his slacks were pressed into knife-edge creases. His wide silk tie and poufed-out pocket square, which would have been stylish on a straighter body, were borderline flashy on Eli, as were his gleaming, expensive shoes.

Once they were seated, cold bottles in front of them, Eli said, "I just flew in from Israel. I don't travel much, and I always forget how much it tires me out."

"How long are you staying?"

"I'm not." His eyebrows lifted, self-mocking. "I'm a big security risk."

"Well, Eli, I've never been on the short list of things to see in New York. Aaron said you had some questions. What do you want to know?"

"It's related to the Van Gogh you connected to its owner. Good detective work, by the way."

"My computer and I thank you."

"First off, I should say that I have no interest in either the painting or Dr. Meredith. The person accused of stealing the painting, however . . ."

"Udo Luscher?"

Eli kept his expression impassive, even as a spasm shot through his left shoulder. "Yes. It was the first time we'd heard his name in twenty-eight years."

"That's a pretty cold trail."

"For any other man, yes."

"A note came with the painting. It said that the man who'd held the painting was dead a long time. *If* that man was Luscher."

"The letter from a Señora Reyes-Martinez," confirmed Eli. "The old woman who did the vanishing trick in Buenos Aires."

Neither Luscher's name, nor that of the Argentine woman, had been released to the press. On the other hand, no one had treated them as classified information, either. "Should I assume you're familiar with Madame Bergère's accusations at the Jeu de Paume?"

"Only since the story broke. We've always been more interested in stolen lives than stolen pictures."

"If you know so much, why did you—"

"Travel so far? To ask for your cooperation—off the record, of course."

Clay poked at two beads of condensation on his beer bottle and watched them race down to the tabletop. Even though the fan was doing its job, he had that fried, queasy, up-all-night feeling, as if he, rather than Eli, had dragged himself through airports and time zones. *Off the record* had whizzed by fast, like a figure of speech. "Sure, I'll do what I can, but nobody beats you guys at this stuff." He jabbed his finger toward his front door. "Aaron just made me feel like you know which brand of underwear I'm wearing. You have all the experience, all the resources—I don't see how I can help."

"The Van Gogh, coming out of nowhere the way it did . . . that's a whole new angle. I don't know where it goes—God knows I've had my share of stumbling down blind alleys after Udo Luscher." Eli's shoulder twitched again, and he shifted on the chair's cane seat. "Damn airplanes! I can't get rid of this cramp!" Twisting his neck, he produced an audible crack. Then he tilted his head back even further, so his words drifted toward the ceiling. "He's like grabbing at smoke rings. There's nothing human about him. Only his will to survive."

Clay took a swig of beer to erase a flash-image of Luscher in the black Mercedes. "Twenty-eight years, you said? Nineteen seventy-one . . . that's almost right in the middle. Twenty-six years after he allegedly drove off to Nazi Valhalla on his way to Munich. What was Luscher up to in '71?"

"Doing something he had no right to. Living a normal life in Argentina. But let me back it up a bit for you. Nineteen sixty-nine. The year we started trailing an Argentinean neo-Nazi by the name of Pedro Mueller. Have you heard of the *Kameradenwerk*?"

"Only a week or so ago, for the first time. While I was reading up on post-war Argentina. Everything on the subject was unsubstantiated . . . sketchy."

"Yes, I'm sure it was. That's always been the desired effect. However, the *Kameradenwerk* was—still is—very real. Once the war ended, and the Nazis scattered, it was their only link to one another. Just as you'd expect, it proved to be an extremely efficient network—and particularly well organized in South America. If you ever wondered how so many Nazis managed to wind up there, the *Kameradenwerk* was their conduit. Aided by the Vatican, of course." He paused. "Does that surprise you?"

"Go on."

"The Nazis hated the communists second only to the Jews. The pope viewed communists—card-carrying atheists, all—as first among the Church's enemies. To use today's jargon, an opportunity for bonding presented itself. In every Nazi the Holy See helped to escape, there was the potential for the elimination of God knows how many godless Bolsheviks."

"Like they say, politics makes strange bedfellows."

"Even among those sworn to celibacy." A trace of a smile crossed Eli's face. "Anyway, moving those men required papers. The way it worked was that the Vatican supplied Nazis with its own identity cards. They were like vouchers that could be exchanged for International Red Cross passports. That's what the war criminals, posing as priests, used to cross into Italy from Switzerland and Austria. Can you picture them, blessing the border guards who let them pass?"

"Nice touch. And then?"

"Hid out in monasteries until they had their Argentine travel visas and their ships were ready to sail. Usually out of Genoa."

"What about Argentina's government? It had to know what was going on."

"Absolutely. After World War I, waves of Germans emigrated there, to get away from the economic collapse in Europe. By the mid-Thirties, Third Reich operatives had a strong base in Argentina. It was all very simpatico—not one was ever detained by the *Coordinación Federal* for espionage. In '46, Perón came into power. He and Evita made a bloody fortune importing the Nazis and all the war loot they carted along. As for the *Kameradenwerk,* the more Nazis filtering in, the more manpower they needed. The source they tapped was Argentine natives born to German parents. As kids, they belonged to scout groups whose top merit badges were awarded for essays praising *der Führer.* As they grew up, they came to view themselves as the cornerstones of the Fourth Reich. And whenever anyone got too close to the original Nazis, they'd move them. New names, new papers, new jobs. Moved them around like chess pieces. Argentina's a big country."

"If they were so good, how'd your guys get Eichmann?"

"Good question. Back in Europe, prison sentences for war crimes were being cut in half, some even commuted outright. Cold War politics. If prisoners were being released faster than new ones could be prosecuted, it was logical to conclude that the bloodhounds would relent. Also, Israel wasn't considered a genuine threat—Nazis old and new viewed Jews as *Untermenschen,* not quite human. I wouldn't say the *Kameradenwerk* became complacent . . . just a lot less vigilant."

"Like Eichmann working in Mercedes-Benz's Buenos Aires factory? 'Less vigilant?' God, did he go to work in his old SS uniform?"

"He was a foreman, no less. But we've come around to suspecting that maybe he was hung out to dry. High-ranking Nazis didn't consider him in their class. Plus, if he was accused of killing every Jew in Europe, how many others could be tried for the same crime? As for Argentina, Eichmann's kidnapping made her stand victimized before other nations—but subsequently we learned that the *Coordinación Federal* knew every move the Israelis made, from the first moment they set foot on Argentine soil."

"What are you saying, Eli? That they turned their backs and let your guys carry off Eichmann to make it *safer* for the rest of the war criminals? That making him the scapegoat insured that Argentina wouldn't become Israel's private Nazi poaching preserve?"

"Illogically logical, wasn't it? Proof that no matter how smart you think you are, there's always someone who can outsmart you. Which brings us back to Pedro Mueller, the neo-Nazi I mentioned. He spent his life on the road, driving from war criminal to war criminal—some were hundreds of miles apart. He kept them up-to-date about what was happening in *der Vaterland*, played Nazi mailman, brought them wursts and stollen. Who knows? Maybe they read *Mein Kampf* aloud to one another out on the pampas."

Eli stopped to drink some beer. Like moving on his crutches, swallowing required sheer doggedness. Clay kept his eyes on Eli's face; averting them would have indicated revulsion, or, far worse, pity.

"Mueller was good—one of the *Kameradenwerk*'s original recruits. He shook our guys off several times. When we started tailing him, in '69, he drove a new Buick—they always drove American cars. By the end, its odometer probably reset itself to zero. With switching and all, we must've used twenty cars to tail him. It took us nearly two years just to figure out who lived on his route. Unfortunately, our top suspect drowned, but another piqued our interest: he went by the name Javier Delgado, and ran a winery up in the hills outside Córdoba. An extremely isolated place.

"Mueller always waited until after dark to drive onto his property, and Delgado never left, never went to town. All we could find out about him was that he'd been there about ten years, which made sense. The *Kameradenwerk* probably moved him up there right after the Eichmann incident."

"So you suspected it was Luscher?"

"We had no idea. Obviously someone important, given Mueller's precautions. For a while, we even thought it might be Bormann."

"Bormann? Still alive in '71?"

Eli sighed. "Sadly, yes. Anyway, we desperately needed a photograph that we could send to Israel for verification. Surveillance was impossible—the winery was enclosed, guarded, and at the end of a mountain road. We couldn't figure out how to get a man in. So we came up with something better."

"Which was?"

"A woman," Eli grinned. "You know the Avon Lady?"

" 'Ding-dong! Welcome your Avon representative when she calls.' "

"In Argentina, they had *Fascinación*—same idea—makeup and perfume right in your own hacienda. The saleswomen wore pink—at the time, polyester pantsuits were all the rage. So a sample case is snatched out of a car in Buenos Aires and turns up in Córdoba, hauled around by one of our female operatives. She's the color of lox head to toe, a miniature camera very ingeniously concealed in her shoulder bag.

"The *Fascinación* agent gets in, chats with Señora Delgado. Her older sister, one Señora Suarez—not half as pretty—strolls over from the other house on the winery grounds. Their kids are running in and out, all ages, boys and girls. Miss Pink shows both women the new lipsticks. They all have a cup of coffee— still no sign of Señora Delgado's husband.

"They get around to perfume. Which to choose? 'Let your husband decide, dear,' says *La Fascinaciónista*. 'After all, isn't he's the one who's going to smell it?' Wink, wink. So the husband's dragged in—much older than his wife, late forties, but tall, blue eyes, blond hair. Click, click. On the way to the car, as much of the layout of this very private compound as she can get. Click, click. By diplomatic pouch to Tel Aviv, and, to our amazement, Udo Luscher is positively identified."

"Okay. So your people went back to . . . export him? He caught wind of it, and took off again?"

"No . . . that's not the case." Eli breathed in sharply. "An extraction party was planned. Seven men, plus two drivers in two cars. It was set for the night of the new moon. Tremendous risk, only a sketchy knowledge of the surroundings, the defenses . . . the consensus was that getting Udo Luscher was worth it. Plus, we had something invaluable on our side: the element of surprise. Or so we thought. But even with all our stealth, leaving our cars well down the hill, and a night black as pitch, the people inside knew what was up. The first men to reach the winery gate went down like tenpins."

"Shit! What the hell happened?"

"To this day, we still don't know."

"So your guys walked into a trap?"

"Into a bloodbath. Nearly annihilated in the first twenty seconds. No one would have survived if our side didn't have an M-79, launching both explosive and incendiary grenades. The explosions and the fires they ignited exposed Luscher's positions, forced his men out. After that, it was our turn to do some damage . . . until the winery team stopped the man with the M-79. Only two badly wounded Israelis could still return fire. They managed to radio the cars and then cover the drivers while they removed the dead and severely wounded. They shot at everything that moved and encountered weak resistance. At a time like that, you get the hell out as fast as you can. Not a good time to check if Luscher was among the dead.

"We finally got a man back in the area about a week later. He learned that the local doctor was called up to the winery the day after the attack. No mention was made of a fire. The place is a very long drive from town, so when the doctor didn't return that night, no big deal. The morning of the third day, the constable went up to check. Burned ruins, bodies charred beyond hope of identification, not a living soul. One of the few recognizable objects was the blade of a dagger, with engraving in German. Himmler's name was on it."

"*Le Découpeur*'s?"

"The same. The doctor's car was gone. So was the doctor. He was never seen again." Like a man eager to purge away a bad taste, Eli downed the rest of his beer.

Some time passed before Clay could ask, "Can I get you one more?"

"Thanks, but I'm only allowed one a day." He looked at Clay's empty bottle. "Go ahead, it doesn't bother me."

Clay remained in his chair. "If Luscher died in the raid, or under the doctor's care, then no need to off the doctor." Like a man who catches himself dozing, Clay's head snapped back. "You don't think Luscher's still alive?"

"I rule nothing out. I hate the word 'closure,' Ryder. It's become so trite—a synonym for all-purpose, feel-good healing."

Was he wrong, or had Eli just looked right through him? "Yeah. Ain't it."

"This situation with the painting, it's hardly enough to let in a pinpoint of light. That Luscher was—or is—such a survivor complicates things. I'm here because you're one link closer to him than anyone else."

"Officially, the book is closed on the Trabuc case."

Eli took a deep breath. He forced his twisted body forward. "Clay, any help would be appreciated, any crumb of information about Luscher that might turn up. Of course, without compromising you or the NYPD."

He was tempted to ask Eli exactly when a crumb turns into compromise. Instead, he blurted out, "I only have one thing rolling around in my head right now. Luscher stole two paintings. Only one showed up. I don't know where that goes, but—"

"That, or anything, please, do me the favor of keeping your eyes open." He reached for the canes he'd leaned against the table.

"What's your closure all about, Eli? *Le Découpeur*'s handiwork in Europe, or the Israelis in Argentina?"

"You mean, is it personal?" He looked into Clay's eyes for a long time. The only sounds in the room were the low thrum of the fan and Eli's labored breathing. Impulsively, he reached into his suit jacket and pulled out his billfold. He threw it down on the table, then turned his head away. "Open it. Left side. Behind the Visa card . . . the photograph."

Clay removed a picture of two young men perched on the hood of a jeep. They were tussling with one another, laughing. It looked as if they were in a military post in the desert. They wore shorts and combat boots, and both were good-looking guys, muscular enough to look like they'd just gone through intensive basic training.

"The young man on the right is my brother," Eli said. "He was the agent operating the M-79 in Argentina. The other one . . . that was me . . . before I met Udo Luscher."

CHAPTER
NINE

"Hi, Mom."

Clay's mother was asleep. Or pretending to be. He'd long since stopped trying to tell the difference.

On his last visit, another health care aide had sat in the big, upholstered chair next to the bed—Berenice, who came after Carlette, who came after Marla, if he had the order right. A replacement appeared from the employment agency every month or so. The current aide, wrapped in a heavy cardigan sweater, blinked up at him with puffy eyelids. She'd been catnapping herself, as if his mother's disorder were contagious.

Clay introduced himself. Her nametag read GWEN. "I'll be here at least an hour," he told her. "Take a break, and I'll let you know when I'm on my way out." It was a short walk back to the station, and he knew the train schedule by heart.

Pushing down hard on the armrests, Gwen, a tall black woman in her early forties, got to her feet. Her sweater parted, revealing a blue polyester uniform, one interchangeable with those worn by office cleaners, shampoo girls, and counter-ladies in donut shops. "I'll be in the kitchen if you need me." Her voice was unexpectedly light and sweet, like a girl's. She pulled the sweater tight around her again. "He—your grandfather, I guess?—he sure likes it cold in here, huh? June outside, December inside." She shook her head, as if contemplating what so many wasted kilowatt hours would do to her own utility bill.

"How's my mother been?"

Gwen shrugged. "I only started a few days back. She don't eat much. Mostly lies there, like she's asleep. I don't even know what color eyes she has. Actually, I was surprised she wasn't in Depends. But she gets up to go do her bathroom business. Keeps her eyes closed, like she's sleepwalking. If that's how she was, she's the same."

Once the door was closed, he bent to kiss his mother's forehead. Her light brown hair was fanned out over the pillow; Gwen must have filled some empty time by brushing it smooth. Outside the blanket, her arms lay straight along her sides, and the nightgown's full sleeves did little to conceal how gaunt they were. When Clay took her hand, the fingers felt as thin and inflexible as number 2 pencils.

In the hope that his voice would be therapeutic in some small way, his visits had become verbal rambles—monologues about his week, items in the news, whatever came into his head. This week, it was mostly about the closed case, the Trabuc. As usual, he meandered on, ever hopeful for the slightest squeeze of acknowledgment.

He knew his mother was in there.

Once or twice a month, she had brief, inexplicable windows of wakefulness, lucid enough to pick up the phone and call him. As if they chatted daily, she'd ask, "Did I miss your call, dear?" or, "When's your next visit? I don't want to make any other plans for that day."

Her tone was always pleasant, tinged with concern—like any mother who wasn't playing the lead in the AARP version of Sleeping Beauty.

His reply was always a straightforward, "I was there last week, Mom. You were asleep."

"Oh. Why didn't you wake me? Did Lauren come, too?"

"I was alone."

"She wants to move to Westchester. But I told her it's far too cold here."

"That's the air-conditioning, Mom—Grandpa Ryder keeps it turned up."

"Who?"

"Your father-in-law. The CEO of Ryder Air Conditioning and Refrigeration. He considers anything over sixty degrees tropical."

"I thought he was dead."

"No, Mom. Lauren died."

"Who's Lauren?"

"Mom, I—"

"The next time you visit, do you think we could go out for dinner?"

"Sure, that would be great. How about right now? Anyplace you want. Get yourself all dressed up. I'll be there in—"

By the time he arrived, she'd be in her sleep state, deeper than ever.

Her doctors found no evidence of a brain tumor. Her condition couldn't be traced to any physiological cause. Repeated bloodwork showed no indication of substance abuse. Treatment for narcolepsy, involving both stimulants and antidepressants, was unsuccessful. Her selective semicoma could only be diagnosed as psychosomatic.

Jonas Ryder, legal guardian of his daughter-in-law Betsy since she sank into her sleep affliction/addiction, arranged for a doctor to make house calls weekly. However, he refused to have her placed in a psychiatric facility, not even for an evaluation. Shortly after the onset of his ward's strange self-sedation, she was ensconced in the east wing of his large Westchester Colonial—a suite hastily created from a renovation combining the former library and an old-fashioned screened sun porch.

Legal guardianship wasn't new for Grandpa Ryder: he'd assumed financial responsibility for Scott, Clay's younger half-brother, shortly after his birth. Scotty had repaid the old man by not only trotting happily down the path originally intended for Clay, but by following it all the way into the family business.

At an early age, the obedient Scott had learned to take advantage of his favored status—the slight thaw he produced in his grandfather. He never missed an opportunity to taunt Clay with childish riffs on *I-may-be-younger-but-I've-got-the-juice-in-this-house*. Now barely thirty, a chip off the old block of ice, he'd already started a family in his own Colonial, a suburban stone's throw away.

"Half-brothers," Jonas liked to say, "but only one has a whole brain."

Although he bridled at the absolute authority his grandfather exerted over his mother, Clay knew he could never come close to providing her with the same level of care. Jonas Ryder might not have always outmaneuvered Clay, but he'd always been able to outspend him.

Clay let go of his mother's hand only once, when the temperature plunged even lower. Taking a second blanket from the foot of the bed, he gently spread it over her without a pause in his narrative. When he came to Luscher, he again pictured Jonas Ryder alongside him, on the backseat of the staff Mercedes. Suddenly he realized why imagining them as Best Buddies came so easily to him, and it wasn't because they were born barely a year apart.

Their bond was their cold, steely rage, their relentless drive to punish. Luscher used a knife; his grandfather wielded an icicle. Luscher's devotion to the military and his grandfather's contempt for it ultimately came to little more than opposite sides of the same coin.

Shortly before the war, right out of high school, his grandfather was hired by a small manufacturer of refrigeration units. He married young and already had an infant son when Pearl Harbor was hit. The local draft board rejected him because of a childhood injury which left him able to walk, but unable to run. Long after the war, whispers persisted about how he'd used his gimpy leg as an excuse to shirk his patriotic duty. A deep, unwavering hatred for the armed forces still festered inside him.

By 1947, he had enough scraped together to open his own repair shop. Except for home refrigerators, cooling was a fledgling industry: Frozen pizza, waffles, and burritos were as futuristically weird as science fiction, and air-conditioning was a luxury limited to movie theaters and overpriced restaurants.

Although he was no inventor, Jonas Ryder had a knack for adapting cooling devices to just about any space or need. When it came to his small family, however, he was neither so flexible nor accommodating. As business expanded, the rare appearances he did make at home transformed it into a permafrost zone, cold and silent as the tundra. That Clay's dad would join the family firm as soon as he finished college was foreordained; all other options were frozen out.

Shortly after the start of 1962, Jonas's long-neglected wife died of uterine cancer. Six months later, the day after graduation, his son phoned from Fort Dix to inform him that he would not be reporting for work at the new headquarters of Ryder Air Conditioning and Refrigeration. His image would not be captured in the massive blue-tinted mirrors flanking the RACR entrance; he would not join the blue-skinned reflections, to the left and to the right, in which one's entire body appeared to be flash-frozen in a giant cube of ice.

Clay's father, who'd graduated in the top 10 percent of his ROTC class, had been offered a regular Army commission. He was twenty-one years old, en route to Fort Benning, Georgia, and there wasn't a goddamn thing the son of a bitch who'd visited his dying wife once during her last six days in the hospital could do to stop him. Knowing how much contempt his father had for the military, he subsequently mailed him a series of three postcards. The first arrived after he completed his Officer's Orientation Course, the others after Airborne School and Ranger School. A short interval followed before the wedding invitation went out, but he knew the old man wouldn't even consider attending.

Three years after that, the daughter-in-law he'd refused to meet sent Jonas another letter, informing him that his only child, Captain Jonas Ryder Junior, had been killed in action in Vietnam. She'd signed it, "Betsy and your grandson Clay."

When it was time to go, Clay kissed his mother's cheek. "Give me a call, Mom, anytime you want to talk." With her face relaxed, she looked even younger than she had in the years before she'd drifted off to sleep. Maybe she was dreaming of Clay's father, and never had a bad dream.

He stopped in the kitchen, to let Gwen know he was leaving. As he passed the living room on his way to the front door, he heard the clink of ice. His grandfather was in his wing chair at the far side of the large, unlit room, nursing a drink and sulking. Despite all his clout, his most recent legal stratagem to prevent Clay from visiting his mother had failed. The judge, like all the others before, had not been able to pick up a pen to sign that order.

"So the cop had his picture in the paper." Jonas Ryder's voice was still strong, his words measured. Like a glacier, he had no need to rush; everything in his path could eventually be crushed. "The brave cop. Formerly the brave sailor."

Clay wheeled around, and a few long strides brought him to the living room threshold. If he took one more step—if one foot even brushed the intricately patterned border of the Persian carpet—he'd fall right into the trap. Entering the same room with the old man, just like speaking threateningly to him, would make this the last time he'd see his mother.

"Brave? That sounds awful strange coming from you," he said to the figure shrouded in the shadows. "Every time you couldn't get your hands on the person you really wanted to hurt, you just reached out and grabbed her—my mother, your daughter-in-law—always your favorite victim. Your son was dead, so you punished her instead. When I was just a little kid, if I pissed you off, you punished her instead. It must have really fucked up your day when I was finally old enough to catch on to what you were doing, and you had to give her a time-out and punish *me* instead. And I didn't give a shit what you did to me, because all that mattered was that I was keeping her away from you."

Clay's throat ached from choking down the rest of what he wanted to hurl at the miserable son of a bitch. Across the room, his grandfather's white hair glowed faintly, a nimbus against the chair back, like the flat, round saints' halos in medieval paintings . . . a halo he deserved about as much as Udo Luscher.

He knew Jonas Ryder always had to have the last word—and braced himself for it.

"She could have left anytime."

The old man hadn't lost his knack for finding the raw spot, and for rubbing it rawer still. What those words implied was vile; the offhand way he said them was vicious. But Clay wouldn't let him win it all.

"No," he managed to whisper, "she was always your prisoner. She was just as much your prisoner when she could walk out on her own as she is right now."

"She could have left anytime," Jonas Ryder repeated.

But the backlit silhouette had already disappeared from the doorway, and the front door was clicking shut, sealing out the steamy summer night.

CHAPTER
TEN

" 'Beauty is truth, truth beauty,' " the phone voice solemnly intoned. "There-fore, the noxious garbage passing for art today is a pack of lies. Don't you agree?"

"We live in a free, First Amendment society," replied Clay, "which sup-ports this inalienable right: beauty is in the eye of the beholder."

Bloomie, weaving her way through the nearby desks with a bulging file clutched against her chest, shot an apprehensive look at Clay.

"Yes, Clayton, a free country—but one with abominable taste."

"Then I guess we'll just have to make do with the free part, Oliver." No-body else called him Clayton. "I'm sorry I haven't kept in touch as much I want to. How are you?"

"I'm seventy-three. That says it all. No longer an antique dealer. Just an an-tique who deals."

"Come on! I don't want to hear you, of all people, talk like that!"

Nevertheless, the sign above his caller's shop, which was tucked into the ground floor of a brownstone just off Madison, did indeed proclaim, OLIVER PLUMWORTH ~ ART AND ANTIQUES ~ EST. 1956.

"I saw you in the paper last week. A fascinating case, Detective."

"I wouldn't be on cases like that if not for you."

"I wouldn't be seventy-three if not for you."

Clay had been on patrol when their paths first crossed. Freshly assigned to the Nineteenth Precinct, he was to be the Official Street Presence of a glitzy up-town stretch of Madison Avenue and its environs, a strolling Cerberus with a two-way radio. The merchants often flashed tight little smiles at him through their plate glass—most of them, even the fishmonger, kept their doors locked during business hours.

As he froze his ass off, he concluded that his protectees viewed him as little more than an extension of their elaborate security systems, a mobile motion detector with a gun. Even though he had yet to experience one moment of regret over leaving Esterbrook-Grennell, the outside-looking-in existence had brought him to a low point in his life, and he feared going lower still. When he dressed in the morning, he often found himself blinking at the image in the mirror, momentarily confused about whose blue uniform he was wearing—the Navy's or the NYPD's. Making it to detective grade seemed his only out, except that prospect appeared—for him, at any rate—tougher than making it through SEAL training.

One bone-chilling January morning, Clay was squinting through the grill-work of Oliver Plumworth's gate to get a better look at the painting in the display window. The hour was well in advance of the "11–6, Tues–Sat" on the door.

"Shall I wrap that up for you?" asked an amused voice.

Clay turned to face a sprightly old gent in a floppy-brimmed hat and a double-breasted black overcoat. Definitely cashmere, perfect fit. The previous week, Clay had watched as he greeted a customer with a deftly executed bow and a fleeting kiss on the hand. An octogenarian, she'd blushed like a girl.

"A William Merritt Chase? Doesn't exactly work with my weekly pay."

The man's eyes were tearing from the cold; maybe they were twinkling, too. Between gloved thumb and index finger, he held up the key for the gate, and Clay stepped aside so he could unlock it. Slowly, he stooped down and turned the key. "I've seen you looking in my window. You're new to the neighborhood." With the release of the catch, the metal barrier began to roll up like a window shade, needing only a little push to glide completely out of sight. "A shame we have to barricade ourselves like this," he said, as he straightened up. "This need for a gate . . . as I recall, it started sometime in the Sixties." He leaned forward and peered into his window. "Just as I thought! It's signed 'W. M. Chase.' How do you know William Merritt?"

"Popped into my head."

A sharp wind ripped around Madison, lifting the man's hat. In the nick of time, he caught it by the brim. As he readjusted it over his white hair, he asked, "Anything else in my window that's caught your fancy?"

"The Childe Hassam you had up a couple of weeks ago. That was incredible, Mr. . . . you are Mr. Plumworth, right?"

"Indeed." A nostalgic smile spread across Plumworth's face. "I held that Hassam for a very long time. Now I regret having parted with it." After a one-shoulder shrug, he plucked out another of his twenty-odd keys.

Clay knew that the dealer would have to punch in his pass code within seconds of opening his door, and he started to move away. Alarm Etiquette, part of Life in the Big City. "Have a good day, Mr. Plumworth."

He still held up the key. "Hassam and Merritt. Both were members of . . . ?"

"The Ten." The Ten was a group of American Impressionists who exhibited together annually. "Hassam was a charter member. When Twachtman died, Chase took his place."

"You didn't show off and tell me the year."

Clay couldn't resist. "1902."

"Officer, when you're not protecting Madison Avenue's fifty-dollar cheeses and hundred-dollar brassieres, come in from out of the cold, and we'll talk."

From two doors away, Clay answered with a thumbs-up.

"You think that's an idle let's-do-lunch-someday?" Plumworth had to shout to be heard over the wind. "I never invite people to stop by unless I absolutely mean it!" With that, he thrust the key in the lock, gave it a hard twist, and pushed at the door with both hands. The alarm-delay whined, and he rushed inside.

The next week, on a day when the snow was so heavy even the thieves were hibernating, Clay lightly tapped his nightstick on Plumworth's door. With a broad smile, the old gent hit the buzzer. Clay was still stamping snow off his thick-soled shoes when the dealer launched his first question about his impressive art background.

"Impressive?" Clay responded. "Two whole painters?"

"And now?" he asked, after hearing Clay's abridged bio, "do you keep up?"

"I read a lot, go to museums on my days off, gawk at only the finest gallery windows . . ."

Acknowledging the compliment with a smile, Plumworth gestured toward two chairs upholstered in moss-green velvet. Grouped with an embroidered footstool on a pale Tabriz carpet, they formed a snug island in the middle of the narrow shop. Assorted antique tables, not one much wider than a chessboard, roosted around them, each displaying a small bronze or an assortment of collectibles.

Clay shook his head. "Thanks, it'll look better if I stand. The uniform. I'm just coming off duty." He leaned against the counter, which took up the rear half of the right wall. "But I'd feel more comfortable if you sit down, Mr. Plumworth."

"Oliver, please."

"Clayton. Clay."

They paused to shake hands, and Plumworth took a seat. At his back, on the opposite wall, were a handful of extraordinary paintings, mostly by American Impressionists. Clay couldn't keep his eyes from wandering in their direction.

"Go on, have a look." Like an impresario presenting his leading lady, Oliver swept his arm toward the pictures in a broad, graceful arc. "Why stare at an old man, when you're beckoned by lovely faces surrounded by sunlight and flowers?"

Clay, bulked up with cop gear, carefully lumbered toward the paintings. He lingered over a portrait of a young woman in a lacy white summer dress. She was seated in an open carriage near Washington Square Arch, in sun-dappled shade. "God, why'd they stop painting like this?"

Oliver sighed. "Because it's easier to paint a green blur and a brown smudge? Or because some of our tastemakers deny beauty even exists?"

After that, Clay looked in on Plumworth regularly, no more than a wave if he happened to be on the phone or with a customer. Besides paintings and *objets de vertu,* he did a brisk trade in Art Nouveau jewelry. Many times, Clay watched from the street as a trophy wife who'd been exercised, colorized, and plastic surgeonized to the requisite flawlessness pored over a velvet-lined case of earrings as if it were a box of chocolate bonbons.

On another chilly day, roughly a year later, Clay was drawn to Plumworth's window by an illuminated Tiffany table lamp. It was only midafternoon, but dark clouds were already freezing the slush underfoot, and the leaded glass—a pattern of spreading daffodils—was the only warm, bright spot on the entire block. Like a man holding up his fingers to a fire before facing the cold, Clay basked briefly in the lamp's promise of springtime. As he turned away to trudge toward the avenue, he glanced through the glass door to see how Oliver was doing.

For the first time, someone else was behind the counter.

Clay couldn't place the young man in the white shirt and tie, but he wasn't a total stranger, either. As if he hadn't seen him, the man reached under the counter. Bringing forth Windex and a roll of paper towels, he lowered his head and put real muscle into scrubbing the countertop. Clay wavered, then tapped on the door. The young man looked up—too suddenly and too startled. He also hesitated, then buzzed Clay in. He had no trouble locating the control button.

"Hi," Clay said, as the door closed behind him, "owner around?"

"I'm an associate of Mr. Plumworth." As Clay came closer, he noticed the tie was a clip-on, the shirt rumpled, and the pants rode low, hip-hop style. "He had to go to the doctor today."

"The doctor? Does he have that Alzheimer's that's going around?"

"Uh-huh. Hurt too bad to come in."

"Sorry to hear that." Clay ambled around the shop, eyeing the paintings, lifting a bronze to feel its heft. "You know about this antique stuff?"

"Pretty much." A brown paper bag, lunch-size, was on the counter near the young man's elbow. He moved it, and, with a fresh paper towel, wiped away a circle of condensation. Plumworth ordered in every afternoon, always a sandwich and coffee from the busy coffee shop two blocks south on Madison. Clay strolled back toward the display window. "So what's the deal on this lamp here?"

Judging by his blinking eyes, his query started the guy's brain spinning faster than the reels in a one-armed bandit. While he calculated how much a cop on the beat carried around in his wallet, Clay checked out the back of the shop.

On the left, a painting on a partition was askew. On the right, perpendicular to the end of the counter, an Art Nouveau screen concealed the rest of the narrow rear. A door frame was visible above it. Clay had never been back there, but it had to lead to a bathroom, perhaps to a supply area, as well. *And to a safe?* All those ladies, bent over trays of earrings and bracelets. Unquestionably it led to a safe.

"We talking cash?"

A smile from Clay prompted the man to respray the spotless countertop.

"Four hundred."

"What? You've got to be kidding!" Feigning astonishment was easy, since the lamp had to be worth at least seventy-five thousand.

"Three-fifty. Police discount."

As he drew closer, Clay glimpsed a familiar object behind the counter: a floppy-brimmed hat perched in its regular place, atop a crooked pile of art books. "No, I think you can do better." In one swift movement, Clay pulled out his gun.

Mr. Plumworth's associate looked genuinely disappointed, as if he thought he'd been doing really well so far.

"Put your hands on the counter. Now."

As the young man complied, his eyes darted right, toward the rear.

From the corner of his eye, Clay saw something edge out from behind the screen: a man wielding a sawed-off shotgun. Before he could take aim, Clay swung around and fired a burst at him. Clay never saw his face. All his concentration was on the center of a long leather coat, exploding, disintegrating. With a roar, the shotgun fired wild, riddling the ceiling, knocking out half the overhead lights, bringing down a hailstorm of plaster and glass.

Clay immediately swung his gun back toward the clip-on tie behind the counter, just as his right arm swept forward from behind his back, a gun in his hand. Clay fired another burst, and the guy smacked back against the wall, his head a wet brush splattering the wall red. In the same moment, pain erupted in Clay's right leg—the guy had gotten a shot off. Face-to-face with the cracked glass showcase where the thug's bullet had exited, Clay hit the floor hard.

A third man dashed out from behind the screen. Clay fired the remainder of his clip at him, but he kept on going, hurtling right through the front door. In a torrent of glass, he crash-landed on the sidewalk. Cold air blasted in. Before Clay could get at the gun in his ankle holster, he was out of sight.

Gripping the countertop, Clay struggled to his feet. He managed to stumble around the screen, where Oliver lay on the floor, barely conscious. His mouth was gagged, his hands and feet bound. A big welt, deepening into purple, stood out over one eyebrow.

———

Hours later, Oliver, sporting a large gauze patch on his forehead, was waiting when Clay was brought down from Recovery. After the nurse left, he asked, "I guess you're wondering how they got in?"

Still groggy, Clay answered in a thick voice, "Crossed my mind."

"My coffee shop order. The one you were talking to—he's been working there a week or two. No doubt he observed me showing jewelry to my clients."

"Delivery guy . . . knit watch cap . . . now I place him," Clay slurred.

"Indeed. I gave him a tip, and he pulled a gun. *I* thought it was a good tip." Clay laughed along with him. "Then he buzzed his friends inside. When they saw the safe, they demanded the combination." Gingerly, he touched the bruise on his head. "I knew they'd kill me once they had it. Thank God you came along."

All the drugs pumped into Clay made his head loll back onto the pillow. A thumbs-up was all he could muster.

"He was captured before he made it across Central Park."

"Who?" Clay mumbled, his focus unraveling.

"The third man. The one with the unique method of going through doors."

Plumworth was released the next day, but not Clay. The mayor came, kicked everybody out, and spent half an hour with him. Oliver visited daily, often twice.

"Clayton," he said near the end of the week, "your visitors—a good many fellow officers, some very attractive young ladies . . . but no family?"

"My mom. She . . . it's hard for her to get away."

"No one else?"

"My father died before I was born. Vietnam."

"So your mother had to bring you up all alone?"

He couldn't keep down the rancor. "Not exactly."

Embarrassment flared in Oliver's cheeks. "I do apologize . . . I didn't—"

"No, not that. My grandfather—my father's father—he took over."

Oliver's eyes flickered. "Too vast a generation gap?"

"Think the Grand Canyon."

"In that newspaper account, I was pleased to learn that your current duties seem to have removed you from the line of fire," Oliver's voice continued through the phone. "What you encountered in my shop was more than anyone's share of violence for a lifetime."

Incisive as he was, the old gent never could have parsed out the multilayered silence the same Trabuc front-page story had thrown over the squad room.

Glancing around, he felt his anger reignite, the weight of the gun in his holster triple.

"Quite a story, the way you traced the Van Gogh to that lovely college professor," Oliver was saying. "But like all stories that go back so far, perhaps it has a missing chapter or two?"

Clay's back straightened in his desk chair. He'd spent too much of the morning in SoHo, where a gallery had reported the disappearance of a red medical waste bag filled with hypodermic needles—part of an installation entitled "Get Well Soon." The gallery manager had prickled when Clay asked if the cleaning crew might have mistakenly thrown it out with the trash. The office wall clock was nearing twelve-thirty. "What kind of sandwich do you want with your coffee?" he asked Oliver. "I'm delivering, I carry a gun, and I'll expect a damn good tip."

Outside, Manhattan was hot, hazy, humid, and hostile; Plumworth's shop was a calming oasis. The two of them settled in the green chairs, and Clay dispensed sandwiches, napkins, his friend's coffee, and his own soda.

As Clay was about to take his first bite, Oliver calmly announced, "Clayton, I don't believe that this is the first time that the famously lost Monsieur Trabuc has been found."

"Thanks for sharing that with me before I had a chance to choke on my sandwich, Oliver. But how the hell is that possible?"

"Over the years—the eons—I've been in business, I can't tell you how many people have walked into my shop and offered me items that they might feel . . . well, *uncomfortable* about selling to the larger galleries." He sighed. "And believe me, I've had some tempting offers. Some of these visitors are quite knowledgeable about the art world . . . especially the part that isn't written up in the glossy magazines." Holding up his sandwich in two hands, he took a small bite. "They want to know what my customers are looking for, how I price particular pieces, et cetera. Naturally, I'm curious about *their* business as well." He pointed a warning finger at Clay. "For the record, Mr. Officer of the Law: these people may be nefarious, but my interest is purely vicarious. At any rate, we compare notes. We chat. We gossip." He sipped his coffee. "This is a delicious lunch, Clayton, and I do thank you."

Clay toasted Oliver with his soda, but didn't drink.

"When the Trabuc appeared in the papers with such fanfare, my memory was jogged. I'm not sure exactly when, but sometime in the Seventies, it was up for auction."

"That can't be, Oliver!"

"Oh, not a *public* auction! This was one where the bidding was limited to the handful of collectors in the world who not only can afford to pay millions for a painting, but who also don't give a damn about ever having to sell it. That a painting's been stolen means nothing to them. Owning is all."

"Their own little black market. A sort of private club?"

"Aptly put. These collectors are extremely rich . . . and extremely powerful. Therefore, it would be ill-advised to offer them anything that is not"—Oliver raised a knowing eyebrow—"right. At any rate, this Trabuc was snatched up and locked away by one of these remarkably avaricious individuals, without the slightest concern for the way it was wrested from its rightful owners." He shook his head. "So much money, so few scruples!"

"Who bought it?"

"Ah! Better to ask who sold it!" He took another bite, another sip. "The truth is, Clayton, I never found out for sure. It was all out of my league, of course, but nevertheless, it was quite an intriguing rumor. And it certainly heightened my conviction that, just as there are few collectors wealthy enough to indulge in this game, there are even fewer dealers with the international connections to get away with playing its gamemaster. I doubt there are more than three or four. Needless to say, your sleuthing has sent shock waves through certain small, rarefied circles."

Clay still hadn't touched his sandwich. "Let me get this straight. Are you saying Trabuc was bought sub rosa in the Seventies, and this private collector felt guilty and *dumped* it?"

"*Saying?* I'm not saying anything. But rest assured that guilt, like goodness, had nothing to do with it." Plumworth dabbed at his mouth with his paper napkin. "Please, eat your sandwich. Chewing will take that look of stupefaction off your face. Besides, my coffee's getting cold."

When Clay's mouth was full, Oliver leaned toward him. "Is the name Toshio Hashimoto familiar to you? No? Doesn't ring the old wind chime? Well then, you must remember the Japanese businessman who paid the highest price ever for a painting, also a Van Gogh?"

Nodding, Clay swallowed hard. He hadn't tasted a thing. "Sure. The *Portrait of Dr. Gachet.* The spring sale at Christie's, 1990. The Eighties bubble, at its bursting point. Eighty-two and a half million bucks. Shit, they talked about it all the time when I was at Esterbrook-Grennell. It was like the Holy Grail, getting back to haywire prices like that." He thought a moment. "Didn't the buyer die?"

"Oh, indeed. Fortunately, his macabre wish to have *Dr. Gachet* buried with him went unfulfilled. What I was getting at is this: for all his wealth, *Gachet*'s buyer was just a little fish compared to Hashimoto . . . who is very much alive. Clayton, did I mention that he is an art lover?"

"You didn't. But the blinking neon arrow is pointing that way."

"Such a perceptive young man! At any rate, two of Hashimoto's representatives flew in from Japan two days ago. They're staying in a suite at the St. Regis."

"It's a hotel. People stay there every night."

"Exactly. But let us focus our attention on the adjoining suite. I assume you've heard of Galleries Grauberger?"

Clay balled up his sandwich's paper wrapper and stuffed it into his empty soda cup. "Sure. Swiss-based, several showrooms—Fifty-seventh Street, London . . . other cities I can't exactly recall. Stodgy image. Expensive, old master stuff."

"Gregor Grauberger Senior is a fossil who makes me appear a mere stripling in comparison. Years back, he relegated all of the international business to his son, Gregor Junior, who's based in New York. No one can remember the last time Papa Grauberger set foot outside of Zurich."

"Let me guess. He recently checked into the St. Regis. Next door to the Japs."

To hide his grin, Oliver looked down and busied himself with his tie.

"I'm hearing sushi and Gruyère. An unsavory combination. And . . . ?"

"I've nothing more to tell—except that Hashimoto is reputed to be an exceptionally ruthless businessman."

"What if I'd bought you two coffees? Would that've gotten me another chapter?"

Oliver remained silent. Clay's gaze drifted down to the small table at his right elbow. Several small Art Nouveau silver pieces, mostly bud vases and picture frames, were arranged on it. Among them was a two-dimensional cherub, only a few inches tall, holding a wine bottle in one hand, its cork aloft in the other. Reaching out, Clay picked it up and examined the curved stand that supported it. "What's this for?"

"To perfectly honest, I'm not quite sure. That slat in the back was made to hold a card. To identify a decanted wine, perhaps? Display a handwritten menu? I lean toward the piece being one of a set of name-card holders, to show guests where to sit at a dinner party—in the interest of creating the most agreeable pairings."

"Ah. That was important." Clay pictured a long table set with several of the cherub-stands, a name written in calligraphy in each. Did they hold the names of the Graubergers, father and son? Hashimoto? And who else? Could Luscher be at the head of the table? "That handful of black-market collectors— where do you think they are? Geographically, I mean."

Oliver waved a hand. "Japan, Europe, Manhattan, Texas."

"What about South America?"

"No, Clayton. Hardly among the first places that come to mind."

ELEVEN

After ten that night, Rachel Meredith left her co-op with Lulu and a man on the far side of fifty. Despite his age, he was the big, burly type only a fool would pick a fight with. Another good reason for keeping on his good side was the creature he held on a short leash: though others might mistake it for a woolly mammoth, Clay knew a rottweiler when he saw one. The big man called the dog Rolf.

Hanging way back, he tailed them as they took a leisurely stroll around the neighborhood, then headed into Washington Square Park. They drifted past the fountain, the guitar players, and the old men playing chess under the street lamps. Offers of "smoke, smoke" floated in the air like the buzz of insects. Two black men in dreadlocks, wearing the official drug dealer gear of sleeveless white undershirts and baggy camouflage pants, were doing the selling.

"Watch out," Dr. Meredith said to her fellow dog walker, loud enough for even Clay to hear, "those might be cleverly disguised undercover operatives, attempting to lure us into purchasing an illegal substance."

One of the faux Rastafarians muttered at her under his breath, and both beat a rapid retreat to another part of the park. Lulu stopped to sniff a candy wrapper, but her owner kept walking. When she turned to tug her along, Clay's cover was blown, as well. "Detective Ryder, is that you? Tell me you're not with those guys!"

"Not my department. But I agree, they're pretty easy to make."

She arched an eyebrow and smiled at his sports jacket and tie.

He attempted a return smile, keenly aware how out of sync he was with the mellow nighttime atmosphere of the park. "How are you, Dr. Meredith?" His attempt to sound casual was a dismal failure.

"Pretty good—now that the spotlight's died down. I'm not the stuff of which celebrities are made."

He nodded. The melancholy, high-strung woman he'd faced on their last encounter was gone.

"What about you, Detective?" she asked. "Any new art crimes?"

"Only the prices they get for Descartes-art these days." He answered her puzzled look with " 'I think it, therefore it's art.' Conceptual stuff. No brush. No chisel. No talent."

Something jostled his slacks. Glancing down, he caught Lulu backing off from a quick, anxious sniff. Her negative reaction had Rolf inching closer, straining his leash. Even with all his heft, the dog's master had to work to keep him in check.

"Rolf has this protective thing about Lulu," the man explained.

"That's a lot of protection."

"I'm sorry," Rachel Meredith jumped in. "Detective Ryder, this is Dr. Renaldo Corelli. Fellow dog owner and my upstairs neighbor since I can't remember."

"You still had braces on your teeth when I moved in."

"Of course *you'd* remember that! If you ever need a great dentist, he's the one. Renny, Clayton Ryder. The detective who—"

The dentist pumped Clay's hand, smiling. "Sure. Saw you on the front page."

Clay pointed toward the arch. "If you're on your way home, I can offer a police escort. Not that you need one with Rolf."

At the mention of the dog's name, Clay heard a low growl, followed by blood-curdling snarls. He hopped backward, in time to catch Rolf and Lulu muzzle to muzzle. The Weimaraner had jumped up so that her forepaws were on Rolf's massive shoulders. Clay tensed for the ugly spray of blood, fur, and bone—all Lulu's. Only when she began to chew the big, meaty roll of neck that hung over his metal-studded collar did Clay realize that all the savagery was coming from Lulu, the psycho dog he'd subdued with a snarl. Rolf—the dog he'd been rooting for—responded by crumpling onto the ground. Lulu, outweighed three to one, danced around him, mouthing hunks of rottweiler fur.

Corelli and Meredith stood by idly, leashes slack in their hands. "You have no idea how much this used to embarrass me," Corelli explained, "Rolf wimping out like this. I live on the top floor, and until Lulu came along—a mere puppy— Rolf was top dog of the building, literally and figuratively. Then this happened . . . the first time was in the elevator, no less. God, I thought the cable was going to snap when he collapsed on the floor. We can't figure it out. He's like her love slave."

"But didn't you just say how Rolf was so—"

"Oh, yes, he's very protective of Lulu," Dr. Corelli confirmed. "Won't let another dog near her. Very few people, either."

"My brother gave me Lulu for my birthday," Rachel Meredith sighed, "back when I was plowing my way through my dissertation. I'd turned into a total zombie. Michael saw her as my return ticket to mental health."

Clay pretended to nod in agreement. *Sure, if you needed a partner to bounce back and forth against the walls, head first.*

The one-sided dogfight ended as abruptly as it began. Lulu and Rolf shook themselves, and the short walk back to the apartment building was congenial for man and beast. As they said good night, the doorman swung the door open.

Dr. Meredith stepped inside, then glanced back at Clay. "I'll catch the next elevator," she told her friend, then quickly conferred with the doorman. Back out on the sidewalk, she said, "You have this look on your face. . . ."

"That's the gyro I had after work. How's your husband?"

"Fine. I just asked the doorman to buzz him, so he won't worry. If you ate at that gyro place across the park, I know the feeling—*Revenge of the Silence of the Lambs.*"

A red Porsche rolled by, blasting rap so loud that even the sidewalk throbbed out the beat. As it faded to the west, an unusual stillness enveloped Ninth Street. Without a word, they began to amble along, an extraordinarily calm Lulu in the lead.

"Did we really meet by chance?" she asked.

"When do we not?"

"I meant tonight! Not in a cosmic sense."

"Only in a comic sense?" They were between streetlights, and he couldn't see her face. Hickey's face, however, was quite easy to imagine, no matter how dark a stretch they might walk through. If he'd been on hand to observe the Art Guy standing poised over a Closed Case, metaphorical crowbar in hand, the DI would have turned purplish red with rage. Nevertheless, Clay hooked the tool around the edge, and began a series of tentative practice pries. "What about Trabuc? Your phone stop ringing yet?"

She dug in the pocket of her slacks. "Here. We've joined the rarefied ranks of the unlisted." She handed him a business card with a phone number scrawled on it. "Trabuc is like the prom queen. Everyone wants to dance. Museums I've never heard of want his portrait as a bequest. Auction houses long to sell it, dealers beg to buy it."

"Lots of dealers?"

"A cast of thousands."

Clay took a deep breath, already on edge for his next question. Cautious, still trying sound casual, he probed, "How about Galleries Grauberger . . . heard from anyone there?"

"Them! They're the worst of the lot! Wil and I had one Sunday to spend together—June's his busiest time, shooting Christmas catalogues—and they finagled the doorman into ringing us at eight A.M.! Naturally, we refused to let them come up. When we went out for lunch, this shaky old man and his extremely unpleasant son were camped out in the lobby—they'd waited for us all morning! The doorman's excuse was that he couldn't let someone so old and frail stand out in the heat, but I think they bribed him. They were the ones who drove us over the edge to go unlisted—constantly calling, wheedling, making offers. . . . How did you know?"

"The name came up in a conversation with a friend." Steering a bit off-track, he asked, "Have you decided what you want to do with the Trabuc after the exhibition?"

"No . . . it has to be the most difficult decision I've ever faced." They'd walked to the far corner and back. "The exhibit at the Met is still months away, so I have time to make up my mind. But that's what I want, to make up my own mind—without being pushed and prodded by all these obnoxious people in the art trade."

"If anyone gets too close, Dr. Meredith, let me know."

She gathered up Lulu's leash, and the doorman pushed the door open, but she waved him back. Her eyes locked on Clay's as she asked, "Detective Ryder . . . what's going on?"

Unprepared for such directness, he tensed even more. He gave his stomach a little pat. "Like I said, I was only walking off that gyro. And I don't live too far from here." She didn't look convinced, but he went ahead. "Any other dealers come to mind?"

"There are so many. . . . Well, Rasenstein's the most famous, I guess. He keeps reminding me that he's descended from a family known for doing business with the Rothschilds. I remain neither impressed nor intimidated."

"Good. You mentioned auction houses?" Clay probed.

"All of the big ones. But especially that woman from Esterbrook-Grennell."

"Deirdre Sands? *She* made a cold call?"

"Only after I refused to speak to her top-tier flunkies. Played the woman card big time. When I turned her down, she had the nerve to call Wil at the studio!" She shook her head in disgust. "Why? Do you know her?"

"I once worked at Esterbrook-Grennell. But *know* her? No way." His attempt at casual interest was stretched to its limit, but he dared one last question. "What about Japanese dealers?"

"No, not one Asian name that I recall. But remember that Word War II movie? The hero's being held at gunpoint by a Jap spy. He asks, 'Where'd you learn to speak English so well?' And the spy sneers back, 'I went to UCLA. Ha-ha.' Well, I can't see who's at the other end of the line."

They both hovered in place, staring down at the sidewalk. When he finally said, "Don't forget, Dr. Meredith, there are laws against stalking," he heard echoes of Mr. Policeman visiting the first grade. "Like I said, if any of these jokers gets too close, don't hesitate to call me."

She took a step away from him, a sign for the doorman to open the door at last. "You bet. I'll just dial 911, and ask," she paused to give him an exaggerated wink, "for Detective Clay."

CHAPTER
T W E L V E

Out in the Sound, but within sight of land, commercial baymen harvested clams from wide, low-slung Garveys year round. From the beach near The Shack, Clay often watched them work their heavy professional steel rakes, with thick prongs that curved like talons from the mouth of a deep basket. The baskets, upward of two feet wide and ten inches deep, attached to a series of telescoping aluminum poles that could extend to a depth of forty feet. With enough muscle behind them, the big rakes scooped up a sizable chunk of ocean floor. A single pull in a rich bed might deliver fifty to a hundred clams into the basket, which then had to be hand-hoisted up into the Garvey, a task equal to hauling up a boulder.

Clay had a scaled-down version of a bayman's rake out at The Shack, rigged on a six-foot pole. Half an hour before low tide, he'd carry it to the water's edge. There, he tied one end of a rope around his middle and fastened the other end to a half-bushel wire basket wedged inside an inner tube. Dressed in a baseball cap, T-shirt, cutoffs, and old sneakers, he waded out until the water reached midthigh, then slogged parallel to the shore, the inner tube bobbing behind him. Once he lined up with a particular house, stand of beach roses, or the broken remains of a sea wall—each a marker of a high-yielding clam bed from summers past—he'd begin to scrape away at the bottom.

It was a pretty good place to be, in between the baymen and the beach crowd. He liked the taste of salt when he licked his lips, like the rim of a margarita glass. Working his rake to the steady rhythm of the lapping water, he also found it an excellent place to think when police matters weren't clicking. That was the best part of detective work, that transcendent moment when everything finally snapped together like brand-new Lego blocks . . . maybe better than making the actual collar. The Trabuc case had clicked neatly into place—until his meeting with Eli and his talk with Oliver. And then the stroll with the Meredith woman, the transformation of rumor into . . . possibility, at least.

The case had broken apart, leaving him with more pieces than he'd had when he started. Paradoxically, now there was a missing piece, as well. Without it, none of the others would lock together again.

If the case was closed, did it really matter?

Certainly not to Hickey. Clay understood that his employment status depended on sticking with the DI's script, the one that invariably finished with Closed! The End! and faded to black. But outside of NYPD protocol, endings were not always so clearly defined, not nearly so absolute. Life wasn't a series of little closed boxes. And the one that the Trabuc had been stuffed into wasn't staying closed.

By the time he lugged his basket and rake up The Shack's driveway, Clay had decided to call the number on the business card tucked in his wallet behind Rachel Meredith's unlisted number:

Solomon Computers & Electronics

Professional Installation

By appointment only

On the drive back to the city, he used a gas station phone booth just off the Long Island Expressway in the middle of Nassau County.

"Solomon Electronics," a man's voice answered.

"Is Eli there?"

"Who's calling?" It sounded a lot like Aaron.

"I don't think he'll remember my name. He came to my apartment last month. Gave me his card with this number."

"Okay. I know who you are." Aaron, for sure. "Did you make up your mind about the home theater system?"

"I need you to come back and go over the figures—how's the same time, tomorrow night?"

"I'll be there. Don't eat supper."

Clay swung onto the highway and turned off the radio.

Calling those Israeli guys—that could open a whole can of worms.

Thanks for the advice, Lauren, but the case doesn't fit. Not anymore.

Too bad you didn't take as much interest in our marriage.

Whoever wrote "Til death do us part" never met you, Lauren.

As he waited for Aaron the next evening, Clay examined his half-finished ship, charting out the next phase of work. In the first weeks after Lauren died, he'd sat stock-still in the dark every night, wanting to be the way Lauren was. When the terrible things he saw in the blackness began to swirl around him in the daytime, he put the lights back on. For a long time, he stared at the spines of his art books—Lauren had arranged them on two long shelves, in alphabetical order according to artist. Finally, something made him go to Antonio Jacobsen.

An eighteen-year-old Dane who'd arrived in America penniless in 1868, Jacobsen proved himself talented enough to make a living painting pictures of ships for captains, ship owners, and steamship companies. Considered a commercial artist in his lifetime, he had since risen to the rank of maritime folk artist. Some degree of drama was always in the sea or the sky in his portraits of schooners and clippers and steamships, and the ships were unfailingly heroic. Even if he was the equivalent of a romance novelist with a paintbrush, he'd always been one of Clay's favorites.

The name emblazoned across the paddle wheel housing of a single-stack passenger craft stopped Clay from flipping through the paintings. The *Shelter Island*, the caption explained, ran a circuit from Sag Harbor to Shelter Island, Southold, Orient, and New York. Out east and back to the city she trekked, just like him, but free and clean out on the Sound. Neither particularly handsome nor ornate, the *Shelter Island* transported 250 people to and from a pretty good time.

Clay had never built a model of anything before in his life, but it suddenly seemed very important to build the steamship in the painting. And it absolutely had to be done from scratch . . . no kits, all crafted with his own two hands. Finding the original plans, adapting them to scale, locating New York's dusty basement and second-story hobby shops, got him started. The actual construction—with its splinters, glued-together fingers, hands-and-knees searches for microscopic missing pieces—was the anchor that was helping him to ride out his own personal storm.

When he answered the doorbell, Aaron was waiting in the shadows by the gate. He held up a white shopping bag.

"What smells so good?"

Aaron shot right by him, headed straight for the table. "Second Avenue Deli, the best in the city, and within walking distance." He pulled out two overstuffed sandwiches. "I didn't know if you were a corned beef man or a pastrami man, so whichever one you don't want, I get."

"Thanks, Aaron. Whenever I feel like giving myself a heart attack, I eat Jewish deli. As long as I'm going to kill myself, I might as well die happy. I'll get us some beer."

While Clay made the trip to the refrigerator, his visitor pushed both sandwiches toward Clay's chair. "So? What've you got?"

"I don't know if I have anything. But do I still get to eat the sandwich? The *pastrami* sandwich?"

"I figured a *goy* would grab the corned beef. No matter. I'm listening."

First, Clay recounted his conversation with an "acquaintance in the art world." Next he told Aaron about his un-accidental bump into Dr. Meredith in the park.

"This Grauberger I don't know. But Rasenstein—that's interesting. You've heard about the bullshit lawsuit he's bringing against that writer in Paris?"

"I'm just a provincial New Yorker. Fill me in."

"Rasenstein's suing this author for slander because his book singles out Rasenstein's late father as the only Jewish art dealer in Paris whose gallery the Nazis didn't confiscate lock, stock, and barrel in 1940. Rasenstein's old man not only hung on and did business in Europe for another year, but he also managed a safe sailing to New York—packing enough inventory to set up shop here."

"If it looks like a collaborator, and it smells like a collaborator . . ."

"There's more . . . a little postwar postscript. The same way Orthodox Jews pay a Gentile to turn on the lights and stoke the fire on the Sabbath, Rasenstein had a token Gentile all picked out to step in and run his gallery when he left Paris for New York. In 1945, he waltzed back to France, and his Christian pinch-hitter retired to a villa on the Riviera. Not much, but you can have the pastrami."

As they finished up, Clay mentioned Deirdre Sands's unusual interest in the Trabuc. Aaron started shaking his head. "Swiss dealers, Rasenstein, this Jap collector, a pushy auction *shiksa*. All I can latch onto is the time your pal heard the painting was on the market—the early Seventies. Nothing more points to South America?"

"Zero." Responding to Aaron's scowl, he added, "I know, a giant question mark. Plus, if it *was* sold and shipped out of Argentina, how and why did it wind up back there, to be sent to the Met?"

"You think Luscher survived the firefight with Eli's unit, and offered it for sale? Maybe got a big deposit from some black-market guy, then backed out of the deal?"

Clay mulled the possibility for a while. "I never thought of that. Maybe. From what my art friend said, those black-market boys are not to be messed with."

"You don't buy that letter from the old lady who sent it to the Met?"

"I didn't, I did, now I don't know. It's impossible to peddle a painting like that today on the open market without a bona fide claim to it. If he did back out in the Seventies, like you say, he could've screwed himself out of a second chance to offer it on the black market later. Then again, he might've simply repented. Decided to give it back. To make things right."

Aaron's face darkened. "Out of the question. Anyone else, not him!"

"You know him so well, that you can be absolutely sure of that?"

"Luscher isn't the type anyone can know, beyond what he did to get on Himmler's A-list."

"You mean the story behind the dagger?"

"Didn't Eli tell you about that?"

"No. Only about Argentina."

Aaron pushed back his chair and stretched his long legs, deliberating. "Everyone in our organization vies for the chance to work with Eli—he's brilliant, unselfish, fiercely supportive. He even has a wicked sense of humor—amazing for the shape he's in. Plus, in case you didn't notice, he's thoroughly obsessed by Luscher."

"But the reason for that attack on the winery in the first place—Luscher was already on Israel's Most Wanted list, right?"

"Absolutely. Right near the top. Put there by hundreds of people who'd testified against him—mostly Jews, but there were plenty of Parisians and Poles, and, believe it or not, even some SS men who thought talking would help them sleep better at night. But I said *obsessed*. You know what Eli has in his office, sitting right in the middle of his desk, in a clear plastic case? Take a guess?"

Clay shook his head in disbelief. "Not that."

"Right. The damn dagger. Cleaned up from the fire, so you can read Himmler's inscription—shit about honor and loyalty in old German script." Clay's eyes closed against the image, and Aaron continued. "After Eli was airlifted back to Israel and glued back together—that's his term for it, not mine—he personally translated and transcribed all the testimony from the original Polish, Yiddish, German, and French. Then he arranged it all in chronological order, an exercise he considered part of his therapy, but the consensus was that it had the reverse effect."

Clay tried to keep his eyes from straying to the *Shelter Island*. He'd considered it part of *his* therapy. Aside, of course, from keeping him isolated and introspective, alone in his apartment. "You've read it all?"

"Let's say it was required reading." Pulling himself up, he leaned toward Clay, his face grave. "Look, Luscher was as evil a bastard as ever lived—a one-man Holocaust. The problem is, my coworkers and I have our hands full with . . . let's just say, don't be encouraged by Clinton's peace talks. The way things are going, if anyone other than Eli were involved, events that happened twenty-five years ago in South America and over fifty years ago in Europe would get pushed to the end of the ever-growing line."

"So if I could get Eli his closure, your life would be simpler. It might even get me another sandwich."

Why did he feel like *It might even get me fired* was scrolling right across his face, like the headlines wrapping around the building in Times Square? His job was all he had left, and if he lost it, what were his options? Begging Florene Cope for a job as a security guard at the Met? "Aaron," he asked, his voice tinged with an urgency that surprised him, "how fast can I get an English version of Eli's transcripts?"

"Ryder, what do you think you're going to dredge up?"

"I won't know until I read them, will I? That's the way I work, and I'm going to do it on my time—not yours or the NYPD's." *And I might wind up with all the time in the world if Hickey finds out.*

"I'll get them to you." Aaron's voice was flat with resignation. Eli's Luscher-paranoia had spread, yet another incurable end-of-the-millennium disease.

"Thanks. Give me something to get started. October ninth, 1921 . . ."

"When's *your* birthday, Ryder? They ought to make it National Pit Bull Day."

"My memory must be failing. You mean it wasn't you guys who came to me?"

Shaking his head, Aaron began. "October tenth is just as important. Luscher's mother didn't die in childbirth, but you could say his father did—the day after Udo was born. He was a wealthy man, though, and he left his family well provided for. Udo was the youngest of three brothers, by a big age difference—ten and twelve years. Bright, always near the top of his class, and his big passion was riding. I picture him going straight from diapers to the black riding jacket and the shiny boots and the straight back and the stare. He was good at it—won nearly every junior equestrian event he entered.

"When Germany invaded Poland in '39, Udo had just entered the university. What could be better than to ride a horse for the SS? Quick visit to the tailor for a few alterations to the black jacket, a new hat, and you're all set. Don't laugh. The *SS Hauptreitschule* was considered the finest riding school in Germany. Elite. Crème de la crème. With his background, Udo was just about guaranteed a spot, after officer's training school."

"Intelligent . . . athletic . . . competitive. A prime candidate," Clay agreed.

"Don't forget young and impressionable. The only thing missing from his life was someone or something to hate—a gap the SS conveniently filled. But a whole nation of people far older and wiser than Luscher was sucked down that same toilet." Aaron cleared his throat. "The riding school prepared young men for the *Kavallerie.*"

"Literally a mounted cavalry?" asked Clay. "For a modern, mechanized army like the *Wehrmacht*?"

"Actually, it was an extremely strategic second-line unit. First, the *Wehrmacht* mowed down everything in its path with tanks and planes. Then in rode the SS *Kavallerie*, champing at the bit, eliminating enemy survivors before they could form bands of irregulars, or recruit civilian partisans. Naturally, being on horseback, the *Kavallerie* could cover any type of terrain. Ryder, can you imagine a herd of those bastards in black coming at you over a hill?"

"I think I'd rather take my chances against a whole Panzer division."

"For sure. And once the mopping up was completed, they took on the police functions of an occupying army. In Poland, that involved protecting the *Volksdeutsch*—civilians of German descent. Who they were protected *from* were the *Untermenschen*—the Poles and the Jews. Herding the *Untermenschen* off to the ghettos was another of the *Kavallerie's* duties. For Luscher, the Warsaw Ghetto was just a warmup for Paris."

"And in Paris . . ." Clay mused. "I still can't figure out how Luscher managed to track down Paul Bergère to find the Trabuc portraits in the first place . . . maybe that could lead to something. So far, the French haven't been much help—they're so damned secretive about the Occupation! Do you know they've sealed the Resistance files until 2090?"

"You might not have to wait that long. Let me check with Eli. There's a chance we can get you in touch with somebody useful—if he's still alive."

"In the meantime, I'll keep an eye on all the interested parties here in New York, like the Graubergers and Rasenstein." *Only one eye, because the other one has to stay on the lookout for Hickey.*

"What the hell can we do about Hashimoto—that collector in Japan?"

Like a man who's heard the punchline, but missed the joke, Aaron had an attentive look on his face. "You've got me completely stumped on that one." A quick glance at his watch, and he stood up. "We'll let Eli figure it out. He's an early riser. I'll call him as soon as I get home." On his way to the door, he turned and asked, "Tell me, Ryder, isn't it unusual for so many people to be chasing a painting like that?"

"No. What's unusual is that so many of them are scumbags."

Clay's phone started to ring as Cello rolled toward his desk. He picked up the handset.

"Pastrami King!" the voice on the other end greeted him.

"What's up?" asked Clay.

"The man said thanks, believes your proposals might prove useful. On some, we'll get back to you soon. Others may take a while. I'll give you a hint: if you don't know what a minyan is, it's the minimum of ten Jewish men needed to say the morning prayers. Right now, we couldn't raise a minyan in all of Japan. But you never know."

"You never know. Great. Thanks. Good luck."

As soon as Clay hung up, Cello eased an ample half-rump onto his desk. "My partner's going on vacation, so before I ask Hickey about—"

"Sure, Cello, not only is my dance card empty, but I'd rather dance with you than any of the other hairy guys. Turned up any leads on those express truck jobs?"

"Not yet. We're doing random tails. East Side, West Side. The guy did about one holdup a month. For all we know," Cello bent forward and pointed upward, "he's waiting for the next full moon." As he settled back, a pile of file folders shifted, and one slid to the floor. Clay reached for it, but Cello was closer. "What's this?" He frowned, holding out the faxed picture of Rachel's grandmother that had slipped out. "You're not still playing around with this Van Gogh case? I thought it was closed."

"Yeah. It is," Clay confessed.

"What if it was the DI who saw this, instead of me? Are you a complete putz?"

"No, Cello. That would prevent me from being an organ donor."

"Is it the woman? The college professor chick? That would look bad, but only normal bad."

Clay shook his head.

"Then get it off your desk. Now. Aside from her, everyone else in this case is dead."

CHAPTER

THIRTEEN

A couple of weeks later, Clay came home to Aaron's idea of the perfect place for a cold case: most of the bottom shelf of his refrigerator was occupied by an overstuffed manila envelope; on the top shelf, a Solomon Electronics card leaned against a beer bottle. Not even the landlord had a copy of his keys, so Solomon Corp. had breaking and entering down to a science that nearly eliminated the breaking part.

If he closed the refrigerator door, would the envelope— it could only be Eli's dossier—vanish? Did he want it to? Other than the letter from the old lady in Argentina and the Trabuc itself, it would be his first tangible link to Udo Luscher.

He hadn't just asked Aaron for it, he'd *demanded* it.

"Go ahead, take it," he could hear Hickey urging behind his shoulder, "and save me the trouble of finding a rope long enough."

An international phone number was written on the back of the Solomon card, and from his calls to the Jeu de Paume, Clay recognized the code for France. He glanced at his watch—seven-thirty P.M. He set its alarm for four A.M., late morning there.

Then he reached for the envelope.

The pages inside consisted entirely of statements taken in an interview format, dated between 1948 and 1956; however, they were ordered as the events described occurred in Udo Luscher's life. One of the earliest took place his first week in Poland:

INTERVIEWER: *That day in June 1940—he was the SS Untersturmführer in charge?*

WITNESS: *Yes, Luscher. The Germans were on horseback, marching all the Jews in our village to a train bound for Warsaw. We started at dawn, with no food or water. It was hot, and the old people were very slow. By the time we reached the station, the train was due to leave in ten minutes. Ten cattle wagons, already crammed with people. The officer in charge ripped the papers out of Luscher's hands. "Get your transport on the train immediately, Untersturmführer! If one Yid is left on this plat-form at 1800 hours, you and your men will guard them right here until the next train passes through—four days from now!" Luscher saluted, gave his men an order, and they started shoving us onto the train. They kicked and whipped us, pushed us with rifle butts. The baker's wife, one of a dozen Jews left on the platform, was screaming—she didn't want to be separated from her little boy. Luscher took out his revolver and fired into her mouth. Just like that. Then he put the gun to her three-year-old's head. I can still hear him: "You have one minute to make room—either for eleven plus one corpse, or twelve corpses." We all pressed back so hard, the wagons shook. All twelve were inside when the whistle sounded. Through the slats, I could see the two officers walking down the platform stairs. The senior officer was laughing, slapping Luscher on the back.*

A pattern evolved that first year: instead of competing for equestrian rib-bons and medals, Luscher vied for the attention of his senior officers, impressing them either with his quick thinking or his utter disregard for human life. A defining moment occurred in 1941. It followed a roundup of Polish villagers as they left a Sunday Mass in mid-June.

WITNESS: *While we were in church, the Germans surrounded our town—closed off the roads, cut all communications. They'd come to march us off to the slave labor camps. Anyone too old or sick to work was shot. The priest tried to stop them, and the officer—Luscher, of course—ordered him shot, too. Then they started us on the road to Lodz. When we came over the peak of a high hill, I saw a man with a big bundle in the distance. He wandered onto the roadway from the woods, then ran back. Luscher saw him, too. He left his sergeant in charge, and he and a small squad rode off ahead. No markets were open on Sunday, so we all knew it had to be a Jewish smuggler.*

INTERVIEWER: *Why do you say that?*

WITNESS: *The Germans had the Jews sealed off in the ghettos by then. Everyone knew the Nazis were starving them to death—so smuggling food was a capital offense. A bundle like that had to be filled with food—bread, potatoes, veg-etables. Luscher and his men raced into the woods. There was shooting, then shout-ing. After a while, the Germans reappeared, waving to the sergeant to march us forward. Three of them had big burlap sacks hanging off their saddles. A rope was tied to the back of Luscher's saddle, and a smuggler was attached to the other end, by the feet. His arms were tied behind his back. Once we caught up to them, we saw that he was a Jewish kid, too young to shave. Luscher was white as a sheet—he was shot in the leg, and blood was streaming down his horse's side. He waited for a tourniquet to be wrapped on his leg—without getting out of the saddle—then rode the rest of the way like he was in a parade. There couldn't have been a greater hu-miliation for him.*

INTERVIEWER: *A greater humiliation than . . . ?*

WITNESS: *Being shot by a Jew. With all the stones in the road, it wasn't long before the kid he was dragging didn't have a face left. I remember thinking there couldn't be a more horrible way to die, but that was only 1941. When we got to Lodz, Luscher transferred our custody, and he and his men rode into the ghetto—still dragging the corpse and making a show of the three bundles . . . his message that more dead Jews were back in those woods, and that the ghetto was going to starve.*

INTERVIEWER: *Tell me about the patient Luscher.*

WITNESS: *He was rushed from Lodz to our military hospital in Warsaw—the driver couldn't stop talking about how there was so much dried blood on his uniform, he had to be peeled off his horse. There's this phrase—"SS hard," but Luscher went to the next level—steel balls. I operated on his knee. When he woke up, he was the only one left in the ward. While I was explaining how he'd probably walk again—after a second operation in a few months—he was looking around. All he wanted to know was why the hospital was deserted. "Everyone is off to invade Russia," I told him. I needed an orderly to restrain him, to keep him in his bed!*

INTERVIEWER: *June 1941—the start of Operation Barbarossa?*

WITNESS: *Correct. I was shipped out to Russia a few days later myself, but before I left, Luscher found out that his Kavallerie regiment was attached to Himmler's Kommandostab Reichsführer SS—one of its crack rear mobile units. From then on, he needed a psychiatrist more than a surgeon.*

It was past midnight, but Clay paused to contemplate the countless deaths that Jewish smuggler's single bullet had caused. The irony was, given the failure of Hitler's invasion—the largest military action in history—if Luscher actually had galloped along behind the tanks and planes of Barbarossa, it was unlikely that he and the horse he rode in on would have returned.

After his second operation, Luscher's leg healed. He was promoted, but while the war raged on in Russia, he was stuck in Poland—more specifically, in Warsaw, a bombed-out sewer of a city . . . his own personal ghetto. That troops passed through constantly, on the way to the front, had to be salt in the wound.

INTERVIEWER: *What were your duties under Obersturmführer Luscher?*

WITNESS: *We moved Jews . . . to trains, to camps . . . you know.*

INTERVIEWER: *You were under his command during the 1943 ghetto uprising?*

WITNESS: *Yes. Himmler wanted to give Hitler an empty ghetto for his birthday on April twentieth.*

After reading the SS Mann's account, Clay sat on the edge of his chair with his head in his hands. He stared down at the natural markings in the oak floorboards and the stains and nicks and gouges in the finish. In an already burned and bombed-out square, Udo had fought his own bloody little war, and won. Udo the victor, but not the hero. Not when hatred takes the place of bravery.

His watch alarm began to ping, but he read a little further:

INTERVIEWER: *Describe the occasion on which you met Udo Luscher.*

WITNESS: *At a convalescent facility for the military just outside Berlin, late spring of '43. I was an assistant to Reichsführer Himmler's official photographer. Of course, I thought I was going to be the next Leni Riefenstahl. My job was to carry the medals and make sure everyone looked their best. With a lot of the wounded soldiers . . . you can imagine. Luscher had the blanket up to his neck, and the skin on his face looked scalded. His hair was just growing back—so light, like peach fuzz—but his eyes . . . beautiful eyes. That day, Himmler personally promoted him to Hauptsturmführer. He presented him with a Knight's Cross with Golden Oak Leaves, Swords, and Diamonds. We took a photo of Himmler next to the bed, holding it out to Luscher in the open case. Luscher looked up at Himmler like he was Jesus Christ.*

INTERVIEWER: *How rare was that medal?*

WITNESS: *One of only two I ever saw. The medal was from the Reich, but Himmler also gave him a personal gift, a short, narrow dagger in a scabbard. Just above the hilt, it was tied with a tasseled sword knot. Above that, the handle was decorated with the Third Reich eagle on a swastika-globe and SS lightning bolts. There was an inscription on the blade from Himmler, in ornate Gothic style. Oh, and Himmler told him that when he was recovered and ready for duty, he was to report to Paris, directly to General Oberg. I remember that, because I always wanted to go to Paris.*

CHAPTER
FOURTEEN

Somewhere in France, the phone rang for a long time. Finally, it was answered by a shout of *"Allo!"* but the person at the other end continued to fumble with an unfamiliar keypad. After a few frustrated curses, he blurted out, "You are the person who inquires for Udo Luscher?"

Unprepared for such directness, Clay's response was barely audible.

"My English is not good. You speak French?"

"University French. I'll understand if you speak slowly."

"At my age, I don't do anything fast anymore. Can you really hear me on this little phone they gave me?"

"Perfectly. How did you come to know Luscher, Monsieur?"

"I was in the Resistance. A kid with a broken nose—I looked like a surly little punk. I was one of four infiltrators among the *Gestapistes*. As far as I know, the only one of us who made it through the war."

"Infiltrating the Gestapo, you said?"

"No, *Gestapistes*. Organized gangs of French criminals. Local garbage who dressed up in fancy suits and did a lot of dirty work for the SS."

"I didn't know the SS did any work that wasn't dirty," said Clay.

That made the old man chuckle. "Laffont, the boss I was assigned to, liked to parade around in his SS officer's uniform."

"A Frenchman—in the SS?"

"An honorary Nazi. His reward for informing on the leader of the Belgian Resistance. That capture was a disaster for us. It led to six hundred arrests and collapsed the Resistance network in four countries."

"What else did that get him, besides the uniform?"

"His gang became the most powerful in Paris—he was the king of the black market. There wasn't a string Laffont couldn't pull."

"Sort of an Occupation Al Capone? If you've heard of him?"

"Yes, like him—if Capone also had a torture chamber in his cellar."

"And the connection between Laffont and Luscher?" asked Clay.

"I penetrated Laffont's gang in October '43; Luscher arrived in Paris about a month later. Everyone knew he was Himmler's boy. He reported directly to General Oberg, who was chief of both security and police—a butcher in his own right. Luscher's duties included making regular rounds of all the *Gestapiste* bosses—nothing escaped him. He was always writing in a little black book—observations for his report to Oberg. He also visited each of the city's prisons at least once a week. All that careful scribbling—it was the only thing I ever saw that put Laffont on edge. Otherwise, he was a smooth character . . . smooth as silk."

"Why should Luscher make him nervous, if Laffont was so esteemed?"

"Ah. With the Nazis, Monsieur, no one was untouchable. If anyone had reason to fear what some poor bastard would give up under torture, it was Laffont. For his part, Luscher hated Laffont on sight and made no attempt to hide it. Such a low criminal, holding the same rank? SS Hauptsturmführer? It had to infuriate him! Nevertheless, Laffont put up a jaunty front, always offered him black-market cigarettes and cognac. Luscher never accepted, and that agitated Laffont even more . . . no one refused black-market gifts! Perhaps Luscher thought that put him on a higher plane . . . asserted his superiority. Sure, Laffont was a common criminal, but how could anyone knifing his way through the prisons—a person they called *Le Découpeur*—look down on anyone? Talk about how looks deceive!"

"So he was good-looking? I've never seen a photo of him."

"Monsieur, he was radiant! The perfect Aryan: tall, lean, blond, extraordinary blue eyes. He could've been the model for the poster the *boches* pasted up all over town at the beginning of the Occupation: a handsome German soldier cradling a lost little French child in his arms. But one thing the Nazis never could pull off was looking kind, not even in their own damn propaganda."

"What sort of personality did he project?"

"Does ice have a personality?"

Momentarily, Clay stopped jotting down notes.

"He hardly spoke," the old Frenchman continued, "just stared and wrote. Those eyes! He made you feel *exposed*—like he could look right through you. What do they call those cutting lights they have today?"

"You mean a laser?"

"*Oui! Comme ça!* Frankly, I was scared shitless of both of them. Him and Laffont. And in constant terror of being discovered as a spy." The phone line hummed with unspoken bad memories.

"Monsieur," Clay prompted him at last, "you described Laffont as the king of the black market. Did he handle artworks? Paintings?"

"No, that was all under a special arm of the SS. They confiscated art privately owned by Jews and also seized the Jewish galleries. Art wasn't a black-market item like cognac or cigarettes. But it did come into play between Laffont and Luscher. And I paid close attention, since the matter was connected to the Resistance. One of the ways Laffont's organization served the SS was by infiltrating and smashing Resistance cells."

"I see. And you infiltrated the infiltrators? An even more dangerous job."

"I was too young to know any better. One day, Luscher began to complain about how the gang wasn't being diligent enough about art sales. 'Diligent.' That was the word he used. For whatever reason, he'd driven by the rue de la Boétie, and found it inexplicable how, at a time when bakers had no bread and shoe stores no shoes, every gallery had several paintings in its display window—with wildly inflated prices only German buyers could afford. Luscher insisted that the paintings had to be coming from Resistance supporters. He said, 'They must think themselves terribly clever, charging German museums, German diplomats, and German businessmen exorbitant prices while they take the proceeds and turn them into guns and explosives!' Believe me, that was quite a speech for someone as closemouthed as Luscher."

"So he was accusing your boss of not doing his job?"

"Yes. Which Laffont more or less shrugged off. He said, 'Resistance sympathizers are hardly the only art lovers in Paris. Times are hard, and people are forced to sell things. With all due respect, the Germans enjoy a twenty-to-one exchange rate—so who's gouging who? Everybody's happy!'

"Few people dared contradict Luscher. He was seething. But he stuck to his conspiracy theory: '*Happy*? Yes, especially the Resistance!'

"Laffont had to back down a little. 'In random instances that might be the case, but even then, what will you accomplish? Prevent them from buying a few grenades, a few machine guns? At the same time, you'll prevent your countrymen from salting away something to get back on their feet . . . in case the war ends badly.' Oh, how that made me want to cheer, even if scum like Laffont was doing the talking! 'Besides, do you think the Resistance will ever accomplish anything? Half of them are communists, the other half Gaullists, and they absolutely detest one another! Let them have those art-financed bullets—maybe they'll do us the favor of killing each other off!' "

"I'll bet that produced one hell of a laser," said Clay.

"Luscher nearly lost control! 'Is this the thanks the Reich gets for handing the Jews' galleries over to French dealers . . . to see them turn into middlemen for the Resistance? Enough duplicity! As of now, they're accountable for the origin of every piece in their shops! I want a list of everyone who brought them art to sell in the last ninety days! And I want that list updated weekly!' Then he stormed out.

"All Laffont wanted was to keep Luscher off his back, so he obliged. Since I was the most junior of his underlings, and there was legwork involved, I was tapped for the lists."

"When was this?"

"Late June '44. I only did it a few weeks, because by August, everything fell apart for the *Gestapistes*—the *boches* evacuated Paris."

"So these lists were Luscher's only connection with art?"

"As far as I know. There was a bit of a twist, though. Most of the paintings that drove Luscher so wild—you'll never guess where the dealers got them." He paused for effect. "From the Nazis themselves—at an SS art exchange they ran at the museum of the Jeu de Paume!"

"I know they stored stolen art in the museum, but . . . an art exchange? Are you saying that the SS actually made sales there?"

"Well, that was the story all the dealers told me. Whatever Hitler wanted was shipped off to Germany, but the rest . . . Yes, the dealers could walk in and buy what amounted to the leftovers. The *Einsatzstab Reichsleiter Rosenberg* was the name of the operation—how it worked was too complicated for me. At any rate, every week I dutifully went to the ten largest galleries—the places where Luscher said the Germans shopped—and leaned on them for information."

"Luscher's mandate . . . didn't it compromise your own Resistance people?"

"Thank God, no. Laffont hit it right on the head. Other than those pieces from the Jeu de Paume—by far in the majority—the rest came from people just selling stuff to survive. Luscher collected the list every week, but never discussed it again. The dealers complained to me that people who sold to them were being arrested, and they moaned about how that cut into their business. Never did I hear, 'Awful, how they're picking up poor innocent people!' Not once. Not from them."

"Did he use the Gestapo to make the arrests?"

"Luscher used a small squad of *Milicents*—French militiamen. Another form of Nazi puppets in uniforms."

"Those galleries you went to . . . do you recall their names?"

"Pretty much. I should point out that some kept the old name—the Jewish name—and some changed it. Most of the impostors went out of business after the war . . . and not all the Jews came back."

Clay began writing down the names of the galleries as the old man remembered them. One name stood out. "Rasenstein . . . who was on their list?" he asked.

"My God, do you think I'm one of those computers? Fifty-five years!"

"What if I give you names—on the list, not on the list?"

"I'll try."

Clay took a deep breath. He tried to concentrate on the bottles of Bordeaux in the big liquor store on Astor Place. "Lafite?"

"*Non.*"

"Bâges?"

"*Non.*"

"Dèscombes?"

"*Non.*"

"Bergère?"

"*Oui.*"

Clay swallowed hard. "What do you remember?"

"Bergère was on several times. Lots of drawings, not paintings. That's the reason I remember. I had to keep writing his name down for small amounts. He probably didn't want to dump them all on the market at once. Yes, yes, it's coming back—I'm pretty sure he sold to other dealers as well. The sales must have gone back to May or April."

"Who was the artist?"

"Several artists. Everyone in Paris knows Toulouse-Lautrec—him, maybe Degas. All sketches. Like I said, he didn't get much for them. Probably got screwed."

"Van Gogh?"

"It's possible. Maybe. I wouldn't swear to it."

"But Bergère's name . . . on Rasenstein's list?"

"Yes. That I would swear to."

Mind racing, Clay tried to keep the excitement out of his voice. "Is there anything else you can tell me about Luscher?"

"Occasionally, he would go down to the cellar. Luscher could whisper to a prisoner—even if he knew nothing about him, not even why he was being held—that he had his wife or his brother or half his Resistance cell back at Gestapo headquarters, and the poor bastard would believe him. His interrogation technique was relentless; he was a driver—always made them talk. And Laffont's basement was a playpen compared to what the Gestapo had at the rue de Saussaies. Or so I was told. I was not an eyewitness to what Luscher did there, or in the city prisons—but nothing was too cruel for Luscher."

"Nearly done. Did you ever see Luscher with anyone else?"

"Always, he came to Laffont's alone. I heard he had a cousin stationed in Paris—another Luscher. About him, I can tell you nothing."

"One last question—what happened to Laffont?"

"Executed shortly after the Liberation."

"You're sure?"

"Positive. I killed him myself."

The unashamed satisfaction in the old *Gestapiste*'s voice, preceded by Luscher's ingenious scheme, was enough for Clay to abandon any attempt at sleep in that last hour before dawn. Instead, he went through the rest of the testimonies, horrific accounts of *Le Découpeur*'s cruelty as he slashed his way through the dungeon beneath Gestapo headquarters and the prisons of Paris. Presumably, his anti-Resistance scam—art theft in the guise of duty to the Reich—had been crafted to avoid troubling his conscience . . . the same fastidious conscience which had not been troubled in the least by the bloodiest personal body count of the Occupation.

CHAPTER FIFTEEN

"Eighty-third Street," said Cello, and Clay made the left off Central Park West. Sure enough, there was a FedEx truck parked near the corner. Clay pulled up next to it, to confirm that the driver was following the advisory to keep his doors closed. "Hey," Cello bragged, "do I know their schedules, or what? The next time Rhonda orders something from Macy's, they ought to give me free shipping."

In midsummer, many galleries shortened their hours, and, despite record-breaking museum attendance, Clay didn't have much of a case load. Deputy Inspector Hickey teamed him with Cello on the express delivery shooter—a logical choice, but not one the DI would've made had he any inkling of how hooked Clay was by the Trabuc-Luscher connection. Instead of the tranquil streets east and west of Central Park, Hickey would have dispatched him on a tour of the city's Nine Circles of Hell—perhaps the environs of the Port Authority Bus Terminal, for starters—to burn his closed case–obsession right out of him.

Only the occasional spike of static reminded them that the radio was droning on. Because repairs had depleted the car pool, the only vehicle available had been Hickey's Category 1 Crown Victoria. Even though it had top-of-the-line communications equipment and was only a few months old, there wasn't a detective who wouldn't rather sign out the worst clunker in the fleet. Return Hickey's car with the slightest trace of smoke, food, lint, or pungent aftershave, and even a cop the DI didn't consider half as useless as Clay would land with a splat on his Revolving Shit List. (An exit was possible only when an even bigger fuckup took your place.) Police and Politics . . . they both started out with the same four letters.

Cello jotted down a notation. As he flipped through route outlines, he asked, "Want to grab some lunch?"

"Sounds good." Clay didn't have to look at his watch. All along one side of the block, car engines were revving up, approaching a Daytona-like crescendo. The drivers were primed to make the big switch to the other side of the street the very second the 11-to-12:30 alternate-side parking ban expired. The countdown received the same rapt attention as the final moments before the ball dropped on

New Year's Eve. "I bet some of these cars go years never driving anyplace else—just back and forth across the street," Clay observed. He pointed at Cello's sheaf of papers. "You think Mr. UPS has picked up on all this surveillance—that he's laying low?"

"Doesn't matter—one way or another, we'll get him. I can't wait to call him by his real name: U Piece-a Shit." The younger brother of a cop shot on duty, Cello had pulled all the stops on the guy: in addition to the contingent from Police Plaza, three precincts of cops were keeping an eye on the trucks—on the beat, on bikes and scooters, in unmarked and patrol cars. Under pressure, the shippers had begun placing their own security people in random trucks as uniformed helpers, and some tailed their vans with their own plain cars.

Suddenly a report came in over the radio—jumbled, but the word "Airborne" made them both sit up straighter. The driver of an unmarked express company security vehicle, approaching a parked Airborne van from behind, had noticed a man lurking by a gated delivery entrance further down West Seventy-seventh Street. When the driver returned to the van from a pickup, the loiterer—wearing a black running suit, and fitting the shooter's description—rushed toward him, holding up an express delivery envelope. The moment the uniformed security guards stepped out of the car, the running suit turned and bolted, disappearing around a corner. Clay's mind flashed back to the guy in the janitor getup, whirling back in a shooting stance.

At a risky 12:25, the bravest—or most impatient—of the waiting cars made a diagonal crossing, claiming a spot on the opposite side of Eighty-third Street.

Simultaneously, the security contingent in pursuit—thankfully not the target du jour—reported that the man had hopped into the passenger seat of a waiting late-model Grand Prix, dark blue. The driver was heading north on Amsterdam Avenue. There was a partial on the license plate.

Meanwhile, emboldened by the trailblazing parker, several cars started to edge out into the roadway.

Clay clamped the red light on top of the Crown Vic, switched it on, and bleeped the siren. Startled, a member of the alternate-side advance guard hit the brakes hard, and the car behind him smashed into his rear fender.

The sound of metal creasing and denting prompted Cello to run his finger under his seat belt, checking that it was secure. "Get around these assholes and go!" he shouted. "We'll meet and greet the bastard at Amsterdam!"

The single car that had moved to the opposite side, thinking the siren was a warning for him, pulled out in a panic. In the nick of time, Clay swung Hickey's car away from his front fender. Running the gauntlet of alternate-siders paralyzed by ticket-terror, Clay barely managed to beat the light across Columbus. The next report placed a uniform car from the Twentieth Precinct in pursuit of the Grand Prix at Eighty-first Street. Cello radioed that he'd be joining at Amsterdam and Eighty-third.

The block between Columbus and Amsterdam had other, nonalternate, parking rules, so Clay had a chance to barrel crosstown. But as the Vic closed in on the corner, he and Cello muttered "Shit!" in perfect unison.

Two cars were waiting for the light to change, blocking access to the avenue. Clay hit the brakes hard. The flashing red light, several siren bursts, and Cello's angry orders over the speaker convinced their drivers to move—inch by inch, it seemed—far enough into the intersection to give Clay room to maneuver onto Amsterdam. Just as he was clearing the second vehicle, a dark blue blur sped by. No heading anyone off at the pass. "Okay, so now we go after the son of a bitch!" Cello yelled.

Before Clay started to swing onto the avenue, he instinctively glanced south; the pursuing patrol car, going full-out, was bearing down on them. Clay took off as soon as it passed, and Cello radioed in their new position.

Amsterdam was a broad, six-lane avenue, with lanes one and six reserved for parking. Its lights were sequential, precision-timed to roll from green to yellow to red. By Eighty-sixth Street, the Crown Vic came abreast of the patrol car. Traffic was light, in a midday lull. "How fucking fast is that mutt going?" Cello screamed, outraged. "Two more blocks, and he'll start hitting red lights! Get your nose right up his ass!" Clay shot ahead of the patrol car. The Grand Prix was weaving in and out of the stream of vehicles moving uptown—dangerous even if he'd been going only half as fast. The driver was taking risks—big ones—but darting through.

"Look at that!" Cello said, almost admiringly, as the dark blue car picked another hole in the flow of traffic and slid right through it. "This guy's got all the moves—he's gotta be a pro!"

"Cello, he's also nuts! You've got to request permission to pursue!"

Their speed had them catching red lights before they turned green, and up ahead the Grand Prix ran the stoplight at Eighty-eighth Street, barely avoiding the first car going east through the intersection. The cars waiting for the light to change gave Clay one lane to scoot through, and he went for it, aware of the patrol car at their rear, catching radio reports that another car from the Twentieth had joined the chase back at Eighty-fifth Street, and that Twenty-fourth Precinct cruisers north of Eighty-sixth were zeroing in on Amsterdam to cut off the blue sedan. Up ahead, the avenue seemed to constrict with truck traffic, but the Grand Prix kept on deftly dodging between vehicles, eluding Clay, disconcerting him with split-second disappearances. He managed to stick with it, but narrowing the distance was tough, even though they briefly came close enough for Cello to call in the full plate number.

He'd stomped the Crown Vic's brakes so many times, they were starting to heat and stink. More straining brakes—the skidding, swerving squeals of cars as they unwittingly moved onto Amsterdam from the side streets—just about drowned out the radio.

The lights ahead were all red. Approaching Ninety-first Street, Clay could see two open spaces; the Grand Prix was aimed at one of them, in the right center lane. A taxi was pulling up on its right, to either pick up or discharge a passenger.

Out of the corner of his eye, he saw Cello's steadying left hand on the dashboard, maybe a glint of metal near the passenger door. "That's it—squeeze in there, center lane. Get in fast—before he knows we're there." The unusual calm in Cello's voice was unnerving. It would be their first chance to come abreast of the Grand Prix, and they'd be coming up on its left. A truck was in the lane left of Clay.

Oblivious to the approaching havoc on Amsterdam, the traffic waiting on Ninety-first, prompted by a green light, began to flow westbound. On each side of the avenue, the flashing green "Walk" man beckoned pedestrians to cross, a jaunty promise of safety. A small Asian woman, rebalancing her two bulging plastic shopping bags, stepped from the curb. She looked straight ahead at the east side of the street—no need to glance south, as she trusted in the protection provided by the green man.

Just as Clay raced up near the trunk of the Grand Prix, her bright yellow dress—she'd been totally blocked by the truck to his left—came into view. She was fully in his path as he slammed on his brakes. Her feet kept going another step or two as the peril registered. Then, except for the rapid blinking of her eyes, she froze. The Crown Vic's overheated brakes made it swerve more than stop, and Clay wrestled to keep control of the car as it plowed toward the truck. The Grand Prix's driver, free of Clay on his left, purposely veered toward the woman, striking her with his left fender. Cello was screaming something incomprehensible as, catapulted skyward, the lady in yellow sailed toward them through the air. The shopping bags jettisoned a hailstorm of hand-picked produce. Peaches, tomatoes, and a small melon juggled before their eyes for a second or two before her plummeting body slammed down on the Crown Vic's hood. The impact rushed her straight at the windshield. Mouth and eyes wide open, the nightmare face kept coming at Clay and Cello, monstrously large as it crashed into the glass. The safety glass shattered, then sagged from her continued momentum. With one final lurch, she bulged in at them, trapped in its mesh.

Clay, still skidding to a stop, his view completely obscured, felt the rear of the Vic grate against the truck. Disoriented, unable to see, he lost control of the car. He went from driver to prisoner as it slid and skated across the avenue on a horizontal trajectory, toward where the taxi had been.

Braced for the impact from the front end, he was totally shaken when the rear of the Crown Vic was hit so violently, it skidded along twice as fast, in a different direction.

The impact activated both airbags, the fraction-of-a-second expansion an all-out assault on head, neck, and upper body. A total eclipse overtook Clay, but it must have been brief, because the Vic was still sliding sideways, only slower.

The airbag was deflating, and his neck hurt like hell. Two dead women were on the hood; one if he blinked, then two again. Turning his head was painful, but he managed a glance out the side window. Hickey's car was coming to a standstill in the middle of the Ninety-first Street intersection.

The next block was a slate wiped clean of northbound traffic. No dark blue car, nothing. From Ninety-second Street on, Amsterdam Avenue dropped off like a cliff; the steep incline led down to what was called Manhattan Valley. Clay could imagine how the Grand Prix's taillights looked as they'd disappeared from view, all alone on the avenue. He closed his eyes, trying not to breathe in the stench of the overheated car, trying not to look at the woman on the hood.

"Cello?" he called out. Pain reduced his voice to a whisper. "Cello? You okay?"

CHAPTER
SIXTEEN

With two black eyes and a dressing on his broken nose, Clay walked into Major Case with his head held high—thanks to the cervical collar he had to wear for whiplash.

A partially opened door afforded a glimpse of a frowning Hickey, phone cradled on his shoulder as he transcribed notes on a pad. He filled his office like a thundercloud, darkening and gathering force.

Maybe, Clay was rapidly convincing himself, the way they did it at sea in the old days wasn't so harsh, after all. A drum roll, hands tied to a mast, and twenty lashes. But at least it would be over. In the here and now, even before facing Hickey, he had no doubt that he'd already been transferred from the DI's Revolving Shit List to the On for Eternity version.

As for what had happened the day before, he hadn't expected any concern or condolences from anyone in The Big Room, and he received none. Cello, his single ally, wouldn't be in until the end of the week. Although Martino had blacked out and suffered a concussion, his life had been saved by the driver of the patrol car chasing right behind them: once the Crown Vic had gone into its horizontal skid and collision was inevitable, the cop had done his damndest to avoid crashing into the Vic's front seat. The reward for his quick maneuvering was a face full of scrapes and bruises and a shattered wrist. Because the blue-and-white's passenger seat wasn't equipped with an airbag, his rookie partner had fared the worst—the kid had multiple fractures, and internal injuries still hadn't been ruled out.

Instead of starting his report, Clay crossed to Hickey's office. The phone was back on its cradle, but the Deputy Inspector was still writing. "Enter, Ryder," he said, without looking up, proving that he was a man who could sniff out Eau de Garbage, no matter what the distance.

Clay stood behind one of the visitor's chairs, leaning a little of his weight against its molded plastic back. Like an incoming tide, pain was washing in and out behind his forehead, spreading with each wave. When Hickey deigned to glower up at him, he did not simply ignore his injuries; he left no doubt that the

Art Guy couldn't suffer enough to atone for what he'd done to his fellow cops, to the Department, to the city of New York, to the U.S.A., to Jesus Christ, and to Hickey's car. "I was going to write my report," said Clay, "but I thought you might want to see me first."

"How considerate," said Hickey. "Let's see." He held up his index finger. "One dead woman." He added and subtracted fingers for emphasis: "Three cops in the hospital. Two of our cars totaled. Four precincts involved. More collateral damage than the entire department's annual budget." Joining thumb and index finger to make a zero, he added, "Plus, the perp got away. Report? There aren't enough trees to make enough paper for you to account for everything that went down yesterday."

"The perp . . . got away?" Clay's grip on the chair tightened; a wrecking ball had just smacked square into his stomach.

"The Grand Prix was pulled over at One-forty-seventh and Adam Clayton Powell Boulevard. A rental, of course. We picked it up with three jerks inside."

"But there were only—"

"Yeah, two. After the Mario Andretti type you were following hit the woman—who only happened to work in an embassy, and that's another can of worms—he managed to shake you and snake his way to the Ninety-seventh Street Transverse. The consensus is that after going through the park, he dropped himself off on the East Side, somewhere between there and One-twenty-third Street. That's because the other guy—the one fitting the description of the shooter—double-parked the Grand Prix on One-twenty-third between Lex and Park."

"How do you—"

Hickey waved his question away. "The three aforementioned jerks, who were hanging out in front of a bodega, saw him double-park and walk away from the car. They watch him walk to Lex and turn left—the One-twenty-fifth Street subway entrance is right down the street. Meanwhile, it has not been lost on the Three Amigos that he left the car with the windows rolled down and the key in the ignition. They then took it for what, in my youth, was called a joyride."

"And they made it to One-forty-seventh?"

"Yes, and considering every cop in the city was looking for that license plate, that car, and that dented left front fender, that's pretty disgraceful, too. Of course, when they were pulled over, they swore up and down they didn't do any-thing wrong—like grand theft auto doesn't count. But their description of the guy who walked away from the Grand Prix matches every description we've got of the perp, and the time makes it a slam-dunk. Not only that, but he'd been re-ported wearing a black running suit, and they spotted him in a black T-shirt and black running pants—he dumped the jacket. This mutt manages to figure out every angle."

That, Clay realized, was the first grudging concession that someone other than he might be responsible for what had happened on Amsterdam Avenue. It brought back Cello yelling out, "This guy . . . he's gotta be a pro!" Briefly closing his eyes against the pain surging inside his head, he saw the face of the woman in the yellow dress against the windshield, blood flowing from her nose. Veering at her intentionally with his fender, at that angle, the cold-blooded bastard had to have known that no airbag sensor in the Grand Prix would be activated when he plowed into her.

With no further allowances to the killers, Hickey resumed his tirade against Clay, loud enough for half the detectives on duty to hear every word. "I can't question a man with a possible concussion, but nothing Martino can say will change the fact that this is a total disaster, a total fuckup—and I'm holding you responsible!" The DI had chosen to overlook that Cello had been in charge of the case, and calling the shots on Amsterdam.

Hickey stood up, placed both hands on his desk and leaned his long torso toward Clay. "I don't know who thought up this job of yours. Hanging around museums—what kind of job is that for a detective? It never felt right that a cop with your record would even *want* a job like that. Before this art bullshit, you put your life on the line every damn day, and now how do you spend your duty time? Chatting in hole-in-the-wall galleries. Making long-distance calls to Paris. A regular Michael-Fucking-Angelo. But when it comes to the Department, you revert into your prima donna mode, the same uptight prick all over again."

Outside, The Big Room had never been so quiet. Not the embarrassed quiet that descended when someone was hauled in and skewered without due cause, but a satisfied silence—a hushed, he-had-it-coming appreciation of Hickey's rant against the insufferable prima donna–cum–prick.

Of course, when Cello returned, he'd try to take all the responsibility, mea culpa himself blue in the face. Still, any blame laid on Martino wouldn't linger—Cello was no weak sister. But that was exactly how Hickey and everybody else saw Clay . . . and once you see a guy that way, nothing will change your mind.

SEVENTEEN

"And have the Culture Kingpins decreed when Trabuc will be exposed to public view?" Oliver Plumworth's head tilted back to indicate the edifice looming behind them.

The summer evening was in a suspended state of golden pretwilight; it lingered on, as if the sky would never darken, the stars never appear. Clay sat down next to his old friend on the steps of the Metropolitan Museum. "November," he replied, imagining that autumnal 8 P.M.: dark and cold, the pluming fountains capped, the patchwork groups hanging out on the tiered stairs—seniors, kids, families, would-be hipsters—long gone.

"This puzzle of yours—you'd like to solve it before the opening?"

Clay thought back to Aaron, warning him not to expect quick results. And to Eli, waiting decades for a clue. "Sooner. Before it drives me nuts." *Now there's an option for Hickey, even better than the threat of suspension: put the Art Albatross through a psychological assessment, to prove how unfit he is to carry a gun.*

"Judging from how ragged round the edges you look, Clayton, that is rather imminent."

"Need I remind you who got me going after the case was closed? That little reminiscence about the painting turning up in the Seventies?"

Oliver shrugged. "I believed it at the time. I have no reason to doubt it now."

Keeping his voice low, Clay recounted what he'd learned about Luscher to date. "His only surviving relatives are in Germany, the son and daughter of his cousin. But so far, the son's untraceable, and the daughter slammed down the phone as soon as I mentioned Udo's name. Two days ago—and I've been waiting for weeks—I finally got translations of some old German newspaper stories that might explain their behavior. As a bonus, the stories point to how Luscher was able to sneak out of Europe."

"That far back? Oh, fascinating! And what about Paris?"

"Well, what led Luscher to Dr. Meredith's grandfather, Paul Bergère, is plain enough now—that Resistance scam. But figuring out how a stage designer wound up with two Van Goghs hanging on his bedroom wall . . . that might be a key."

"Perhaps a key which might unlock the whereabouts of the elusive Madame Trabuc, as well? Is it folly to hope that the cranky couple might one day be a matched set?" After a pause, Oliver sighed, "But even if you do accomplish such a splendid feat, there's no telling how many more paintings that Nazi looted while he was in Paris."

"No matter how many, the NYPD doesn't see it as their problem. Nobody does."

"Working single-handedly on an investigation like that . . . it has to involve quite a commitment . . . time, trouble, not to mention the funding."

"Well, so far it's my time, my trouble. And thank God for the Internet." He glanced at his watch; he'd waylaid Oliver on his way to a cocktail party. "Am I making you late?"

"Only fashionably so." Suddenly, a great rustling of plastic ensued: all over the museum's steps, people in T-shirts and Yankees caps gathered up plastic bags and poster tubes. A phalanx of three super-size tour buses was rolling up to the curb in front of the Met in perfect synchrony. "Now, that should be your inspiration," said Oliver enthusiastically, as out-of-towners filed into buses marked A, B, and C.

Clay stared at him, not getting it.

"Be a tourist! Go to Paris—to the Jeu de Paume, to the theaters! *Someone* must still be alive! Go accost that German cousin—just as you accosted me tonight! I repeat, you certainly look as if you could use a little holiday. And even if nothing materializes, you'll at least get it out of your system!"

"Actually, I've been giving a trip some thought."

"Well then, stop thinking!" Oliver rose a few inches, then sat back down. "Ah. Perhaps you need some assistance with the airfare? I certainly can—"

Clay sprang to his feet, and gave his friend a hand getting up. "I've got it covered. But that's a nice gesture, Oliver. Not just the cash. The kick in the pants."

Later that night, Clay paid five or six bills that were coming due. At the bottom of the last one, his credit card statement, was the tally of the points he'd accrued over five years—points that could be redeemed for either cash or air travel miles. Bold letters urged him to cash in or use the first year's points soon, before they expired. With all the moving around he'd done in the Navy, he hadn't had the urge to travel since his discharge. After writing out his check, he stood up, stretched, filled a bowl with water at the kitchen sink, and took the bowl to his worktable.

After he'd finally completed the steamship's hull, Clay had gone on to tackle the eight lifeboats the original plans provided for on the hurricane deck. A diversion, but a good drill in working small. He'd spent the last weeks working on the ship's paddle wheels and their housings, and decided to add her name before moving on. The night before, using an X-acto knife, he painstakingly cut out the twenty-six letters required from his decal alphabets. After soaking the thirteen that would go on the portside in the water for about a minute, he picked up an *S* with tweezers. All his concentration focused on lining up the slippery decals . . . until he came to the first *L* in *SHELTER ISLAND*.

L, as in Lauren.

At the end of 1998, he'd become the beneficiary of a $2,500 accidental death policy linked to Lauren's checking account. It was, he'd learned, a free bank promotion aimed at getting customers to sign up for a policy with a payoff of a hundred times as much. He'd kept the check on his mail pile for months before he deposited it, weighing whether "Accidental Death" defined only the moment of impact, or extended to how the "Deceased" had arrived at that fatal juncture of time, place, and misjudgment. He had that, plus the round-trip ticket to Europe covered by his five years of credit card points.

Lauren and Clay had never flown anywhere together; their honeymoon was a three-day weekend at the Plaza Hotel, a memorable marathon of sex and room service. Shortly after she moved in with him, she proposed starting a nest egg, and that seemed like a logical thing for newlyweds to do. That first Saturday in May 1998, she was right on the course she'd set, working toward a house in Westchester—a goal he had only recently learned of, and certainly didn't share. Their marriage had begun to unravel, but Lauren's plans still included him, despite the way he'd immediately scuttled her Five-Year Plan. Looking back, what scared him even more than what he'd seen evolve in her was how desperately he had fought to counteract it. Did that opening salvo of his boil down to one control freak countering another control freak? And what, after all, was the real threat? Was a single sign that she wasn't the woman he'd convinced himself he'd married—unpredictable, sexually irrepressible—such a terrible menace?

But what if the traits that so unsettled him hadn't evolved at all, but had always been there? Had she deceived him, or had he deceived himself, by failing to perceive them? Maybe he truly was the clueless detective Hickey couldn't abide. Maybe the clock was running out for him at Police Plaza, the same way it had run out on their marriage.

Dissatisfied, Clay kept moving the "I" back and forth, until "SHELTER" and "ISLAND" were precisely separated.

He was positive that their relationship never would have gone so bad so fast if she'd gravitated toward any other objective. Hadn't he revealed enough for Lauren to understand that, aside from being able to visit his mother, he wanted to be as far away from his grandfather's world as possible? Nevertheless, he'd lashed out way too hard. And guilt still kept him from sorting out exactly what his own goal was that Saturday in May 1998, and precisely how Lauren figured in it.

The last letter refused to line up; it wasn't the first time the close work blurred his vision, especially when he was working so late into the night. The kitchen area had a wall phone with a long cord. He dialed the credit card company's 800 number and, while he was on hold for a booking agent, finally nudged the "D" into alignment. After an endless series of questions required to verify his identity, his flight was booked.

The agent didn't ask the one question he had no answer for: "Why the fuck are you going to Paris?"

"You put in for vacation," Hickey said to him the next week, skipping the "Hello, see you're finally out of that neck brace" part of the conversation.

"Yes, Sir. One week. The beginning of next month." Clay had bristled when he learned the mileage program required ticketing at least three weeks in advance. But even though he wanted to leave ASAP, the extra notice would work better with the DI.

A little tic lifted one of Hickey's thick eyebrows. Cello had, as expected, defended him to the max, but his entreaties had done little to lessen the DI's ill will. "And where will you be, Ryder . . . in case a dog takes a leak on a statue?"

The last thing Clay wanted Hickey to know was that his ticket couldn't be refunded, and that the dates were set in stone. "Is there a problem with that particular week, Sir?"

"I asked *where*?"

"Europe." Hickey's frown indicated that was far from specific enough. "Paris."

"Paris." His mouth twisted down, a disapproving mini-croissant. "Do cops go to Paris?"

"I don't know if any research has been done on that, Sir. Perhaps I can—"

Hickey wasn't listening; he was too busy pulling wispy threads together, weaving his own connections. "Hold on . . . this isn't about that painting, is it? The one that turned up at the Met? That's a closed case! Tell me you're not still wrapped up in that, Ryder!"

Hickey was a better detective than any detective he supervised gave him credit for. So effortlessly had he discovered the trip's purpose, Clay was forced to scramble, and any cheap trick would do. "My wife . . . she always wanted to go to Paris. She'll be seeing it through my eyes."

That stopped Hickey cold—he'd sniffed out Clay's lie, but wouldn't lower himself to engage at his shamefully low level.

"If you check my vacation records, Sir, the last time I took time off was when she died. I had to wait until . . . you know . . . I felt ready."

"Make sure I have contact numbers in case I have to reach you," said

Hickey. "And get it all out of your system before you come back . . . whatever the hell it is." He stalked off, without a *bon voyage*.

During his telephone conversation with the *Gestapiste* infiltrator, the old man had mentioned that another Luscher was stationed in Paris during the Occupation. A lot of transatlantic digging had identified him as Albrecht, a major in the *Wehrmacht*. After the war, cousin Albrecht, who'd earned a university degree in economics, settled in Munich and went to work for an import-export firm. At the dawn of Germany's Economic Miracle, he switched to a commercial bank. He died in 1986, leaving a daughter, a son, and three grandchildren.

If the son, Helmut, had a phone, it wasn't listed under the Luscher name. The daughter, identified in Albrecht's obituary as Frau Erika Hafner, was a banker like her father. She was still working at the same bank listed in the obit, at the main branch in Munich's city center.

Clay flew into Paris and then took a train to Munich—airfare for the side trip would have taken too big a chunk out of his budget, and for all he knew, the trip could turn out to be a total waste. He'd hardly slept on the plane, and not at all on the train. After nicking himself shaving in the train's claustrophobic lavatory, he wrenched his back wrestling into a fresh shirt. At the next to last stop, a large man boarded with a wurst the size of a rolling pin and took the seat opposite Clay. His first hearty bite sprayed a geyser of grease onto the clean shirt. The man chortled jovially, then offered Clay a bite. Whatever he read in Clay's reaction made him avoid eye contact the rest of the way to Munich's *Hauptbahnhof*.

Just by using Frau Hafner's name, it was easy enough to make it up to the bank's fifth floor. The short, puffy receptionist fronting for the executive offices asked in English if he had an appointment; he gave his name. Staring at the stain on his shirt as he stood before her, she rang through.

"You have no appointment, Mr. Ryder," she announced, as she returned the phone to its cradle.

"Was that Frau Hafner, or her secretary?"

"It does not matter. Since you have no appointment, you must leave now." Her watery blue eyes blinked at the stain through thick glasses. While he stood firm, not budging an inch, the rosacea splattered over her cheeks heated up. Her right hand was groping for the security alarm that had to be just under the edge of the desktop.

"Try her once more," he pressed. "This time, tell her I came all the way from New York, and I brought all her cousin's newspaper clippings. Tell her that I have enough copies to paper every wall on every floor of this whole damn bank."

The rosacea spread like wildfire. The hand vacillated, then reached for the phone again. All he understood was "New York," but she took far more time to explain what he said than he'd taken saying it. After a long wait, she looked up at Clay. "Since this is a personal matter, she asks that you come back at five." When he turned to leave, she said, "If that shirt is not cotton, that stain . . . it will never wash out."

After her secretary escorted Clay into her office, Erika Hafner rose from behind a marble slab of a desk, neither extending her hand nor smiling. She was about five-nine, and the strained seams of her perky blue suit were proof that she hadn't spent much time battling her body type. Clay knew she was fifty-seven, but her round, calorically unchallenged face appeared younger. The dour man who remained in one of the two Barcelona chairs facing her desk was introduced as her brother, Helmut. One name, like a rock star; whatever he'd changed to from Luscher was not about to be revealed. His thinning hair was the same graying dark blond as his older sister's, and he had the same bulky build on a tall frame. His suit, however, fit better.

Frau Hafner gestured for Clay to take a seat. "Herr Ryder," she began, "let me make two points clear: First, our father's cousin was legally declared dead decades ago. Second, our father had absolutely no connection with any of his deplorable actions." She spoke forcibly, with a British accent, and left no room for contradiction.

"The courts are with us, 100 percent," added Helmut. A thick accent, uncomfortable with English, but equally resolute. "How dare you threaten blackmail against my sister?"

"Blackmail? Since when are newspaper accounts blackmail? They turned up in my research, and—"

"How can we tell you about someone we never met?" Erika interrupted. "Being his only surviving relative was our father's greatest misfortune." Huffy attitude, but reading from an old script.

"Our father was a good man. He had a terrible fight, to clean the Luscher name," her brother chimed in.

How clean, Helmut, if you find it too unsavory to use?

"After the war, the Allies treated my father very badly," Erika lamented. "I was very young, but I will never forget how they frightened me when they searched our home. They suspected he was hiding Udo. Some believed *he* was Udo. Twice he was arrested, then freed—just as he was about to be transported to Nuremberg."

"That was for war crimes," said Clay. "But what happened five years later, when the news broke about the two murdered Germans?"

Her eyes narrowed. "German policemen came to the house. Their questions gave me nightmares . . . a smashed Mercedes going over a cliff, a skull with a bullet hole. Udo's picture—the one with Himmler, giving him that medal—it was in all the papers, and then that waitress recognized him, and they started in with the other murder."

Eerily, Clay's construct of how Luscher assassinated his staff car driver in the spring of '45 couldn't have been closer to the facts. In 1949, shortly after the rusted-out Mercedes being hoisted up the side of a precipice was splashed all over the German newspapers, Udo was linked to a second German homicide, also committed in '45.

It occurred in a village on the shore of Lake Konstanz, the *Bodensee,* which forms part of the border between Germany and Switzerland. The village sits on the lake's narrowest point between the two countries. According to an eyewitness—the waitress—its marketplace was crowded the day of the murder, crammed with tented stands and tables set up for the annual fall festival—the Third Reich's collapse hadn't stopped the harvest. A man in the shreds of an Army uniform, leaning heavily on a metal cane, hobbled into the main square. Apparently exhausted, the man—an ordinary *Soldat*—barely made it to a table overlooking the lake. The waitress who served him remembered him for his limp, as well as his good looks.

Before the war, a nearby dock was popular for its motorboat rentals. With hardly enough gasoline for the police launch, the outboard motors had long since been replaced by oarlocks. After the soldier paid his bill, the waitress watched him shuffle to the dock, where Emil, the man who rented out the boats, pointed to his hourly rates sign. Emil had been discharged from the Navy in '43, after a torpedo blast took his left leg at midthigh. When she glanced at the lake a bit later, both men were in a rowboat, far from shore. At the time, the only thing the waitress considered odd was that the soldier had taken his cane onboard, instead of leaving it next to Emil's crutch, which was leaning against a piling. A large party, hungry and thirsty and ready to admire the setting sun's reflections on the water, kept her too busy to look lakeward again before nightfall.

Two days later, the boatman's body washed up on the Swiss shore; he'd been shot in the heart at close range. Sentiment in the village was that the soldier forced him to row across at gunpoint—to transport anyone across the border was against the law, and would have put Emil out of business in a flash, veteran or not.

When the Mercedes was found in '49, and the waitress recognized the man last seen with the murdered boatman, Udo became notorious: descriptions of his crimes eclipsed all other news in Germany for nearly a week.

"After the *Bodensee* incident, Udo was never seen again," Helmut said firmly.

"Yes, I'm sure he was never again seen in Germany," agreed Clay. "Did the authorities continue to question your father after the news died down?"

"I don't know what he kept from us children," said Frau Hafner. "But I don't recall them knocking on the door after that . . . that terrible disgrace."

"You mentioned your father was Udo's only living relative. I know his mother was a widow who died in 1941. His two brothers died in battle. Wilhelm, in Africa, September of '42, at Alam Halfa. Ernst, on the Russian-Polish border, spring '44. That made Udo the sole heir to a considerable inheritance."

Helmut's face darkened. His big sister sat up even straighter and squared her considerable shoulders. "Yes. We were the poor relations. Udo's family owned a town house, as well as a country property. Helmut runs it now."

Runs it? As in country estate? "And you've taken the town house?"

"My job here is three stops away on the *U-Bahn* . . . it's convenient."

"So having Udo declared legally dead was also . . . convenient?"

Helmut rose halfway out of his seat. Clay figured he was shouting the German equivalent of "You're way outta line, pal!"

"He is dead!" Erika snarled. "If not, wouldn't he have contacted us? Asked about the property? Asked for money?"

Only an idiot would have risked it, and you two, living very comfortably, would have given him up in a heartbeat. Ignoring their outburst, he said, "When I telephoned you, I tried to explain the investigation linked to your father's cousin."

"Yes, yes, something about a Van Gogh."

"Did your father have any interest in art? Did he visit museums . . . galleries? Was painting a hobby of his?"

"Not at all. His hobby was stamp collecting."

"No connection to art at all?"

Exasperated, Erika Hafner took a deep breath. "He was assigned to Paris right after the start of the Occupation, attached to the *Verwaltungsstab,* in the Hotel Majestic. He was an economist. At first, he conducted efficiency studies, projections for staff supplies for the *Wehrmacht.* His thoroughness earned him a promotion—doing pretty much the same work, but for the railways. After the Allied invasion, he was under incredible pressure. On the one hand, the *Wehrmacht* was fighting a war in Normandy, counting on trains to move wounded troops back from that front and to bring in reinforcements and supplies. On the other hand, the SS ordered every available *wagen* to be loaded with Jews and sent east. He couldn't satisfy both."

Her brother pitched in. "He didn't sympathize with the Nazis! He said the Party position was ridiculous. Why give a Jew on his way to a concentration camp precedence over a German soldier?" Catching Clay's look, he added, "My English . . . you know what I mean."

"Sure." Helmut's political incorrectness wasn't the only thing that had caused Clay's reaction. From conversations with Mr. Weinberger of the Met, he knew that art had been moved out of Paris right up to the last days of the Occupation. By train. The SS had demanded precedence not only for Jews, but for plundered art, as well. Four thousand, one hundred seventy-four crates, containing twenty-two thousand artworks, had been shipped by rail from Paris to Germany. Even if Albrecht Luscher didn't know a David from a Da Vinci, he had to know about the wholesale looting.

"Did your father and his cousin meet at any time in Paris?"

"Never," said an adamant Erika.

"Only twice," said her brother, in the same instant, but too late.

"Which is it, then?" Clay asked, looking straight at Erika.

"They didn't *meet*. Their paths crossed by accident." She shot Helmut an *I'll-get-you-later-Dummkopf* look. "Each of them made a dinner reservation at a restaurant frequented by German officers, half an hour apart. When Udo showed up, he was told there was a mix-up, that another officer named Luscher had already claimed the table. He insisted the maître d' bring him to the impostor. After things were ironed out, my father invited Udo to join him for dinner. All he recalled about his cousin was his enthusiasm for riding—a boy with a wall full of trophies and ribbons. The last time he'd seen Udo, he was maybe thirteen or fourteen. He joined the SS because of their riding school. Quite elite. I assume you know all that."

"Sure. Bad Tolz Officer's Training School, the SS Riding School, the SS *Kavallerie*. Poland, Paris, Berlin." *Switzerland, Genoa. Argentina.*

Erika nodded. "He struck my father as a very handsome young man, but also very . . . what you would call 'uptight.' Young for his rank. And that medal he wore"—she touched the base of her thick throat—"my father had never seen one before. They ordered dinner. Udo asked my father where he was assigned."

"And he told him about the trains," said Clay dryly. "Maybe, after a drink or two, about how he was caught in the middle? Between the *Wehrmacht* and the SS? Soldiers to the front, versus Jews to the camps."

Reluctantly, Frau Hafner sighed, "Perhaps."

It was the moment, and Clay pounced. "What about the art transports? They were as high a priority as the Jews! Certainly the approach was equally methodical. Surely he told Udo about the art!"

Erika's mouth compressed into a tight line. Breaking the silence, Helmut declared, "He knew only the numbers. The number of crates, the number of *wagens*. No idea the contents."

Clay could feel links snapping onto links, a chain of connections coming together faster than he'd expected.

Helmut stumbled ahead. "Even if he knew it was art, he was always in the office. He never saw a single crate. No idea where it came from, other than that museum."

"The Jeu de Paume."

Identical *X*s, the Luscher siblings folded their arms tightly across their chests, holding back any further details about the villain who had both plagued them and made them rich.

"That can't be all. What else did they discuss?"

"Being polite, our father asked Udo where he was assigned," Helmut said, with a nod to his sister. "After squeezing so much out of our father, he in turn tells him nothing, only that he reports directly to General Oberg."

"From what I understand, that was saying a lot," said Clay.

"Our father was rather insulated in the *Verwaltungsstab*," Erika countered. "A few days later, a *Wehrmacht* officer he hardly knew asked if he was related to a Luscher in the SS who worked the prisons—whose favorite tool happened to be one of Himmler's ceremonial daggers. When he found out about *Le Découpeur,* Father was appalled! More inquiries followed, and he became increasingly uncomfortable about being confused with someone who'd have to pay the piper at the end of the war. More important, he had the family name to defend."

They'd reached an impasse. Erika looked at her watch. Helmut fidgeted. "What about the second meeting?" asked Clay.

To Clay's surprise, it was Erika who broke the silence. "Just as you said before, Udo's brother Ernst died that spring on the Eastern Front. Udo knew that Ernst and our father had been close in age . . . and good friends. He telephoned when the telegram arrived. They arranged to meet in a small café near the Hotel Majestic. They had one drink in honor of Ernst. Then Udo started in about the art."

"Udo wanted information about the Jeu de Paume?"

"Not exactly. He wanted to know *how it all worked.* Where the art on the trains was going, who was on the receiving end. When he heard it was being shipped to party leaders, that Goering alone had an entire train of art sent directly to him . . . he refused to believe it. He became hostile."

Helmut broke in, "A man with such a reputation, even if he was a relative, made our father nervous. You can imagine . . . every word, like walking on eggs."

"He couldn't mention defeat or corruption," agreed Erika, "or how the men at the top were scheming to get away with as much as they could. He finally told Udo, 'Germany will be victorious. However, *if* the unthinkable happens, currency will be worthless, and gold is far too heavy and bulky to carry on one's person. That's where the art comes in. A good painting can be wrapped up tight and carried under your arm. Like an umbrella for a rainy day.' "

On the Munich-Paris train, Clay considered how Albrecht Luscher had disclaimed his murderous cousin in Paris, only to reclaim him in Germany, in order to gain control of his sizable estate. If there had been any doubt, the meeting with Erika and Helmut proved that something in the whole family was seriously twisted.

His first stop in Paris was the Jeu de Paume. During his hitch in the Navy, he'd spent a leave in Paris and visited the museum, never imagining the chaos and frenzy that had gripped it during the Occupation, when the museum had been the repository for the art the Nazis carted away from Jewish homes and galleries.

Mr. Weinberger of the Met, an expert on Holocaust art loss, had taken the time to explain to Clay what seemed so complicated to the young *Gestapiste*: the operations of the major Nazi looting organization, the *Einsatzstab Reichsleiter Rosenberg*. The ERR was a completely autonomous operation: besides a crew of its own art appraisers, carpenters, packers, and transporters, it had undercover agents to ferret out art, and a corps of crack ERR troops ready to follow up with confiscation raids.

"The Germans are famous for their efficiency," observed Mr. Weinberger. "As it turned out, the ERR was so resourceful at impounding Jewish-owned art, it literally overwhelmed itself. Collections began to pour into the Jeu de Paume so fast, their movers were forced to dump canvases anyplace they could. In no time, everything was shuffled together, like hundreds of different packs of playing cards. At the beginning, they wanted to document and photograph every piece. They never even came close."

"The price of success," Clay had observed, and a slight, wry smile broke out briefly in the midst of Weinberger's salt-and-pepper beard. "Wasn't it all supposed to go to a museum Hitler planned to build?"

"Yes, in Linz, Austria," replied Weinberger. "But not all of it. The ERR's appraisers were to select only art that reflected the Führer's personal taste: German, Flemish, and Dutch Old Masters, mixed with hideous Viennese kitsch. The rest could be traded away for Linz-type art. Or, in case of paintings the Nazis classified as "degenerate"—work by artists such as Picasso, Léger, and Matisse, or anything by a Jew—burned."

Clay's eyes widened in disbelief, but Weinberger held up a hand.

"That's where the French dealers came in. Just before the bonfire was lit, it was pointed out that the French were willing to pay thousands for the Nazi rejects. After that, a gallery at the museum's rear, separated by a curtain, became the scene of very brisk trading. A veritable bazaar, Detective Ryder! Thieves selling to thieves, the Germans to the French!"

"How much made it to Linz?" Clay had asked him.

Weinberger had closed his eyes, and Clay was sure it was against the magnitude of the plunder. "Nothing . . . not a single brick was ever laid for Hitler's museum."

That same day, Clay read the yellowed statements of Paul Bergère's theater associates. Their descriptions of the SS captain exactly matched the officer in the sworn deposition of Madame Delamarche, the Bergères' upstairs neighbor. She attested:

> *The boche officer told me if I let him in, I'd be helping my neighbors. Annette and the girls were on holiday in the country, and I worried something was wrong. He pushed in through the door and marched into my living room, looking all about. A rude young man, impatient, no manners. I asked him about the Bergères, but he ignored me. Then he noticed the two pictures on the mantel, the girls' crayon drawings that their father had framed up. One was a picture of me reading to a girl with long braids. That was Cécilie's. She'd written on it: "To Madame D., Love, Cécilie." Léonore's was a little girl handing me a bird. "Léonore will bring you a country chicken," it said.*
>
> *The officer took the chicken drawing off the mantel. "Charming," he said.*
>
> *I gave him a piece of my mind. "Not so charming, if you saw how skinny that poor child is! She and her sister, they only want me to tell them stories about food! Not about handsome princes or faraway places, but about the confiseries before the war! Over and over, they ask to hear how a girl could choose any sweet from the display case, any time her Papa gave her a few spare coins from his pocket!"*
>
> *Then he took the other drawing, too. He put them both under his arm. "I'm sure they'll eat better in the country," he said, and started to leave.*
>
> *I told him to give me back my drawings. I was shaking, my heart was beating so! He didn't even turn around. He said, "If you care about your neighbors, you'll say nothing about my visit. Or you'll never see them again."*

The statement was dated November '44, when Annette Bergère returned to Paris. In the spring of that year, Paul Bergère's name had appeared repeatedly on the *Gestapiste*'s list, for selling off what was supposedly a collection of sketches . . . most of them to the Rastenstein gallery.

Did Udo, contrary to Albrecht's impression, already believe Germany's defeat was inevitable? Was the hostility Albrecht had seen when he suggested that members of the Nazi high command were making a grab for art no more than a feint? Had Udo actually been inspired to follow their glorious example? Armed with his list from his trumped-up paintings-for-bullets Resistance scheme, and dressed in his impeccable black uniform, he'd managed to track down and murder Paul Bergère to steal the Trabucs.

Just as Oliver had mused back on the steps of the Met, there could be no telling how many more paintings Luscher had stolen . . . and how many more Paul Bergères he'd murdered to get them. When Clay walked outside, it was late afternoon, and raining lightly. The lights blinked on as he walked along the Seine, thinking about the strange and circuitous journey the Trabuc had made to Rachel Meredith. He smiled, remembering what Cello had called her: "the college professor chick." The smile vanished when he realized that was the first time he'd lied to his friend Martino. A half-lie, but a lie nevertheless, because he still hadn't let go of that closed case. It wasn't about the woman, but it was about Udo Luscher. Not *cherchez la femme,* but le fiend.

Eli, clever, calculating Eli, had never put any pressure on him, never tried to compromise him. But he'd read Clay like a book, and the man from the Mossad was no longer the only one who believed Udo Luscher was still alive.

CHAPTER
EIGHTEEN

Rachel Meredith hugged her cape around her shoulders, but Clay doubted velvet could provide much warmth against a November wind determined to rip the last leaves off the trees. High above their heads, it snapped the long museum banners announcing *The Empty Frame: Lost Masterpieces of World War II.*

The Merediths had invited him up for a drink before the limo arranged by the Met was scheduled to show up, but he'd declined, meeting them for the ride only. Even though his attendance at the museum opening was official, he had to be careful that every move he made with a possible connection to the closed case was dutifully reported to Hickey. The doorman rang the Meredith apartment when he arrived, and they'd come down immediately.

"Go on, one twirl of the cape for Detective Ryder," Wil Meredith had urged, and the lobby was briefly awash in black velvet, as it slowly billowed out, then swirled behind his wife, a languid, heavy wake. "Absolutely regal, isn't she? We saw it on a mannequin at Saks, and I told her she had to buy it for tonight."

"I'll never have another occasion to wear it," she'd sighed, embarrassed by the extravagance. "It's . . . I've never owned anything quite so theatrical."

"Remember what I told you, darling? 'V is for velvet and for Visa. Do it for your grandfather!' Tell me, Detective, couldn't she be the star in one of his set designs?"

Less than a half-hour later, Clay hung back a little as he followed the wind-whipped velvet up the tiered stone stairs to the museum's main entrance. Along with her long black silk dress and the carved ebony clips in her auburn hair, he had to agree: the cape was the perfect homage to Paul Bergère from his lone survivor.

A near-stumble in her skyscraper heels—apparently caused by the unaccustomed fabric fluttering around her ankles—made her grab for her husband's elbow. With a grandly chivalrous gesture, he hooked his arm through hers, look-ing like a man who was born in a tux and in the habit of attending a gala every night of the week.

Clay knew that he not only looked like a cop in a plain dark suit, but that there was no chance he'd ever again be mistaken for half of a happy couple.

"No reason to be so nervous, darling," Wil Meredith reassured her, "no one will notice us—they're all on the lookout for celebrities. You'll be able to view your painting in peace."

"I feel like Cinderella crashing the ball—an impostor in uncomfortable shoes."

After presenting their invitation at the door, the Merediths entered, Clay right on their heels. Before them, the monumental Great Hall, which he associated with quiet afternoons, was transformed. High-spirited people in evening clothes with glasses in their hands swirled into and out of loose clusters. A string quartet bowed away near the entrance to the gift shop.

"I never took an actual cloak to a cloakroom before," Meredith said with a smile. His wife opened the clasp at her neck, and he lifted the cape off her nearly bare shoulders. That same moment, the room fell still, and all eyes darted toward the entrance. Surreptitiously, Rachel Meredith lowered her gaze, perhaps to check if something had slipped out of her décolletage. Applause broke out, and, confident that the accolade could not be for one of her breasts, she glanced back at the door. No one was behind them. A young man appeared out of nowhere to relieve her husband of her cape, and Castelblanco was striding toward her, smil-ing exuberantly, arms extended wide. Her face flushed as she reflexively smiled back at him. "No one will notice us, right?" she whispered through her fixed grin, seconds before the director embraced her and flashbulbs popped.

Led by Castelblanco, the Merediths ascended the majestic staircase to the second floor galleries, shadowed by museum staff, the press, and hundreds of guests. Jonathan Haybrook, the museum's Van Gogh expert, greeted them at the top. Florene, smashing in a cocktail dress, pearls, and an earpiece, hovered dis-creetly.

Neither the Merediths nor Clay, whom the director had included in his en-tourage, had been prepared for the scope of *The Empty Frame*: not counting a small anteroom where a documentary played continuously, depicting events leading up to the art confiscations, the show filled four large galleries. To show-case their solidarity with the Met on the reappropriation of Holocaust art, sev-eral European museums had volunteered twenty-three masterpieces never before seen in the United States; they'd raced and beat the red tape clock to have them included. Although the majority of the show was devoted to the Impressionists and those who followed, masters of the caliber of Tiepolo, Raphael, Vermeer, Rembrandt, Goya, El Greco, Holbein, and Ingres were well represented. All were matched as closely as possible to prewar photographs of lost art. Some photos showed the legitimate owners with their paintings in their homes or galleries—intriguing enough to merit an exhibition of their own.

By the second gallery, a somewhat breathless Dr. Meredith said, "I never expected anything like this."

Castelblanco took her hand in both of his. "I thought I had some concept of how much had disappeared in those years, but when our curators came to me with their lists of stolen artworks, I was staggered. We estimate there's enough to fill a phantom museum the size of the Met. And the greatest pity is how many pieces are not on record, because no one survived to claim them."

The director hailed one of his aides and asked him to hold back the crowd, just for a moment. Shepherding the Merediths and Clay ahead, he resumed:

"You pore through the photographs of the lost art, and you come to a point when you say to yourself—correction: when *I*, not as the director of this great museum, but as a human being, say to myself—'But these are only paintings!' Yes . . . *'only paintings!'* Once, they were art, transcendent: they enhanced their owners' lives, spoke to them of the shared human experience . . . they demonstrated how close man can come to immortality. But now, compared to the lives that were cut short, what are they? No more than canvas and pigment, carried off by vandals.

"So add this crime to the Nazis' unspeakable acts: they turned these beautiful, passionate works of art into tombstones." He looked off into the distance. "Tombstones," he repeated flatly, then closed his eyes, as if to block the sight of infinite aisles of them, in cemeteries without end.

The aide reappeared at the doorway. The press and guests were surging behind him, and they had to move on.

The grand finale, at the far end of the last room, was the Trabuc, encased in Lucite atop a plinth. Clay recollected a similar mounting in the Metropolitan's permanent Van Gogh collection, designed for viewing a canvas the artist had frugally painted on both sides. A card on the base explained why the back of the Trabuc was exposed:

> Note the distinguishing mark "Léonore," the name of the younger Bergère daughter, later the mother of the only surviving heir. Madame Annette Bergère reported this mark to the French authorities after the war.

Just to the left of the exit door was another departure from the rest of the exhibit. Instead of a photo of missing art next to a similar work from the museum's collection, an empty frame, the show's namesake, was affixed to the wall.

Next to it was a photograph of the studio copy of Madame Trabuc, and a small, descriptive sign:

> Van Gogh's portrait of Madame Trabuc was also stolen from
> Paul and Annette Bergère. The distinguishing mark "Céci-
> lie," the name of their older daughter, was reported by
> Madame Bergère to be inscribed on the back.
> The portrait is still unrecovered.

Close by was a photograph of a theatrical troupe, enlarged many times over. The ebullient company was crowded onstage for what appeared to be a rousing opening-night curtain call. Beside it was a blowup of an individual who was off to the left in the ensemble shot: a thin, tired-looking man in a double-breasted suit, most likely in his forties, with a neat mustache and dark hair. The accompanying card read:

IN MEMORIAM: PAUL BERGÈRE

Transfixed, Rachel Meredith murmured, "My grandfather! I never saw him before . . . never knew what he looked like."

Her husband put an arm around her shoulders and hugged her to him.

"Detective Ryder deserves all the credit for that photograph," said Castelblanco. "A small miracle, which he somehow discovered and passed along to us."

Tears brimmed in her eyes as she silently turned to Clay.

"Please, could a copy be made for my wife?" Meredith asked.

"It would give me the greatest pleasure," Castelblanco replied.

Soon after they returned to the reception in the Great Hall, Dr. Meredith blanched and grabbed her husband's arm. "Oh, no! Not now! Not at a time like this!"

Charging toward them was a character with a huge head on a waifish body. The lack of proportion was emphasized by a ceaseless lateral tic, like a sideways bobblehead doll on speed. Although they'd never been introduced, Clay knew him well.

"Mr. Meredith, hello again!" was Gregor Grauberger Junior's enthusiastic greeting, followed by a perfunctory "and Mrs. Meredith."

Grauberger was one of those European males of a certain age (and Junior was up there, at least sixty) who spoke to a couple as if only the husband were present.

"Well, well! You said you wouldn't decide on anything until the exhibition opened, and here we are! Tonight's the night, Mr. Meredith!" He patted his breast pocket. "I have my checkbook right here!"

The glance that passed between the Merediths acknowledged that he shared her outrage. "It's my wife's painting," he said coolly, "and her decision entirely . . . as I've already told you and your father far too many times." Scanning the room over the dealer's head, he asked, "Where is your father? I don't see him."

"A severe heart attack . . . a few weeks ago." Briefly, Grauberger's head went off course and wobbled back to front, as if that were a more fitting direction for such grave issues. "The doctors agreed he should recuperate in Switzerland . . . in the mountain air."

Quite pointedly, Meredith said, "Perhaps it's time you both retired."

Clay himself had been finding it difficult to define where Gregor Senior left off and Gregor Junior began. Under Senior, a sleepy Zurich gallery dating back to the nineteenth century had rapidly expanded immediately after World War II. Even little Heidi could've figured out the reason behind the sudden success: no place in the world was more ideally suited for fleeing Nazis to cash in stolen art than Switzerland—so near, so clean, so clandestine. Not only did dealers in Zurich speak their language, but the proceeds of any sale could be conveniently deposited in a Swiss bank account . . . and tapped after their Vatican passports got the faux priests to carioca land.

Something, Clay suspected, must have transpired between Luscher and Grauberger Senior. His son had been too young to participate, but during the intervening decades he'd surely picked up all the dark details. Despite the sycophantic cheer he showered on Wil Meredith, it wasn't his ruthlessness that betrayed Junior so much as his anxiety. Ruthless people were rarely nervous—certainly not on a scale with the spastic-headed Swiss.

"Dr. Meredith," Clay interceded, "a friend of mine who's been hoping to meet you is right over—" Losing no time, he steered the Merediths to Oliver Plumworth, who'd been observing the entire Grauberger encounter over a flute of champagne.

"The second time tonight I'm indebted to you," she whispered.

"Pure self-interest," replied Clay. "I spent nearly seven years in the Navy, and I never felt seasick until I had to watch that head of his."

"Quite a tribute to your grandfather, Dr. Meredith," Oliver said, after the introductions were made. His gaze lingered on her, an elderly man beyond bothering to conceal that he was quite entranced.

"The best part for me was seeing his photograph at the end. I still haven't had a chance to thank Detective Ryder properly. God knows how he turns these things up."

Embarrassed, Clay mumbled, "I hope you don't mind that I didn't hand it over right away. With the opening so close . . . Anyway, I brought it to Castelblanco."

Oliver stared at Clay approvingly.

"Then putting it in the show . . . that was your idea?" Her hazel eyes sparkled.

"Nothing more than a suggestion," he hedged. "That's all."

Oliver, whose eyes had danced back and forth between them during their exchange, glanced back at Grauberger, who was pushing his way into an Old Money circle. "How curious, Dr. Meredith, that Galleries Grauberger is pursuing your Van Gogh. My impression has always been that they specialized in Old Masters." Looking down at his spotless lapel, he flicked away a speck of lint visible only to him.

"With all due respect to you, Mr. Plumworth," said her husband, "nothing about the art world seems to make much sense. All I know is that everyone who's part of it seems intent on driving my wife and me crazy—with or without an unlisted number!"

"Hi, Rachel. Hey, Wil." They were joined by a young man in a black leather jacket and black shirt, the only Asian male in the Great Hall with a bright yellow Mohawk. "Excuse me for butting in, but I have to leave, and I wanted to thank you for the invitation. The exhibit was fantastic. I've never been to a gala before."

"Neither have I," Rachel Meredith laughed, and introduced him as Phil Chang, her husband's photography assistant.

Phil looked down at his black basketball shoes. "I guess I should've rented . . . you know, like, prom clothes." When she took a step back in mock shock, he reconsidered. "Yeah, maybe not. Besides, how could I go back to Chinatown dressed like that? Everyone would think I gave up photography and became a waiter. My mother would be disgraced."

"Please! One look at the shots Phil took last week, when Wil was overbooked," she boasted to Oliver and Clay, "and you'd see exactly why this guy graduated at the top of his class at Rochester—also known as Kodak U! I keep telling Wil, 'Lock him up with the cameras, before someone steals him away!' "

Self-conscious, Phil fixed his eyes on his sneakers again.

"Speaking of stealing people away, may I steal you away for a few minutes, Dr. Meredith?" Castelblanco bestowed an apologetic smile on their small group. "So many people have been clamoring to meet her! I promise she'll be back in a few minutes."

She pecked the departing Phil on the cheek and let herself be whisked away, in the direction of the Egyptian collection. Clay mumbled to Oliver and her husband about his need for a pit stop. After a zigzag through the crowd, he slipped behind a massive column that provided both cover and a direct view of Rachel Meredith.

The faces around her were familiar from the *Times*—the men appeared frequently in the business section, and their sleek non-first wives were regulars on the Sunday society page. It was a safe bet that they were all major museum patrons with art on permanent loan. Also, it was unlikely that the members of their culture-as-tax-break clique had ever "clamored" to meet anyone.

One of the women was different from the rest—her face odometer hadn't been stretched back to thirty, nor was she buffed to a pearly opalescence. Since Clay had last seen the president of Esterbrook-Grennell, Deirdre Sands had transmogrified into a dead ringer for one of the seventeenth-century English kings. A James? A Charles? George Sanders? Her blonde hair hung from a soupçon of dark roots, framing her long face in horizontal waves like one of the mangier wigs of that period. Right up to the moment Castelblanco uttered Rachel Meredith's name, she was doing a fine job of feigning fascination for the man standing next to her.

He was none other than Randall Broyce, his face still untouched by grief—he looked just like the smiling front-page file photos of the past summer, which had appeared under *"Daring Park Ave. Penthouse Murder-Robbery"* headlines. After about two weeks with no arrests, Broyce had held his own press conference, lambasted the police, and offered his own reward for his wife's killer. The case was still unsolved. Clay was positive that if Broyce himself ever turned up dead, Lieutenant Malenkov would break into that squatted-down, leg-kicking dance Russian men do after limbering up with a few bottles of vodka.

As for Deirdre, during the ride uptown, Rachel Meredith had lamented that Sands was so persistent, she'd dubbed her 'Dread-dre': "That woman! Every time the phone rings, I think, Oh, no—anyone but her!"

"Ah! Face-to-face at last, Dr. Meredith!" Sands gushed. To the director, she enthused, "Armand! What a smashing exhibit!"

Clay studied Castelblanco. *If I were in his shoes, how pissed off would I be? There's more solicitation going on here than at the entrance to the Holland Tunnel.* The big auction houses and the museums frequently interacted in ways unrevealed to the public, but he and Sands were both in strong contention for the Trabuc. The director remained inscrutable, the gracious host of a grand affair.

A waiter passed with champagne, and Dr. Meredith snagged a glass, hiding her discomfort behind tiny sips. The moment another couple joined the group, she bolted.

Clay kept a few paces behind her as she wove her way back across the hall. Just as she reached her husband and Oliver, a man blocked her path. *"Madame le docteur* Preminger—I am Rasenstein." The French dealer was everything "suave" used to stand for, before a line of knockoff shampoos irreversibly debased the word. His elegance, however, was all but canceled out by overbearing smugness.

"Have you seen the exhibit upstairs yet, Mr. Rasenstein? The lost paintings?" Her acid tone made it clear that she'd read about Rasenstein's slander suit—his case against the writer who'd exposed the wartime trading between his family firm and the Nazis. "Tell me, how many paintings did your family lose during the war? Can you name one? Paintings saved your grandfather's life, but they cost my grandfather his."

Oliver's eyebrows shot up; Wil Meredith stared at his wife.

"I think you are confused about the way things were, Madame."

"That makes two of us. But not about the way they are now."

Rasenstein blinked, bowed, and beat a hasty retreat into the crowd.

"Bravo!" declared an awestruck Oliver Plumworth.

Her husband exhaled loudly. "Rachel, you were nothing short of magnificent!"

Trying not show his own reaction, Clay joined them with a "What's up?"

A bit breathless, but acting as if nothing had happened, she tilted her head toward the Egyptian wing. "You know who was over there? Deirdre Sands."

"Right. And when I passed by just now, didn't I see Randall Broyce, too?"

"Not only was he there," she winked, "but I'd say old Deirdre was . . ."

"Tell, tell, Dr. Meredith!" demanded Oliver, who often complained that a day without dirt was a day without sunshine.

"Well . . . am I crazy, or was she was putting the make on widower Broyce?"

Oliver cast a knowing look at Clay.

"What, Oliver?" He pretended to chafe with indignation. "You expect me to malign the woman's reputation? Agree she's capable of any act, no matter how low?"

"Let me interpret that for you, Clayton," Oliver volunteered. "Yes, yes, and yes!"

A few minutes later, a magazine editor who couldn't stop praising Meredith's tabletop shots pulled him away to introduce him to editor-friends at another publication. Claiming he'd just spotted a collector he had to see, Oliver kissed Dr. Meredith's hand and, smiling benignly at Clay, took his leave.

"Now that we're finally alone," she asked conspiratorially, ignoring the crowd milling around them, "please tell me—how did you discover that picture? And where?"

"I had miles expiring. Vacation days. Paris seemed as good a place as any." His attempt at casual sounded closer to caustic.

Nevertheless, a smile lit up her face. "So you say. But I think you went for a reason. I think you went for my grandfather." Temporarily safe from the Grauberger-Rasenstein-Sands brigade, she was beginning to glow with her moment. She didn't need the upswept hair or the makeup or the slinky dress to be absolutely luminous.

He was totally unprepared for whatever suddenly stirred in him. The good news was that he wasn't as dead as he thought he was. But no smile would have been bestowed if she hadn't misread his true purpose. The absurdly diligent detective facing her had gone to Paris not to track down her grandfather, but his murderer.

A guest with a paunch wide as an open umbrella used that moment to snake his way around her. Knocked off balance, she keeled forward, coming at Clay so fast that he had to make a quick grab for her wrists. She was laughing, the fat man was red-faced, and Clay had to pretend that he really wanted to set her back straight on her high heels. Her put-down of Rasenstein had reminded him of how strong Lauren had been, but there was a disconcerting vulnerability about Rachel Meredith that had made him want to hold her for an inappropriately long time.

This incredibly desirable woman, he warned himself, was nothing less than a human minefield: A Person Involved in a Case, A Person Involved in a *Closed* Case, A Married (Happily) Person, A Person Who Is Not Lauren.

With the man still apologizing as he moved off, Clay stammered, "Anyway, the Paris trip . . . I guess it just turned into a busman's holiday."

"Sure. I go to the movies for fun. Same concept." Her smile didn't fade.

Stick to the facts—you've got plenty of them. "Your grandfather's career was relatively well documented—that made it easy. Twenty-plus years, over a hundred productions—pretty impressive. Most of the credits were for set design, some for costumes and lighting as well—a triple-threat guy. The name that came up most frequently along with his was one Henri Chaumont, a director. He told me that they worked together whenever their schedules allowed."

"He *told* you—he can't still be alive?"

"God, I don't know how." His meeting with Chaumont, even if it hadn't yielded a speck of helpful information, would have made his trip worthwhile. In fact, just thinking about him eased Clay's apprehension. "Not only is the man a chain smoker, but I nursed a glass of wine the afternoon I was with him, and he knocked off the rest of the bottle. You've heard how the French eat tons of cheese and pâté, and claim red wine cancels them out? Well, with old Henri, I guess the big reds work on nicotine as well as cholesterol. Anyhow, he and his wife, Charlotte—she's about twenty years younger, and he calls her his ingénue—searched through all their photos, but the only one where your grandfather was recognizable is the one upstairs, in the exhibit. No big surprise— actors do tend to hog the limelight. At any rate, Chaumont said painting was why your grandfather came to Paris."

"*Came* to Paris? But I thought . . . wasn't he wasn't born there?"

"He was quite successful at convincing other Parisians that he was."

"Dr. Meredith, excuse me once again." It was Castelblanco, back for an encore. "With all this opening-night hoopla, it never occurred to me that you might want some time alone with your grandfather's painting." He checked his watch. "Our sweep of the upstairs rooms is nearly done. I invite you to consider the exhibit your private domain."

"Thank you, Mr. Castelblanco . . . I'd like that very much."

"An aide will accompany you upstairs and wait at the exit. Take as long as—"

"How about an NYPD guide?" Clay volunteered. "One familiar with the layout?"

"Ah, better yet!" exclaimed Castelblanco. "No finer escort than the man who's contributed so much to our exhibition!" With a jaunty turn on his heel, he returned to working the deep pockets, a silver-tongued beggar with a golden cup.

CHAPTER
NINETEEN

Except for security, the Met's second floor was deserted. Rachel Meredith walked through the exhibit quickly, making straight for her grandfather's photo. She lingered over the sad map of his face—the deep lines radiating out from the corners of his eyes, the hollows in his cheeks, the groove concentration and worry had furrowed between his eyebrows. Several times, she looked from him to Trabuc, from Trabuc to the empty frame.

"Look at them—my grandfather and Trabuc. Two men who saw far too much insanity in their lifetimes . . . one inside an asylum, the other in an entire world gone mad."

"You're shivering," Clay said softly. "Your dress—it's cooler in here than before, with all the people. Want to borrow my jacket?"

"No, I'm not cold," she said, and pointed to the frame. "It's that. Don't think I'm crazy, but I don't think it's empty at all. He's in there."

"Who?"

"That Nazi son of a bitch. He's in there, hiding."

Clay looked at the two gaunt faces, and then at the empty frame. He could almost catch the glint of the diamond-studded Knight's Cross nestled at the throat of the black uniform. She was right. Luscher was in there, a monster who could cast a shadow anywhere, even in the dark.

As if she'd seen it too, her hand flew to her throat. "No! I want to concentrate on my grandfather! Please, tell me more about that director . . . Chau—?"

"Chaumont. Henri Chaumont."

The scent of newly fallen leaves permeated Clay's memory of the afternoon spent in the stylish neighborhood near the Bois de Boulogne. He could hear the creak of Chaumont's wheelchair as his wife pushed it around the walled garden, keeping him in the sun. The weather had been so mild, he'd been in shirtsleeves, but the frail Henri wore two heavy sweaters with a hand-knit throw over his legs.

"Chaumont said he was the best he ever worked with. And a great friend."

"Did you find out when he and my grandfather met?"

"They teamed up together for the first time in 1924. The thing was, it took your grandfather years to trust Chaumont enough to mention anything about his past. Even then, he'd only drop a word here, a hint there—he was extremely secretive. Bit by bit, Henri found out why. His friend was born Paul Berger in Stuttgart, Germany."

She looked at him in surprise, and Clay was sure he'd had the same expression on his face when he learned about Bergère's real name and origin. "He came to Paris in 1922, with enough money to live on for a week. Barely twenty, and raring to become the next Degas. The closest he came to painting for a living was a backstage job, slapping paint on scenery. The theater must've hooked him hard, because he read every book he could on stage design, sneaked into plays, and eventually put a portfolio together. All his first job as a set designer paid was two weeks of free lunch. It was an experimental, one act deal. The critics tore the play to shreds, but they praised the set designer, Paul Bergère. The playbill misspelled his name."

"Berger to Bergère—that easy?" asked Rachel.

"He told Chaumont he read it out loud over and over again. 'Bergère' had a good Gallic ring to it. By then, he'd spent two years in Paris. The bad feeling for Germans hadn't faded much in the six years since the war ended. Also, it was no secret that a number of French producers excluded Jews from their companies. Being a German *and* a Jew . . . that wasn't exactly a fast track to success. Your grandfather spread out his papers, dipped his pen in some ink, and added an *e* to the end of his name and an *accent grave* in the middle . . . he was an artist, after all. His French was good, and it became perfect—the man lived surrounded by actors. His next play didn't pay much, but it was in francs, not lunch—and he was on his way."

The gallery's sole bench was positioned to view Monsieur Trabuc. Rachel Meredith sat down and gestured for Clay to join her. "And his citizenship?"

"I guess at some point he managed to find a forger. Hey, nobody's perfect, not even grandfathers." He paused, grateful her eyes were fixed on Trabuc. "Anyway, it's unlikely that he would've ever been questioned, considering the reputation he eventually acquired—a knack for being able to find absolutely anything in Paris. Every time he had a new script, he'd wander around the city for inspiration. Museums, antique shops, the flea markets—he knew them like the back of his hand.

"According to Chaumont, your grandfather thought the rue de la Boétie was the most irresistible street in Paris. It was lined with art galleries where he could see paintings by his favorite artists—all far beyond his means, of course. Their drawings cost only a fraction as much, but they were way out of reach for someone still getting established. One day, he fell in love with a Van Gogh sketch of an orchard. On a whim, he asked the gallery owner if he could buy it on time payments. The dealer considered, then agreed. As soon as it was paid off, he put down a deposit on a Lautrec pen and ink. He was working seven days a week, juggling a couple of projects at once, and his sole extravagance was collecting quality drawings. Before long, he had an installment plan going at one gallery or another at all times. And that brings us to the Trabucs."

Rachel's eyebrows shot up. "Don't tell me he bought those on time!"

"Hardly. Actually, Chaumont was indirectly responsible for the Trabucs. His next play was a Chekhov adaptation, and he wanted to set it in Provence, where he'd spent summers as a boy. It was late April, and Bergère was overworked and exhausted, unable to shake a cough that had dogged him all winter. Henri insisted he hop a train south, and soak up some sun along with the atmosphere. He worked it out so the producers would pay for the trip if his friend sent back a few props by truck.

"The only way to get around was on a bicycle. Your grandfather rented one from the local blacksmith. Each day, he pedaled in another direction: Nîmes, Avignon, Saintes-Maries-de-la-Mer. His cough disappeared. He could have sent back a fleet of trucks with all the antiques the locals thought of as junk. When he asked if he could sketch their homes, no one refused, and he filled two sketchbooks. Chaumont thought they were great—enough to set five plays in Provence."

"Those sketchbooks . . . did Chaumont have those?" Rachel asked.

"Unfortunately, they disappeared when . . . Anyway, he wires Henri, tells him how much he loves Provence, how good he feels, et cetera. He'll return in five days.

"The next night he's back in Paris. Tracks down Chaumont working late in the theater. Instead of looking relaxed, he's all jumpy. Henri wants to take him out for a drink, but your grandfather insists they stay in the empty theater. 'Something's happened,' he says, 'and I'm worried sick. I don't know if I did the right thing. Maybe I'm in trouble. I need to talk to you . . . but you have to promise to keep it strictly confidential.'

"All Henri could say was, 'We've worked together for eight years! If we can't trust one another, we can't trust anyone. What the hell happened down there?"

Back in the Parisian garden, the old director, quite the *jambon* himself, had acted out what he finally pried out of his friend Bergère. Clay tried to tone down Chaumont's overwrought version, rife with every broad gesture possible from a wheelchair:

Paul was making a sketch in a rundown farmhouse. It belonged to an old fellow, all alone, badly crippled by arthritis.

Chaumont had crumpled up his hands—a very old man playing someone even more ancient.

He looked over Paul's shoulder at his drawing. As usual, he was putting it all down: dirty dishes, cobwebs, broken chair, the whole sorry clutter. He's shocked: "Mon Dieu, is that how it looks? So shabby?"

Paul started to close his sketchbook. He was afraid he'd unintentionally insulted the old farmer. But no, he urged him to carry on: "It's a good thing my wife isn't alive to see it . . . this was her family's home." Eventually, he asked Paul, "You paint colors, too?"

Paul tells the truth, that he used to, but wasn't all that good.

"Too ugly?" Before Paul can think up how to answer a question like that, the old man says, "I bet they're not as bad as some. Come, I'll show you."

He walked Paul over to a half-door, like a cupboard, set in a wall . . . pretty common in the South. The kitchen was so cluttered, Paul hadn't noticed the knob. "Go on, open it," he says. But the wood was swollen in the frame. Whatever was inside that door hadn't seen the light of day for years.

Struggling with Herculean effort, Henri opened it after repeated tries.

At last, Paul's hit by a rush of cold air and a smell like a wine cellar. Inside, he sees stacks of empty canning jars. The old man points inside, to the right of the door.

The director pointed, a sailor sighting land after a year lost at sea.

Paul reaches in, feels something stiff and light . . . two canvases, roughly the same size. They'd been facing the wall, so he saw the backs first. The old man warns him how ugly they are.

As soon as he turned the first one around, Paul knew instantly! No one could have painted it but Van Gogh! He faked coughing from the dust inside the cupboard, to hide his reaction. Then he shifted the rear canvas to the front—another Van Gogh! Two masterpieces! A portrait of a man and of a woman, locked away God knows how long! Paul kept coughing to compose himself. "Ugly? Thank God there are only two! They keep getting worse! Should I put them back with the jars? Out of sight?"

The farmer gives that some thought, then says no, he might as well use them to start the fire in the cookstove.

Paul tells him no, that's like committing suicide! He makes up some story about how the oils they used back then give off poison fumes. At the very least, he warns, they will permanently damage the lungs. He advises the old man to bury them, instead. Of course, the farmer was so feeble, he couldn't dig a hole to bury a mouse. Then Paul tapped the woman's portrait with his finger. "This canvas still has a little life left to it. Actually, a wash of white paint, and it could be reused, painted right over. Hopefully, with a prettier picture. Naturally, only the poorest artist would buy a used canvas. Three francs for the two."

The old man countered with five, and they settled on four. Paul paid him from

the coins in his pocket, and put the canvases under his arm, trying to act nonchalant.
"By the way," he asks the farmer, "whose faces will I be covering with white paint?"

"Some relatives of my wife's aunt. Don't ask me their names. There's no one
left to remember. The man, I think he worked in hospitals. Maybe the crazy house,
too."

"Crazy house?" Paul asks.

"Twenty kilometers or so from here," the old man says. "At Saint-Rémy."

Rachel Meredith sat perfectly still. After a while, a tentative smile crept onto her face. "He didn't know if he'd done the right thing?"

"Yes. He made Chaumont swear never to tell anyone about the paintings. He couldn't bring himself to return the pictures, but he felt guilty about cheating the farmer. Felt he hadn't acted in good faith and purposely deceived a poor old man. What if anyone found out? Would the portraits be impounded? Would he be arrested? Was he nothing better than a confidence man, a common crook?

"They went back and forth for hours, mostly Chaumont trying to convince him that if he hadn't gone to Provence, the canvases would still be collecting cobwebs in the cupboard. Not only that, if he hadn't taken them, they would've been destroyed one way or another, because who in the area had any idea of their value? Chaumont kept reminding him how the farmer wanted to burn them, and how ugly he thought they were—it wasn't as if Bergère had walked in and talked two cherished family heirlooms off the wall. Quite the contrary—he'd saved them, preserved something precious. Nevertheless, the whole incident obsessed your grandfather. The only thing that helped him out of his ethical morass was meeting your grandmother later that same year, 1932."

"And twelve years later, the irony of ironies," she said softly.

"You mean that they were stolen from him?"

Silently, she inclined her head in agreement.

"In the interim, he lived with his misgivings, as well as the Van Goghs."

She looked up. "That one photo my grandmother had—if he felt that way, why did he keep them out in the open?"

"How many people would have gone into their bedroom? And of that handful, who wouldn't have assumed that they were reproductions? Or even guessed who the artist was in the first place?"

"True. And the farmer? Any more about him?"

"He died within two years—sadly, when his farmhouse burned down. Chaumont inquired during a trip south . . . he thought knowing might put his friend's mind at ease."

"So he actually saved the paintings! Did that change things for my grandfather?"

"Henri didn't think so. But during the Occupation, your grandfather shifted his worrying to his wife and daughters." He paused, readying to tread carefully. "From what I've learned, if he was an observant Jew, he wasn't openly so. If he were alive today, he'd probably call himself a 'secular' Jew."

"I'm pretty much the same. My father . . ."

"I know. Ravensbruck."

"That can change one's view of the world. Of religion."

Clay nodded. "Your grandmother came from a traditional background. Your grandfather had her papers altered long before the Germans invaded. But he became increasingly nervous about people in Paris who might remember seeing her walk into a synagogue or a kosher butcher's. Those were desperate times for Jews. They were barred from any work in communications—newspapers, magazines, radio, movies . . . and, of course, theater. Chaumont knew he was a Jew, and kept him working right through."

"What if anyone had found out?"

"His repertory company would've been shut down . . . at the very least."

"Then he was a true and great friend."

"Dr. Meredith, you have no idea. Under the Nazis, instant deportation was the penalty for any Jew who didn't wear the gold star. And collaborators could collect one hundred francs a head for informing."

"Who'd stoop so low? One hundred francs for a death penalty!"

"People were starving. The rationing was very harsh, and there were terrible shortages. So yes, the Germans paid out plenty of hundred-franc notes. At first, arrests were limited to foreign-born Jews, and for a while, French Jews thought they were safe. Then they, too, started to get the knock on the door in the middle of the night. Your grandfather lived in constant fear that his wife and daughters would be picked up. According to Henri, he was pushed over the brink the day a World War I veteran from his neighborhood—an old man who wore his Croix de Guerre from the Argonne above his yellow star—was arrested right in front of him on the street, in broad daylight. Anyone could be stopped at any time, for any reason. Jews were herded into a big bicycle-racing stadium, the Velodrome. Horrible, filthy conditions. No food, no water, no sanitation. From there, they were shipped east to the camps.

"The more the war turned against the Germans, the more they stepped up Jewish deportations. This was early spring, '44. Your grandfather saw smuggling Annette and the girls out of France as the only way to protect them. The one border the Germans didn't have totally sealed off—thanks only to the Pyrénées—was the frontier with Spain. Annette wanted to stay with Paul in Paris. She didn't see the sense of taking such a risk, especially when there were so many rumors about an Allied invasion."

"He didn't think he himself was in any danger, staying in Paris?" Dr. Meredith asked.

"No. He had no way of foreseeing that the way he planned to save his family would put him on an express track to Udo Luscher."

"How?" she gasped. He was sure she felt the pull of the empty frame, that she was struggling not to look its way again.

"He financed the three passages out of France by selling his collection of drawings. Getting people out of Paris cost a fortune. New, totally different identity papers were necessary. The trip was broken into several stages across France and over the Pyrénées, which required being passed from guide to guide, so that they were constantly in the hands of strangers. By the way, Chaumont thought Annette was right, that his friend was insane, paranoid. But Paul went ahead—sold the drawings, made the arrangements without telling Annette. Chaumont never saw him act so impulsively, or so unilaterally."

"Giving up his drawings . . . that had to be a major sacrifice."

"No," Clay's voice dropped to a whisper, "an act of love."

For a long time, Rachel Meredith's eyes seemed to lock with her grandfather's in the photo on the gallery wall. "And understanding what he'd done out of love, no matter how opposed she was, what could my grandmother do? I mean, there was no way for my grandfather to reverse what he'd set in motion, was there? She had to go with the girls." She paused. "But I still don't see the Luscher connection."

Clay explained the Resistance deception.

"So while innocent people were being dragged into Gestapo headquarters, Luscher could help himself to whatever they had left at home?"

"That's how he set it up. Unfortunately for your grandfather, the idea occurred to Luscher shortly after he sold off his drawings. Not wanting to flood the market, he'd sold some here, some there, over a period of several weeks. His name turned up more than once on Luscher's lists of names. That probably made him appear to be a major collector."

"My God!" she cried out, "you're saying that if he hadn't sold the drawings, Luscher never would have known Paul Bergère even existed?"

"I'm afraid that's where I'm at," Clay agreed.

"And the chances of his wife and daughters being arrested in Paris?"

"That's impossible to know."

"But what he did to save them was . . . instrumental in his own death?"

"Once Luscher got hold of the Van Goghs," Clay answered, "I'm convinced there was no way he would have let him live."

"Oh, God! What kind of inheritance is this, if every time I look at Trabuc, all I see is Luscher?" Sobbing, she lowered her head into her hands.

"I'm sorry," Clay said repeatedly, keenly aware that he was the last person in the world to console anyone. Meanwhile, her trembling loosened the antique clip holding the hair over her left temple. He grabbed it just before it fell to the floor, and ran one finger back and forth over its deeply carved roses until she began to compose herself. "You know," he finally said, "cops are probably the only people these days who still carry real cotton handkerchiefs. Here."

She blinked up at him as if she'd completely forgotten he was there. After a nearly inaudible "Thank you," she blew her nose and wiped under her eyes. One hand reached up to push the hair back from her face, and he held out the clip.

"You won't be able to line it up right without a mirror." Reaching out, Clay lifted back her heavy auburn hair and refastened it. He looked from her left to her right temple and back, then gave a nod of approval. "Okay. Perfectly balanced."

Her hands went to both clips, feeling the exact alignment. "Either you have a lot of sisters, or you're married. And now I feel completely egocentric for never having even thought to ask."

"No, no. It's not the kind of thing that comes up. It shouldn't come up on a case. It's essential to maintain objectivity."

"Are you?" she persisted.

"Married? I lost my wife about a year and a half ago."

She started to say something, but it turned into a sigh.

"Dr. Meredith, I was nearly finished. It's how Chaumont's wife, Charlotte, expanded on what happened."

"Please, of course. Were they both in the Resistance? The Chaumonts?"

"Neither was. The only thing they knew about Luscher was that he was the officer who arrested Paul Bergère. It was July, more than a month after D-Day. Chaumont and the stage manager were in the third row of the theater, where they always sat during rehearsals. It was afternoon, and the only light came from an open skylight . . . the Nazis had the electric power rationed, down to barely an hour a night. Actual performances used candles as footlights.

"Charlotte was onstage, rehearsing her big scene in a new play. During a break, she saw a red spot a few rows behind Chaumont. A cigarette."

Clay did his best to relate Charlotte's account:

I pointed out that we had a visitor . . . in a black uniform. He stood up and walked forward, asking for the set designer, Paul Bergère. An officer, young and tall, over six feet, military bearing. As he came into the light from the skylight, I could see that he was handsome. Exceptionally so. But after four years of Occupation, any SS officer made my blood run cold. At the time, my relationship with Henri was strictly professional, so I knew nothing about Paul Bergère's secrets, but my God, I was scared for him.

Henri lied, said the designer was out buying props. Less than a minute later, Bergère was marched onstage at gunpoint by a Milicent—a Frenchman in the German-run militia. Two other Milicents came on from the opposite wing. The SS officer had been playing cat-and-mouse with us. He had a search going on backstage all along.

The officer ordered the soldier holding the gun on Paul to put the prisoner in his car. The other two Milicents were to detain everyone in the theater, get written proof that the play had Propagandastaffel *approval, and check everyone's papers—the actors, the stagehands, and especially the director. I'll never forget the last thing the officer said: "If you find a single Jew among them, close the whole mess down." That was the last time any of us saw Paul Bergère alive.*

"Then Luscher had no idea he was Jewish?" Rachel Meredith whispered.

"Most Jewish-owned art was confiscated in '41, and your grandfather managed to hold on to his collection. Not only that, but if he'd been known as a Jew, there was no way he would have been able to sell it, as he did in '44. I'm convinced his effort to appear Gentile was completely successful. Further proof is that it's impossible for me to believe that Udo Luscher, with his blind dedication to the Third Reich, would have stolen Jewish property. No way."

"I don't get it. A member of the SS? The Gestapo?"

"Oh, he would have *confiscated* Jewish property. Turned it over to the authorities. But in his demented moral code, *stealing* art from a Jew? No, that would be like stealing from Hitler himself. Hence his Resistance charade."

"Stealing from a Jew you don't know to be a Jew . . ." She shook her head, trying to make sense of Udo Luscher's twisted justification.

"What happened to your grandfather underscores how vulnerable everyone was. One more ironic twist, isn't it?" With a sigh, Clay continued, "Two days after the arrest in the theater, Luscher forced his way into the neighbor's apartment. He confiscated two drawings your mother and your aunt gave her before they left for Spain—your grandfather had them framed with the Van Goghs hidden behind them. The old neighbor lady never knew.

"Henri tried to trace his friend, but if someone was arrested by an SS officer . . . When Annette returned from Spain, he was the one she went to, trying to find Paul. He had to give her the bad news. They lost touch after she came to America.

"As I was leaving, Henri said, 'My friend was gone forever, and his precious paintings, too. But I never broke my promise of silence, not once during all these years, not until this afternoon. And I now speak freely and easily, because I have no doubt that if Paul were alive, he'd want his granddaughter to know. Oh, he'd still be worrying, stuck in his needless moral dilemma, but how pleased he would have been, to learn she has one of his secret Van Goghs.' "

"Not so secret anymore," she murmured. Clay rose and waited for her by the exit to the adjoining gallery. When she joined him, they both looked straight ahead, as if the walls lined with masterpieces were bare. They proceeded at a steady pace, gliding from one grand gallery to another, from one epoch to another, immune to the pull and the roll of the centuries on canvas.

"I don't know how to say this without sounding ungrateful," she said at last. "Your kindness, your concern for this case . . . it only reminds me that I haven't done a thing to deserve all this . . . attention. Tonight, when we walked in . . . all those people applauding—why? I didn't survive the Holocaust. I never stood up to the Nazis. I didn't even track down the picture. Thanks to you, it found me."

He tried to interrupt, but she didn't give him a chance.

"As far as we know, my grandfather's bravest act was to do all he could to keep those two paintings for his family. I'm sure it was all wrapped up with protecting his daughters' legacy . . . being a loving father. But in the greater context of the war . . . I know you understand what I mean. I'm sure he was a good man, a wonderful man, but he was no hero, and I'm certainly no heroine."

"But you're a symbol, Dr. Meredith! You represent the hope that more paintings will be returned someday. That's what the applause was for. Tonight wasn't about heroics. It's reaffirmation that the bad guys lost."

She smiled at him, and Clay smiled back, not at all sure that what he'd said about the bad guys was true.

CHAPTER
TWENTY

While he fumbled with his keys in the hall, Clay's pager beeped. It was past midnight, he was beat, and it could only be trouble. For weeks, a hijacking ring had been hitting the Garment District, and Hickey had loaned him to the team assigned to it.

As he walked to the kitchen phone to dial the number, his shoes squished and his coat dripped from the first real snow of the winter. Christmas might be little more than a week away, but on Seventh Avenue, it was high season for resort wear. The ring's latest heist had been a truck jammed with $200 bikinis—far beyond the $100,000 threshold for Major Case involvement. Thong jokes were all over the office.

The unfamiliar number on the pager turned out to be Wil Meredith's cell phone. About a month had passed since Clay had last seen him—and his wife—at the Met opening. When he answered, his voice, tight and shrill with desperation, was barely recognizable: "I'm in a cab, on my way to St. Vincent's. It's Rachel . . . she was attacked!"

"Jesus! What happened?"

"I'm not sure. She called the studio just before ten-thirty, working late. Then the police called . . . someone . . . right there, in a university building!"

"Busy night," Clay said, as he put his shield between the emergency room computer and the face of the woman ignoring him. She lost her place, and the pounding on the keyboard halted abruptly. Behind her, cutout letters encrusted with red and green glitter dangled from a string, spelling out "Happy Holidays!" to everyone in medical crisis. "I'm looking for Dr. Meredith. She's a patient, not a physician, and she arrived by ambulance."

Annoyed, the woman pointed to a door. "In there. Ask at the nurses' station."

Once inside, Clay didn't have to ask; Meredith's agitation rose over a curtained partition with a female police officer stationed before it. "Why haven't you sent her for X rays yet? What if my wife has a concussion, for Christ's sake?"

A barely-there Rachel Meredith murmured, "Wil, he knows what he's doing."

After flashing his shield, Clay announced his name to the curtain.

It parted just a slit, and Wil Meredith gestured him in. His wife was lying on a gurney, while a young, unruffled Indian doctor checked her pulse. "Look at her, Detective Ryder!" The doctor, chubby enough to evoke a junior Buddha, remained serene in the face of Meredith's shrill belligerence.

An IV was attached to the back of Rachel Meredith's right hand. One cheek was discolored and swollen; the other cheek and her throat were scored with a hatchwork of scratches. Blood was smeared at one corner of her mouth and across her chin.

Clay tried to close the curtain behind him, but someone else was pulling it open, a man in a white coat with a small lab kit. He set to work taking blood samples, concentrating on the blood around her mouth. When he was finished, swabbing her with alcohol, she proudly told the technician, "I bit him. I bit the bastard on the hand."

"Good for you, Missus!" he replied softly. All his equipment was neat, prelabeled. He looked up at the doctor. "Has someone already taken the . . . other samples?"

The doctor shook his head. "Not needed." Clay knew the lab man meant the hospital's rape unit.

"That's good." He gathered up his samples and equipment. "Feel better, Mrs. . . ." after consulting one of the labels, he added, "Meredith."

She gave him a big, brave smile, but winced when it spread across her battered cheek. Turning to Clay, she asked, "What was Wil thinking, asking you to race down here so late? That you're our own private police force?"

"Maybe he thought it'd make you feel better—and that's all that matters. Tell me, did you see—"

"I only saw his hand, and the cuff of his jacket. Black leather," she blurted out. "The black or white question they keep asking? The hair on his hand stood out against his skin. That's it—except that he was very big . . . and very strong."

"You never lost consciousness?"

"No. I kept thinking, 'This isn't happening to me!' and I ran like hell."

Again, the curtain parted. Two attendants from X-ray positioned themselves at each end of the gurney. "Your statement, Dr. Meredith," he asked, "did you finish?"

"The police and the ambulance showed up the same time. I guess I wasn't totally coherent. The policewoman who rode in the ambulance with me started to—"

Impatient, the attendants began to wheel her out of the enclosure.

"She's right here. Give her the rest of your statement," he said, moving alongside her. "I'll check the reports and give you a call first thing tomorrow." Like a relay race, the officer slipped into his place beside the accelerating gurney.

Before eight the next morning, Clay had read all the paperwork. The attack took place at 721 Broadway, the Tisch School of the Arts, on the ninth floor, between 2230 and 2245. It was determined that the perp escaped via a fire door which opened onto Mercer Street. His jacket was thrown over his head before he came in range of the door's surveillance camera. No one had been seen fleeing the building. In fact, no one was even aware of the assault until Dr. Meredith ran into the main lobby, bloodied, bruised, screaming, her blouse and bra ripped open. The police investigation continued past the building's 2300 closing time. The hospital discharged her shortly after 0300.

After several calls to the Meredith apartment yielded nothing but busy signals, Clay tried the photography studio, not really expecting an answer.

"Meredith studio," a voice answered after the second ring, "Phil speaking—Wil?"

"No, it's Clay Ryder, NYPD. We met at the Trabuc opening last month."

"The detective, sure. You're calling about Rachel?"

"I took a chance—I can't get through to the apartment. You're in early."

"Actually, I've been here all night—but that's a long story. Anyway, Rachel checked out okay. Wil said she's exhausted. I guess he unplugged the phone."

"And Mr. Meredith is . . . where?"

"NYU. He went to read them the riot act about their security. He was going to wait by some dean's door, then ambush him when he comes to work."

"And you're expecting him after that?"

"I can't leave until he gets back."

"Mr. Chang, if he gets there first, please tell him to stay put—I'm on my way."

Stopping at Bloomie's desk, Clay learned that Hickey wasn't expected back from City Hall until lunchtime. He left word that he would also be out until noon, at a new downtown satellite museum. No one had to know that it didn't open its doors until 10:30. Let the old man think that he was still up to his neck with Art Guy stuff, even as he worked his butt off on hijacked thongs.

Meredith Photography was on West Twentieth Street near Fifth, the only nonresidential floor in an old commercial building converted into floor-through lofts. The lobby was small and grimy, its cobalt blue paint peeling in big, scaly patches. A form inside the elevator certified that its last inspection took place in January 1988. With a lurch, it stopped at the fourth floor. Chang was on the other side of the folding steel gate, holding an oversize padlock. Two more dangled from hooks on a nearby pegboard, and an alarm light blinked green next to the elevator. As the gate ratcheted open, Clay got a better look. The studio had to be three thousand square feet, at least.

The young man's hair, now neon orange cut in a short brush, reminded Clay of the sweeper part of the ice scraper–snow sweeper he kept in his car. "Wil just called," he reported. "He's in a cab headed uptown."

"You look beat, Mr. Chang. How come you can't leave?"

"We were just finishing up a really long shoot when Wil got the call about Rachel. He split before he could lock the cameras in the safe." Phil shrugged off Clay's inquiring look. "It's not a matter of trust about the combination—it's some insurance thing because the equipment's so expensive. The last assistant got fired because he left the cameras out overnight without waiting for Wil to lock them up. Want some coffee?"

"Thanks. Milk, no sugar. Okay if I look around?"

"Sure. Just watch your step—in between naps, I got a head start on the next shoot. There's stuff all over the floor."

The entire area to the left of the elevator, about thirty by fifty, was open space. Cartons spewing Styrofoam peanuts and stacks of dishes and pots and kitchen gadgets were on the wide-planked floor, grouped around a large makeshift table—unfinished wood boards on sawhorses. A roll of black paper, suspended from a ceiling rig, was unfurled enough to form a backdrop and cover a wide section of the table. On the paper, a perfect potato pyramid rose, with a single potato and a heavy-duty stainless steel peeler before it. Mounted on a tripod, a camera was positioned directly in front of the composition, light stands clustered right and left. White tape marked their exact positions on the floor. Strolling past several wheeled, multidrawered utility cabinets, Clay glanced up at more giant rolls of colored paper suspended from a ceiling that had to be twenty feet high.

"That's all no-seam paper, for backgrounds," Chang called from the kitchen area. "Those"—he pointed to the thicket of spindly metal stands in the corner—"are umbrella rigs, reflectors, strobes . . . you know, lighting stuff."

"Hell of a lot to photograph a potato peeler."

A small conference table stood in front of the three big gated windows overlooking the street. Although compact, the kitchen contained two of everything: sinks, refrigerators, ovens, and butcher block workstations. "For food shots," Phil explained with a sleepy grin, as he filled two mugs. "Lots of leftovers."

Sipping his coffee, Clay slowly walked toward the other half of the floor. In contrast, it was partitioned off into a number of small rooms: an office with a large safe (cameras and lenses, precisely arranged, waited on the banged-up desk), a darkroom, a bathroom, a dressing room, and a room barely wider than its single bed. Returning to the photography area, he asked, "Who lives back there?"

"Nobody now. I think Wil did, before he got married."

Clay turned in place, a sweep around the studio. It was difficult not to be impressed by how much Meredith had accomplished professionally. *Okay, maybe more envious than impressed. And maybe envious of more than the studio.* He studied a large corkboard covered with dozens of Polaroids. Every one was a shot of a woman's wrist adorned with watches. In several, the watches extended past her elbow. "Are these test shots of what you did last night?"

"Yeah, the shoot from hell. Don't take this the wrong way, but if that call about Rachel hadn't come in, we might still be shooting."

"How many variations? Forty? Fifty?"

"Wil wanted to try it with three watches, five watches, watches up to the elbow, the shoulder, the pink watch on top, the green watch in the middle," Chang explained. "The clients had no complaints—they were getting their money's worth, plus all the takeout sushi they could eat. I had to beg Wil to yell 'Wrap!' before he flew out the door."

The elevator opened. Meredith walked in, dark circles under his blue eyes.

"Fresh from a heart-to-heart with the university folks?" asked Clay.

"A half-hour of canned excuses about Fortress Tisch. More security than any other NYU building, blah-blah-blah, because that's where they store all the film school equipment. I had a virtual tour of the security desk, the surveillance cameras, the security force"—his voice rose in anger and exasperation—"all the extra vigilance needed so a film student with a pass and a pierced tongue can walk out onto Broadway with a twenty-five-thousand-dollar movie rig."

"Cameras? You should appreciate that more than anyone."

"Sure I do. But they're paying more attention to who's leaving than who's coming in," Meredith said defensively. "Resulting in the gorilla who nearly raped my wife roaming free in the building."

"I looked at the reports, Mr. Meredith. Maybe he wasn't a gorilla off the street. Maybe he even had the ID to get in."

A man who suddenly recognized the extent to which anger had distorted his judgment, Meredith deflated.

Clay gave him a little time, then asked, "Does Dr. Meredith have any students who might be considered . . . vindictive?"

"Rachel? No, no way! If anyone's having trouble, she makes herself available—if any of her students fail, it's only because they've given up on themselves."

"What about her colleagues?"

"Faculty? I've met the whole department at one school function or another." He appeared to be checking through a mental list. "No. Not one I can imagine doing such a thing—not to mention the size or the strength to drag my wife around like a rag doll. Rachel's slim, but she's stronger than you'd think. She's at Coles—the NYU sports center—every morning, running or swimming or both."

"Well, it paid off . . . she got away from the guy." Clay finished the rest of his coffee. "I know she's resting today, but I'd like to talk to her tomorrow. Actually, what do you think about her walking me through, showing me what happened, right on the scene? While it's still fresh?"

Meredith paced back and forth. "Her decision, but I think it's a good idea. The winter break just started, and it has nearly a month to go. . . . That way, it won't be looming over her—her first time going back into the building." He walked past the previous night's Polaroids without a glance. "I'll remind her that she's helping the next woman this bastard stalks. That's all the motivation she'll need." He paused. "What about the cop who took her statement?"

"Give her your full cooperation, Mr. Meredith. But right now, you might want to . . ." he gestured to young Chang, asleep on his feet.

"Shit! Phil, go home. I'll see you at two."

Chang pointed at the camera on the tripod, and his boss gave him a thumbs-up.

When they were alone, Clay asked, "What's happening with the Trabuc? All those people still hounding you?"

"Most have taken the hint, now that Rachel's decided to keep it."

"Keep it? She made her decision? When?"

"More or less at the museum gala. What you told her about her grandfather made up her mind."

"Ah." Clay walked to the kitchen area and rinsed his cup. "So who's left? Who doesn't understand the 'not for sale' sign?"

"Not many. Primarily, Grauberger and Rasenstein. But that's enough. Those two! Like having jock itch and athlete's foot at the same time. They both claim they have serious buyers, keep asking us to name our price. Oh, and the big auction houses haven't let up, either, especially that annoying Sands woman. She jabbers away about how no one in the world can sell Trabuc for a higher price than Esterbrook-Grennell. Totally writes off the galleries and keeps asking us if the other houses can match her marketing plan. Like we've bothered to read any of them."

"Really? You still have the proposals?"

"Hers is probably around here. She's the only one who mails copies to the apartment, Rachel's office, *and* here. All by express delivery. Entire families could live well on the woman's shipping bill." After a quick trip to his office, he returned with a wastepaper basket, and was already sorting through its contents. He pulled out three FedEx packets. Not this . . . not this . . . gotcha! All yours."

"Want it back?"

Meredith dumped the rest of the basket into a big kitchen garbage container. "Hardly." He suppressed a yawn. "Sorry. It's been a long, upsetting night."

At five-thirty the following afternoon, Clay picked up Dr. Meredith at home and walked her to 721 Broadway. From his nametag, Clay saw that the man at the security desk wasn't the same guard listed in the police report. Nevertheless, the man didn't have to check ID to know who the lady with the shiner and scratched cheek was. His strained greeting indicated that the whole security staff had taken flak over the incident.

They crossed the deserted lobby to the elevators. "You know that I arrived here earlier that night," she volunteered. "More people. And it was still light out."

"I know. I purposely waited until dark, so everything upstairs would look the same as it did when the black leather jacket turned up."

"Lightning doesn't strike twice," she said, but held up crossed fingers.

"Your statement says, 'I was working on the Avid.' What's that?"

They entered an empty elevator. "An editing machine. Tape, not film."

"What were you editing?"

"Next term's clips. Wil was working late. I figured I'd get a head start. I was grading finals all day, got about halfway through, and had to get out of the apartment."

When they reached nine, Clay let her go first, and watched her head swivel left, toward the adjacent stairwell door. Nearby, double doors sectioned off the rest of the hall. Through their glass panels, he saw the long corridor beyond, a stretch of at least a hundred feet.

"I had to stop to pick up the key to the Avid room." The area they entered widened and led to the Post Production desk. Behind it, two students were slumped in chairs, reading. One was a slight young man with long hair and a dot of blond hair under his lower lip. Dr. Meredith introduced him as Jon Armbruster; the pretty Asian girl next to him was Fran Kim. The day of the attack, they'd taken the Post desk at four. Besides Dr. Meredith, only three others had used the editing rooms during their seven-hour shift: a trio of African-American students, all females, who'd come in together at seven to finish their fall term projects. At ten, they'd regrouped, returned their keys, and left. When questioned after the attack, neither they, nor Jon, nor Fran recalled seeing anyone else on the ninth floor.

Fran froze when Dr. Meredith requested the keys to 979 and the Script Library.

"It's not the fruit cellar from *Psycho*, Miss Kim. Besides, this gentleman is a genuine New York City police detective. Without him, I'd be scared shitless."

Gesturing for Clay to follow, she turned left into another corridor, one long enough to run parallel with the hall beyond the double doors. Editing rooms were to their left, offices to their right, all apparently unoccupied and locked. After two more quick lefts, they started down a much shorter and poorly lit interior hallway together. One side was lined with more editing rooms, but the other, past a doorway under the glow of an Exit sign, was nothing but unbroken wall. Even in the dim light, he saw how her face had drained, making the scratch marks stand out like purple ink on white paper.

"One moment, Dr. Meredith." A push revealed that the exit door opened onto a narrow connecting stairwell. "Got it. Go on, please." To her back, he said, "I had no idea this place was such a maze." Room 979 formed the end of the hall. As she unlocked it, he said, "This room has to be right behind the Post desk."

"It is. The walls are so thin, you can hear right through them." Room 979 was equipped with a large screen, several chairs, and computer equipment. With a solid click, its door shut behind them.

"All the rooms lock automatically?"

"Yes." With a shaky hand, she indicated the bank of chairs. "There are other Avid rooms, but this one's used mostly by faculty. The screen and the chairs are for demonstrations—seminars on how to use the software." She sat down at the computer. "I walked in here a little after five. I was totally into my reel, and I didn't look at my watch until ten—I heard women's voices."

Clay nodded. The three girls, leaving.

"All of a sudden, I felt absolutely starved—I'd only planned to work a few hours. But I was right in the middle of a segment, so I finished it up. Then I called Wil on my cell phone, the way I usually do, to touch base. I was really hoping we could meet for a snack, but when I heard all the people in the background—the shoot wasn't over—I figured I'd just pick something up." Gripping her chair's armrests, she pushed herself up. "All right! Let's get to the juicy part!"

She strode out, forgetting the keys. Clay grabbed them.

"I was heading back to the check-in desk the same way I came. Just after I passed the Exit sign, about here"—she suddenly halted—"he jumped me from behind. I was completely . . . overwhelmed. Confused. And scared. His left hand was clamped over my mouth, and it blocked part of my nose, so I had to really struggle for air. His right hand was . . . he had it over my left breast, like it was a goddamn handle, and he was squeezing it, hard. It was horrible, the way he was totally in control." Her head drooped, and she reached for the wall.

He thought she was going to be sick. "Deep breaths."

"No, I'm fine," she protested, but it was a while before she straightened up. "I was screaming for help, but he had my mouth sealed off with his hand, and I don't think much sound came out. I guess I was only spitting onto his hand and fighting to breathe. Then he . . . *propelled* me toward the Script Library. . . ." She shuddered. "He was so strong . . . I almost gave up." She turned left. The Script Library entrance was diagonally across from her. The room extended along the exterior wall of the building, all the way to the long hall with the double doors.

"The Script Library also has an automatic lock, right?"

"Yes. But he walked right in, just gave it a push."

"The lock was jimmied and a small wood shim turned up. It's a good bet he kicked it away when he dragged you in. So the door would lock behind you."

She nodded. "That click! It meant I didn't have a chance—that no one could hear us or see us. And he was moving me past the checkout desk, toward that long table. He let go of my breast, but only to rip my blouse open. Then he was pulling at my bra, and the clasp popped, and I felt his bare hand on my skin. . . . I kicked him, hard as I could. I was wearing my heavy boots—it was snowing—and I kicked backward, aiming for his groin. I think I got him in the knee—he staggered a little. All along, I was still trying to scream, and his hand was all wet with my spit. It slipped just a little, just enough for me to move my mouth. I bit down as hard as I could. I got him right here"—she held up her hand—"on the web between his thumb and his index finger. I bit right through—it was disgusting! He tried to shake me off. The hand that'd been on my breast . . . he let go and punched me in the head. I lost my balance and landed on the floor. I rolled under the table"—she walked around it, and touched one of the small computer desks—"and crawled under this." She moved to the Script Library's second door. "I remember pulling myself up on this doorknob. Then I ran out the door. I never turned around. I didn't have to. I knew he was coming after me."

"Hold on." Clay pivoted around slowly, trying to absorb as much of the Script Library as he could. Instead of bookcases, file cabinets lined the walls, even under the windows. "The scripts are in the file cabinets?"

"That's right."

He was stalling, waiting for it to come to him. *Why this room? Why not one of the editing rooms?* He rotated once again. It was the only room so far that had windows. "What about the windows? Were any of them open?"

"I don't remember. Maybe my back was to them."

"It was cold, nasty out—your boots, remember? Go on, walk through it again."

Her look said she didn't want to spend another minute in the library, but she obliged, walking back in. Repositioning herself at the first door, eyes shut, she once again resisted her attacker as they advanced toward the table. Her eyes opened. "Yes. I felt it when he ripped off my clothes." She swept a hand across her breasts. "I felt it here. A gust of cold air."

"Thank you, Dr. Meredith. Sorry. We're done in here. Please, continue."

She walked out the far door. "I took off down the hall that leads back to the elevators. I heard the library door click shut. I heard it open again, after I'd only gone about twenty feet. I remember thinking, What if the elevator doesn't come right away? Then I came to my senses, and thought of the stairwell. I can run, but he was fast—knee, hand, and all." She approached the double doors. "I crashed through hard, so they'd swing back at him and slow him down." Giving them a violent shove, she ran through, forcing Clay to wait for them to rebound.

"You saw that in a movie, didn't you?" he asked, once he caught up.

"A cartoon—and it worked," she smiled triumphantly. "I ran for the stairwell door. I just made the first landing when he came through. By the time I got to eight, I remembered to scream, and never stopped. You know those dreams when all of a sudden you can fly? That's how fast I went down those stairs. Once I passed four, I had a feeling he wasn't after me anymore."

"But you kept on running."

"And screaming. The security guard was already coming across the lobby when I came through the door. I couldn't stop running. I think he sort of tackled me. I guess the rest is in other people's statements."

When Clay and Dr. Meredith rounded the corner onto Ninth Street, her husband was in front of their building, paying a taxi driver. Clay called to him, and he walked back, meeting them midway.

He put an arm around at his wife, then turned to Clay. "How'd she do?"

"I was fine," she answered for herself. "We slid down nine floors of banisters to the lobby. No, I am not traumatized. In fact, I was about to ask Detective Ryder to join us for supper, maybe at that new place on—"

Clay looked at his watch. "Hey, I didn't realize it was so late! I was supposed to meet someone five minutes ago! Listen, I'll do what I can on this. Someone from your precinct might ask you to do another walk-through. We could avoid a lot of red tape if . . ."

Rachel Meredith winked at him. "Detective Who?"

"That's right. If I don't get in touch with you folks before, Merry Christmas!" He walked away briskly, a man in a hurry. Once he was out of sight, he doubled back to Tisch. Too much of what had happened to Rachel Meredith up there just didn't add up.

CHAPTER
TWENTY-ONE

"Ryder, we just got our first and only break on the Broyce case. And guess what it's going to make you say?" Malenkov ratcheted up his gravel-pit voice, not even approaching a feminine range. " 'Oh, it was soooo good for me, honey— was it good for you?' " Speaking to someone else, he said, "Great. Tell them to make sure she doesn't leave." Back to Clay, he asked impatiently, "How fast can you get up here?"

"That's it? Not even a hint?"

Either there was very noisy static on the line, or the lieu's answer was a dismissive throat-clearing.

Clay glanced at his watch. The February days were steadily lengthening, but he knew it was already twilight outside. "Okay. Soon as I clear it with the DI, I'll be on my way," he replied. As if it were no big deal. As if he could actually do his job without Hickey scrutinizing his every move.

Up at the Nineteenth, Malenkov handed him a newspaper clipping that had gone to press exactly three months earlier. Its focus was the "grotesque and heartbreaking final hour" of one H. Sorcher.

Just after two o'clock on November 8, 1999, Herbert Sorcher, known to all as Buddy, sat in his doctor's office, staring at an X ray. He was forty-eight and physically fit, except for the newly discovered tumor metastasizing in his brain. Three months was the doctor's most optimistic prognosis.

Half an hour later, a distraught but pragmatic Sorcher phoned his lawyer while en route to a Midtown business meeting. He scheduled an emergency five-o'clock appointment that would be the first step toward putting his estate in order. The legal agenda was to include the immediate dissolution of several highly leveraged corporations, as well as special instructions to accompany his will.

Neither was accomplished.

Moments after Buddy exited his limo and pressed END, he met his.

Half a block away, a bus driver in the grip of a heart attack had no idea that his thrashing foot was hitting the accelerator instead of the brake. His bus lurched onto the sidewalk and bulldozed its way into a brick wall. Whether Buddy, a somewhat shady megamillionaire, was headed for heaven or hell, he got there on the bumper of an M-103.

Except for the mysterious source of his fortune, there hadn't been much else to the Sorcher saga: twice divorced, he left no children. His sole heirs were his brother's son and daughter, both in their mid-twenties, who had no comment.

Clay read over the grisly newspaper account, recalling that even the *Times* had painted Buddy's end as a lurid, you-can't-fuck-with-fate event. "Sure, I remember this."

"Tax-wise," Malenkov explained, "Sorcher's estate was a mess. He dabbled in stocks and bonds, but for the most part, he invested in real estate and"—he pointed at Clay—"art. The IRS bill was a shocker, and there were almost no liquid assets to pay it off. The tax boys gave his niece and nephew less than a year to settle."

"I assume you got this from the heirs."

"Uh-huh," Malenkov smiled. "Neither had the slightest interest in Uncle Buddy's paintings, so selling them was the quickest way to raise cash. Otherwise, 'Heir today, gone tomorrow.' Sorcher kept his entire collection in a twenty-room mansion in Connecticut, his weekend retreat. The housekeeper is living there until it's sold, and she was politely asked to give us a little tour." He jingled a pair of car keys. "Shall we?"

On the trip to Connecticut, Malenkov gradually filled out the story: "Sorcher didn't keep any organized records of his art purchases. The niece and nephew turned up receipts for less than half the pieces." After putting a winding stretch of the Merritt Parkway behind him, the lieu added, "But every receipt they found came from Esterbrook-Grennell. So consigning the paintings back to that institution seemed the logical choice for the niece and nephew, especially after they found out that one of their top executives had personally advised their uncle on his acquisitions for years. About two days ago, Esterbrook-Grennell's own movers efficiently packed up every painting in sight. And even though the paintings are gone—sorry to disappoint you on that, Ryder—I'm hoping the housekeeper might throw a little light on Sorcher's relationship with the addressee. You see, all the crates were flagged to Deirdre Sands, President. *She* was Buddy's buddy."

In the confines of the car, the only way a speechless Clay could demonstrate his glee was by thumping the dashboard hard, many times.

Malenkov pulled off the Merritt and raced along a series of country roads. "All we know right now is that the Sorcher collection arrived while she was out of the office. One of her assistants, a Ms. Archer Bigelow, took it upon herself to supervise the unpacking. Before four this afternoon, Bigelow followed E-G's mandatory drill for all new consignments: she checked off the manifest, then entered the paintings for a search against the computer files of the Art Loss Register. I guess she figured a clean report would be waiting on her computer tomorrow morning, because she left to run errands for her boss. She told the secretary that she wouldn't be returning to the office."

Clay pictured one of Sands's typical industrious post-deb underlings reaching into the bubble-wrap. "Which one was it?" He started to laugh uncontrollably. "The El Greco, or the Hals?"

Malenkov joined in, laughing so hard, only Clay could have known what he was saying. "The Hals! The fucking Hals!"

Evidently, while Bigelow was ducking in and out of cabs, her Art Loss Register search had triggered the art world equivalent of America's Most Wanted high-kicking into FBI headquarters like a Radio City Music Hall Rockette.

The lieu pulled into a long driveway. A castle-size Norman creation loomed at the end, extra-heavy on the turrets and leaded windows. Malenkov offered Clay a tissue before they got out of the car. Both of them had tears in their eyes from laughing.

Clay and Lieutenant Malenkov showed up at Esterbrook-Grennell early the next morning. As soon as Ms. Bigelow hurried in—a toothpick with short dark hair and huge gray eyes—they personally escorted her to her computer. Her email brought bright pink spots to her gaunt cheeks, but her effort to compose herself verged on the heroic. Her response was pure Esterbrook-Grennell: "Shall I put you in touch with the consignors?"

"Oh, we've already been in touch." Malenkov's usual croak barely disguised his euphoria. "But right now, the painting is in Esterbrook-Grennell's possession. And we're ready to pay a visit to Ms. Sands."

"She gets in at nine-fifteen." On full self-defense alert, Bigelow crossed her arms, the long fingers clamping over bony elbows.

"Well, then," said the lieutenant, "let's all wait right outside her office, so no one beats us to delivering the happy news."

As predicted, Sands breezed in at a quarter past nine. The sight of two grim, unexpected visitors in off-the-rack suits clearly rattled her, but when they identified themselves as NYPD, her anxiety appeared to dip a notch or two. Their request for an unscheduled audience in the presidential office was granted—although they were forewarned that it would be brief.

After a few warm-up questions, Malenkov got out the sledgehammer, and began smashing her pedestal to bits: "Ms. Sands, did you consider yourself Mr. Sorcher's primary advisor on art purchases?"

"I frequently advised him. However, I'd be surprised if he didn't avail himself of other sources, as well."

"But weren't most of the paintings on this list bought right here?" Malenkov waved a printout of the Sorcher collection, which had been provided by the heirs.

Sands snatched the paper out of his hand, then carefully scanned every item. "All but the three undocumented works."

"And you knew the stolen painting—the Hals—was in his collection?"

"What? How dare you! Absolutely not!"

"You know nothing about where it came from, or how he came to own it?"

"That's an outrageous question!" Once again, she put Clay in mind of a bewigged English monarch. Red faced with rage, she appeared ready to scream for the Royal Executioner to chop off Malenkov's head.

"What about the other two paintings on this list without histories?"

"Without provenance," she corrected. "I know nothing about them."

"But advising Mr. Sorcher as you did, wouldn't knowledge of everything he owned be a necessity"—Malenkov tipped in the phrase Clay had suggested—"to ensure a well-balanced collection?"

Momentarily, her lips pressed in a thin line. "Yes. But only if you assume that all collectors pursue balance."

"What about Buddy Sorcher? What can you tell me about him?"

"Obviously, we shared an interest in art. It was a business relationship."

"We have a statement from the housekeeper up in Connecticut. According to her, you were a regular visitor."

"I grew up in Connecticut. I have family there. I stopped by the Sorcher home from time to time on my way back to the city."

"And you never saw that painting? It was hanging right there."

"It must have been in another part of the house—a part I didn't see."

"It was in the master bedroom," countered Malenkov.

"What's that supposed to mean?" she snapped.

Clay, who so far hadn't said a word in her presence, glanced over at Malenkov. One of the first things the lieu had asked him was if he thought Sorcher and Sands had slept together. Clay had pointed out that since her clients got more fucking than anyone could handle in the course of an ordinary business transaction, there seemed little reason to go to bed with her, too. However, he didn't rule it out.

Sands tuned right in to their private channel. She jabbed a finger at Clay. "You! *Now* I know who you are! You used to work here! No doubt you find this interrogation remarkably amusing!"

"Detective Ryder is aware of the gravity of this situation, Ms. Sands," Malenkov interceded. "But let me put that another way. *If* you'd gone into Mr. Sorcher's bedroom, would you have been able to identify the painting?"

"For goodness' sake, it was all over the papers last year!" No doubt exactly what she intended to scream at the unfortunate Ms. Bigelow before she axed her.

"You also saw it at the home of Randall Broyce. Another valued client."

Pointing to a Rolodex big as a truck tire, Sands said, "One of many. Yes, I attended a little reception after the painting's installation. Over the years, Mr. Broyce has bid at many of our auctions."

The lieu turned to Clay and nodded. They rose from their chairs in perfect unison. Thrown off balance by what seemed a sudden departure, Sands glowered up at them, not sure if she'd won or lost the round.

"Understand, Ms. Sands, I'm obligated to follow up on everything that relates to the Broyce case." Malenkov slipped into his overcoat. "That was a nice picture of you and him at the Park Avenue Armory Show." Appraising her, he rubbed the chin he was never able to shave clean. It scraped audibly. "But so was the one from Christmastime, too—that Tavern on the Green shindig." He hooked a thumb toward Clay. "And Detective Ryder here, although he rarely hobnobs with the rich and famous, also had the opportunity to observe you and Mr. Broyce at the November Metropolitan Museum gala." He rummaged through his pockets for his gloves. "That blurry line between business and personal you Haves cross so easily . . . us Have-Nots just don't get that at all."

Neither spoke until they were outside, striding toward Clay's car. "God, you had to work for that woman?" Malenkov asked, genuine sympathy in his voice.

"I was beneath the bottom of the ladder, Lieu. Not even the mud under her shoes. Next down. The dogshit layer."

"Boy, no wonder you became a cop. A clean, safe job, compared to being around her." When Clay was right next to him, unlocking the passenger door, he asked, "You see Sands connected to the Broyce job?"

Clay jogged around the car, and they both slid in. "Selling stuff to Broyce on the up and up, stealing it, then turning around and selling it to Sorcher on the sly?"

"Yeah. Am I being desperate, just thinking that?"

"Desperate? No. Anything more ever turn up on that climbing gear?"

"Nah. The line that was dangling over the side comes from Europe—it's not even sold in this country. Grappling hook's from Japan. Available in the U.S.A., but only west of the Rockies. It added up to a lot of work that went nowhere. But this Sands woman . . . she was a guest in Broyce's fucking apartment! She knew where the picture was! She's the only link between Broyce and Sorcher!"

He waited while Clay turned the ignition key. "How much would she make, brokering a deal like that? Broyce paid Esterbrook-Grennell eight million for the Hals."

"That's like full retail. Figure much less than half on the black market," Clay ventured. "Maybe three, tops."

"So let's say a thief that good, taking that kind of risk, could hit her for fifty-fifty, even if she did draw him a fucking map of Broyce's place. Worst scenario for her, one and a half million, tax-free. And she wasn't the one playing slide-for-life twenty stories up. Then Sorcher's death comes out of the blue. His estate's all in knots. No fucking way she can get the painting out of the way, except stealing it all over again. Maybe by the time she gets it all set up, it's too late. It wouldn't surprise me if she was accidentally-on-purpose out of the office when that skinny Bigelow kid opened it up."

"Hard to say. A million and a half's a lot of money. But Sands probably outearns the annual payroll of your entire precinct."

"Man, it's cold for such a sunny day! Your heater broken, Ryder?"

"It's already on. You'll feel it soon as I pull up to the station house, or in ten minutes, whichever comes first." Clay eased out into heavy traffic. "Lieu, I'm interested in Sands on something else."

"Oh yeah? What's she need money for? I don't exactly peg her as the Atlantic City type. Drugs? Kids in trouble?"

"The problem is, I haven't come up with a money angle. Her ex is raising their kids in Connecticut. He's loaded, and the kids are only seven and ten. I never rule out drugs, but she's too on top of things for a habit that big."

A red light temporarily stopped both car and conversation.

"No, that doesn't work either," Clay said, as it turned green.

"What?"

"Her getting in line as the next Mrs. Broyce. Get it? Not a robbery that turned into a murder, but a murder disguised as a robbery."

"Anything's possible, Ryder, but casting Sands as a jealous lover?" He winced. "I'll admit I did play with Broyce wanting to get rid of his wife, though. That was a possible for a while. He offs Long Tall Sally, and he gets a double payoff—her life insurance, plus his fine arts policy."

"So?"

"Couldn't stick." He turned up his coat collar against the car's chill. "As for Sands, if not for love or money, what's left? The girl just wants to have fun?"

"Her? Fun to that woman is fucking the competition, period." Clay pulled up in front of the Nineteenth. Warm air finally flowed from the heater.

"Ryder?" Malenkov was saying, "Ryder, did you hear what I said?"

"Sorry. I just realized I was wrong. I mean about Sands wanting to screw the competition. Back when I was working there, a reliable source told me about a certain list of Sands's. Names of megabuck collectors. She was sharing it with the other two big houses. If that's still going on—and I have every reason to be-lieve it is—she's been in the middle of all sorts of price-fixing and collusion for years."

"White collar crime?" asked the lieu.

"A whole dirty laundry bag full of it."

"You think she's worried the government might be on to her?"

Clay thought for a moment. "Did you catch how she was practically re-lieved that we were NYPD? Sands thought we were Feds!"

Malenkov whistled. "Then money might be a motive, after all."

"Right. Because there's one hole you can't pour enough money down."

"The law hole."

"It's still only a hunch, but in the near future, Madame Sands might need the services of a very expensive lawyer. Maybe two. Maybe a whole damn firm."

As he drove back downtown, Clay shifted from Malenkov's case back to the Trabuc. And, of course, to Udo Luscher.

The more he learned about the Broyce crime, the more Oliver Plum-worth's words about a handful of unscrupulous international dealers and collec-tors rang true: together, they could pull off just about anything.

Whether or not Sands was one of them remained to be seen.

Certainly, she had the client contacts, Esterbrook-Grennell was global, and she was dirty enough. If all the games she'd been playing since the early Nineties were about to catch up with her, getting Rachel Meredith to consign the Trabuc was exactly the kind of big media splash old Deirdre needed to hold onto her job. All her double-dealing aside, however, he still couldn't find the thinnest thread to tie her to Luscher. Plus, in '72, she'd have been finishing finishing school.

In contrast, the current Rasenstein, though only in his twenties that year, could easily have been keeping up the family tradition: cozying up with the Nazis. Like *père*, like *fils*.

But he really liked the Graubergers best: the Zurich gallery's international postwar expansion had put them at the top of their game in 1972. Furthermore, the Rasensteins had been among the more eclectic Parisian dealers since the Twenties, while the Grauberger specialty—as Oliver Plumworth had pointed out at the Met—was Old Masters. That provided a very interesting cover for peddling Impressionist and Post-Impressionist paintings.

In days, the Hals portrait was returned to Randall Broyce. No arrests were made, because Buddy Sorcher was not around to either explain or be detained.

His niece and nephew were in the clear. But the Broyce case wasn't a single step closer to being solved, and Clay, increasingly frustrated by the possibility that he'd overlooked or forgotten some detail, began to understand the temporary refuge Lauren had found in her lists.

CHAPTER
TWENTY-TWO

In May, Clay drove out to open The Shack. Both on the way out and back, Lauren's frequency had faded out completely. Going over the fatal stretch of highway, he focused hard, even gave the turned-off radio a whack, but she remained incommunicado. The second anniversary of her death had just passed. He didn't know if he had let go of her, or if it was the other way around.

A few days later, he was on hand at a SoHo gallery, watching as the handcuffed owner did the perp walk out to the precinct squad car. No windbreaker over that lady's head. She was all dressed up for the occasion, in a slinky sleeveless dress and stiletto-heeled sandals that made her fifty-something legs look great. As soon as she neared the news crews, she began to protest that yet another "temple of art" had been desecrated. Her lawyer followed the high priestess, invoking the First Amendment.

The police had shut down her temple because of an installation composed of real guns and G.I. Joe action figures. Also, a large glass bowl near the entrance was filled with a mix of bullets and Bazooka bubble gum, a hand-lettered HELP YOURSELF card perched next to it. Clay's attendance had been requested for the removal of the unlicensed weapons and the live ammo, art-as-evidence. Shortly after he walked out onto the sidewalk, the yellow crime-scene tape went up and the remaining onlookers scattered.

"My kid would've liked that kneeling artilleryman," whispered a voice just behind him. "They don't make that G.I. Joe guy anymore."

Clay walked away, his eyes looking straight ahead. "Long time. How you doing?"

"Considering you just closed down a great source for free bullets, not bad," answered Aaron. "I have something for you."

"I assume the content isn't kosher?"

"Nope. Two visitors from the Land of the Rising Sun flew into town on the seventh."

The date was familiar to Clay; Sunday, May seventh had been the final day of the Met's *Empty Frame* exhibit. "What about them?"

"Must be art lovers. Every day they pay a visit to Galleries Grauberger."

Halfway down the block, Clay paused in front of a boutique, straining to conceal his excitement. Aaron's news could only mean the Mossad finally had a strong lead in Japan, significant enough to be carefully monitored. Once again, the Japan-Grauberger connection. "Every day?"

"For a whole week. And while we're on the subject, guess who yodeled his last yesterday? A hint: old and frail, at home in a big villa with a mountain view, in a travel poster village called Engelberg. Couple of hours from Zurich."

"According to his son—this was back in November—that old man was pretty ill." Clay moved on again, toward the din of lower Broadway.

"Yeah. Stuck in a wheelchair. Taking meds for depression. The Swiss police think that was what did it."

"Did what?"

"Pushed him over the brink. He's bundled up out on his terrace, getting some sun like it's Miami Beach. Asks his day nurse for a cup of cocoa—probably Swiss Miss. She comes back, and her patient's not in the chair. He'd become forgetful, too."

"What did he forget?"

"His parachute. Crash-landed a couple hundred feet down the mountain. Oh. One other thing—I'm becoming forgetful, too. A tour bus stopped in Engelberg yesterday afternoon."

"Didn't you say it was a touristy place?"

A tall, dark-haired man stepped around Clay and hurried across Broadway just as the light turned red. His words drifted back. "A tour bus full of Japanese tourists."

Clay watched as Aaron slid into the passenger side of a car idling at the curb. It pulled away immediately, leaving him to wonder how the hell Aaron had turned up at that particular gallery, at that exact moment. But far more important was his news that Grauberger Senior's header down the mountain was a Nipponese warning to Junior that he was about to follow right in his daddy's skid marks. Luscher had set it all in motion. Either in 1971, or now. And Aaron had been determined not to hang around to answer any questions, which really pissed Clay off. Eli had asked Clay for a crumb, any crumb. And now that's all the Mossad was throwing to Clay.

————

May hadn't been a lucky month for Lauren, nor for the other woman in Clay's life: later in the month, his mother died.

"Betsy's gone. I'm so sorry. She just slipped away." The wife of his half-brother, Scott, was the one who called with the bad news. "The nurse's aide thought she was asleep, she went so peacefully." He heard a deep intake of breath. "Do you want to know about the funeral arrangements?"

"Does that mean my grandfather and your husband don't want me there? Or is it just that they made you the designated caller?"

"I hate being in the middle," she sighed. "Both."

"Well, I'm coming—they can damn well count on that. You can tell them not to worry—things won't get ugly. Not on my part. But only out of respect for my mother."

During the service, he sat off to one side of the chapel. Few of the guests knew who he was, so long had he been frozen out of the Ryder Air Conditioning and Refrigeration loop. True to his word, Clay kept his silence and lobbed back his grandfather's stone-cold stares. Surrounded by peonies and sprays of lilac, his mother slept on, unaware that she'd traded her bed for a casket.

Clay was pulled back to his first sketchy memory: him and his mom coming to Grandpa Ryder's big house in the country. (That part of Westchester had been a suburb for decades, but to young Clay, anyplace with more than one tree qualified as country.) At first, he loved the Colonial. With its endless halls, rooms large and small, and towering, tantalizing cupboards filled with fragile (and thus forbidden) objects, it was a place made for a boy to explore. The only drawback was his tall, unsmiling grandfather. His most vivid memory was of the old man chasing him out of darkened rooms . . . rooms he wandered into, searching for his mother. Sometimes she'd be just out of sight, a pale blur in the corner shadows; sometimes, under Grandpa Ryder's shouts, Clay was sure he heard her sobbing. Back in the room she shared with Clay, she would stuff their tired-looking clothes into her worn blue Samsonite. Crying and packing, time after time.

It had to be during his fourth year when he took direct action against the old man who kept hurting his mother. After she returned to their room, eyes red and still sobbing, he commenced a long search in the gloom of a snowy afternoon. He found his grandfather in the hall, already in his overcoat, pulling on his galoshes. Clay ran at him, and lashed out with fists and feet. His grandfather stood up, looming so high above him, he couldn't see his face. Long, bony fingers grabbed Clay's collar and transported him at arm's length, still kicking and flailing, out of the house. The snow was so deep, the old man had to lift his feet as if he were marching. He trudged all the way to the snow-covered garbage bin on the far side of the garage. After hoisting Clay up so high that he could look down on the ugly intensity of his grandfather's fury, he released his grip. When Clay hit the top of the bin, it shuddered, but the snow cushioned him from the impact. His grandfather was out of sight before he was able to sit up. He was immediately terrified by how far his perch on the bin appeared to be from the ground. Only after he saw his grandfather's car drive away, and he realized he was stuck there, shivering in his shirt and pants, did Clay summon the courage to jump to the ground. Half-frozen, he slogged through the hip-high snow to the front door. Too small to ring the bell, he screamed and pounded on the locked door until his mother, already looking for him, pulled him inside.

She left him only once.

When Clay was five, he woke up one morning to discover that both his mother and the suitcase were gone. Inconsolable, it was his turn to cry, and he didn't stop until she reappeared a few days later. Having her back made him so happy, he hardly paid any attention to the baby in her arms: Scott, his new little brother.

By eleven or twelve, when his own body began to push him toward an awareness of what happens between men and women, he began to wonder about what he might have glimpsed in those darkened rooms. But even at that age, revulsion trumped curiosity. Maybe it had never really happened, after all. Maybe it was only what he thought he saw, back when he had to stand on tiptoe to reach the doorknob.

All those years, the old man kept coming at Clay like a bulldozer. Quashing disobedience wasn't new to him—Clay's own father had given him plenty of practice.

Jonas Ryder always postponed his grandson's punishment until evening, when the chill in the house reached its peak. The object of his scorn was ordered to stand completely out of sight, between the back of his wing chair and the soot-free fireplace.

(The only time the Colonial's hearth had been warmed by so much as a twig was the day Clay tried to surprise his mother with a cozy fire. Because he was neither aware that chimneys have flues, nor that opening them was very important, the surprise ended with a bucket of water and billowing, black smoke.)

The old man would sit there, nursing a Scotch in total silence—except for the clink of ice in his glass. There were times he'd pour another glass, even a third, although he was not by habit much of a drinker. At such an unhurried, deliberate pace, this presentencing phase could drag on for an hour or more—enough time to make Clay fear that if the old bastard didn't acknowledge him soon, he'd be forgotten there forever. Or at least long enough to have to be taken out with the trash.

In the end, whatever discipline was ultimately dispensed, far worse had already preceded it.

Clay was eventually allowed to join the outside world—the right schools, closely monitored friends. Although limited, the exposure was liberating. Shows of defiance were replaced by plans for escape.

The day after Thanksgiving of his sophomore year in college, Clay told his mother about his intention to change his major, and asked for her help.

At first, he thought she didn't hear him. Without a word, she put on a heavy sweater and walked out through the old sunroom, crossed the empty terrace, and paced back and forth along the tall hedge that formed the rear property line. He followed, falling in step alongside her. Earlier in the day it had snowed without sticking, and for once the outdoor temperature was lower than the Ryder thermostat. They were both shivering by the time she finally replied.

"Clay, you were fourteen months old when I found out your father had been killed in Vietnam. I had trouble holding on, but concentrating on you . . . that pulled me through. I truly did try to cope, but I started to worry that I'd lose *you*, too. I applied for a teaching job, and I was hired to start the next term—second grade, just what I'd always wanted. But then the thought of leaving you with strangers all day . . . I never showed up at the school district office to sign the employment papers. A foul-up in the system delayed our benefits from the government, and I ran out of money. I had no place to go. So I wrote a letter to your grandfather.

"Many times," she sighed, "your father told me horror stories about him—how incredibly manipulative he was, how he tried to control every last detail of his life. I assumed he was exaggerating—after all, who's ever truly objective about family?"

"Dad was right."

"Oh, Clay—you have no idea!" The remorse and loathing in her voice brought it all back.

By then, he'd lived in his grandfather's house long enough to understand. It had all been real, horrifically real, far beyond anything his young mind might have imagined. To the rutting old man sprawled over his mother, sex was only another way to inflict punishment. Lose a son who wouldn't obey, beget a son who would, all the while imposing as much degradation and humiliation as possible.

"For Christ's sake, Mom, why didn't you leave?"

"He provided food and shelter, but I never had a dime. I kept writing to the government, but my claim for our survivors' benefits was completely tangled up—I've always suspected your grandfather was responsible somehow. I owned nothing. I couldn't get a credit card. I became his financial prisoner. I despised him, but if I locked my door, he'd take it out on you . . . just a little boy! He was that cruel. When Scott was born, I was so ashamed. I'd stopped fighting. That was my biggest sin. Giving in. Giving up. Then, after I came home from the hospital, it was over. He had what he wanted. And that's why I'll do anything to help you. That's what I love about you, Clay. You're just like your father."

"And Scott . . . is he just like his father?"

She lowered her head. She didn't have to say a word.

Still hanging back by himself, Clay followed the hearse and all the Ryder Air Conditioning and Refrigeration mourners into the cemetery. Their show of grief was as heartfelt as a corporate Christmas card. The midafternoon temperature was pushing ninety, with no promise of relief in the cloudless sky. The thick, still air would have been a bruiser even in July; the unexpected heat quivered over every car hood like gelatin.

A little revenge for his mom, the sunshine glinted off the brass fittings of her casket and warmed the earth of the open grave.

From a distance, Clay watched as the chauffeur of the mourners' car helped Scotty's wife, Scotty, and his grandfather emerge into the harsh light. The old man visibly buckled at the knees. *What's this? Certainly not remorse. Only the unpleasantness of having to leave your ice locker for a few minutes.*

To steady himself, Jonas Ryder grabbed for the limo's roof, only to immediately flinch back from the searing black metal. Scott rushed to brace him. Despite the supportive hand under his elbow, the old man swayed, more than a little shaky.

Clay squinted up at the sun. *Come on, blast him with a few more degrees. A little foretaste of which way he's heading straight after his own funeral.* Inspired, he felt a smile spread across his face. *And to get him on his way, I'll make sure the heartless old bastard is cremated. If it's the last thing I ever do, I'll have him burned to a crisp.*

After the burial, he went to a bar in the next town—not as nice a town as the one he'd grown up in.

Clay drank to his mom. Maybe the one good thing in his life was that she knew he returned her unconditional love. Supporting him when he wanted to go down his own path had been an act of great valor for her. His mom had loved him so much, she'd helped him run away.

He toasted his dad, for resisting and escaping Jonas Ryder's domination.

He cursed his grandfather, who'd purposefully crushed his daughter-in-law to get even, and fucked up his son's son in the process.

Ah, but he'd resisted, like his dad. He lifted a glass to himself for that . . . even though he hadn't really escaped, and was still fucked up.

A couple more rounds, to the guys in the bar.

The last toast he could remember, around midnight, was to Scotty, his younger, controllable half-brother.

He still remembered what he'd asked him on his twelfth birthday:

"When are you leaving, Clay?"

"What do you mean?"

"Grandpa says he can't wait for you to be even older than twelve," Scott said in his squeaky voice. "Old enough to get out of the house for good. So he won't have to look at you every day."

Clay had stared at his half-brother. He and Scotty looked more alike than other kids who were full brothers. But unlike those other brothers, his grandfather made sure they were separated in every way possible: they had their own rooms, their own toys. When he was younger, his mother had saved the clothes he outgrew for his little brother; the first (and only) time his grandfather saw Scott in Clay's hand-me-downs, he'd yelled at her until his voice went hoarse, and wouldn't stop until she put everything in bags for the trash. "What about you, Scotty? Do you want me to leave?"

"Sure. That's what Grandpa wants." He looked around Clay's room. The one gift he'd received, from their mom, was on his bed. "That's not a real Walkman. Grandpa gave me a real one, and it's not even my birthday."

The way it looked now, thirty years of compliance had made his brother the perfect Jonas Ryder clone. And didn't that ultimately put Scotty in control of the man he called his grandfather? Little Bro had actually beaten the old man at his own game.

A nice twist, worthy of a toast to how a thoroughly contemptible self-made man would be responsible for his own unmaking. Before he had a chance to raise his hand once again for the bartender, his stomach backwashed all the booze he'd poured into it.

Rachel Meredith followed him outside. She was wearing her black velvet cape, still lamenting, "What kind of inheritance is this, if every time I look at Trabuc, all I see is Luscher?" Words slurred, he called back to her, "Can't be. The bastard's too busy showing up every time I look at my grandfather."

Halfway to his car, he threw up in the parking lot. As soon as he slid behind the wheel, he passed out.

The early sunrise hit him square in the eyes, jolting him awake. The car keys jangled as they fell from his lap. Just before he woke, he was in Paris, in a cramped, dark cell. Udo Luscher's prisoner. Or maybe he was in Westchester, locked in the interminable wait by the fireplace. In the dream, they were pretty much interchangeable.

CHAPTER
TWENTY-THREE

Rubbing at the deep imprint dug into his forehead by the rim of the steering wheel, Clay glanced back over his shoulder. Even if he looked only half as bad as the taste in his mouth, he still wanted to avoid the troll waiting to stare back at him from the depths of the rearview mirror. His car was the only one left in the parking lot. The bar sat next to the Interstate on-ramp, and the exhaust fumes of a big truck lumbering by shot straight from his nose to his uneasy stomach.

He was just sober enough to realize he should have called in hours earlier, but his phone wasn't in his jacket next to his wallet. As he felt for it, he remembered that he'd turned it off and tossed it onto the passenger seat when he drove into the cemetery. At some point, it had slid to the floor. In his condition, lowering his head would be unwise, so he stretched out his arm and groped for it blindly, through the loose change and torn cellophane and sand.

Penny Bloomberger answered when he called in.

"I'm very sorry about your mother," she told him, "but no one's been able to contact you for hours."

"I screwed up, Bloomie. Please—who was trying to reach me?"

"R. Meredith, R. Meredith, R. Meredith. Same message: 'Please call ASAP.' Looks like the first one came in at three A.M."

"Dr. Meredith—sorry, a mix-up," he lied. "Are you and your husband okay?"

"I'm okay . . . Wil's out of town. But Lulu . . . she's dead!" Her sobs made it difficult to understand the rest: "The police are going to take her body . . . but his . . . it's still down there."

"His?"

"The burglar's."

Clay stared down through the gaping hole where the Merediths' bedroom window had been. A double row of yards ran behind the block's north- and south-facing buildings, a patchwork defined mostly by sagging plank fences. One section was made up of mismatched interior doors, their paint weathered into a pastel rainbow. The weeds, where they hadn't been trampled down by the crime scene unit, were surprisingly high for May. In the narrow space below, a body was sprawled out between a garden hose and a broken Adirondack chair.

A crime scene tech pointed Clay to the study, a small room made smaller by built-in bookshelves. Rachel Meredith, in an oversize T-shirt and jeans, was perched on the desk. Dr. Corelli, her upstairs neighbor, filled the high-backed desk chair. Although both of them looked as if they'd been up all night, her eyes were noticeably puffy and red. Maybe she wouldn't notice his bile-green complexion; the quick stop he'd made at his apartment had done little for his own bleary appearance.

"They keep moving us from room to room," said Corelli, "and every time, someone new asks us the same questions."

"Looks like they're wrapping up," said Clay, "but I'm afraid I'm going to ask those questions all over again. You've both been down to ID him?"

"Yes. I've never seen him before," he answered. "And neither has Rachel. The police keep asking her if he's the Bell Atlantic man."

"As in the telephone company?" Corelli nodded, and Clay paused before he asked, "And Lulu . . . is she still here?"

Dr. Meredith looked away. "They finally took her . . . right after you called."

"I'm sorry." As much as he'd initially disliked Lulu, she was a feisty little dog, and her owner had seen her as an anchor of sorts. "You said your husband is . . . where?"

"On his way back from a shoot in Florida."

"Do you recall telling anyone that he'd be away?"

"I didn't even have the chance. It was a rush shoot. Not even twenty-four hours' notice—a new client. Way too pushy . . . very demanding. I didn't think it was a good idea for Wil to take the job, and I told him so."

"When did he leave?"

"Yesterday morning. Seven-thirty flight."

"And what about this Bell Atlantic guy?"

"While I was getting ready to leave for school, around nine, the doorman buzzed me that the telephone repairman was on his way up. I had no idea that anything was wrong, but sure enough, I picked up a phone, and no dial tone. I asked how long it'd been off, and he said some tenants noticed around seven."

"This was the regular daytime doorman?" Clay asked.

She nodded.

"If a bottle of Bushmill's could speak, it would sound like Jimmy," her neighbor confirmed. "His voice is unmistakable."

"Were you one of the folks with a phone problem?" Clay asked him.

"If I was, I didn't know it. I was out of town myself, at a dental seminar."

"He showed me his Bell Atlantic photo ID through the peephole—I didn't even have to ask," said Dr. Meredith. "Andy Allen. Before I opened the door, I warned him, 'I have a dog.'" At that, she burst into tears. Dr. Corelli reached out to pat her hand while she tried to compose herself. "He made a big fuss over Lulu. Anyway, he had a toolbox and that telephone-thing they always have dangling off their belts. He used it, my phone rang, and he answered it. Then he said the line still wasn't clean, he had to check out all the extensions. By then, Lulu was glued to his side. He tested the phones in the living room and our bedroom and in here. Of course, they dusted them all for fingerprints."

Clay nodded in agreement.

"Every extension, he had to wait longer and longer for the callback. I was getting a little crazed because I had to leave. At the same time, I started to really worry about Angelina. She'd never cut it that close before."

"Who's Angelina?" asked Clay.

"The lady who comes to clean for me every week. She worked for my mother before she moved to Florida, so she's like family. She's retiring at the end of July, and I'm already starting to miss her. Anyway, just when the last phone rang in the study, Angelina was at the door. She looked awful. The subway broke down and the air-conditioning went off. That same moment, the repairman walked into the hall. Lulu was with him. I remember exactly what he said: 'Your troubles are over.'

"I wasn't sure if he overheard Angelina, or if he was talking to me. He said good-bye, and let himself out. Lulu sat by the door for a while—that old 'His Master's Voice' pose." Lifting one shoulder, she swiped at her eyes with her T-shirt sleeve.

A forensic tech stuck his head in to say that the living room was finished, and they all trooped down the hall toward more comfortable quarters. Clay stopped at the archway leading into the living room. The room's neutral shades were no match for the blue of Trabuc's coat and Van Gogh's exuberant background. Back in the same showy frame the Met had dressed him in one year before, Saint-Rémy's head orderly glared at him so reproachfully, whatever was left of the postfuneral booze began to rumble in Clay's gut. After they sat down, he said, "I noticed you had an alarm installed. State of the art."

"Wil insisted on having it in place before the Trabuc left the Met."

"Good move. So the phone guy left, and you went to school. What then?"

"Do you remember how hot it was yesterday afternoon?"

"Only too well."

"When I came home in the evening, it was an oven in here. Lulu's usually wild to go for a walk after being cooped up all day, but she was lethargic—I blamed it on the heat. I turned on the air conditioners, and out we went. Going around the block, she perked up. I gave her supper and fresh water. She went for the water first, which was unusual, but it was so hot. . . . Then I checked to see if Wil had called." She reached over to a compact answering machine on the end table.

"Hi, Sweetheart." The sound quality was great: Wil Meredith's voice filled the room. "Hope I didn't make too much noise this morning. Jesus, were you ever right! I never should have taken this job. The man who hired me read somewhere that I have lots of experience with pots—except he didn't figure out they were the kind you cook in. His pots are big ceramic monsters, like those urns the Egyptians kept spare parts in . . . mummy parts. His are new, though, made—excuse me, *sculpted*—right here in the Sunshine State. He wouldn't let Phil or me even touch the ugly things—claims they're too valuable. Plus, he wanted to get in the pots *and* his art gallery, so the pictures are going to look like crap. Chances are I'll never get paid unless I come back down here and demand my fee, which I'll never do—it's hot as hell, with whirring insects the size of helicopters. The worst part is, this madman nitpicked so much, we missed the last plane! Phil and I are going out for dinner and drinks. Lots of drinks! Love you, miss you, see you tomorrow."

In the background, Phil Chang called out, "Hi, Rachel!"

She clicked the machine off. "The heat knocked me out. I had work to do, but I caved. *Bullitt* was just going on. I stayed awake for the car chase, then I fell asleep. When I woke up, credits were rolling—not for *Bullitt,* but the next film."

"What time was it?"

"My VCR clock actually works. Twelve-twenty-eight. My throat was parched, and I went to the kitchen for a glass of water. While I let the water run, I had a feeling . . . I looked around—I had trouble adjusting to the bright light in the kitchen. Lulu's food bowl hadn't been touched. Not only that, but she would have been right next to me the second I got off the sofa—I'd slept long past her bedtime walk. When it's hot, she sleeps in the study—small room, more air-conditioning. I ran in there . . . she was . . . dead." Her voice fell to a whisper. "Mike—my brother—gave her to me. Didn't I tell you that? A nutty, funny little dog. But every day, she sort of . . . brought him back."

Her neighbor waited for her sobs to taper off. "Rachel used that thing that gives you the number of the last incoming call to get in touch with Wil. A Holiday Inn. The manager told her Wil asked not to be disturbed until his wake-up call. So she called me. Luckily, I'd just gotten back from the seminar."

"I hated bothering you so late."

"Shhh . . . that's what friends are for. I rushed down with Rolf. He started pulling on his leash, and I could hardly hold him. Rachel said it was okay, to let him go, and it was amazing, the way he ran straight for the study. When we walked in, he was lying next to Lulu, his head down on his front legs."

"If I hadn't fallen asleep watching TV, maybe I could have . . ."

"Rachel, stop blaming yourself," Corelli cut in. "She was a very intelligent dog . . . smart enough to come to you if she was in pain."

"I just brought her to the vet for her annual checkup, Renny. A-OK."

"A patient can come in for a cleaning, X rays, everything's fine. A couple of days later—an abscess." He spread out his fingers, perhaps considering the occasional futility of regular checkups. He turned toward Clay. "Anyway, we went into the kitchen and I made Rachel a cup of tea. Rolf wouldn't leave his little friend. He kept sighing—that's a sound like he has a broken accordion inside him. And Rachel was so upset, all I wanted was to get her out of here. I finally convinced her to come upstairs and rest on my sofa. While she went to get a pillow and a throw, I tried to separate Rolf from Lulu, but he wouldn't budge. We both felt that he was keeping a vigil, and Rachel thought he should stay the night."

"It was impossible to sleep," Rachel said. "I heard Renny's clock strike two. A little later, there was a horrible crash. For a split second, I thought it was thunder, that the heat was breaking. But then . . . shattering glass and that long, awful scream. I heard a dog—a big dog—barking nonstop. Renny came running in, yelling, 'That's Rolf! That's Rolf! That crash—it had to come from your apartment!'"

Though they'd repeated it many times, they both shook their heads in disbelief.

"And that's how the body wound up in the backyard." Clay got to his feet. "Thanks for telling it all over again. I'd better find the officer in charge."

Reaching into her jeans, Rachel Meredith pulled out a business card. "Precinct Commander T. McFeeley," she read aloud.

"And the 'T' definitely doesn't stand for touchy-feely," Dr. Corelli complained. "The man's completely insensitive. My first patient's due at my office in half an hour, and he won't let me leave for work."

Going through the building superintendent's basement apartment was the only way to get to McFeeley. As soon as Clay set foot in the small backyard, the precinct chief barked at the bald black man next to him, "Brewster, find out who the hell that guy is, and what he's doing here."

Since he was only a few feet away, Clay introduced himself directly.

McFeeley's hair was a black helmet, more Kiwi shoe polish than Lady Clairol. "Right. The detective she's been trying to reach. Detective Brewster here will fill you in."

Clay pointed up toward the broken window. "Dr. Corelli asked if he can leave for work now, Commander."

McFeeley looked at his watch. "Time flies." After ordering the nearest uniform to go up and release the dentist, he took off himself.

"Name's Marcus Brewster." The detective, a heavyset man in his forties, thrust his hand at Clay. His gray suit was a little too snug, his stylish steel-rimmed glasses slightly undersized for his face, but nothing was small about his smile—a welcome change from McFeeley. "Dr. Corelli—nice guy, but have you seen the size of his dog?"

"Big one."

"Easy he outweighs this guy." Brewster gestured toward the body.

"I saw the marks Rolf's claws left in the bedroom floor, putting on the brakes. Whoever this guy is, I guess you could say he broke in . . . and broke out."

Brewster laughed, then turned serious. "You probably don't know about this." He kneeled down. "The medical examiner doesn't think he died from the fall." He pointed to a bullet hole in the dead man's temple. "No exit wound," Brewster noted. "Someone with a .22 was waiting for him down here."

"The person waiting to catch the Van Gogh?"

Brewster straightened up. "That's where I'm at. I'm thinking, maybe this guy broke his back, but his mouth was still working. Bang-bang, shut him up. The killer used a plastic soda bottle as his silencer. They checked it for prints. Wiped. And now it's not even good for the five-cent deposit."

"What about the Bell Atlantic guy? Was he legit?"

"Nope. Nobody was dispatched. Phony ID. When he screwed around with the phones, he disabled the Meredith alarm system call-out. Looks like he poisoned the Meredith dog so this guy here"—with a spit-shined toe, he pointed to the corpse—"wouldn't have any interference. What they didn't count on was the Rottweiler." Shaking his head, Brewster asked, "Man, can you imagine that Godzilla jumping you in the dark? Which would you take, the broken glass and the long trip down, or the four-legged meat grinder?"

"Might have been the right decision—if not for his pal with the .22. But what I don't get is this: The phone guy was inside in the morning. The Meredith dog died well over twelve hours later. . . . If she was poisoned, how could it be him?"

"Bothered me, too. We had some vets scratching their heads, but it turns out it's possible. Something called Humilin-L. Extremely slow-acting. They're doing an autopsy on the dog. But if that's what they used, they were able to schedule the death to some time after the Meredith woman's ten-o'clock dog walk and then her usual lights out. You can see the bedroom lights from down here, and you can get back here from more than one building on the block . . . if you're a pro."

"And this guy was a pro."

"Look at him—a skinny little shit, the type who can Spiderman his way up and down a wall. See that small ripple-glass bathroom window that's open, next to the one where he played Peter Pan? That's where he got in. Meredith says she was positive it was closed—checked it when she turned on the AC. No way *I* could fit through the opening, and even you would have a hard time. Plus, he had no ID, and all the labels were razored out of his clothes. All that is pro enough for me."

"Yes!" Clay couldn't suppress a smile. He wanted to high-five the guy—his rundown had just unleashed a whole runaway freight train full of connections.

"Detective Ryder," Brewster finally asked, "other than his being dead, what is it about this guy that makes you so damn happy?"

Hickey would have gone nuts if he'd found out that Clay had rushed over to the closed-case apartment just because Rachel Meredith called him, so this was enough to keep him grinning all day. The dead man had to be the finest, the most legitimate link possible to the burglar in the Broyce case. Even though the Hals had been recovered, that robbery-murder was anything but closed, and the DI had already loaned him out to Malenkov on it twice.

"You remember the Broyce deal—the Park Avenue murder-art theft?"

"That big penthouse? About a year ago?"

"You got it. Whoever pulled that wasn't exactly scared of heights, either. Crossed the street from one building to another—twenty flights up, and on a line a lot thinner than your little finger. Lieutenant Malenkov up in the Nineteenth might want a look around here."

"Sure. Give me his number."

"If you don't mind, let me give him yours. We go way back, and we haven't spoken in a while. I see it as a small way to personally bring joy into his day."

As Brewster reached for his card, two men appeared in the super's doorway. "Hey, thanks for showing up," he greeted the body bag crew, as they maneuvered a stretcher through. "Even the corpse asked what was keeping you."

Less than a minute later, a shaken Wil Meredith appeared, escorted by a uniform. He squeezed around the stretcher and rushed up to Clay. "Detective Ryder, I didn't know you were here! I wanted to go right up to Rachel, but the cops in the lobby told me I had to see a Detective Brewster first. My wife—is she all right? I don't understand any of this!"

"I only arrived a little while ago myself, Mr. Meredith. I just spoke with your wife upstairs. She's . . ." Clay searched for the right word, unable to say that Rachel Meredith was all right. "She's unharmed. This is Detective Brewster, from your precinct. He's been on the case since three A.M., so he's way ahead of me."

The two men with the body bag had been blocking their view of the dead man. Grunting, one of the pair bent to position it over the feet. When the corpse's face came into view, Meredith looked away, then snapped his head back and stared. Crime scene bodies always had a raw, unquiet look, unlike their

peaceful, flower-wreathed funeral home counterparts. There was something beyond the usual morbid curiosity in the way he'd fixed on the dead man's face.

The bag's zipper started to buzz upward.

"Hold it!" Clay cried out. The worker was approaching the corpse's neck.
"You, with the damn zipper—stop!" Startled, the guy backed off. "Mr. Meredith, have you ever seen this man before?"

"I'm not sure. I think so."

Clay and Brewster exchanged a glance; both then regarded him with great
interest. "Do you recall anything about that encounter, Mr. Meredith?" asked
Brewster.

"Grauberger—the son," he replied. "I think this man was with him."

Brewster pulled out his notebook. "Could you repeat that name, please?"

Clay answered for Meredith, whose face was flushing an angry red. "Until
about a week or so ago, it was Gregor Grauberger *Junior.* The father just died in
Switzerland. Sonny is about sixty. Swiss art dealer, Galleries Grauberger, Fifty-
seventh Street. He and his father have been after the Van Gogh right from the
start. Very aggressive."

Eyebrows shot up over Brewster's little steel frames. "Mr. Meredith, can
you be more specific—was the deceased *with* this Grauberger, or simply in his
proximity?"

"I'm trying to remember. As soon as the museum exhibit was over,
Grauberger started . . . well, *lurking* around our building. He'd be here at all
hours, double-parked in his Mercedes, and he pounced as soon as he saw me.
The problem is, different people were with him at different times . . . except for
one big thug, who always kept close to him. A bodyguard type."

"Obviously, this was not the big guy," said Clay, glancing down.

"No . . . I think this creep was in the front passenger seat. Grauberger always sat in the back." Meredith bent a little lower, as if a closer look might jog
his memory. He recoiled with a jerk. "Oh, God! He's been shot!"

"Unlike cats, cat burglars don't have nine lives," said Clay. "How many
times did you see him around Grauberger?"

"Once. Just that one time."

"Was your wife with you?" Brewster asked casually.

"It was dusk, I'm pretty sure I was on my way home from the studio, walking down Fifth. . . ." He closed his eyes. "Yes. When I turned onto Ninth, I
could make out the Mercedes, down the block. Coming home from work . . . I
would have been alone." He turned up his hands, an apology for his inability to
recollect anything more. "That's it."

"Okay. That's good. Thank you, Mr. Meredith." Brewster turned to the
tag and bag team. "Gentlemen, zippity-doo-dah." With a snap, he closed his
notebook.

"I'm going upstairs with Meredith—you heading that way?" Clay asked Brewster.

"I want one more look around after they finish here. Go on ahead."

The boiler and utility rooms were on one side of the super's apartment; the laundry room was on the other. Dryers were tumbling clothes, breathing out warm air scented with fabric softener and lightly toasted polyester. Before they reached the elevator, Wil Meredith stopped and turned to Clay. "Detective Ryder, before we go up . . . I still don't understand what happened here."

"I'll do my best to explain, Mr. Meredith, but let's get out of the way before the stretcher comes through." Clay glanced into the laundry room. "There's no one in here."

Four machines took up one wall, four the other, with a table in the center for folding clothes. Meredith leaned against it, blinking at Clay.

He did his best to summarize what had taken place in the Meredith apartment in the last twenty-four hours. "So with the alarm knocked out, Rolf thwarted a well-planned attempt to steal the Trabuc," he concluded, just as the body-bag team jostled past the doorway. Following Meredith's gaze, he looked back over his shoulder, adding, "That's how it ended. And unfortunately, the other casualty was your wife's dog. They think Lulu was poisoned."

"Oh, God! All that dog wanted to do was play!" Meredith put his hand to his forehead, and rubbed it back and forth. "Rachel adored her."

"But if your wife hadn't been in Dr. Corelli's apartment, chances were the burglar might've killed her, too."

Meredith's color drained. "What about me? How did they know I wasn't there?"

"You usually work in the city, right? In your studio?"

"Yes . . . oh, shit!" He blinked, deer-in-the-headlights. "That assignment . . ."

"Your wife said it came up all of a sudden."

"Out of nowhere." His voice was strained and bitter. "A rush job. The client insisted yesterday was absolutely the only day we could shoot. That son of a bitch! 'Reshoot it this way, now try that.' He was stalling until we missed the last plane!"

"Dr. Meredith explained that the job . . . it wasn't exactly your line of work."

"A misunderstanding, I thought. But now it looks like I was—"

"The usual phrase is 'set up.' You away, the dog dead. A lot of trouble, but fifty million makes up for the inconvenience."

"Detective, more than anything, I want to go upstairs and reassure my wife, give her a hug and promise her that everything's going to be okay. But I have the feeling that as long as that painting is up there, that's not going to be the case."

Clay said nothing, but gave Meredith a nod of agreement.

"The Van Gogh . . . at first, I thought of it as a huge and unexpected dividend—one that came along after I married a woman who was pretty incredible to begin with. But we've barely had it in our home two weeks, and this . . . nightmare!" His eyes narrowed. "You think it was Grauberger, don't you? No one's as determined to get his damn hands on that painting as he is! If he knew I was out of town yesterday—maybe even was behind sending me on that shoot—then maybe that wasn't a drunk driver after all!"

"What are you talking about? What drunk driver?"

"Late one night, about a month ago. Phil and I left the studio together, heading toward Fifth. I heard a car coming up behind us, fast enough for me to turn and look back. All of a sudden, it jumped the curb. We both dove for cover behind some garbage cans—the car knocked down half of them, then took off around the corner."

"You called the police, didn't you?"

"Neither of us could see the plates, just that it was some kind of SUV. Its lights were off, and no one else was around. What was the sense of reporting it?"

A clinking sound was coming from the closest dryer, maybe a quarter forgotten in a pocket.

Was the brush with the car a warning? A warning from a man who couldn't comprehend Meredith's respect for his wife's attachment to her grandfather's legacy?

Meredith moved from the table, close to Clay. "It was him, wasn't it? You can't come out and say it, but Grauberger's behind all this, isn't he?" His right hand came up, a threatening, solid fist. "That scuzzy little cocksucker! That despicable black-market bastard! I'll kill him!"

Clay looked down at his fist, then pushed it down firmly with the flat of his hand. "You didn't really mean to say that." His eyes fixed on Meredith's. "Calm down. You're not killing anybody. You're not going to talk to anybody, or make one single accusation. You're going to go upstairs and take care of your wife, and let the police take care of Grauberger. He's a very dangerous man, and he obviously has very dangerous friends."

Or enemies, Clay thought to himself.

That afternoon, Brewster faxed over a photograph of the dead burglar. On a hunch, Clay stopped at Oliver Plumworth's shop, bearing two large coffees. It was the kind of day he couldn't get enough caffeine.

"Terrible! How distressing for Dr. Meredith!" Oliver said, hearing the events of the morning. The creases in his brow deepened. "Being reunited with the painting . . . that was her first good luck in quite a while, was it not?"

"So it appeared."

"And now the painting itself seems to be turning things bad for her."

"Worse than you can imagine, my friend. Anyway, we still don't have a match on the burglar's fingerprints. Europol might have something, but they're not the speediest guys. With all your shady visitors, I wanted you to take a look at his photo."

Oliver didn't flinch at the corpse photo. "No, I've never seen that man before."

Clay stuffed the photo back in his jacket. "Well, Wil Meredith thinks he saw him in Grauberger's car." If he'd blinked, he would've missed Oliver's smile. "That doesn't seem to surprise you."

"You recall my observation that only a few dealers worldwide are capable of brokering artworks that can never appear on the open market?"

"Yet another of your countless pearls of wisdom, my friend."

"Perhaps I have another. Some speculate that at least one of those select, enterprising dealers has taken it yet a step further . . . accommodating collectors who feel a pressing need to fill specific gaps in their collections."

"What are you getting at, Oliver? Dial-a-Picasso?"

"Indeed! The ultimate wish list. Dial-a-Tintoretto, what you will. It might be no more than Dial-a-Rumor, of course."

"Hold on. If Grauberger is that 'enterprising dealer,' he's gone beyond being a middleman. Do you mean he's actually setting up robberies? Stealing paintings on demand?" The door opened, and Clay couldn't tell if Oliver was grinning at

him or at the attractive brunette breezing in. Oliver's revelation and slugging down
the rest of his coffee had certainly perked him up. "If the dead man turns out to be
a bona fide art thief," he whispered, "the gossip wouldn't be gossip anymore."

"And for those with profits to hide," his friend whispered back, "how convenient if a Swiss bank account is but a yodel away."

Clay walked down the parkside of Fifth Avenue, in the mottled shade of
newly leafed out trees. A perfect spring day, the exact opposite of the slushy,
wintry night Rachel Meredith was attacked at NYU. That morning, Wil Meredith's ID of the dead burglar as one of several creeps in Grauberger's employ
made Clay think back to the Tisch assault. Both had been meticulously
planned . . . like Swiss clockwork.

Galleries Grauberger packaged itself like the somber Old Master paintings
that were the mainstay of its business: the floors and wainscoting were chestnut
washed with black stain, to simulate centuries of exposure to wood smoke and
oil lamps. The walls, faintly marbled aubergine covered with layer upon layer of
thick lacquer, closed in the showrooms like ancient bed curtains.

Featured in the main gallery was a Dutch or Flemish flower painting, probably seventeenth century. Out of his period, Clay guessed Jan Brueghel or one of
his contemporaries, simply because he had no more guesses. With coyness that
made his skin crawl, the bouquet in the painting was replicated on a table in the
center of the room, a duplicate shallow wicker basket with the same pink and
white peonies, feathered cream-colored tulips, and blood red carnations. A
middle-aged couple stood before it, gushing over the likeness.

More people than Clay had anticipated were wandering through the
rooms, and, like the couple, they all looked like tourists, albeit Gucci-
accessorized tourists. Many clutched shopping bags from the neighborhood em-
poriums: big FAO Schwarz bags for their grandchildren, little bags from Tiffany
and Cartier for themselves.

"May I help you?" The modulated voice belonged to a tall, slender woman
in a black suit. As per the year's Look, she wore neither stockings nor blouse, and
he detected distinct evidence of a Miracle Bra. In turn, her nose discreetly
screwed up, she was scrutinizing Clay's linen sports jacket as if he'd nabbed it
off one of New York's more fragrant homeless people. Her disdain reminded
Clay of Esterbrook-Grennell—not the most pleasant association.

He pointed at the painting. "Do you think that would work over a plaid
recliner?"

"What's a recliner?" Frosty. Not only a snob, but a humorless snob.

"I'm here to see Gregor Grauberger."

"Pertaining to?" Her thin smile made it clear that she wanted him outside, unsuccessfully dodging traffic in the middle of Fifty-seventh Street.

"Just a minute, while I reach into my non-Armani jacket," He smiled back, matching her warmth. With a great flourish, he produced his gold shield. Ratcheting up his voice several decibels, he repeated, "I'm here to see Mr. Grauberger," then added a booming "NYPD!"

Every head swiveled around, and all the arrogant gatekeeper could do was lead him toward the back as fast as her five-inch heels would carry her. She punched a few numbers into a wall phone, announced the visitor, and huffed off. No good-bye.

After a few minutes, a shadow fell across the space where Clay was waiting. A giant had passed through the closest doorway, but only by ducking his head. This had to be Wil Meredith's big guy, for sure. "You . . . po-lice?"

Clay assumed he'd bypassed English lessons to devote more time to quantum physics. "I am reaching for my shield," he said slowly, "po-lice badge."

A stairway behind the door led up to an open office where men and women worked at computers, a surprisingly large operation. He followed the giant down a long, carpeted hallway. The man waiting at the end was in his mid-thirties. Average height, slim build, just starting to show gray at the temples. Not a remarkable face, except for the heavy, hooded eyelids: the kind of lids that make eyes look sleepy . . . except when they're on a cobra. With minimal movement, he swung open the door to Grauberger's office, then left it open enough to monitor what went on inside.

Ensconced behind an oversize desk that dwarfed him, Grauberger neither rose nor made a motion for Clay to sit. "Detective Ryder, why do you look so familiar?" he asked, as if he expected nothing more than a parking ticket.

"I was with the Merediths at the *Empty Frame* gala. One of the innumerable times you've intruded on their privacy." Grauberger didn't react. "You left some of your garbage in their backyard last night." Clay reached into his jacket and showed him the dead man's photograph.

The dealer's head lowered for a better look. "I have no idea what you're talking about. If this is the only reason you're here, I'm a very busy man."

Clay pointed at his bodyguard. "What's his name?"

"Lothar."

"You have a permit for that gun, Loathsome?"

Grauberger did a snappish translation in German, and Lothar did a quick check to see if his weapon was indeed visible, like a teenager at the prom worried about his erection. He replied in German.

"The permit is in his wallet," the dealer said, bored by the exchange.

With amusement, Clay noted that while Grauberger had a big head on a little body, Lothar's head was markedly undersized for his.

"Tell him to take out the wallet and show it to me with his left hand."

"*Ich verstehe,* boss," Lothar replied. As he lifted his hand to reach into his jacket, Clay examined the web between his thumb and Index finger. No bite marks; of course, they would have had months to heal. He pulled a big, European-style billfold out of his jacket, removed the permit, and held it before Clay's face. His cuff was pulled back slightly; he was fair, but the hair on his wrist stood out against his skin. Clay snatched the permit. "This is for a Walther .380. Where's the permit for the .22?" Clay barked.

"*Kein* .22, only Walther."

Clay held the permit between his own thumb and forefinger, letting it dangle until the bodyguard held out his hand flat to receive it when it dropped. No scars on the palm side, either. Thinking back to the Tisch School's ninth floor, he had serious doubts that Lothar could have mastered its layout. Nor was it likely such a giant would have made it past the security desk unnoticed.

Turning back to Grauberger, Clay said, "The owner of the Pelican Art Gallery down in Florida won't deny that he knows you." That finally raised a flicker in the little man's eyes. "I believe he did you a favor yesterday." He flashed his you-thought-I-was-a-really-stupid-cop grin.

"People everywhere know me—by name. Especially in the art world."

"Oh, I'll bet they do." Once again, Clay displayed the photo. "I'll ask you a second time, Mr. Grauberger. You know him?"

Grauberger made no attempt to disguise his impatience. "Why should I?"

"He's been seen in your company. Outside the Meredith home."

"That's preposterous!"

"Call it what you will, but for nearly a year now, your interest in Dr. Meredith's painting has gone way beyond the norm."

"I'm an art dealer! The United States is a free country, and New York City is not a police state! I have a right to solicit art wherever and whenever I choose!"

"You're harassing those people. A judge might even call it stalking."

"Are you finished, Detective?"

"Not yet, Grauberger. Not before you know that you're about to get a dose of your own medicine." He bent, putting his face square in front of the dealer's. The bodyguard took a cautionary step forward. "From now on, you'll be watched every time you go to *your* apartment, *your* business, *your* appointments. And I'm not the only member of the NYPD who's going to be keeping an eye on you."

Clay retraced his steps to the showroom. He blew the Esterbrook-Grennell type a wet kiss. As he exited, he thought back to the flimsy, makeshift fences separating the yards behind the Merediths' building. It was impossible to imagine someone Lothar's size scaling any of them without bringing them down in a heap. On the other hand, Cobra-eyes could've made the hurdles easily enough. And there was no reason to rule out the possibility that Grauberger had yet another man in his nasty entourage, one who'd simply remained out of sight during his visit . . . the man in the black leather jacket at NYU.

After the synthetic shadows of Galleries Grauberger, the sunshine was blinding. Clay's tired eyes blurred with lurid spots. Most of them were filled by Monsieur Trabuc's watchful, suspicious face. Fatigued as he was, it occurred to him that the head orderly of Saint-Rémy was no stranger to the way cops feel, or come to feel, at one time or another. *We're witnesses to the worst in human nature, and our greatest fear is that worse is yet to come.* Even the swirling paint around Trabuc's head reminded him of a world spinning out of control.

He'd held back on the one question that he'd been itching to ask Grauberger. The timing wasn't right—maybe it never would be.

More than anything, Clay wanted to know if he or his father had ever met Udo Luscher.

CHAPTER
TWENTY-FIVE

Intensive Grauberger-watching commenced immediately. Marcus Brewster and Malenkov coordinated tails that were conspicuous, ubiquitous, and continuous. If nothing else, the effort paid off by keeping Grauberger's crew off Ninth Street.

The autopsy confirmed that the dead burglar survived his desperate leap from Rolf's jaws, only to be executed by the shot from the .22. During the wait for the thief's prints, Brewster showed his picture to the entire staff at Galleries Grauberger, only to be met by blank stares. The single lead he sniffed out came from a tail on Cobra-eyes (his name, on an Austrian passport, was Florian Koors) and Lothar: both were holed up at the same address, a cheap hotel in the West Fifties. "So far west," as Brewster put it, "even the fleas have to take a stagecoach to get there."

A door-to-door of their neighbors didn't turn up anyone who'd seen the burglar, but Brewster persisted. Fanning out, he finally connected when the clerk at another seedy hotel two blocks away gave a nod to the thief's picture. Without any prompting, he groused that "the Frog" had overstayed the three days he'd paid for in advance—in cash, of course—and that he still hadn't checked out. By his calculation, the missing guest owed for an extra night, plus a property storage fee. The property consisted of a nylon carry-on bag with more label-stripped clothes. After viewing surveillance photos of Koors and Lothar, all Brewster could get out of the clerk was, "Maybe I seen them around the neighborhood," an observation with all the sticking power of sugarless gum.

After two days, the dead man's prints were a match with those of Edouard St. Charles, a native of Belgium. His criminal history began young, as a preteen prostitute and drug abuser. He progressed from reform school troublemaker to window washer to circus high-wire performer. By the age of thirty, St. Charles headed Europol's list of suspects in three different art thefts valued at over a million dollars apiece—two in France and one in Germany. (He was suspected of starting out with lesser works in Belgium, but had somehow slipped out of the country without being convicted.)

Clay checked on the three big-ticket paintings with the Art Loss Register. Tapping away at his computer, he eventually concluded that St. Charles had nabbed them from country estates relying on high walls and low-tech security. Discovering that one of the break-ins involved a poisoned dog surprised him not at all. But when he studied the provenance of the Rubens that had been lifted from a retired industrialist outside Mannheim, he wanted to kiss the monitor. The German had purchased the Rubens thirteen years before, from none other than Galleries Grauberger, Zurich. Evidently, one of its many services was providing a database for Dial-a-Theft.

Still wary of giving Hickey anything to stew over, Clay restrained his joy. He had continued to inform the DI the minute he was available for non-art assignments. Hickey seemed to like him for extortion cases—perhaps an expression of how he viewed the Art Guy's paycheck. Among his coworkers, his status was that of the kid who was always picked last, and only when there was absolutely no one else to play right field.

Most of his evenings were spent working on his steamship. After weathering the single smokestack and assembling the pilot house, only decorative details and flags and rigging would be needed to finish the *Shelter Island.* He tried not to think about what he'd do with his time after that. Another ship might not be a good idea . . . it would lead to another, and more after that. A whole fleet, with no rescue in sight.

"I'm really trying," he'd updated Cello. "Things have been on the upswing since the day the whole squad heard Hickey dump on me. It's been slow, but when I look around, I can see the rejection turning to distaste. Hey, after that, who knows? Pity? Maybe someday I'll rise from pariah to outsider . . . if I don't give Hickey an excuse to boot me out first."

"Hickey doesn't like anybody," Cello replied. "He just doesn't like you a little more. You're doing your job. You're not breaking any of the Department's rules." Cello stared at him. "You're not that stupid, are you, Ryder?"

Right after the break-in and a few times after that, Rachel Meredith persisted in inviting Clay for dinner, but he always wriggled out of it. When she called before the last weekend in June, the mechanic had just given him the bad news that his car would be stuck in the shop until the next Tuesday; an out-of-stock part would rob him of his time at The Shack.

"Dr. Meredith, I appreciate the gesture, but accepting an invitation from someone who's connected to a case . . . that's frowned upon."

"But it's been over a year since the case was closed! And I wasn't a suspect, or a victim, or—"

Another phone picked up. Wil Meredith boomed, "Detective Ryder! Please, no more excuses! Saturday—no, Sunday, the twenty-fifth—let us take you out to brunch, lunch . . . whatever! We know it's because of you that we haven't seen that Swiss jerk for weeks! We owe you . . . don't say no!"

"Refuse once more, and we'll find where you live, and drag you out!" his wife threatened.

Grauberger might no longer be a threat as far as the Merediths were concerned, but the man's penchant for carefully choreographing criminal acts well in advance had Clay on constant alert. If the couple made any plans or changes in their lives that might increase their vulnerability, it was important that he find out about them before Grauberger did. Besides, who was going to tell Hickey, anyway? And the Merediths would only keep pestering him until he relented. "Okay," he was answering, "thank you. Sunday will work. How's between twelve-thirty and one?"

"Perfect. Couldn't be better."

As Rachel Meredith welcomed him in, her husband appeared at the other end of the hall. After greeting Clay, he asked, "Rachel, wasn't there a bottle of aspirin in the medicine cabinet?"

"You put back an empty bottle . . . again. I've got it on the shopping list for tomorrow. Same headache-thing as during the week?"

"Same, but worse. Well, there's got to be a store open between here and the restaurant. Between an aspirin and a margarita, I won't feel a thing. Ready?"

"Oh." Her eyes darted between her husband and Clay. "I thought we were going to ask Detective Ryder in for a drink."

"No, I don't want to prolong your husband's agony," said Clay. "Let's take off."

"A second!" She dashed into the room that Clay remembered as her study, then reappeared carrying a circlet of silk flowers, each a different color of the rainbow. Raising it high, coronation-style, she slowly lowered it over her head. It settled over her auburn hair like a May Queen's crown. "It's a canine Hawaiian lei. A couple of years ago, Renny gave it to Lulu to wear to the Gay Pride parade. She never marched, but she wore it every year. She was one hell of an enthusiastic spectator."

"It's not that day, is it?" Clay groaned. "The gay thing?" The disappointed look in her eyes made him quickly counter, "Hey, you're taking that the wrong way. Put on a uniform and do parade duty first."

Her husband dashed to his rescue. "Lighten up, Rachel! I'll take a camera for the lesbian bikers. They're the only women who turn me on—besides you, of course."

Ignoring them both, she dropped her eyes to where her dog would be standing, right by her side. "Renny marches with Rolf every year. He doesn't dress up, but Rolf always wears a costume. This year, he's going as the Tooth Fairy."

Clay wanted to say that the dead cat burglar didn't exactly see Rolf that way, but held his tongue.

"We had a sneak preview," said Meredith. "Giant toothbrush wings and a tiara made of cardboard molars. I'd say old Rolf managed to keep his dignity intact, didn't he, Rachel?"

"Yes, absolutely." His wife looked up, then checked her watch. "We're eating in a great place Wil discovered not too far from his studio. I'm hoping we'll see them along the way."

"Do you feel that? The parade's getting close—I feel the rumble under my feet!"

"Rachel, a chunk of your psyche stopped developing around the age of eight," her husband observed. "But that is part of your charm."

Under a scorching sun, they neared Sixteenth Street, walking along inside interlocking metal crowd barriers that didn't yet have much of a crowd to contain. A woman walked out of the corner store with a Cosmetics Plus shopping bag.

"They're open—terrific!" said Meredith. "I'm going to buy two bottles of aspirin, sweetheart—and I'll never put back an empty bottle again—I swear it!"

Across a Fifth Avenue devoid of traffic and parked cars, Clay took in windowsills and balconies draped with rainbow banners, a show of solidarity with the advancing marchers. He noted that there was a good police presence; like him, the uniforms kept a vigilant eye on the roaming clusters of young men in tank tops and baseball caps. Still a sparse crowd, but a trickle of people kept coming from the side streets. Families with kids in strollers gravitated toward the front of the barricades. Clay wondered if the parents had any idea what was to come.

Like the clowns who warm up the crowd before the official start of the Macy's Thanksgiving Parade, a dozen figures approached from the north, all on rollerblades, all male. Half of them were trailing bunches of balloons—a Gay Pride rainbow mixture—and the rest had sheaves of flyers, which they distributed to spectators every twenty feet or so. Clay guessed the leaflets promoted the gay-lesbian street fair and other West Village events taking place after the parade.

As soon as the crowd got a look at the skaters' costumes, a cheer rippled southward, like the old Wave at ballgames. Three were burly and barrel-chested, with shaved heads—big bullet heads, so bare Clay hoped they'd remembered the sunscreen—and they sported fishnet minidresses (extra-wide fishnet, more striped bass than minnow size). That was it, except for hoop earrings and the rollerblades. Sheer jockstraps were all that protected the six guys carrying the balloons from charges of indecent exposure; other than that, they wore only purple, blue, green, yellow, orange, or red body paint. The remaining three, all brown-skinned, had on feathered collars and codpieces, along with headdresses of radiating gold spikes—the Aztec Sun God Look.

The Merediths and Clay wandered up to the corner of Sixteenth, for a better look uptown. Walkers followed the skaters, some marching, some dancing; all wore platform shoes or boots with the highest heels Clay had ever seen.

"How do they do that without breaking their necks?" Clay asked.

"Forget that," Rachel Meredith replied. "The *pain*! You have no idea!"

"You've got to admit it certainly does something sexy for the shape of the leg," said her husband, focusing his camera.

"Yeah. If you try not to look at their football scars," Clay noted.

Meredith clicked a series of shots of a bald male bride floating by—it was obviously a big year for shaved heads. A half-skirt (the rear half) of white lace, tiered like the layers of a wedding cake, flounced out from just above his butt. He wore white opera gloves and a veil, and carried a bouquet.

Men and women along the route begged, "Throw the bouquet!" A *basso profundo* bridesmaid wannabe implored, "Please! Throw it to me! Let it be me!"

The more northerly spectators were cheering an outfit that was a mass of dryer-vent hoses, sprayed gold. Some were shaped into a Medusa–Star Wars headpiece that was at least three feet tall and four feet wide. Meredith snapped him, then craned his neck to look up the avenue. "Good a time as any to run in for my aspirin—I'll be right back."

Newcomers had quickly filled in the spaces around them. Some were pressing forward, wedging Clay and Rachel Meredith between a wire garbage basket and the base of an aluminum streetlamp. Two free newspaper dispensers also took up the crowded corner: one was a bright magenta plastered with stickers; the other was white, with "The Learning Annex" printed on it. A melon-breasted young woman in a jogging bra and cutoffs was climbing up onto the white one. She reminded Clay of the honey-skinned California girls who used to wave at the SEALs when they ran in full battle gear on Coronado Beach. She offered a hand to her girlfriend, who wasn't bad either, to boost her up onto the other newspaper box. Before reaching out, the friend tilted back her head to finish her can of soda, then tossed it into the garbage basket. It was already two-thirds full with paper and plastic bags, newspapers, a broken umbrella, and most of a Whopper.

"C'mon, Detective Ryder, you've got to applaud the marchers' imagination," Dr. Meredith encouraged him. "You never know what to expect."

"That's why I prefer the Thanksgiving parade. I like knowing Santa will be at the end. A dignified dude in a suit, even if it is red."

"I always cry when I see him."

"*Cry?*"

"That beautiful goose sleigh . . . the big wreath and the reindeer . . . so perfect, so sentimental. It always made me nostalgic for holidays we didn't even celebrate. To be honest, it made me feel sort of—" she stopped abruptly. "God, I thought John Belushi was dead!"

Sure enough, a dark-haired man with Blues Brothers sunglasses was dancing their way, the sun glinting off his towering, multicolored turban. Behind him, the male bikers were crossing Eighteenth Street, their lesbian counterparts bringing up the rear. Orange glitter platforms aside, the guy could have been Belushi's long lost twin. He certainly acted the same—audacious, borderline psychotic, but nevertheless, a likable superextrovert. Between his frantic boogie and the temperature, his chipmunk cheeks were overheated to a feverish crimson. He was dressed in a short, big-shouldered bolero top and a scant bikini bottom, both covered with masses of sequins the size of half-dollars in every color of the rainbow. In between, his belly was completely exposed. It was big and round, but looked hard as a medicine ball, a still-youthful beer drinker's gut. Without cease, he alternated between caressing, squeezing, and spanking it. At the same time, his twinkling feet did snazzy cha-cha moves, mambo steps, and meringue slides; he was a swaying, swinging, one-man conga line. From his knees to his platforms, his legs were also covered with sequins, and the clatter of the metallic discs grew louder with every approaching step.

"There he is! Hey, Bobby! Wave to us, Bobby!" a deep voice above Clay's head called out. Clay turned. The California girl's melons were definitely imported. A faint patch of stubble was visible on her friend's chin. "Ooooh! Bobby!"

The man in the sequins heard them, looked up, wiggled his hips as a greeting, and began to shimmy toward the curb. His buddies jumped down off the newspaper boxes and rushed up to the metal barricade. Clay and Rachel turned sideways, to give them room. Giggling, the pair leaned over the metal frame, throwing big, slurpy kisses to Bobby-Belushi. In no time, they'd firmly wedged their way between Clay and Rachel Meredith and the wire trash basket.

Without warning, a roar erupted, a thunderclap so painfully loud, Clay's every nerve reverberated with it. An eerie silence accompanied the brief sensation of the sidewalk ripping and churning beneath his feet, just as a mighty rush of air rocketed him off the ground.

Shiny blue, green, and purple sequins were flying all around him, but they suddenly all turned one color.

A thick, wet red.

CHAPTER
TWENTY-SIX

A woman in a white doctor's coat brushed by Clay's gurney. Seconds later, she went by in the opposite direction, and he knew that the fresh smear of blood on her coat had come from him. Clay tried to tell her about the knife cutting into his back, but no sound came out. Nor was sound coming from anyone or anything in the chaotic room—he was surrounded by the grim silence of a deep dive, without the pressure. The pressure would have squared the silence, countered the commotion raging inside his head.

Two aides jostled him, pushing through a gurney with California Girl's unconscious friend. His skin, wherever it wasn't bloodied, was ash-gray. Triage. If they were taking more serious cases ahead of him, maybe he wasn't in such bad shape after all. He lifted his head to locate Rachel Meredith, but the silence grew black, and it pulled him under.

The next time he opened his eyes, a woman's face was directly above his. Her lips were moving, and she was doing something annoying—lightly slapping his cheek. Even though Clay felt groggy, the throb in his head was sharp, and her insistent little smacks were making it worse. That was reason enough to tell her to go fuck herself. Her response was a grin and a gentle, reassuring pat on the shoulder. By the time he formed the words to ask where Rachel Meredith was, she'd hustled away. Lots of beds were in the area, all connected to machines. A recovery room—but a recovery from what? At least nothing was jabbing into his back anymore, and his fingers and toes were still attached—concentrating long enough to count all twenty was a colossal effort. He remembered where they'd stopped to watch the parade, which meant he had to be in St. Vincent's Hospital. Without the woman striking his face, staying awake was impossible.

He woke in a small room. The light was dim. Another woman was leaning over him. He said, "Hi, Mom," but no sound came out. Later, the mayor was at his bedside. He held up two fingers, pointed at Clay, then himself. Right. The second time he'd visited him in a hospital room.

By Monday afternoon, his head was a lot clearer, the pain intermittent. Doctors and nurses shuttled through, checking his IV, holding bright lights in front of his eyes, probing and poking every part of him. When they spoke, he strained to hear, eyes squeezed shut, as if that could pull their words through the brick walls in his ears. Later, when a nurse looked in on him, he made writing motions.

She smiled, disappeared, and came back with a pad and pencil.

How's Rachel Meredith? he wrote.

You both have concussions and multiple lacerations, the nurse wrote. *She had metal fragments removed from both eyes—whites only. Broken wrist. Should be OK.*

How's her husband?

He was in here a little while ago. Don't you remember?

Clay shook his head.

Released. Shoulder in a sling. Minor cuts. Don't you want to know about you?

My bra is killing me.

The nurse tilted her head back and laughed, but he couldn't hear it. All her movements were smooth and graceful, and with her reddish brown skin and amber eyes, she had to speak with a lilting Caribbean accent. *Two cracked ribs,* she wrote. *No physical damage to your ears. A huge shard of glass was removed from your back, very close to your spine. PS—Someone was here before I came on duty and left this.* She handed him a copy of the *Daily News,* and pointed to a scrawl near the masthead.

They say you're going to be okay, Ryder. See you tomorrow—Martino.

The mere sight of Cello's name reminded him he was starved. *When's lunch or supper or whatever's coming up next?*

Smiling, she raised a hand, fingers splayed, for "five minutes," and took off.

Clay glanced down at the front-page headline:

BOMB AT GAY PRIDE PARADE KILLS 3
12 SERIOUSLY INJURED

The accompanying photograph showed rubble where the front of the Cosmetics Plus once stood. Inside, the article explained that a bomb powerful enough to destroy the store's facade and part of its interior had exploded in a curbside wire trash basket. As a precaution, the parade was immediately ended, and marchers and spectators disbanded along side streets. The entire parade route was sealed by the police. With the help of bomb-sniffing canines, they discovered another bomb in a trash basket six blocks away, at Fifth and Tenth.

The dead were Robert Brevetto (Bobby, the Belushi-man), Roy Warrenton (California Girl, a.k.a. Cindy), and Germaine Krasner, an exiting customer. A female police officer who'd been directing crosstown traffic on the corner was in critical condition; Ted Trumbell (most likely California Girl's friend) wasn't expected to live.

Clay put his head back on the pillow and closed his eyes. The bomb had been in the garbage basket. The garbage basket had been so close, he'd brushed up against it several times. By pushing up to the barricade to greet Bobby Brevetto, the two transsexuals, poor bastards, had created a buffer zone for him and Rachel with their bodies. The reporter implied that separating two packs of hamburger mushed into a meat loaf would be easier than distinguishing between Bobby's and Cindy's remains. Clay lay still for a while, then finished the account. The rest consisted of statements from gay activists decrying the violence, quotes from the police commissioner and mayor about the breadth of the investigation, and a brief history of the parade and the Stonewall Riot that was its genesis.

Smiling, the graceful nurse returned, disconnected his IV, and wheeled it away. Clay was starved; he hadn't eaten since Saturday night. Skipping Sunday breakfast, he'd worked out and hit the Academy pool before meeting the Merediths. After a short wait, an aide with a tray balanced on one hand walked in, Deputy Inspector Hickey right on his heels. Hickey took charge, centering the tray on the wheeled, over-the-bed table. When they were alone, he touched his forehead—an informal, encouraging salute. Only too well did Clay remember how the DI had ignored his cervical collar and black eyes the previous summer. Had too many higher officials put Hickey on the spot, asking how his detective was doing? Or did the old man have a well of compassion to draw from as long as his Crown Vic wasn't involved?

Grabbing his notepad, Clay wrote, *Any leads on the bombing?*

Hickey was a slow, careful writer. Acknowledging Clay's impatience, he fed him one sentence at a time:

Express mail timed to reach all metro newspapers this AM.

Responsibility claimed by Society To Retaliate Against Indecent Gay Homosexual Trash.

That's S.T.R.A.I.G.H.T.—get it?

Their charter date is October 16th—10/16.

Bombs were at Tenth and Sixteenth.

But the president of S.T.R.A.I.G.H.T. denies their involvement.

Clay immediately responded: *What do you think?*

Hickey pointed to the ceiling, which Clay interpreted as, "God only knows!"

What kind of bomb? he scribbled. This was the best conversation with his boss he'd ever had.

Hickey shaped a C with two fingers, then held up four, for C4, a moldable plastic explosive much favored by the military—and terrorist groups. Then he wagged a finger at the tray, a command to eat, get healthy, and get back to work—maybe even Art Guy work.

The turkey and vegetables differed only in color; their taste and texture put him in mind of an overused kitchen sponge, but he was too hungry to care. Using a straw, he drained the little carton of milk. The scratchy, sputtering gurgle of the straw as it pulled up air instead of liquid was a relief—the first postbomb sound he could hear.

His eyes felt heavy again, and he closed them for only a moment, wondering if Hickey would jot down *What the hell were you doing with the Merediths?* or if he'd wait for his hearing to return, so he could scream it at him, full-throated and crimson-faced.

Next time he looked around, the light in the room had turned golden, and the DI was gone. Wil Meredith was in the open doorway, his left shoulder in a cloth sling and his left cheek covered by a gauze square. Gauze was also taped onto the back of his left hand, no doubt a defensive wound: Clay imagined him holding it up to shield his eyes against the glass hurtling into Cosmetics Plus. His shirt and khakis looked fresh and pressed, as if he'd recently returned from a shower and change of clothes back at the apartment.

"How's your wife?" Clay asked, holding up the notepad.

Uncomfortable. Can't wait to get the bandages off her eyes on Wednesday. Are you OK?

A few stitches. Sore shoulder, but the X rays say it's OK. I keep getting the shakes, thinking what could've happened.

"Me, too," Clay said. His voice was like the fading back-end of an echo, but it was there. "As soon as they let me get up, I'll visit her. Where's her room?"

Meredith pointed to the hall, and kept jabbing his finger—the end of the corridor.

In the evening, Clay was given permission to walk around his room. Two nurses braced him on either side. A few laps back and forth didn't stretch his legs much, and he steered the nurses out into the hall. He ached all over, but his ribs weren't as painful as he'd expected. The last time he dropped from such a height, he'd been attached to a parachute.

Twenty feet away, diagonally across from his room and directly across from the elevators, loomed the nurses' station, a large, high desk. Two outsize mirrors on sturdy chrome mounts that would've looked sharp on an eighteen-wheeler were at either end; they gave the duty nurse long views down the hallway to the left and right. The nurse on watch was frowning at his reflection in the right mirror, maybe because he was taking too much of a hike. His nurse-walkers tried to lead him back, but he wanted more of a look around. Shaking her head in disapproval, the duty nurse returned to her paperwork. Behind her, in a glass-enclosed inner office, another nurse checked over a tray of medications. The elevators were flanked by fire-stair doors, and Clay made the farthest one his goal, but it was a struggle. Getting to Rachel Meredith's room would be like running the marathon. *Mañana.*

Every part of the breakfast that appeared a little after seven on Tuesday was watery: the juice, the tea, the poached eggs. When Oliver Plumworth sneaked in with a bag from a neighborhood patisserie, Clay practically ripped it out of his hands. The aroma of fully caffeinated coffee and something buttery and fresh from the oven was irresistible; his sense of smell was definitely over-compensating for his hearing difficulties.

"I was here yesterday morning, Clayton," his old friend explained in a clear, loud voice, "but you were asleep. You didn't even stir when they wheeled your chariot off to do tests. Sunday's event was horrible, horrible." He pointed to his watch. "My apologies, but I won't be able to stay as long as I would like to-day. I have an appointment at the shop with an enchantingly pulchritudinous young lady. Her husband—a man twice her age, who, I regret, is nearly half mine—will also be in attendance."

"It's the thought that counts, Oliver. At least I'll have one decent meal to-day."

Fortified by Oliver's croissants, Clay managed to walk him to the elevator, rest a bit, and continue on to Rachel Meredith's room. He arrived a little spacey—that concussion had rented a room in his head, after all—and he grate-fully accepted her husband's chair. While Clay regained his equilibrium, he as-sessed her condition.

She looked limp, as if the bomb had blown her right onto the bed, all the way from Fifth and Sixteenth. Big pads shaped like aviator glasses were taped over her eyes, and her left wrist was in a cast. Dressings covered most of her arms and neck.

"Dr. Meredith? It's Clay Ryder."

She stirred, and turned her head toward the chair. "It's really you?" Her voice was weak and groggy, and he moved his ear closer to her mouth. "Oh, that's wonderful! I thought you . . . that they weren't telling me . . ."

"I'm okay."

"And Wil . . . is he just putting up a front? Is he really all right?"

"He looks good to me, but your patches are coming off tomorrow—hang around, and you'll be able to see for yourself."

"But he's not making any sense. He wants us to move . . . out of the city! With him so close to the studio . . . and me practically next door to school!"

"I only urged her to consider it," Meredith countered. He moved closer to the bed. "For safety's sake. I didn't mean to upset you, darling."

"But it's not the *city*! It's my own personal black cloud! It can follow me to New Jersey . . . Connecticut . . ." She was starting to drift. "It covers the entire Tri-State Area."

"At least think about a vacation," her husband persisted.

She lifted her wrist. "Tennis, anyone?"

"You'll be swimming in a month. Anyplace you want to go. Promise?"

"Okay," she slurred, "surprise me."

"Fly me to the moon, on the twenty-fifth of June . . ." a voice sang directly into Clay's ear. "NOW HEAR THIS! NOW HEAR THIS! Picasso landed on his ass-o! You in there, Ryder? Guess who?"

"Hi, Cello." Clay opened his eyes. He'd dozed off when he returned from Rachel Meredith's room, and hadn't heard his lunch tray arrive. Rhonda Martino was lifting the lid with one finger and scrunching her nose, as if she'd poked it into a bedpan. "Rhonda! You too! Hey, I feel better already!"

She pecked him on the cheek and spoke close to his ear. "I'm glad you didn't eat. I brought a big homemade vegetarian hero. It's to die for." She pointed to the yard-long object wrapped in silver foil she'd deposited on the air-conditioning unit. Rhonda's hair was a couple of shades too red, but the brass was offset by a sweet face. How she managed to stay so trim while living under the same roof with Cello ranked as a major Unsolved Mystery.

"What's in it?"

"Crispy Italian bread dotted with minced garlic, drizzled with extra virgin olive oil and balsamic vinegar. It's topped with grilled zucchini and plum tomatoes, mozzarella, and the first fresh basil from my garden."

"Sounds fantastic."

"It's the best," Cello confirmed. "It goes better with beer, but we brought a six-pack of Coke instead." With a pious upward roll of the eyes, he crossed himself. "After all, this *is* St. Vincent's." He pulled the soda and several newspapers out of a supermarket bag. "Today's papers, too."

"Hey, this is great! And Cello—thanks for stopping by yesterday." He winked at Rhonda. "Lady, how about coming back tonight with one of those little hibachis? Grill me some pinwheels."

"What, and spoil you for all other women forever? You're still the only eligible bachelor around, my dear Claytini." She pulled paper plates out of the bag and headed for the windowsill.

"When I came here yesterday, I thought you'd be all cut up," said Cello. Like someone played tic-tac-toe on you. You don't look so bad."

"Clay is like a chambray shirt," Rhonda called over her shoulder, "he gets better and better with age."

Clay laughed, then gestured for Cello to bend lower still. "What's going on? Was it those S.T.R.A.I.G.H.T. guys?"

Cello shook his head, a disgusted look on his face. "Frankly, I don't see those pathetic jerks toasting a marshmallow without setting themselves on fire. They're all from Staten Island, have a rally in a dinky little park there every October sixteenth, and they write the newspapers about gay conspiracies in Hollywood and on Wall Street. In their book, Washington is A.C.–D.C., and all wrestlers and quarterbacks are queer.

"Monday morning, they all go to work like nothing happened. The papers get the express letters, and shazam! they're all arrested. But they're all yelling that they're innocent. Plus, it's checking out that most of them spent the weekend with their kids at a Little League tournament in south Jersey. Why pay twelve bucks a letter to say, 'I did it!' and then say, 'Whoops! Wrong hate group!'? Sorry, wrong number."

"Then who?"

"Hey, it's not my case! I just think the S.T.R.A.I.G.H.T. men were straight men for someone else's sick trick."

Rhonda came back with a big hero wedge. After one bite, Clay asked her to leave Cello and marry him, but she turned him down.

Clay napped, read Cello's newspapers, slept some more. Wil Meredith stopped by, and they trekked down the hall for another visit to his wife, who was less disconnected. Not at all fatigued by the walk, he made it back on his own. His hearing popped on and off, the way it did if he didn't shake all the water out of his ears after a swim. Little by little, it was more on than off.

While he was away, his supper tray had been delivered. Figuring it was cold anyway, he turned on the six-o'clock news. He only had to turn up the volume a couple of notches to hear. Closing his eyes, he stretched out and enjoyed the sound, commercials and all.

He even heard the click when someone shut off the TV with the remote that was inches from his fingertips. Grabbing the retreating hand, he held it tight, although his grip was more mush than muscle. He opened his eyes. "You shouldn't sneak up on people like that."

"Just checking your reflexes—not bad. Now for your intuitive power. What would I bring you, all the way across town?" Aaron held up a white paper bag.

"Pastrami on rye?"

"I would schlep ham on Wonder Bread so far?" Holding the hospital food tray as far from his body as possible, Aaron removed it from the room. When he returned, he carefully closed the door.

After Clay took his first bite, the Mossad agent said, "I've got an art thing."

"It's been a long time."

"I warned you it wouldn't happen overnight." Aaron poked a straw into a can of Coke and handed it to Clay. "And once we found out what we were dealing with . . . frankly, if not for Eli, we would have dealt ourselves out. The guy in question is more than an incredibly wealthy businessman with a yen for art."

"They usually don't stop at one dirty habit."

"That's not exactly what I meant. The guy owns several legitimate businesses—finance, real estate, manufacturing—but he's been a Yakuza kingpin for decades. No matter how many millions he's put into his collection, it was only petty cash to him."

"Yakuza—the Japanese Mafia?"

"Don't you love the way that almost rhymes with *mezuzah*? Even in good years, they're boys who don't play nice. With the bad economic situation over there, they're nastier than ever about protecting their turf: sex, gambling, extortion, smuggling—of human beings, as well as merchandise. All I'll say is that it took us three agents before we could penetrate the subject's security. The last one had to go very deep. You're a detective. You'll want to ask questions. *Don't.* Some I can't answer. The rest, I won't."

"The agent is still inside?"

"Yes. No way we'll compromise such a valuable operative."

"It's between you and me and Eli, the way it's been from the start," Clay reassured him. "You have my word."

Aaron stared at him for a long time. "Okay. It wasn't easy, but our agent finally made it into the private art gallery. The *secret* art gallery. They were there."

"They?"

"Monsieur Trabuc. And Madame. Together, like Mickey and Minnie. 'Cécilie' on the back of Madame's canvas. Nothing on Monsieur's."

Clay bolted forward. "My God! That means . . ."

"Remember you're in a hospital bed, my friend—take it easy! You said Monsieur was offered in the early Seventies."

"My source placed it around that time. Aaron, what you just told me means that somebody sold Hashimoto a fake!"

"I never said that name."

"So that's what this is about! A hood who was hoodwinked! No more matched set! He's pissed! He's ballistic!"

"I've brushed up on art forgers lately. An interesting line of work. One that takes great patience, in more ways than one. I learned that fakes of certain artists take much longer to cure than others." He pointed at the pickle that came with Clay's sandwich. "Like a sour, versus a half-sour. A Van Gogh forgery, for example, is a sour-sour. Up to ten years! Did you know that?"

"Aaron, will you get to the point! You're driving me nuts!"

"You strapping on your gun and going somewhere, cowboy?"

Clay leaned back on the raised bed. "Yes," he sighed, "I've heard of cases where an insurance appraiser stuck a pin in an alleged Van Gogh, and it came out wet. Lots of Impressionist and Post-Impressionist works look as if the paint went on with a trowel. They take forever to dry."

"And Van Gogh wasn't one to chintz on the paint. Maybe because his *meshuga* brother was paying for it." He shrugged. "Some of his paintings look like a bagel with a heavy *schmeer*."

"Okay. You've done your homework, Aaron. Ten years to safely age a Van Gogh. Early Seventies. Take away ten years, and you're in the early Sixties."

"Coinciding with the Eichmann extraction. Think about it. All the Nazis are nervous, worrying about escape hatches. Worrying how safe their money is under the old SS mattress. Ah, that got your attention. Go on, eat."

Clay obliged as Aaron continued: "A very short list of world-class forgers was operating then. The one acknowledged to be the best was a Spaniard. Lived all over Europe, but his real home was his mother's house on Minorca. Ever been there?"

"No. It's supposed to be a pretty place."

"Not bad. At any rate, in the late Fifties our forger got into trouble. Seems a big London auction house bought from him regularly. They neglected to age one of his fakes long enough, and got caught by the old pin trick. Naturally, they fobbed the blame off on him. He slipped out of London one step ahead of Interpol."

"Hid out with mom on Minorca?"

"Right. By the time Interpol tracked him there two years later, he'd been gone for months. Several locals remembered he left with an extremely attractive woman. A tourist from South America."

"Never surfaced again?"

"Not a trace."

"The raid—Eli and his brother—that was '71. The forger disappeared—what?—around ten years before? It fits!"

"It's promising," Aaron agreed.

"Luscher's aware the Nazi hunters could turn up any time. He hires the forger to make a copy of the Trabuc. As soon as he puts down his brush, *Le Découpeur* strikes—and now only Luscher knows there's a Van Gogh and a faux Gogh."

"What about Madame Trabuc?" asked Aaron.

"If he still had her then, she would've been copied, too. My gut is that he was forced to sell her earlier, either to get out of Europe, or set himself up in South America. Luscher was smart enough to figure the collector who wound up with Madame would snatch up Monsieur if he ever popped up on the black market. So Luscher had the forgery on hand—an insurance policy for the day he needed cash quick. Like after the raid on Córdoba."

"Assuming this forger was all that good."

"Museums make mistakes all the time," said Clay, "but they don't exactly advertise it. Let's say Hashimoto—"

Aaron winced.

"Let's say this mystery collector employed the expert of experts to check the Monsieur. A world-class forger would've used a period canvas and made his own pigments. The copy could've slipped by. Twenty-five plus years ago, they didn't have the precision testing they do today. Plus—very important—if Trabuc was being brokered by a prestigious dealer, that had to carry a lot of weight. Even more, if that dealer was the same one who sold the collector Madame Trabuc."

"That's pretty good for a guy with a concussion. Now finish your sandwich."

As Aaron cleared everything away, Clay confided, "All this pretty much convinces me that the Trabucs were the only two paintings Luscher had when he left Paris. That has to be why he pursued Paul Bergère so relentlessly. It was more than a month after D-Day, and he was running out of time. Plus, the names on his art gallery lists—those Parisians with art to sell—many were likely to have been in bed with the top Nazis . . . sometimes literally. That was the only juicy thing I turned up at the Jeu de Paume. In July of '44, a woman had a painting stolen while she was brought in for questioning about Resistance activity. It turned out that the woman was a German general's mistress, a well-known couturière. She was released immediately. The incident had Udo's fingerprints all over it, but the painting was listed as recovered two days later."

"I've heard about her affair," Aaron confirmed. "Whenever I see those matching initials of hers in the fashion ads, I think they should read 'SS' instead." He reached inside his jacket and pulled out a small, square envelope, the kind invitations come in. "I didn't forget dessert." He extracted several photographs from the envelope. "Here. This is what we've got." His eyes stayed on Clay's face as he flipped through the photos. "Are you having multiple orgasms?"

"They're coming too fast to count." Clay went through the pictures backward, forward, backward again. He laid the Trabucs side by side on his blanket. Monsieur appeared to be an impeccable copy. Beneath them, he placed a photograph of the same Rubens that the art thief Edouard St. Charles was suspected of robbing from a German industrialist, the one that listed Galleries Grauberger in its provenance. An Ingres portrait he remembered from his search of the Art Loss Register's files, stolen in the early Eighties, floated down next to it. The Grauberger name was in its history as well. "These two," Clay said, "the Rubens and the Ingres—"

Aaron smiled. "I know—Grauberger."

"Had to be! When the lost Trabuc turned up in New York, there was lost face in Japan. Grauberger was expected to remedy the situation."

"His father's dive down an Alp was a warning. And he's still getting daily reminder visits from the Yakuza. Our Swiss friend is trying to outski an avalanche."

"So where do you come out on all this?" asked Clay. "What about Eli, and his closure? Is he still looking for a Luscher connection?"

"The current situation—the collector's vendetta against the dealer—seems to have finally ruled Luscher out . . . either as a player or as a survivor. Nearly thirty years have gone by since Córdoba, without a single attempt to sell the genuine Van Gogh. Eli's resigned to giving up as soon as our agent is safely extracted. I think he's finally convinced Japan was his last wild goose chase after Luscher." Aaron slumped back in his chair. "What about *you*, Ryder? You think Luscher's finally out of the game?"

"Luscher. With Eli, it was personal." *With me, my grandfather's personal. And the only difference between Luscher and my grandfather is that Luscher has a rap sheet.* "But I'll take these pictures in his place any day. Think of all the art they'll bring back into the daylight again. Plus, they're going to put Grauberger and all his black-market cronies out of business. I'm not exactly going out of this empty-handed."

"You make me awful nervous about our agent, the way you drooled over those photos."

"I swear, Aaron. I won't do a thing until you let me know she's out."

"How do you know it's a she?"

Clay winked. "I can almost smell her perfume."

Clay had a hard time falling asleep that night, but indigestion was only part of it. Finally, he drifted into a dream. He was seated across from Aaron at a stone chess table in Washington Square Park, trying to build a house of cards with the photos from Japan. Taking turns, each of them came close, but every time the last picture was added, the structure collapsed. Clay's turn came up again, and in the split second he released the final photo, a woman's scream rang through the hall.

Instinctively, he reached over to the nightstand for the gun that wasn't there. Forgetting that his hospital bed was higher than the one in his apartment, his feet hit the floor hard, and pain speared straight up to his bandaged ribs. Once out of his room, he saw nurses and orderlies converging past the elevator, at the far end of the hallway.

All of them were running toward Rachel Meredith's room.

Moving at a pace that was maddeningly slow, he chased after them. As he passed the nurses' station, he noticed a wall clock that read one-thirty, not too far along into the night shift. No one was at the desk.

A gray-haired nurse was sprawled out on the floor, half in and half out of Dr. Meredith's room. She was the screamer. "Her IV! Her IV!" she kept shouting. Patients who could walk were leaning out of their doorways. Some gaped at the confusion; several looked terrified.

A young Asian nurse bent over the nurse on the floor, struggling to calm her and move her while other members of the hospital staff stepped over her like a rain puddle. While Clay was still making his way down the corridor, a hospital security guard finally pulled her out of their way. The Asian nurse got down on the floor, the guard propped the hysterical nurse's head in her lap, and then he rushed back into Rachel Meredith's room.

Clay didn't follow him inside; people in white had the bed surrounded, and the security man was wheeling an IV stand into a corner.

The nurse supplying the lap ordered Clay to get away from the doorway. "You shouldn't be here! Go right back to your room!"

"Look, Nurse," he bristled, "I'm a cop first, a patient second—is that clear? I'm not going anywhere, even if I don't happen to have my shield right now." He pointed to the woman on the floor. "How about calming her down, so I can find out what the hell's going on?"

Her eyes widened, but she clamped her hand over the other nurse's mouth. White-stockinged legs instantly thrashed out in protest "Patty, stop! It's Irene! Patty, this patient is a policeman. He needs your help! Tell him what you saw!"

Patty gradually stopped resisting, and the hand over her mouth was removed. She gasped, "I never saw him before! The stairs . . . not right . . . so I went to look. The patient's IV bag—he was putting something in it!"

"Okay, Patty." Clay's voice was low, encouraging. "You did great. They already took the IV out. It's *out.* But you're the only one who saw him, and we need to know what he looks like, so he doesn't hurt anyone else."

"A doctor. He was a doctor. One I never saw before."

"White coat?"

She nodded. "And a stethoscope."

One question at a time, Clay learned that the man was probably Hispanic, medium height, and wore glasses. He was wearing an ID tag, but she hadn't been able to make it out.

"You're sure he was medium height? He couldn't have been over six feet?"

"My husband's six-two. I can tell. No."

"What did you mean before, about the stairs? Where were you?"

"At the desk," Irene volunteered. "She's duty nurse tonight."

"You saw him in the mirrors?" Clay asked, "coming from the stairs?"

"That's it, yes."

"You said 'the stairs . . . not right.' You meant the left stairway?"

"No, no!" she shook her head impatiently, "I meant the doctors and interns always take the *elevators*. A doctor taking the stairs—*that* wasn't right." Trying to explain how illogical the situation appeared to her seemed to have a calming effect. "No reason for him to be there. The floor was quiet right from the start of the shift—no alarms, only a few requests for pain medication. And then, when I saw him in the mirror, the way he looked both ways . . . I went to have a look. I walked in behind him—he was fiddling with the IV—and I said, 'Excuse me, Doctor, is something wrong?' You know what he did?" Outraged, Patty lifted her head from Irene's lap. "He hit me! Knocked me down! Jesus knows what I broke! I started screaming, and he ran!"

The security guard who'd pulled Patty out of the way had been listening from Rachel Meredith's doorway. His nametag read Riverton, and he was young and shy. Without coming any closer, he said, "Everyone inside thinks he was trying to mix another bag in with her IV, but dropped it when Nurse O'Connell came in. They're hoping the patient will be okay."

"Thank you. That answers a lot of questions." Clay had been leaning over Nurse Patty, and his ribs were aching. Slowly, he straightened up. "Mr Riverton, I need your help. Two things."

The young man nodded.

"First, secure that bag. Second, get hospital security posted outside this room. A police officer will take over ASAP."

"I hope someone called down to Emergency for Nurse O'Connell," Irene piped in. "She has to be X-rayed."

"I called," Riverton replied. "They're probably still holding the elevators while they search, but I'll double check."

"Thanks, Riverton," Clay called after him. "And thank you, Patty. I hope you check out fine."

"Me, too. Lord, I don't want to be a patient here—the food is awful!"

All Clay wanted was to crawl back into bed, but he hobbled to the glass-enclosed office behind the nurses' station and picked up the phone. The calls to the police were easy. Being a patient, he asked the head of hospital security to come to him. Then he took care of the hard part—calling Wil Meredith.

Meredith was half-asleep when he picked up. As Clay began to explain what had happened, he exploded and slammed down the receiver.

Conferring with the security chief occupied Clay for about fifteen minutes. Moving as fast as he could, he made his way back to Rachel Meredith's room.

"How are you doing?" he asked. "It's Clay Ryder again."

"No one will tell me what's going on! That screaming! I thought another patient was in trouble—then all those people rushed in here. I still don't understand! Did you call Wil?"

"He's on his way."

"If only I could see . . . then things wouldn't be half so damn confusing!"

Her husband burst into the room and rushed to her side. Once she assured him that her condition hadn't changed since he'd left a few hours earlier, he kissed her on the forehead and ushered Clay out into the hall.

"Enough of this!" he said between clenched teeth. "I can't believe it's happened again! You—the police—were supposed to stop this!"

"A police officer will be here any minute to guard her room."

"Really? And what about the next executioner Grauberger sends in dressed as a doctor? How's your cop going to know the difference?"

"He'll know. And when your wife goes home, we'll keep your building under surveillance."

Meredith's eyes narrowed. "Locking the barn after the horse runs away?"

"You're right. I'm not making excuses. I should have seen it coming. Listen, until I'm discharged, I can only do things by phone. But I can guarantee that if Mr. Grauberger isn't being questioned as we speak, someone will be knocking on his door very soon."

Thankfully, the uniform arrived, and Clay said good night. He couldn't wait to get back to his room, but not to sleep.

Maybe things weren't all that they seemed. Maybe someone had taped gauze pads over his eyes, too.

CHAPTER
TWENTY-SEVEN

Rachel Meredith was ten minutes late, and the restaurant was only three short blocks from her building. Under his breath, Clay cursed his failure of judgment. Although it was still light out, he never should have let her walk there unaccompanied.

Even before his release from the hospital, he'd dug right in, determined to probe all his hunches, no matter how unpromising or unlikely. He still didn't have all the answers, but the information that had finally started flowing to him in the last few days was chilling. And Grauberger's race against the clock set ticking by the Hashimoto gang was only part of it.

Just as he was about to signal the waiter that he was leaving, Rachel Meredith walked in. Clay stood up so that she could see him. He'd asked for the last booth in a dimly lit rear corner, as far from the dinner crowd as possible. While the maître d' led her back, Clay's eyes shifted from her to the door. Except for the cast on her wrist, she appeared fully recovered. About a month had passed since Gay Pride Day, and their only contact—polite inquiries about one another's recuperation—had been by phone.

"Detective Ryder, I apologize for being late," she said, easing onto the bench. "A fellow instructor called the second before I keyed in the last number of the alarm code. She was out of town last month, and just found out about the parade . . . the bomb. I had to reassure her that I was one of the lucky ones."

"No problem," he lied. "How are you doing?"

"Better every day. I can see clearly. I started running again this week. But I can't swim until this beast comes off." She held up her cast. "Monday at eleven-thirty. I can't wait. It itches like crazy."

"You need a knitting needle."

"For what?"

"Scratching. Nothing beats a knitting needle for getting under a cast. I speak from experience. I broke my ankle when I was nine. The only problem is, where do you find a knitting needle in Manhattan these days?"

"That's easy. Angelina knits."

"The cleaning lady, right? You worked that out? The way it sounded, you had to bodily snatch her away from the other people she works for."

"They finally relented. We all have to let her go eventually, because she's retiring soon. Hard to believe, after all these years. She's been staying with me Monday through Friday, in the guest bedroom."

"That has to be a big help."

"You have no idea! Otherwise, all the things I can't do with one hand would pile up until Wil comes home and . . ." She averted her eyes. "Thanks to her, that doesn't happen."

"Speaking of your husband—where is he tonight?"

The waiter stopped by their table with a basket of warm bread. After a brief consultation, he went off after a bottle of wine.

"Wil's been involved with a youth group up in Harlem recently—a photography workshop for disadvantaged kids. It's held in a church on Thursday evenings. When you called, you said it was important we meet right away—so he's there and I'm here."

The waiter returned with the wine. As he uncorked it, Clay told him, "We won't be ordering for a while, Ray."

"That's fine, Mr. Ryder. You and the lady, enjoy the wine."

"Sounds like you're a regular here," she said, as the waiter headed off to a table near the front. With one hand, she worked at breaking off a piece of bread. "I must have passed this place a thousand times. Funny, how some places pull you in, and others just don't register." She looked around. "But there's a good feeling in here. I bet the food is good, too."

"A neighborhood secret." He'd frequented the restaurant ever since he moved into his apartment, but it was the first time in more than two years he'd been there with a woman. Clay motioned toward her wrist and offered to butter her bread.

"Please. Just slather it on. After the last couple of months, not even cholesterol scares me. Sorry—me, me, me. How's your recovery going?"

"Not quite ready to bench press four hundred, but I'm nearly back to my old routine. Actually, I've been pretty busy." He concentrated on the butter, swirling it into small ivory waves, cresting left, cresting right.

"The reason you had to see me . . . is it about Grauberger?"

"That's part of it." He nudged the bread plate toward her uninjured hand. "Dr. Meredith, what do you know about Grauberger's business dealings?"

"Other than his fixation on the Trabuc? Not much."

"Ever heard anything connecting him with the black market?"

"Didn't that go out around 1945? Lucky Strikes and silk stockings?"

"What about a black BMW? Or Lloyd Harbor?"

She smiled uncomfortably. "Black is a sharp color for a BMW. I've heard of Lloyd Harbor, but I'm not sure where it is, exactly. Detective Ryder, these questions! I think you have me mixed up with some other Rachel Meredith, who's leading a much racier life."

"Racier? With everything that's happened to you?"

"That bomb didn't happen to *me*! That was the work of some crazy hate group! It was a case of wrong place, wrong time."

"And that incident at NYU? Also wrong place, wrong time?"

"Yes. And something I work damn hard to forget." She paused, perhaps regretting the sharpness in her tone. "But my insistence on bringing my grandfather's painting home—I have no one but myself to blame for that. It was a terrible mistake, and I paid with Lulu."

"As we cops say, hindsight sucks." He lifted his glass. "To Lulu." After their toast, he kneaded his stray bread crumbs into a ball, looking up only when the restaurant door jangled. "I've mulled over everything I want to tell you tonight a hundred times," he said at last. "The hard part is deciding where to begin."

Almost imperceptibly, she drew back, flattening against the booth. Maybe she'd taken his words the wrong way, and thought he was putting the make on her. If she despised him for that, okay. After all, it'd only be a warm-up: in five minutes, give or take, she'd flat-out hate him. Her hurt would go deep, and the damage would be irreparable—too many layers of scar tissue were under that resilient facade of hers.

"Dr. Meredith, as soon as I got out of the hospital, I started checking around. What got me started was . . . well, certain things your husband said."

"Wil? What things?"

Experience had taught him never to tell a woman she had lipstick on her teeth. She'd thank you for telling her, rub it away, then bear a grudge against you for the rest of the evening. The edginess tingeing her voice—he suspected the Wil-thing was the same deal, but on an entirely different level.

"Back in May, after the break-in at your apartment, he met up with me while I was talking to Detective Brewster. He identified the dead burglar as a man he'd seen sitting in the front seat of Grauberger's Mercedes. After that, the two of us had a talk in the laundry room. Naturally, he was upset. He spoke about how the painting had changed your lives . . . my impression was that the negatives outweighed the positives."

"He never wanted it in the apartment. But he left the decision up to me."

"Right. And at the time, a dead body was just beyond the dryer vents."

"Just like you said, hindsight definitely sucks."

"Dr. Meredith, out of curiosity, how did you and your husband meet? And when?"

"Why does that matter?"

"Humor me."

"I guess he picked me up," she admitted, "at the opening of an exhibit at the Photographer's Club. Four years ago." Two questions, two answers, and her mouth clamped tighter than a fresh-dug clam.

"I understand why he would have been there . . . what about you?"

"I hadn't been out for a long time. The invitation sat on my desk for weeks. I went on a whim." She closed her eyes. "The exhibit was a collection of movie-star publicity shots from the Thirties and Forties. I'd just written an article on stills. *The Myth Behind the Myth* . . . something like that."

Clearly, she wasn't about to volunteer any more. "And?" he persisted.

She sighed. "It was such an interesting show, I was halfway through before I realized a man was behind me, tall enough to see straight over my head. I moved to the right, he moved to the right—sort of like the Big Apple Square Dance. We slid through the rest of the show that way. At the end, he asked me, 'If you could you be anyone on these walls, who would you be?' "

"Quite an opening line," said Clay.

"I turned around, and there was Wil. Six-foot-three, at least. Too short to play center for the Knicks, but half a foot taller than me in my heels. And those I-see-through-your-clothes blue eyes . . . My answer was 'Norma Shearer, the girl who married the boss,' but he didn't buy that. Finally I admitted to Myrna Loy, got him to confess to Cary Grant, and we decided we could costar in *Mr. Blandings Builds His Dream House.* I hope that's not so meet-cute it makes your teeth ache."

He thought back to the morning in Criminal Court when he'd first seen Lauren, encased in her prim gray suit, casting her spell over a willing jury. Less than fifteen minutes later, whatever he wanted to think was under that strait-laced exterior had snared him, too, a willing victim. "No . . . but why hadn't you been out for a long while?"

"That had to be the busiest summer of my life. I wrote half a book and took on a full class load."

"Any particular reason for committing yourself to all that work?"

She squirmed on the booth's bench seat. "A relationship I was in ended that March. It ended badly. Work was a good way to push it out of my mind. Actually, my former fiancé showed up at that same exhibit. I've always suspected he was the one who sent me the invitation—he wanted us to get back together."

"Is he a photographer, too?"

"No, a creative director at an advertising agency—but the bastard works with photographers all the time."

"Should I assume his desire to patch things up was one-sided?"

"All I'll say is that I can handle a lot of things, but humiliation isn't one of them. Anyhow, there I was with Wil, laughing and drinking wine, and my ex had no idea we'd just met. You can't imagine how satisfying that was—watching him skulk away from firsthand proof that he'd been replaced by a new, improved model. Wil didn't exactly have to twist my arm to get my phone number."

"And a year later you were married."

"Actually, the wedding was set for Christmas break. But a few days before my mother was supposed to fly up, she was killed in a hit-and-run."

"I know about that. I'm sorry."

"We were such a small family to begin with. My mom was always my best friend. I miss her terribly. Every day." After a sip of wine, she resumed: "Anyhow, the next summer, we took a spur-of-the-moment subway ride to City Hall." Lowering her eyes, she edged her little finger inside the rim of her cast and rubbed at the skin. "Why this side trip down memory lane?"

"I'm getting there. But back to the laundry room. Your husband's ID of the burglar tied Grauberger to the break-in. That pointed to seeing him as a possible behind the NYU incident as well."

She gasped. "Why would—?"

"Dr. Meredith, I never believed your attacker was just some horny guy who wormed his way into Tisch, looking for a woman to rape. He was on a mission to kill someone. That someone was you. It was very carefully planned. Otherwise, why choose the Script Library, the only room with windows? Why not any one of the editing rooms? While you were working on your film clips, he popped the library door's lock, set up a shim to keep it ajar, and opened one of its windows. Yes, he mauled you and ripped your clothes, but after he roughed you up, he was going to send you for a ride on the sidewalk express. When you hit the ground, any bruises and torn clothes would make you look like a desperate woman who jumped or fell in a struggle to get away from a rape attempt— like you just said, a woman in the wrong place at the wrong time. A victim of rape . . . not premeditated murder. That incident happened about a month after the museum opening—a month after you informed all the interested parties that the Trabuc was definitely not for sale.

"The break-in at your apartment took place shortly after the Van Gogh arrived. Also meticulously planned—except no one counted on old Rolf." She was staring at him, her face ashen. "Your husband didn't mention our talk to you?"

"I was so heartbroken over Lulu and crazed over the break-in . . . he had to figure it would upset me even more. After that, you and the other detectives started putting pressure on Grauberger, and—well, it's not that surprising Wil didn't bring it up."

"I see your point."

"What I don't understand is Grauberger's obsession with the Trabuc. There has to be more to it than—"

"Dr. Meredith," Clay cut in, "first of all, I can't answer all your questions right now. I wish I could, but I still don't have everything worked out. Second, to protect my sources, I've given my word to keep certain details secret . . . at least for the time being. I have to ask you to just trust me on that. And third, I needed to talk with you before my investigation could go any further. Not only for information that only you can provide, but to make you aware that from now on, you're going to have to be very, very careful." He waited while Ray hurried by on his way to the kitchen. "Your husband hasn't tried to hide the fact that, unlike you, he has no emotional attachment to the Trabuc. Do you think he could be persuaded to sell it if something happened to you?"

"Something fatal, you mean?" she whispered.

"I'm afraid so. This is New York; there must be about a hundred ways—"

She shrank back. "You think Grauberger's made other attempts on . . . ?"

"On your life? Why rule it out? He's so damn cautious, he'd abort before we were onto him, then try, try again, until the day comes—after an appropriate mourning period—when he shows up at your husband's door with a blank check."

"What would 'appropriate' be to Grauberger?" Five minutes?"

"He's a sentimental guy. Maybe ten. However, you've proven very resilient, Dr. Meredith. And Grauberger—this is one of those things I can't discuss—is just about out of time. Someone's turning the screws on him, tighter and tighter." As he drank some wine, Clay studied her face. Wary, frightened. Angry, too, but not at him. Not yet. "In the laundry room again. When your husband put two and two together and figured out that Grauberger set up the job that kept him in Florida overnight, he ranted and raved. Called Grauberger a black-market bastard. Then, last month, there was the IV bag incident. I was the one who phoned your husband. I told him someone had tried to harm you in the hospital, but that you were okay. Period. Fifteen minutes later, he storms into your room, demanding to know what the police were doing to stop the next executioner Grauberger sent in, disguised as a doctor."

"I'm trying, but I don't see your point."

"Over and over, he kept pointing at Grauberger. Now I realize he was feeding me exactly what I wanted to hear, right down to that alleged attempt to run him down outside the studio."

"Alleged? Phil was there! He told me how close that car came!"

"Like I said, he was throwing it all at Grauberger. And it fit like a glove, too, except for a few small details. After the burglary attempt, I tailed that Mercedes for weeks. The windows are too deeply tinted to see anyone inside. The black-market remark? I'm very covertly investigating Grauberger as an insider in a damn serious crime ring. At the very least, your husband is a lot more knowledgeable about the dark side of the art trade than he's letting on. The doctor? No way he could've known that man was dressed as a doctor. I never mentioned it on the phone."

Rachel had the limbo look of a battery-operated toy with its batteries removed.

"Okay. Maybe the Mercedes's door was open, or the window rolled down. Maybe 'black-market' just popped into his head. Maybe a nurse said something on the elevator he rode up to your hospital room. Once, I could have accepted all that, chalked it up to me being an overzealous cop, or totally paranoid, or simply because I was recently knocked unconscious. But that's no longer possible. Because a few weeks ago, I learned your husband isn't Wil Meredith."

"What are you talking about? We've been married three years!"

"That's the only thing we *do* know about him. I did thorough background checks on the Bergères and the Premingers when the Trabuc arrived at the Met, but I was focused on tracing an heir. I knew you were married, but it wasn't about your husband—it was all about you."

Not much light shined on Rachel Meredith in the booth, but what little there was suddenly gathered and haloed around her. Her image wavered in it, like a match in the wind. The hospital neurologist had warned him about the unpredictable aftereffects of head trauma.

"At first, it seemed so implausible, but why not rule out such a crazy notion once and for all? I keyed in a standard computer background check. Wil Meredith, West Twentieth Street—he was in there, all right. The only catch is that he was born in Queens, in 1943. Your husband's considerably younger than fifty-seven." Suddenly, he riveted his eyes on the door.

Over her shoulder, she followed his gaze to the man who'd just walked in. Only after the maître d' seated him with a woman waiting near the window, did their eyes meet again. "Wil's thirty-five," she said. "There has to be an explanation—a glitch in the system."

"My check revealed that Wil Meredith also owns a car. A black 1985 BMW 635."

She sighed, exasperated and relieved. "Then it's definitely someone else! We don't own a car! We're in the city 99 percent of the time!"

"There's a parking garage on the same block as the studio. For years, a Wil Meredith has rented a space there. Same car, same plates. Your husband's been taking the car out once a week, Thursdays, around seven P.M. He usually gets back by midnight. When I questioned Phil Chang, he didn't have a clue, because *he's* the one who spends Thursdays with underprivileged kids. Your husband's never been near that group in Harlem. Tonight the BMW left right on time. I knew he wouldn't be here."

"You've been following him?"

"For the last three weeks. He goes to Lloyd Harbor it's on Long Island's North Shore, an hour plus from Midtown. If you keep going on the main village road, it turns into a causeway between two harbors, and then you're on Lloyd Neck. Very quiet, very private, water all around. He drives nearly to the end, turns onto a dead-end road, goes to the very last driveway—a long, steep one that leads down to the water. Partway down, he parks, then walks the rest of the way. I can't get too close because of a very alert dog. You can't see the house from the road."

She put her hand to her forehead. "And then?"

"I don't know. It's just turning dark when he gets there. An hour and a half, two hours later, he leaves."

She closed her eyes. "I see."

"This is not about another woman. The man who built the house in 1956 still lives there, and . . ." He cut himself off, then resumed. "By the time you hear the rest, if your husband was screwing every woman in North America, it wouldn't look half so bad."

She started to get up; he pulled her back down by her good wrist.

"Not yet! This is too damn serious for me to sugarcoat it! The Wil Meredith who was born in '43 is the BMW's original owner. The six series—that's a pricey car. Around the time Meredith purchased it, he was a successful photographer; he could afford it. But the man had a little problem with marijuana that escalated into a big problem with cocaine. Thanks to an extremely lenient judge, the charges against him were dismissed. Meredith got a second chance."

"Detective, I know this! Wil never mentioned his name, but he told me about the photographer he worked for, and the judge ordering him into rehab. After he got out, he retired upstate, and let Wil buy the business over time. Isn't that true?"

"In part. The best lies are built on truth."

Tears welled up in Rachel's eyes, but he didn't stop. "Meredith signed his first lease on the studio in 1969. One managing agent or another has received Wil Meredith's monthly check for thirty-one years."

She looked queasy, as if she were on a boat that continually threatened to capsize, but kept on righting itself.

"Where did your husband go to school?"

"The University of—"

"Rochester. Kodak U., you called it, when you introduced Phil Chang at the Met. Wil Meredith—our junkie—graduated in 1965. No one else by that name has been registered there since. What else did your husband tell you— where's his family?"

"His mother died of cancer when he was a teenager. Her illness wiped them out financially. His father couldn't cope. He died a couple of years later."

"So you agree he wasn't driving around in a new BMW in '85?"

"He would have been working his way through school . . . he had a late start professionally."

"Even later than you think." He rolled the rest out fast, not giving her a chance to protest. "The real Wil Meredith had a wife. She divorced him after the drugs started to get out of hand. I tracked her down in Virginia. Nice lady, very forthright. My big question was whether she and Meredith had any children together—you know, the Wil Junior angle? Negative. No kids with her, not with anyone." Clay stopped briefly, studying a couple entering the restaurant. "Every Christmas, Meredith would get stoned and phone her. From the *studio*. Still on the blow—selling off photo equipment to stay high. The last Christmas he called her was the one before you met your husband."

Her eyes blinked rapidly. "There's nothing I want more than to walk out on you and all the crap you've laid out on the table! Why should I believe you? Why the hell—" Behind her, a woman three booths away turned around. Aware that Clay was staring someone down, she cut herself short. "All I want is to go home—but now I don't even know who's living there!" To muffle her sobs, she held her napkin to her face. When she spoke again, she gulped for air, as if she couldn't quite catch her breath. "I've known something wasn't right . . . for a long time . . . but, my God, you're talking about things . . . things I can't even begin to comprehend!" With one hand, she hoisted her purse onto the table and searched until she came up with a packet of tissues. "Even though we were both in our thirties . . . we didn't want a baby right away. We just wanted to get to know one another first. . . . How ironic is that? But the end of last year, things started to change. No, *Wil* started to change."

She crumpled a little, but she didn't cry anymore. Blowing her nose and wiping at her eyes, she continued. "It began right after the museum gala. I told him I'd made up my mind not to sell the painting. Up until that point, we'd never disagreed on anything significant. For a few days, he tried to dissuade me—mostly from the security angle. Then he refused to speak about my decision at all—maybe stonewalling was supposed to change my mind.

"Everyone else saw a caring, protective husband, especially when I was . . . threatened. That was an excuse to go off the deep end, accusing the university, the police, the hospital. . . . Totally enraged as long as somebody was listening— exactly what you saw. I wound up feeling guilty for what happened to me! Guilty for getting him so stressed! That's how twisted our relationship's become. As for the actual marriage, he hasn't . . . we haven't . . . It's been quite a while. And that's okay with me."

Embarrassed, Clay stared down into his wineglass.

"Who is he? Why is he doing this? And why *me*?" she demanded. "Assuming another person's identity—isn't that against the law?"

"Criminal impersonation is a misdemeanor. But when the person being impersonated drops off the face of the earth—it gets complicated."

"This hasn't even sunk in yet, and I'm already scared stiff! And I don't even know who I should be more scared of—Grauberger or Wil!"

"Since your husband's personal bio is a total blank, I've considered the possibility that Grauberger might have enlisted him."

"*Enlisted?* As in working together?"

"You didn't figure the guy out in four years. Whoever he is, he had me conned, too. And if it's any consolation, even the truest love can falter when tempted by fifty million dollars." He lifted the wine bottle to refill their empty glasses. "*Finito*. I'll order another bottle."

"No! Water, please. I'm parched, but I've got to keep focused."

"Can you handle dinner?"

"Outrage and insult sure give a girl one hell of an appetite. You choose. I'm too damn pissed to concentrate on a menu."

She downed half the sparkling water in her goblet. With her good hand, she dipped one corner of her napkin in the glass. Eyes closed, she pressed the damp cloth over her forehead and cheeks. Another dip, and she rolled the Pellegrino compress across the nape of her neck. "Cooler heads shall prevail," she said. Both of them sat in silence, not looking at one another. Finally, she sighed, "It's the painting—it'll always be the painting. What happened to my grandfather . . . the same thing is happening to me. Please, can you explain how such a source of joy can turn into such a curse?"

"Would it have been better if I'd never found you—if you and the Trabuc hadn't been brought together?"

"Never! But you're here because you want to protect me, and you don't understand how impossible that is. I have to protect *myself*, and there's only one way to do that. I have to get rid of the Trabuc."

"Your grandfather's painting?" he blurted out, incredulous.

"Not get rid of it literally. What I mean is, I have to hide it. I'm not going to wait around for something terrible to happen to me, and let it go right to the Man with No Name. God, I wish I could just bring it up to the Met, but that doesn't solve a damn thing!"

"What about making a will? Or, if you have one, changing it?"

"A will without Wil? I'm no lawyer, but since the Van Gogh became my property well after we were married, and since I have no other heir, I bet that could be contested. No, I don't see that as a safety net." Her eyebrows lifted ruefully. "My only hope is to get a final divorce before our dinner is served." Her gaze shifted beyond him, and he heard the kitchen door swing open. "Too late."

With a flourish, Ray presented them with two entrees. "I tell the chef to pound this cutlet paper-thin, so the lovely lady with the cast no need a knife."

He stood in attendance, beaming, while she effortlessly broke off a piece of chicken with her fork, took a bite, and declared, "The best *pollo ai limoni* I ever tasted!"

Ray winked at Clay as he moved off toward another table, a sign of approval, as if she were a date. While they ate, he weighed her proposal about hiding the Van Gogh, apprehensive because he still lacked so much key information. "Taking the painting out of play has its risks," he ventured.

"Hardly any more than the alternative!"

"If you go through with it, you'll have to hide it from everybody—not just your husband. You've got to be the only person in the world who knows where it is."

"I can't tell you?"

"Not me, not Dr. Corelli, not Angelina. Being the sole key to its whereabouts . . . I think that's the only way to stop another attempt on your life."

"Me alone—that makes it a hell of a lot harder. I can't imagine where . . . That's going to take some thought."

"Just be prepared. Once Trabuc's off the living room wall . . . all bets are off."

"Right now, my biggest worry is just going home tonight—how the hell do I keep up the pretense? Especially with a man who's been acting up a storm for years?" She lowered her eyes. "I must look like a fool. Totally gullible. Absolutely pathetic."

"You'll get your chance to get even, I swear to you. But right now, the guy is way ahead of us, and neither of us knows exactly where he's heading."

"How far ahead now, how far ahead then?"

"What do you mean?"

"What made him zero in on me four years ago? Drop-dead gorgeous I'm not. I inherited a nice apartment, but it's not the Trump Tower. Let's assume he wasn't sticking around for my 401(K) plan, either. The only thing a grifter would want me for is the Van Gogh, and you didn't connect us until last year."

"That's right. I didn't."

"By that, do you mean that he did?"

"That's why I was asking all those questions. I still have a few left. I need your help, but some are going to be . . . uncomfortable."

Ray swept in to remove the dishes, asking if they wanted anything more. Complimenting the entrée once again, she refused. "Then only one espresso, like always, Mr. Ryder?" Clay nodded, and he headed back to the kitchen.

"Did you just say some of your questions might be 'uncomfortable,' Detective? Fine. Since I feel absolutely devastated, that sounds pretty easy. Shoot."

"At St. Vincent's, the guy masquerading as a doctor was trying to add potassium chloride to your IV. It would have killed you. Most significantly, it would have killed you by stopping your heart—simulating a heart attack. That's how your brother died, at an even younger age than your father. Tell me about his medical history."

"Michael dropped dead in the middle of a run in Central Park."

"A *run*? The report only said he died in the park. Had he just started running?"

"God, no! My brother was an incredible athlete. His death came out of the blue, a terrible shock. He ran the park every day. He was cross-country in college, a starter on his high school basketball team—still played with his old friends. But as much as we'd like to have one, our bodies just don't come with a seventy-five-year warranty."

"So it wasn't necessarily congenital?"

"Hard to say. My father survived Ravensbruck—he was one of those living skeletons when the camp was liberated. Who's robust and healthy after that?"

"And what about you? Your heart?"

"I run or swim every morning. After Michael died, my mother begged me to quit. She knew all the health benefits, walked every day herself. But she had a crazy fear that what happened to Michael would happen to me."

"Crazy? Not to the person trying to poison you." He counted off on his fingers: "One, heart problems run in your family. Two, the trauma of the bombing could have easily precipitated a heart attack. Three, potassium chloride is virtually untraceable. Add them up. Another Preminger dying of a heart attack. It wouldn't even have raised an eyebrow, medically speaking."

"How could they know all that about my family?"

"Information like that is easy to come by. You were a sitting duck in the hospital. Next question: the breakup with your old boyfriend. What happened?"

She shook her head in refusal.

"You never know where something will lead, Dr. Meredith."

"You don't let go, do you? And please, it's about time we dropped the formality. After this interrogation, I have no doubt you're an excellent detective—but I prefer to address you as I think of you, as my friend Clay. And since you've turned me inside out and thoroughly rummaged through the last four years of my life, Rachel will do fine."

"Okay . . . Dr. Rachel."

She sighed. "Okay. Josh and I were engaged, living together. Then it turned out that he was seeing another woman. No, that's not quite correct—he was banging her every chance he got. He denied it, even when I replayed the sleazy messages she left. Pretty humiliating, right?" Rachel looked away, and her voice betrayed all that was raging inside her. "But that was only kid stuff compared to this . . . being married to a stranger for three years!"

Ray was coming their way with one espresso, and Clay asked for the check before he even placed it on the table.

"Rachel, as soon as I pay, I'll walk you home," he said, as the waiter hustled away.

"No, have your espresso. Please. I need a little more time."

Clay never took sugar in his coffee, but the thick brew in the little cup was always too bitter to go without sweetening, and he stirred in two full teaspoons. How many times had he sat across from Lauren here, in the almost mystical glow of her green eyes? Maybe they were just were two people who didn't understand each other, or expected too much of one another, or were simply incompatible. But whatever they had together, it was real . . . even if it hadn't lasted as long as their marriage. He looked up, almost expecting to see her.

Rachel was there, her profile white as a cameo. Rachel, who'd never had anything real. Rachel, who'd never had anything but a lie.

TWENTY-EIGHT

The following Monday, Rachel called Clay at Police Plaza. "I'm back from the doctor's office," she announced, "and cast-free. Under any other circumstances, that would make me deliriously happy."

He could hear car horns and the unmistakable digestive churn of a garbage truck in the background. She was where she shouldn't be—out on the street, exposed. "What about that place we discussed?" asked Clay.

"I came up with one. I had to buy some stuff, though, and the store was closed over the weekend, so—"

He cut her off. "Stop. Don't tell me any more. Are you being careful?"

"I left the doctor's building through a coffee shop, took a bus and a cab." A brief gap followed—perhaps turning, checking her back. "Clay, I've been doing a lot of thinking, and we have to talk—right away, in person. Can you get away?"

Turning his chair, he took a sideways glance at Hickey's closed office door.

For three weeks after the bombing, he'd waited for the DI to rip into him for being with the Merediths that day. Simply being off duty wouldn't hold up as an excuse. He'd rushed back to work to pursue his investigation by phone and computer; that, combined with coping with his injuries and avoiding Hickey's scrutiny, had him totally on edge. When Cello mentioned that he looked like shit, he told him how the DI had him spooked.

"Oh, I took care of that the next day," Martino replied. "I saw the Meredith names in the paper, and figured the old man would get on your case . . . your *closed* case. So I went to see him early, all shook up. I said that I was working in your neighborhood Saturday night—which was true. By the time we wrapped up, Rhonda and the kids were at church, so I called you to meet me for brunch. Also true—you didn't answer."

"I was working out at the Academy. But I went home to change and take care of some laundry. I must've just missed your call."

"Good. Then there's only one little fib: on the way back, who do we run into on that same corner, but the Van Gogh duo. Yakkety-yak, boring, I say good-bye, head for the subway. Wow, I can't believe how close I came to being blown to smithereens." He shrugged. "I guess I should've told you, but a damn bomb—well, even Hickey wouldn't give you grief if you forgot where you were, who you were with, or how you got there."

Figuring he could squeeze a little more mileage out of his injuries, he said, "Sure, Rachel, where?"

"It's so hot, the vendor across the street's using the sun to grill his hot dogs. How about the place I couldn't wait to go to today—the NYU pool? You swim, right? The Navy and all that? Could you meet me there? I'll tell the desk I'm expecting a guest."

A woman with a lock of auburn hair straggling out of her swim cap was doing laps when Clay came out of the men's locker room. It was a little after two, obviously an off-peak time at the sports center; the lane next to her was free. He paced her until she flashed him a quick, wet smile. When they both climbed out, her skin was city-white against her black tank suit, but sleek—her running-swimming regimen paying off.

He caught her checking him out at the same time. "Your ribs look good," she said, suddenly intent on examining them. "I thought you'd still be black and blue." He reached for his towel, and she got a look at his back. "That scar—from the bomb?"

"Flying glass. How's swimming with that wrist?"

"Doctor-approved. The bone's healed. And what's that? On your leg?"

"Gunshot. Work injury."

"You make it sound like a paper cut."

"No. Paper cuts really smart." He walked her over to the bleachers, then up a few rows. Even though no one was within twenty feet, Clay kept his voice low. "Does he suspect you're on to him?"

"I don't think so. Friday was easy—he worked late. By the time he came home, I was in bed with a phony cold. For the rest of the weekend, all I had to do was act miserable—hardly much of a challenge. I wadded up two boxes of Kleenex, inhaled chicken soup, and played a pile of movie tapes . . . without seeing one. I was too busy working my way through the stages: shock, grief, outrage, retaliation. Plus lots of self-pity. Not to mention coming up with where to stash Trabuc."

"Busy weekend. So you think you slipped all that under his radar?"

Nodding, she lowered her head and peeled off her tight white latex cap.

Red-gold waves exploded in every direction, broadcasting the light perfume of her shampoo. "I think I have a way to find out who he really is. That's my first step toward slamming the son of a bitch with an annulment. Fast track. I want to dissolve the marriage, get him out of my life, and make sure he's locked up long enough to stay out of it for good."

"Any cop will tell you that's a good plan."

"All his paperwork is at the studio. Bills, correspondence, bank statements—it's all mailed there. He takes care of it in that little office."

"The room with the big safe?"

"Right. I never thought about it before, but I've never seen the inside of that safe. It was always either locked, or Wil was just closing it. I can just picture the way he'd fling it shut with a little flourish—as if my visit were so much more important than anything else he could be doing. Sure."

She paused, anticipating some sort of reaction, but he wouldn't give her anything until he saw where she was going.

A tinge of exasperation in her voice, she exclaimed, "Clay, it's so obvious! He's got to have stuff locked up in that safe! I know where he keeps an extra set of keys to the studio, and I know the alarm code. The only thing missing is the combination to the safe." She leaned forward, her eyes locking his. "Thursday night, when he's out of town . . . Do you know how to do that? Crack open a safe?"

"Jesus, Rachel, are you serious? You know what you're asking me to do?"

"I'm his wife—damn it! Don't I have the same right to look through his safe as he has to kill me?"

Standing up, he removed the towel he'd draped around his waist and made a show of briskly drying his back and chest. If her notion about smuggling the painting out of sight had surprised him, this scheme had him totally blown away. Only a few days before, he was worrying about hurting her feelings; now he was thinking of ways to keep his own ass out of trouble. He also wanted to hug her for her burgeoning chutzpah.

"That safe," he said at last. "Phil Chang has never seen the inside, either, not in all the time he's worked for Wil. I took him out to lunch in Chinatown yesterday. Made him pick the restaurant and order in Chinese. We had a long talk over an incredible dim sum meal. He's a good kid."

"At least someone is who and what he appears to be."

"Actually, Phil is a lot more than an assistant who graduated at the top of his class. Wil knew exactly what he was doing when he hired him. Right from the start, he's been setting up Wil's shots, lighting and all. I've asked around. That's pretty much unheard of. For the most part, Wil looks through the lens and walks away. Clicks the shutter only when a client's in the studio. It took seven or eight courses to pry that out of Phil. Naturally, it's great for him. Where else could he get that kind of experience?"

Once again, he sat down, closer to her than before.

"The night you were attacked at Tisch, Phil had to stay at the studio overnight because he couldn't leave until Wil came back to lock up the cameras. When I got there the next morning, the place was plastered with Polaroids. Phil told me they were variations *Wil* had insisted on. In the light of what I learned over lunch, that no longer made sense. I asked him outright, and he said that he couldn't explain why Wil had continued that particular shoot either, especially since Phil kept whispering to him that he already had the shot covered ten ways. I believe Phil. My guess is that Wil was stalling . . . waiting for a call about you."

Goosebumps bloomed all over Rachel's body. *"Waiting?"*

"Has your husband ever been up to the ninth floor at Tisch?"

"Dozens of times . . . My God! All the times he'd show up a little early, and tell me to take my time finishing up. He'd walk around! Does that mean he was—"

"Casing the place? That's how it looks, all right."

She jackknifed forward at the waist, as if she had a sudden, severe cramp. "That creature who was trying to rape me," she groaned, "was Wil behind *that*, too? Who is he? Who the hell is Wil?"

"I've been working on that ever since I got out of the hospital. That's why I brought up the safe at my lunch with Phil yesterday. I wanted to know why a guy who hardly knows the difference between lenses is so damn paranoid about who puts them in the safe. Phil told me he once asked Wil what he'd do if he forgot the combination. His answer was, 'I could never forget my mother's birthday.' "

"Great! We don't know who *he* is, no less his mother. Except . . . are you thinking it could be the mother of the *real* Wil Meredith?"

"Anything's possible. I've been waiting for a search of some old records. Maybe a wild hunch. But I've been promised I'll have it by then."

"By when?"

"Thursday, when we're going to break in."

"Clay . . . thank you."

"There's a catch. I want you to postpone hiding the Trabuc until that evening."

She looked uneasy. "But what if he tries to—?"

"So far, whoever's after you has planned every step methodically. The cast just came off today. Your daily routine is going to change. You're going to be watched. Don't give anyone a chance to get your moves down. If you have to go out —no matter where—take a cab. Is Angelina still with you?"

"Yes, another week or so."

Before he'd joined Rachel in the water, he noted that spectators could look down onto the entire pool area from the floor above. Trying to look relaxed, he stretched out his legs. "Thursday evening, I'll call you right after his BMW leaves the garage. I'll pretend I'm one of those suppertime phone solicitors. Right after you slam down the phone on me, job one is to get Angelina out of the apartment. Send her on a long errand—a few stops. As soon as she's gone, hide the painting. Then grab the keys and meet me at the studio." They both rose and walked toward the door leading to the locker rooms. "Remember," he added, "even if it takes you two hours to get to Twentieth Street, we'll still have at least two hours more. And that's if Wil comes back early."

When the door to the pool closed behind them, they found themselves alone in the narrow corridor. "Okay," he said, "I'll see you Thursday." That didn't seem enough, so he held out his hand. All of sudden, his arms were wrapped around her, his hands roaming over her naked back. Rachel's hands were behind his neck, pushing down, bringing their faces close. Her eyes were closed, her lips parted. Resisting the need to kiss her never entered his mind. He hadn't kissed anyone so long or so hard for almost twenty years . . . back at an age when kissing really counted.

"From Here to Eternity," Rachel whispered when their mouths finally separated, "the low-budget version—wet bathing suits, but no crashing surf."

"I heard crashing surf," he whispered back, and he kissed her again.

The second kiss would have lasted even longer, if the door hadn't burst open.

Laughing and waving a pair of goggles over his head, a male student ran right by them. On his heels, another teenager rushed through, barely keeping his balance after skidding across the wet floor.

"Thursday," Clay said once more, and they broke apart.

At six-fifty P.M. on Thursday, Clay scarcely got out, "Mrs. Meredith, if you're paying high interest—" before the phone was slammed down hard.

He waited in the shadow of a storefront at Fifth and Twentieth until she emerged from a cab at eight-twenty. Minutes later, he followed her into the studio building's small, dingy lobby. Once they were alone in the elevator, she pulled a set of keys from her purse.

"How'd it go?" he asked.

"Mission accomplished. The taxi ride calmed me down. Handling Trabuc—I was absolutely scared to death of doing any damage. And then I didn't stop shaking until it was hidden. I've looked over my shoulder so much the last week, my neck aches."

"What about Angelina?"

"No problem. After lunch, I removed the black ink cartridge from my printer, then pounded away at the computer in my study all afternoon. After you called, I hit Print. The printer made a racket, and I started slamming my desk drawers, pretending to look for a replacement cartridge. I was moaning away that the article I'd just finished, plus another one I still had to correct, both had to go out tomorrow morning by FedEx."

"So you sent her to Staples?"

"And to the drug store, for a prescription refill and a shampoo I can never find myself. And to the grocery, to replace the orange juice and muffins I tossed in the incinerator. It was a low thing to do to an old lady. I hope she got back before dark."

The elevator jolted to a stop on the fourth floor. With shaky fingers, she unlocked the gate and the oversize padlocks, then pressed in the alarm code.

In the waning light, a bank of light stands confronted them like sentinels. Grouped on a nearby tabletop were cans, bottles, jars, and cellophane bags. Squinting at their bright red and yellow labels, Rachel said, "They're all in Chinese."

"Phil's been building up a client base through friends and relatives," Clay explained. "At this point, Wil's only concern is the illusion of a busy studio."

They moved toward the small office, and he closed the door before he flipped on the light, so that their visit would go unobserved by anyone in the buildings opposite or down in the street. "Do you have it?" she asked. "His mother's birthday?"

"I'm pretty sure I have the right date. But getting the correct sequence of turns . . . that's going to take some time." Pulling up the desk chair, Clay settled himself in front of the safe door. "I'm going to need your help. If you keep a record of the turns for me, like one to the right, two to the left, I won't lose track and waste time." He reached in his jacket and handed her a pad and pen. Next, he took off the jacket, exposing the gun in the shoulder holster beneath. "Don't do that," he said softly, as he draped it over the back of the chair.

"Don't do what?"

"Stare at my gun like that. It's part of who I am."

With the air-conditioning shut down and all the windows locked, the studio had been stuffy. Right from the start, the closed and cramped inner office was stifling, the stench of darkroom chemicals nauseating. He glanced at his watch. Half of what had seemed like so much time was already elapsed. His head was throbbing from the frustration of countless failed combinations. "Rachel, it's nine-thirty, and I'm a lousy safecracker." He stood up and stretched, then shut off the light and opened the office door. It felt at least ten degrees cooler out in the studio. "I don't know if it's worth continuing," he muttered. Close to defeat, he abruptly walked away.

"How'd you do that?" she asked, after his footsteps came to a halt.

"Do what?"

"Walk across the studio in the dark without bumping into all that equipment?"

"We did a lot of night exercises in the Navy. You learn to look to the side, instead of straight ahead. Old Indian technique."

Every now and then, a car would hit a loose manhole cover in the street below at just the right spot, producing a rattling, rolling clank. Traffic was sparse on West Twentieth Street, and the sound was an irregular but constant marker of the minutes slipping by. "That's it!" he yelled, racing back to Rachel. "The Navy! Military time, military dates! Her birthday . . . not month-day-year, but *day*-month-year! Come on!"

Less than fifteen minutes later, a crisp, sharp click sounded. Clay pulled down on the latch, and the safe door creaked open.

"You did it!" Rachel was jubilant.

"Yeah, I did it," he said. His voice was flat.

"Clay, what is it? Why so disappointed all of a sudden?"

"That date . . . being right about it . . . Rachel, you have no idea."

The safe was divided into four shelves. Three were lined with cameras and lenses. The bottommost, the deepest one, was stuffed with legal-sized, reddish cardboard file folders. All were the expandable type, with briefcaselike flaps and string closings. Clay lifted one out and opened it. Bypassing a Meredith Studio checkbook and bank statements, he selected a stack of cancelled checks. "January rent, Con Ed, Phil Chang, Bell Atlantic, model agency, photo supplier, parking garage, February rent, et cetera." Fanlike, he spread out several checks. "Is this Wil's signature?"

"No. But the dollar amounts, the payees . . . that's his handwriting. I imagine we're looking at the real Wil's signature. I mean, a forgery of it by the phony Wil."

Clay reached into the folder again, a grim magician pulling rabbits out of a hat. He held a plastic baggie up to the light. "Here he is—the real deal." They both studied a New York State Driver License with a picture of a haggard, watery-eyed man born in 1943. "Motor Vehicles does five-year renewals by mail. This license still hasn't reached the expiration date. I'm afraid that the real Wil already passed his. Here's his birth certificate, the BMW's title paper, the studio lease, credit cards . . . everything you need to be Wil Meredith."

"Real proof that he's a fraud," said Rachel. "Everything about who he isn't, but nothing about who he is."

Clay glanced at his watch. Almost ten. The second folder was filled with thirty-five-millimeter contact sheets and negatives. He couldn't make out the stamp-size pictures on the sheets, even when he tilted them under the light. He put the negatives on top of a file cabinet. "Didn't I just see a magnifying glass?"

"Here." She angled it over the top sheet, so both of them could look through it. "What's this? A lake?"

"Yes . . . no!" He took the glass. "See? Buildings above the treetops. That's the reservoir. Central Park." Rapidly, Clay roved back and forth over several sheets. "I know that bridge. It's just past the reservoir, near the tennis courts. And this open area? The trees bordering it are the same ones you see just beyond the bridge." He flipped forward. "These shots are definitely in some kind of sequence. Look—that same guy is running in most of them."

That runner's path veered onto a narrow offshoot trail, up past a big rock outcropping, down a steep incline, out through an exit onto Central Park West.

Wildly, furiously, Rachel struck out at Clay's hands. She slapped at them frantically, until the sheaf of photos scattered over the floor, and the magnifying glass clattered after them. Chest heaving, choking on her rage as if it were a sharp bone stuck in her throat, she transferred her soundless, relentless attack to his chest. He pulled her to him and held her tight until her thrashing ceased.

The runner could only be one person. Her brother Michael.

When she was finally able to cry, he rocked her gently for a while before he whispered into her hair, "Rachel, I have to get some idea of what's in the other folders. I'll be fast. Then we'll leave." He eased her down onto the chair. The next folder also held contact sheets. He retrieved the magnifying glass from the floor. "This looks like your apartment," he said, moving through them quickly. "The movie posters in the hall . . . your study . . . a bedroom."

Distraught, she hardly glanced at the pictures. Then she made him flip back for a second look. "That comforter on the bed . . . Lulu cut her paw on glass one night—not a deep cut, but it was a bleeder. The streets were all icy, and I slipped and hurt my knee rushing her home. I couldn't stop her—she ran straight into the bedroom and bled all over everything. Nothing could get the stains out of that comforter or the shams. I had to get rid of them, and they were brand-new."

"Icy streets, winter—do you remember the year?"

" '96, I think. But I didn't meet Wil until that summer! How'd he . . . ?"

"Get in? Any number of ways—all he had to do was wait for you to walk Lulu. He only needed five minutes inside. If someone studies the NYU course offerings, timing your moves is a no-brainer."

Through the office door, their ears picked up the grinding of the elevator. Rachel froze. Clay pointed to his watch and shook his head. But neither of them breathed until it worked its way up, at least two stories higher.

He returned the contact sheets to the folder, then opened the next one. "Phil was right. He doesn't take very good pictures." Clay leafed through a series of Rachel and a man outside her apartment building, in a restaurant, on a movie line. "You and Josh. And these . . . Josh alone. He was tailed all over the place."

"How do you know that's Josh?"

"I went to his office. He's been married nearly a year. But from the way he spoke, I think he still has regrets that she's not you."

The elevator began its descent; neither of them paid any attention to it.

"But he—" she began to protest.

"Josh swore to me that those phone calls were a frame-up. These photos make me believe he was telling the truth. Wil probably hired some phone sex operator to leave those messages. Good-bye Josh."

Before she had a chance to react, he moved forward to two-shots of Rachel and a tiny older woman on a street corner, hailing a cab. "Who's this lady?"

"Oh my God!" She snatched the sheet out of his hands.

"Rachel, is that your—"

"Yes, it's my darling wife's departed mother. Sweet little thing, wasn't she?"

They both spun around. Wil and an even taller man blocked the office doorway. Each had a gun trained on Clay and Rachel, and Wil's had a silencer. The other man was thickset, with a thatch of coarse black hair, a heavy brow, and a broad nose. His bowed, thin-lipped mouth didn't quite fit the rest of his features, and when he saw Rachel studying his face, it twisted into an ugly smirk.

"Raise your hands," Wil ordered.

Clay complied, his mind racing. He couldn't understand why Wil was back so early . . . or how the hell he knew they were in the studio.

"You bastard!" Rachel sobbed. "What did you do to Michael?"

Wil's eyes, icy blue, narrowed. "No, Rachel dear, I'll ask the questions. Let's start with, 'What have you done with my painting?' Go on, search them."

His companion immediately moved in on Clay, indicating with his gun— an Uzi—that he should assume the standard search position. In no time, he'd jammed both Clay's Glock and the .38 he carried in his ankle holster into his waistband. All the while, Rachel kept screaming her brother's name.

The goliath pushed Clay down on the office chair, then took her by the shoulders and spun her around. After pulling her back to him for added momentum, he heaved her against the wall so hard, her cries died in a grunt. He came up behind her, and Clay saw the moment of terror when Rachel recognized who he was—even before his hands began to move all over her.

Two men were at her back, side by side—the man with the smutty grin and the faceless, nightmare memory from NYU. Together, they loomed over her, powerful, evil twins.

Her panic wasn't lost on Wil. "See, we're all old friends here, aren't we? Now let's try again." His voice rose, no longer a question, but a demand. "Where's my painting?"

The hulking man stepped back to the doorway, and Rachel turned from the wall. Almost imperceptibly, Clay shook his head, a reminder of his warning in the restaurant—keeping the Trabuc's location a secret would save her life. Wil moved, blocking her from Clay's view, escalating his harangue about the Van Gogh, but still able to anticipate her knee thrusting up toward his groin. Not missing a beat, he stepped out of range, then landed a slap on Rachel's cheek that made her stagger backward.

"Ah. You have no idea how much pleasure that just gave me," he said.

"What did you do to my brother?" she shrieked at Wil. "And my mother—why do you have pictures of her? Did she get run over before you could kill her, too?" She kept screeching, even when he put the barrel of his gun to her temple.

"Stop your hysterics, or your cop friend dies." Pivoting on his heel, he took aim at Clay. The silencer made a loud pop, like a swollen wine cork freed from the bottle. Something on the wall behind Clay's head shattered. "Just a demo. I'm quite capable of putting a bullet right between his eyes. One of many accomplishments you weren't aware of. Even the most loving husband has to keep a few secrets from his wife."

For the first time, Clay spoke. His voice didn't come out as calm or as controlled as he wanted, but at least the bullet hadn't made him piss his pants. "You're taking a big chance there."

"Really? Because you're a cop?"

"No. Because maybe I know where the painting is. That might be a big asset, since you're on the fast track to knocking her senseless."

Wil stared at him, considering what he'd said. With a nod to the gorilla, he walked out of the office. Clay heard a cell phone beep. His ears strained, but Wil must have relocated to a far corner of the studio. A few minutes later, he reappeared at the office door, his right hand behind him. "Let's see," he smiled, as he approached Rachel. He tilted his head, as if considering the lighting. "Last time, I hit you on the left. This time, dear wife, why not turn the other cheek?"

Pressing her back against the wall, Rachel turned her head away and squeezed her eyes shut, bracing for his blow. Instead of a gun, his hidden hand produced a roll of silver duct tape. Before she realized what was making the ripping sound, Wil had her wrists wrapped tight. Nevertheless, she continued to put up a fight. The tape curled around itself, making it impossible for Wil to break it off the roll. "I need one of those razor blades," he said to his cohort, and stretched his chin toward a small plastic caddy on the desktop. It held paper clips, stamps, and single-edge razor blades with cardboard guards on their sharp edges. Still holding the Uzi on Clay, the man slipped the shield off one and cut the tape. Wil slapped another strip over Rachel's mouth, garbling her protests. This time, he broke it off clean, and his companion tossed the blade into the pocket of his windbreaker.

Assuming he had Rachel under control, Wil reached back to retrieve the gun he'd stuck in his waistband. Seeing a chance to catch him off balance, she once again tried to knee him; he retaliated with a swift punch to her stomach. She gagged horribly, probably pushing down vomit.

"Ah, poor thing. Did my love-tap upset your stomach?"

That made his big buddy chortle.

"Since we're not getting anyplace with you here, we're going for a ride. A pleasant change of scene. Before the night is over, you'll be begging to tell me where you put the Trabuc." He held out his hand to his pal. "The cop's guns." Once the weapons and the folders were stuffed in the safe, he said, "Move them out to the elevator. I'll take another look around before I lock it."

With his Uzi, the goliath gestured for Clay to get up and help Rachel out of the office. She was having difficulty breathing, and, even with his support, she barely stumbled along. Moments after the elevator clanked into place, Wil rejoined them. He herded Clay and Rachel inside, then slid in at their rear, holding them at gunpoint. The big man positioned himself squarely in front of Rachel, easily blocking her taped mouth and wrists from view.

The lobby was empty. Wil's friend walked out onto the sidewalk, just beyond the pool of light outside the lobby door. After several cars passed, he swept his forearm back and forth, a signal for them to exit the building. The street was deserted, with plenty of parking spots. No cars were coming; he'd delayed their departure until the light controlling the crosstown traffic had turned red. A black BMW was parked close by.

Wil threw his left arm around Rachel, forcing her head down onto her chest. "Cat got your tongue, Hon?" The gun in his right hand pressed into her ribcage. "Ryder, walk ahead. No tricks, or I'll be forced to shoot out your kneecaps. Move, both of you."

He remained at Clay's rear while the big man unlocked the car. "Ryder, you're driving. You, my lovely wife, shall share the backseat with me." Clay slid in behind the wheel, and Wil prodded Rachel inside.

The big man filled the front passenger seat, his weapon on Clay. After the rear door closed, he jammed the key in the ignition and pointed down, a signal to give it gas. After the engine turned over, Wil barked, "Midtown Tunnel—use an exact change lane. Coins are in the well by the gearshift. Don't even consider any fancy cop maneuvers."

Before he pulled out, Clay checked the rearview mirror. Once again, his eyes met Rachel's. Wil caught their attempt to communicate, and he forced her onto the floor. Her struggle jarred the front seat, but from his calm reflection, Wil was holding her down with his feet with little effort.

"Darling," he said, "how can you possibly resist my charm?"

Something pressed into and rotated against the upholstery behind Clay—he was sure it was Wil's knee, turning as he ground his heel into the small of Rachel's back.

Her resistance slowed at another tear of duct tape. Then it stopped.

CHAPTER
TWENTY-NINE

About an hour and a half earlier that same evening, the woman who called herself Serena answered her cell phone on the first ring. Glauberger had given her the phone, and only he had the number.

With her olive skin, black eyes, and fluent Spanish, she'd never had any trouble passing as a native of any Latin American nation. No one had ever guessed that she was an Italian, traveling on a Portuguese passport.

At present, she was miserable. Half an hour before, the overworked fan had died, and her cotton top and shorts were soaked through with sweat. The accommodations were absolutely insufferable; if the pay hadn't been so good, she never would have accepted the assignment. However, short of living in a car, she couldn't have been positioned any closer to the target.

Her room was in a building crumbling through its last years as a university dormitory, so decrepit it made the worst hotsheet hotel look like a palace. During the summer, the school rented its rooms for less than the tax charged on a night in a two-star Manhattan hotel, and an occupant didn't even have to be enrolled in a class. The catch was—aside from the peeling paint, threadbare carpets, and stained mattresses—it wasn't wired for air-conditioning.

The phone slid in her sticky hand. "Yes?" she answered in English.

"We've had a little twist in the plan for tonight."

"What do you mean?"

"Koors was in his car, ready to follow our photographer friend as soon as he left the parking garage. But then it turned out that we weren't the only ones keeping an eye on Meredith. Who does Koors see on the corner? That cop, Ryder—the fucking thorn in my side. We made a quick decision to wait and see what he did next, instead of trailing the BMW. He hung around until *she* showed up in a cab. Our *heiress*. Ryder followed her into the studio building. God knows what they're up to. All I know is, no one's left in the apartment but the old lady."

"I'm on my way."

She pulled the ugly dress over her head. It was made of stiff, synthetic turquoise fabric with little yellow suns machine-stitched on the yoke and all around the hemline. No padding was needed; the cut would make an anorexic look dumpy. She jammed on the big Eighties eyeglasses, and secured the wig—coarse black hair, with a hideous henna rinse. Swallowing hard—it always made her gag a little—she clicked the dental prosthetic over her dazzling, professionally bleached teeth. She could carry off any age between thirty-five and forty-five; the stained teeth pushed it to fifty. Tucking the phone into a vinyl handbag, Serena raced down the stairs in her discount store sneakers—waiting to find out if the elevator was still out of service was a waste of precious time. She sprinted the two short blocks, slowing only as she turned the corner onto Ninth Street.

Shoulders stooped, she meekly waved to get the doorman's attention.

He barely acknowledged her, a man whose good cheer was reserved for tippers. Opening the door a crack, he said, "If you want the Meredith maid, she went out."

Haltingly, she asked, "Angelina . . . she come back soon?"

"Couldn't say." He let the door swing shut.

After a moment's hesitation, she turned and walked toward the middle of the block. In five or ten minutes, it would be dark. Once she passed out of the doorman's range, she crossed to the other side of the street and moved into the shadowy recess provided by a columned entryway. She unclasped the purse, in case Grauberger called. If the old lady didn't show up by dark, she'd contact him.

The cars going by were putting on their headlights when an elderly woman in a black dress, walking slowly, came into view. The sweep of a taxi's beams revealed that she had at least two plastic bags in each hand. She stopped, rested them on the sidewalk, and began to rearrange them, to redistribute the weight. Serena recrossed the street, approaching her from the rear.

"Angelina! Is that you?" she called out in Spanish.

Still bent over the sacks, the old lady looked back over her shoulder, "Serena! I didn't see you at church today. What are you doing out so late?"

"No, why are *you* out so late? Let me help!" She snatched up the packages.

Angelina slowly straightened. "Oh, thank you! My lady needed some things. She just had a broken wrist, you know." Extending a hand, she said, "Please, let me carry at least one."

"No, no!" Serena smiled, swinging the bundles. As they walked back toward the Merediths' building, she added, "I got a letter from home today, but I was stuck inside all day, waiting for the decorator to come hang the new drapes—and the old ones only six months old! *Ay!* How that woman throws away money, and what she pays me!"

The doorman opened the door, but made no attempt to help them.

"I stopped by a little while ago . . . about the letter. So many words I don't know . . ." The two women moved toward the elevator.

"Oh, sure! Come up with me. I'll read it for you."

Angelina rang the apartment doorbell and waited. "She'll come right away," she explained. After waiting a minute, she rang again, listening for the sound of footsteps inside. "Maybe on the telephone," she shrugged, and rooted in her purse for her keys. Serena stood aside while she fumbled with the locks. "Rachel, I am back!" the old woman sang out when the door was open. Cocking her head to hear a reply, she called, "Señora, where are you?" She stood just inside the doorway, looking left and right.

Serena stepped inside and put down the bags on the parquet floor. "Angelina, is something wrong?" Reaching back with her foot, she prodded the door until it closed behind them. "Go ahead," she said reassuringly, "look for your lady. I'll wait right here."

With a nervous smile, Angelina headed off to the left. Doors opened and closed. She passed by Serena again, fingering the little gold crucifix around her neck. The moment she reached a large open archway at the far end of the hall, her hand shot up to the wall to brace herself. A long, low moan escaped her.

"God, what's the matter?" Serena rushed to her side.

Even in the gathering dusk, it wasn't difficult to make out the lone decoration on the opposite wall: a gilded frame. The frame was empty, filled only by the white wall beneath. If not for its strangely hollow look, it might have been a new canvas awaiting its first brushstroke.

Angelina put a hand to her temple, where a vein was throbbing. Taking a step forward, she flipped on the light switch. "You leave now, Serena, please," she said. Her eyes were darting all around the room.

"You're sure you don't need my help?"

"Please, no." Angelina was already looking behind each love seat.

"I'll let myself out. I will see you in church tomorrow, yes?"

There was no reply as she retreated down the hall. She opened the apartment door wide, then gave it a solid shove, hard enough to make it slam. Seconds later, her sneakers were silently gliding back down the hall. Keeping out of sight, she watched the old woman's frantic hunt continue.

As Angelina moved her search to the adjacent dining area, she pulled a cell phone from the pocket of her black dress and pressed a speed-dial number. While she waited for an answer, her free hand tore through the sideboard's drawers, displacing neatly ironed table linens. "The painting's gone! And she's gone, too!" she groaned into the mouthpiece in Spanish. "Of course I'm trying to find it! Why else have I been doing her damn cleaning for seven years?" Bending down with effort, she pulled one of the sideboard doors open and peered inside. "I have no idea where she— Alone? Yes, as far as I know, she was." She consulted her wristwatch. "She sent me out on errands around seven. I just got back a little while ago. Hold on—I just realized . . ." Using the top of the sideboard, she pulled herself up straight. Returning to the top drawer, she tossed aside tablecloths and ripped out the paper liner. "The keys! The keys to the studio! Gone! Yes, I'll keep searching, but what should I do when she—hello? Hello?" She switched the phone off and tossed it onto the dining room table.

Her face contorted as she again painfully lowered herself to her knees. Crablike, on all fours, she scrutinized the undersides of the table and chairs. Taking a deep breath, she braced to hoist herself up, gnarled fingers digging into an upholstered seat. For the first time, she looked straight ahead. A pair of scruffy sneakers confronted her; angling her head, she saw a hem embroidered with suns. "Serena! Didn't you leave?"

Hurrying around the table, Serena grasped her wrists and raised her. "You were so aggravated, how could I? Let me help you find your painting, dear."

For a moment, Angelina tottered on her feet. Suddenly wary, she blinked at Serena. "No! You shouldn't be here! You go, right now!"

The younger woman pointed to the phone on the table. "Who did you call?" Her smile revealed more of her yellow teeth than Angelina had ever seen.

Frightened, Angelina began to back away, but Serena kept moving toward her, closer and closer. Her smile was fixed, menacing. "Who did you call about the painting? Tell me!"

"You're no housekeeper!" Angelina screamed.

"Neither are you!"

Angelina backed into the kitchen, calling for help from God or anyone within the sound of her voice. Desperately seeking a weapon, she wavered between the knives in the slotted holder and the cast-iron skillet she'd been about to put away when Rachel started crying about her printer. She lunged for the more accessible of the two, the skillet. Grabbing it in two hands like a baseball bat, she swung it, but the arc of her arthritic swing was so narrow, it didn't even graze Serena.

As Serena wrenched the pan away, she warned Angelina, "Stop the noise, old witch, or I'll shut you up for good!" That only made Angelina's mouth widen into a wordless, terrified howl. A .22 was in the pocket of the ugly turquoise dress, but the heavy pan—the quiet pan—was right in Serena's hands. She slammed it against the side of Angelina's head so hard, the old woman's face smacked into the cooktop. Her body went limp and slowly slid to the floor.

It suddenly became so still in the kitchen, Serena could hear the tinkle of cubes shifting in the icemaker's dispenser tray.

She went back down the hall, where she'd dropped her purse with the bags. The apartment was cool, but she was sweating profusely. She dialed Grauberger.

"You're inside? You have it?" Triumph already tinged his voice.

She tensed for the explosion. "It's gone." Succinctly as possible, she explained what had happened, and waited for the furor on the other end to abate.

"All those weeks spent setting you up, hanging around that damn church . . . we finally get you inside—" His next words sputtered out, as if he were choking on each one. "And . . . it's . . . not . . . on . . . the . . . fucking . . .

wall?" After a pause, Grauberger's tone shifted from rage to irony. "But why should I be surprised? Everything else I tried to get my hands on that painting turned to shit! Now you call—no goddamn painting! Do you know how long I've been living on borrowed time?"

"The Meredith woman . . . did Koors say she was carrying anything?"

"He would've mentioned it. But I'll check and get right back to you. In the meantime, start searching the place."

After grabbing a kitchen knife, Serena did a quick check of the apartment. The easy, obvious hiding places yielded nothing. She'd barely had a chance to slash the mattress in the master bedroom when Grauberger called back.

"Koors is sure all she had was a small purse. And she was wearing light summer clothes, no jacket. The painting has to be in the apartment! Lothar and I are leaving now. We'll be parked right downstairs. Tear up every square inch of the damn place, if you have to! Just get me that wretched curse of a painting!"

Playing a hunched-up, hard-up servant woman had been tiresome, and Serena had no trouble shaking off the repressive role by smashing mirrors and old movie posters. She slashed the love seats and chairs, sliced and stripped back the carpet. Occasionally, her thoughts wandered to the body sprawled in the kitchen. Angelina was no more a sweet old lady than Serena was an illiterate Guatemalan toilet scrubber. Long before she'd played up to Angelina to get into the apartment, Angelina had been playing up to the Meredith woman. How long, had she said? Seven years? But that, after all, was none of her concern.

When the next call came in, she'd made good progress—more accurately, bad progress, because she still hadn't found the picture. She was halfway through the last room, the kitchen, which she'd hoped to avoid. The digital clock on the microwave blinked to six minutes past ten as she answered her phone.

"Since I haven't heard from you, I'm assuming the worst."

"Just a little more to go—but it's not promising." With her foot, she shoved aside Angelina's corpse to get at the cupboard above the range.

"Meredith came back. He pulled up with a character Koors never saw before, a man Koors says is nearly as big as Lothar. They went up to the studio, then came down with the cop and the wife. Koors said there was something funny about the way the four of them walked back to the BMW, the woman especially. At first he thought she was drunk or sick. Then the husband shoved her into the back seat like a sack of potatoes."

"I don't get it."

"Neither do I. Just finish up and get down here. I'm parked just down the block. Koors is already tailing them."

"I'll be downstairs in a few minutes."

Twenty minutes later, her high-heeled sandals clicked along the street as she caught up with the taxi she'd hailed. Settling into the cab's backseat, she adjusted her short skirt and dug the phone out of her Prada bag while the seedy dormitory disappeared in the rear window. Her fingers spiked up her short platinum hair. The phone beeped; the call went through.

"Where the hell are you? Koors has phoned twice! They're already on the Long Island Expressway, and I want to get going after them!"

"Gregor, this is a courtesy call. Let there be no misunderstanding: I did what I was paid to do—I'm done. When they find the old lady, they're going to be looking for me, not you. I'm in a taxi, on my way to Kennedy, and I plan to be out of the States before they find her." Her next and last words to the Swiss could have been, "Hey, fondue!" or Italian for something else. She rolled down the taxi's window and dropped the phone so that the car tailgating them would crunch right over it.

"Did I say Kennedy?" she asked the driver. "I meant Newark."

CHAPTER
THIRTY

The gorilla with the Uzi hooked his thumb toward the middle of the street. Clay looked in the rearview mirror and adjusted it slightly, away from Wil, who looked as relaxed as if he were at home on one of the love seats, sipping a glass of wine. Traffic-wise, the street behind him was dead: nothing in sight. He eased out onto Twentieth Street. Before he reached the avenue, he noticed a car following him, headlights off. Such a sudden appearance could only mean it had pulled out immediately after he did. As the BMW passed through the brightly lit intersection, headlights popped on behind it.

Clay turned north, east, and north again; several tunnel approach streets were barricaded, squeezing him onto Thirty-sixth Street. The car in his mirror, a dark gray sedan, took the same circuitous route. It was a late-model midsize, a typical rental. In the no-pass, white-tile glare of the Queens-Midtown Tunnel, it was the third car behind him.

The Queens toll plaza was only moderately backed up. As Clay inched forward in an exact-change lane, the gray sedan maintained its three-back position. Once clear of the tollbooth, the eastbound traffic broke free over the tunnel's elevated access ramp. The Manhattan skyline twinkled in the rearview mirror; so did the sedan's headlights.

From the backseat, he was directed to take the Long Island Expressway. Careful not to exceed the speed limit, Clay kept in the right lane. After initially falling in behind him, the tail switched from the right to the center lane and back again. The driver let the distance expand and contract like a concertina, but never came up parallel, never ventured close enough for Clay to see who was driving.

Wil finally broke the silence. "I can't deny it—I'm impressed! How the hell did you figure it out, Ryder?"

"Ordinary police work. As soon as I ran a check, it was obvious you weren't the real Wil Meredith." No response came from the backseat, so he ventured, "Where is the guy, anyway?"

From the corner of his eye, he saw his front-seat mate smirk back at Wil.

"Exactly where he's supposed to be. Upstate."

"What's he up to . . . upstate?"

"Let's just say that where he is, he won't be getting a reading on his light meter. But you had to have more to go on than that."

Two cars, going at least eighty miles an hour, careened by in the left and center lanes, horns blaring. Clay waited until their taillights shrank to tiny red dots. "It was the way title to the painting narrowed down to Rachel." Treading carefully, he asked, "This plan . . . how many years has it been in the works?"

"Take a guess." He was playful, amused—the affable old Wil.

"At least five, as many as ten. Someone had to sift through the records at the Jeu de Paume, sniff out the trail to Annette Bergère in the States, locate her daughters, and make the connection to the Preminger family. That was back before the Internet made it so easy to find people."

"Today it would take a fraction of the time, absolutely. Go on."

"Rachel's grandmother died long before you started. And I'm reasonably sure that her father and aunt were already dead, as well. In fact, having so many of them already out of the equation had to be the catalyst for your plan. If anything happened to the mother—not a stretch for a woman of sixty—the painting went to Rachel and her brother. Joint ownership was a distinct impediment, so you had to get rid of Michael. Out of sequence, as it were, his death was less suspect. Depression over her son's death increased the mother's vulnerability."

"Well, well. You certainly did your homework."

"By marrying Rachel, you'd put yourself right in line for the painting. Getting your ring on her finger was your objective, so your profile of her had to be airtight. Inconveniently, she already had a boyfriend, but you turned that into a learning experience. What did she see in him? He worked for an ad agency, but in the creative department. So being commercial was okay, as long as there was a creative link. The film industry? Not without connections. Publishing? Start in the mail room. Fashion isn't macho enough. Photography . . . perfect!

"Hundreds of photographers are listed in the Black Book, but Meredith was a brilliant choice. If you have to get into someone's life, a druggie gives you plenty of chinks to squeeze through. According to his ex-wife, Meredith was in a haze most of the time, going downhill fast. If you laid down a line of cocaine at the job interview, he would've begged you to become his assistant. You're a good-looking guy, so from there all you had to do was read up on photography and keep tuned to American Movie Classics. Hiring a sexy voice gets the boyfriend into deep shit, and before you know it, you're the new Prince Charming. Ansel Adams and Clark Gable, all rolled up in one."

They were on a dark stretch with a long distance between exits. The tail was taking it easy, hanging way back. A bank of clouds moved in, obscuring the thin slice of moon that floated above the trees.

"Well done. Very thorough. Your only problem is that you're too smart for your own good. Otherwise, you wouldn't be taking this ride."

"Not smart enough to know how you faked the brother's heart attack."

"Ah. Brother Michael, the family CPA. I phoned him as a prospective client looking for a new accountant—business and personal. He accepted my invitation to a breakfast meeting at a Midtown hotel at seven-thirty. I knew he ran the same route at the same time every morning. Our appointment would push him out much earlier, before most of the regular runners. I waited until he passed under that bridge in the photographs. He was tired; I was fresh. Also, I had cyanide in a small aerosol bottle. I came up next to him on the most isolated part of his run and sprayed it directly in his face. Cyanide is extremely effective as an inhalant."

Rachel thrashed out wildly against the back of the seat. A thump followed—a brutal kick from Wil.

Doing his best to sound unruffled, Clay asked, "Cyanide—didn't the Russians use it a lot in the Seventies? Cold war stuff?"

"Defectors, traitors, spies—one whiff, and it shut them down, dead before they hit the ground. Sprayers were rigged into umbrellas, rolled-up newspapers, cricket bats, even French bread. The Soviets made a habit of getting away with murder on the busiest streets in the West."

"And the mother? I spoke to the defense attorney for the Cuban thug who was nailed on the hit-and-run. The guy admitted to everything else under the sun, but the one thing he swears he had nothing to do with was Léonore Preminger's death. Either your friend here in the front seat—Mr. Tisch—or the other bit player who played doctor at St. Vincent's ran her down."

"Our plan was simple: find the flashiest car within a short drive of her apartment—it turned out to be a three-year-old Firebird with so much detailing and gang insignia you couldn't tell what color it was. The bonus was that the Cuban who owned it never went outside without his gang jacket. Cream-colored leather, for *La Crema*, the name of his ridiculous gang. He stayed out all night, every night, partying until the clubs closed. Just as he'd be falling asleep, Mother Preminger was in the habit of power-walking along the beach at sunrise. A perfect overlap. So a little after the Cuban came home, his car went for a spin—by a driver wearing a vanilla leather jacket. My beloved fiancée's mother steps off the curb, and ka-pow!" Wil's fist smacked hard into his open palm. "Two witnesses on the street. Plus the doorman and the taxi driver dispatched to the building for a fare, who both caught the Firebird's license plate. The police were at the Cuban's house so fast, the car's hood was still hot. And oh, that telltale dent!"

The movement from the backseat floor was too weak to merit another stomping.

They drove along in silence for a while, until Wil told him to take the next exit. Clay feigned unfamiliarity with the route. As they entered Lloyd Harbor, the dense canopy of trees made the night even darker, and he switched on the BMW's high beams. The tail was hanging way back, its parking lights no more than a glimmer.

"What about the combination?" Wil asked. His bantering tone had an edgy undercurrent. "How'd you figure it out?"

"Figure it out? A safe like that? You'd have to be crazy to even try! No, I learned from a pro on an undercover job," he lied. "Cops acquire the darndest skills."

They passed over the narrow causeway connecting Lloyd Harbor to Lloyd Neck; a few minutes later, they ascended the last hill, a series of corkscrew turns. If the other car was still behind them, the driver was navigating by the BMW's taillights, tricky on a road with so many twists. For the first time, Clay drove down the long, steep driveway.

A simple ranch-style house spread across the base of the drive, a low-wattage lamp glowing in one window. Clay was ordered to pull up directly in front. He waited while a hand the size of a baseball mitt killed the engine and pocketed the keys. Wil pressed his gun into the back of Clay's neck, and said, "Okay, Raul." Goliath had a name. Raul left the BMW and lumbered around its hood, the Uzi in plain sight.

"Get out now, Ryder," Wil ordered, as the driver's door opened.

Clay smelled pine trees and the sea. He watched Wil climb out of the car, stretch, then reach back inside. Using a fistful of her hair as if it were a towrope, he yanked Rachel off the floor. As Clay had guessed, he'd bound her ankles shortly after they entered the car.

A man appeared in the doorway. Backlit, it was hard to tell much about him, except his medium build and height. A huge German shepherd darted around him and bounded toward Rachel. Wil had left her lying flat on her back on the brick walkway. Sniffing madly, the dog burrowed its nose into her face, her neck, her crotch. Terrified, she flinched and tried to thrash away. No longer merely inquisitive, the animal bared its fangs and growled. The man by the door pivoted around and summoned the dog back with a low whistle. Something about the way he moved was vaguely familiar. The dog sat reluctantly, still eager to pounce.

Wil questioned the man, whom he called Benito, in Spanish. Clay saw a striking resemblance to Raul as he moved toward them. They had to be brothers; the single visible difference between them was that Benito was half a head shorter than Raul. Clay caught only the word for telephone and *tu mama*—the latter part of the first Spanish vocabulary lesson a New York City cop learns on the street. He'd picked up words and phrases from signs and shops and a pocket dictionary he once carried around on the beat, but Wil's Spanish was too fast and colloquial for him to piece together. Benito's answer was negative. Next, Wil pointed to Rachel.

"*Tengo.*" Raul pulled the razor blade from the studio out of his jacket and bent over Rachel. Terrified, she rolled up into a tight ball, but all he did was cut through the duct tape around her ankles.

"Ryder," said Wil, "your damsel in distress needs help getting inside."

Clay stooped behind Rachel and briefly rested his hands on her trembling shoulders, a futile attempt to calm her. Gently as he could, he reached under her arms and gradually raised her to a standing position. Her knees bent, and she swayed precariously. As he steered her toward the door, he whispered, "Get ready to meet the rest of the family."

As soon as they entered, Clay caught a whiff of alcohol and disinfectant; it masked something far more unpleasant. Anton Baranowski, the house's original and only owner, had been admitted to the hospital in neighboring Huntington three times in the past eighteen months. Nearly ninety, Baranowski no longer held a valid driver's license, but two cars were registered in his name at the Lloyd Harbor address. One of them, a Jeep, could have been the curb-jumping SUV Wil professed to have so narrowly escaped near his studio. As Clay helped Rachel down the hall that led into the living room, the sickroom odor faded.

The decor was pure Sixties, a time capsule of earth tones and walnut veneer, fiberglass drapes and wall-to-wall shag. A man sat in the curve of a nubby burnt orange sectional sofa, his back so straight, it barely touched the overstuffed upholstery. While his guests were prodded into the room and positioned directly before him at gunpoint, he smoked a cigarette and took little, if any, interest in them. His hair was white with a yellow tinge, like the pages of an old book. It stood out against a deep tan—the kind that layers over itself, year after year, without fading. Piercing blue eyes, cold and alert, were his most remarkable feature. Overall, he appeared to be a fit man in his middle sixties, but Clay knew that he would turn seventy-nine in a few months.

Transfixed, Clay stared at him. Self-possessed and aloof, the man had an air of undeniable elegance; he and Anton Baranowski's dated house definitely didn't fit. Without knowing his true identity, it would be easy to imagine him presiding over a country club membership board, the reigning local aristocrat.

Before speaking, he smoked down his cigarette and stubbed it out. "You have nothing to gain by your recent subterfuge, by this childish game of hide-and-seek," he said in a low voice. His English had a slight, indeterminate accent. "It is over. Where is the Van Gogh?"

Clay, his eyes fixed on the man, said "Rachel, let me introduce you to your father-in-law—Udo Luscher. The Nazi who killed your grandfather in a Gestapo prison. Who plotted the murders of your brother, your mother, and the real Wil Meredith. And those deaths don't even make up 1 percent of all the innocent victims he butchered in Europe." Inclining her head forward, Rachel lifted her arms over her ears, to block out his words. He turned and gently pushed her arms down. "If you reveal anything about the painting, this criminal won't hesitate to kill you."

Luscher's face remained impassive through Clay's accusations. The blue eyes didn't even flicker when the butt of Wil's gun arced up, on its way to smashing the side of Clay's head. He saw it coming, and ducked just in time, only to swivel his stomach into a direct line with Raul's ham-sized fist. He doubled over in pain. Not far from his face, the German shepherd snapped frantically, straining on the leash Benito had attached to his collar.

"You couldn't have figured this out on your own!" Wil shouted at him. "Who are you working with? Who's helping you?"

Luscher shook his head. "First the Van Gogh." He turned to Clay. "If you know who I am, surely you know my reputation for extracting information. I never fail. Save yourself unnecessary suffering."

Clay straightened up, glaring at him defiantly.

"You," Luscher pointed at Rachel. Battered, dazed, and unsteady on her feet, she regarded him with eyes that weren't quite focused. "You look as if you're ready to talk." Glancing at Wil, he touched a fingertip to the side of his mouth.

Wil worked a corner of the duct tape free from Rachel's mouth and savagely ripped it away. She whimpered in pain, then tentatively moved her lips. Drawing her bound wrists up against her chest defensively, she began to scream at Luscher, venting all the rage that had been bottled up by the tape. She lunged at him, hands open wide.

"Restrain her! Silence her!" Luscher barked at Wil, not shifting an inch.

Wil's fist stopped Rachel's charge, his punch landing on her cheekbone with such brutality, Clay felt the impact in the pit of his stomach. She crumpled to the floor, and another piece of tape was hastily slapped over her mouth. The neighbors' homes were spaced far enough apart to be out of earshot, but Luscher wasn't taking any chances. In Spanish, he gave Raul an order, and the big man left the room. Also in Spanish, Wil was told to telephone *Tía*—Aunt—Somebody.

By now, Clay had no doubt that had to be Angelina . . . and that she'd been spying on Rachel for Luscher far, far longer than he'd suspected—after all, Rachel's mother had hired her, before she retired to Florida. She'd been the linchpin in *Le Découpeur*'s study and analysis of Rachel Preminger, a one-woman, once-a-week surveillance team. Scrub a toilet, score some photos of the apartment. Vacuum, get the dirt on the fiancé. Whistle while you work. On your day off, hop a plane to Buenos Aires and bring that package into the UPS office. Shake with phony palsy, so all they notice is your wrist.

"No responde," Wil reported. He tried the call twice more, letting it ring longer and longer each time. *"Dónde está?"* he demanded, frustration in his voice. Before he hit speed-dial again, his father put up a hand to stop him.

Udo Luscher rose and made for the floor-to-ceiling drapes. One leg dragged slightly, but his back remained ramrod straight. As the waffle weave panels parted, light from the living room flooded over a flagstone terrace. With an impatient shove, he slid open the glass and aluminum doors, crossed the terrace, and vanished.

"Get her up," Wil ordered Clay.

Groaning with pain, Rachel resisted his attempt to move her. She was woozy, and she dry-retched as he lifted her to a standing position.

With his gun trained on them, Wil moved them outside. The daylight view had to be spectacular, judging from the lights twinkling at them across a broad harbor. Clay held Rachel tight as they started down the steep stairway Luscher had taken, twenty steps or so that ended on a bulkhead. Benito and the snarling dog remained on the terrace, both ready to spring if there was any trouble. Again, something about his stance struck Clay as familiar, making him wonder where the hell he'd seen him before.

A rough storage shed was tucked under the stairs, and Raul, carrying rope and two sacks, exited as Clay and Rachel descended the final steps. Before Godzilla closed the shed door, Clay caught sight of at least a dozen red plastic five-gallon gas tanks.

A short pier extended from the bulkhead. Luscher was stepping onto the boat moored alongside, a Grady-White, probably a twenty-eight footer. Though not brand-new, it appeared to be extremely well maintained, and, in marked contrast to the house's interior, fitted with advanced features. Its twin Mercury two-twenty-five engines were powerful enough to transport them far out into the Sound with astounding speed . . . to a place where no one would be able to hear what Udo Luscher had planned for Paul Bergère's granddaughter.

CHAPTER THIRTY-ONE

The Grady-White was barely under way when Rachel tried another wild run at Luscher, who was at the wheel in the forward cockpit. Wil and Raul were stationed on either side of him, facing aft to guard the prisoners. Nothing more than a slight shift of Raul's massive torso had been necessary for him to thwart her attack. With one hand on her shoulder, he pushed Rachel backward and slammed her down on the portside storage locker, opposite Clay.

Luscher, ensconced in the center helm chair, didn't even glance around during the brief scuffle. He concentrated on the console before him, which was rigged with considerably more than the depth finder, VHF radio, and built-in compass usually found on such a boat. Besides the depth finder, with its constant graphic of the ocean floor, two more backlit screens glowed up at the captain.

Wil spoke to Raul in Spanish, and the big man handed him the Uzi. He moved aft, giving Clay a better view of Luscher's toys.

The second screen was radar, particularly useful at night or in fog. Besides other vessels, it could detect any obstruction bigger than a lobster pot. The third screen was a Global Positioning Satellite Navigator, an electronic map accurate within fifty feet. The GPS provided a bird's-eye view of a boater's course, a course easily preset by punching in coordinates. Clay also recognized the buttons for an autopilot that interfaced with the Navigator—theoretically, no one even had to sit at the wheel. On the cockpit's left side window, both a Coast Guard courtesy inspection sticker and a Sea-Tow sticker were visible. On board as well as on shore, Luscher left nothing to chance.

In the glow of the running lights, Clay could see the swelling that Wil's blow had left above Rachel's cheekbone, almost obscuring her eye. But before Raul returned with a hank of rope, she moved both her thumbs straight up and managed a nod his way. Her steadfast refusal to give in made it all the harder for Clay to resist the urge to lash out at their kidnappers. He nodded back.

The Grady-White's hardtop canopy was supported by a stainless-steel framework. After tying rope over the duct tape that already bound Rachel's wrists, Raul looped the line up and around the portside canopy support, stretching her arms straight up over her head—preventing any more runs at Luscher. Again, he made a quick cut with the razor blade he'd tossed into his jacket at the studio.

With Rachel trussed up, Raul faced Clay to demonstrate how to cross his wrists together in front of his chest. Clay did exactly as ordered, right hand foremost, but while Raul wrapped the rope, he strained to keep his wrists as far apart as possible, to keep some slack, if only a millimeter.

Observing the five-miles-an-hour limit posted on buoys, the Grady-White chugged between a rock-bound lighthouse and a flotilla of boats moored off Lloyd Neck, all sleeping until the weekend. The square, squat lighthouse stood at the entrance to an inner harbor, where marina lights shimmered in the distance. Once clear of the speed restrictions, Luscher revved the engines, and they broke into a low, well-disciplined roar. The breeze was so light, it barely rippled the water, and the boat made excellent headway due north, toward Long Island Sound. A little more moonlight, and the conditions couldn't have been better for night fishing: the half-dozen rods secured in pole holders camouflaged a more sinister objective.

Kneeling before Clay, Raul bound his ankles. Once again, he resisted the pressure of the rope, to maintain some flexibility. The secure knot ended in a five-foot leader, which Raul cut, as he had the rope around his wrists, with the blade. He hoisted himself up and walked back to the stern, where he collected the large coil of rope and the two sacks Clay had watched him carry onboard.

The sacks were made of red plastic netting, the sturdy type farmers used for fifty pounds of onions or potatoes. Baymen bundled up their daily clam harvests in them; a bag was strong enough to hold five hundred littlenecks. After dropping the rope, Raul briefly held up a sack in each hand, to tell them apart. One contained two ordinary red bricks; the other, four. Raul placed the lighter bag by Rachel's feet. He threaded the leader he'd left at Clay's ankles through the drawstring of the four-brick bag and tied it with a square knot, an umbilical cord attaching him to about twenty pounds of dead weight. Next, using the new line, which was considerably stouter than the wrist-and-ankle rope, he fastened a sort of harness around Clay's upper body, looping it over each shoulder and around his chest, like a double bandolier. From a knot at his midriff, he measured out a trailer of roughly fifteen feet. Again, he held the blade to the rope. But after only two or three saws back and forth, a shard of the razor snapped off in his hand. Cursing in Spanish, Raul shook away the splintered-off particle, flipped the rest of the broken blade over the portside, and walked forward into the cockpit.

Now that the behemoth no longer blocked his view of Rachel, Clay saw that she was rapidly blinking her good eye. She looked down to her right, up at him, down again. Something was on the seat, inches from her right hip . . . the broken razor blade. Whether it had glanced off her shoulder, or the wind from the boat's forward thrust kicked it back, it hadn't gone overboard after all.

Raul lumbered past Wil, and Clay worried that Udo Junior had seen part of Rachel's furtive signal. To distract him, Clay called forward, "I've been in touch with some of your favorite guys."

"Really?" Wil asked, skeptical. "The *Kamaradenwerk?*"

"No, the Mossad."

Clay couldn't hear what Wil said, but it wasn't a compliment.

"They think your father is alive, you know," Clay lied. "That he survived the winery raid in Córdoba back in 1971." As he spoke, Clay looked for anything he could use to his advantage to get at the blade.

"And have you confirmed their suspicions?"

"I'll be happy to—if you loan me your cell phone."

Wielding a filleting knife, Raul was on his way back. Before he came between them again, Clay blinked at Rachel, then at the blade beside her. All the while, he kept on talking:

"The Israelis still can't figure out what happened in Argentina. My impression is that it was a real bloodbath. But you were just a kid then—around six. How did you survive?"

One swift cut with the knife, and Raul finished with Clay. He paused as the boat rounded a headland dominated by a lighthouse with a powerful beam. A series of long, low buildings nestled into the hillside above had the look of a military installation, most likely a Coast Guard station.

"I wasn't there," Wil replied. "Neither were Raul and Benito. We were visiting our grandmother with my aunt."

"They're your cousins? And their mother—the aunt—is Angelina?"

"That's the name you know her by. Yes."

"And she's the one who called the doctor in Córdoba. The doctor who disappeared."

Wil's shoulders went up, a no-big-deal shrug.

"How the hell did you—did your father—know the Israelis were coming?"

"Sentries using an infrared scope," Wil answered matter-of-factly.

Clay considered that for a moment. "In '71? That had to be ultra high-tech back then. Restricted to military use."

"Perhaps. But the *Kamaradenwerk* could get its members anything. Especially," he added with pride, "a member held in high regard."

Everyone knew he was Himmler's boy, the Gestapiste infiltrator had said of Luscher. Clay pictured a mail-order catalogue, thick as the one Sears used to put out, but with a swastika on the front. "So your father had a lookout with night vision? And that's how they spotted the Israelis coming up the hill?"

"The lookout alerted our men, and they took their positions and waited for the Jews to march up to the outside wall. While they were closing ranks, the ambushers became the ambushees."

Clay glanced forward, but Luscher gave away nothing. Never had he seen a man his age with a back so straight, a head so unbowed. He steered east by northeast, widening the distance between the boat and the shore. As the second lighthouse receded behind them, he accelerated. The Grady-White, evidently not a boat that liked being held back, purred. Raul hunkered down on one knee in front of Rachel. She'd shifted slightly to her right, and the razor blade was out of sight. As with Clay, Raul wrapped the rope around Rachel's ankles and fastened the two-brick sack to her legs. Her bondage and the way she shrank from his touch evidently excited him, and he fondled her legs. Clay had to look away.

"Your side was well armed?"

"AK-47s. Took them down like tenpins. They didn't get a single shot off."

"You make it sound as if you were there yourself, part of the action."

"Raul and Benito had two older brothers. Only one survived. He was wounded and burned, almost didn't make it. We could listen to him talk about that night a million times. It's in our blood. We see it with his eyes, as if we were there."

"Did he tell you about the Israeli with the M-79? The one who let loose with explosive and incendiary grenades? After that, fire blew your cover of darkness."

"My father shot the Jew with the M-79. Then he was hit." In a hollow voice, he added, "The two houses at the winery—my father's and my aunt's—caught fire. My mother and my sisters burned to death. My uncle and my other cousin were killed."

Rachel's legs were bare under her summer skirt. As soon as the rope to the sack was knotted, Raul's groping fingers pried between her thighs and disappeared under the folds of cotton. Any resistance—even squirming an inch or so away from him—and she'd expose the blade. The Grady-White's amidships beam was at least nine feet, but the space between the two built-in lockers he and Rachel sat on was narrow.

Jumping up, Clay shouted, "Enough, you perverted fuck!" With all the momentum he could muster, he lunged forward, aiming for a landing just to the gorilla's left. Because of his half-kneeling position, the impact was enough to knock Raul off balance, and he thudded to his right. Clay heard Luscher cursing as Raul crashed into his cushioned helmsman's chair—his first reaction so far. Clay's legs were wedged in the aisle, his torso on the seat to Rachel's right. Desperate, hands pinned under his stomach, he clawed for the scrap of metal, scrambling to reach under her raised hip. A hand grabbed his collar just as his fingers closed over it.

In a flash, Wil had Clay righted and twirled around. Using the Uzi like a cudgel, he smashed it against the left side of his face. The force sent him staggering back onto his seat. "Chivalry is dead, asshole—and you'll be wishing you were, too, if you pull crap like that again."

Briefly, Wil stood over Clay with the barrel of the Uzi pressed between his eyes, then returned to guard duty at his father's side. Letting his head hang down, Clay slowly unclamped his left hand, thankful that he hadn't dropped the razor blade when Wil slugged him, even though the price had been slicing his palm with the cutting edge. Blood trickled from his gashed cheekbone onto his shirtsleeve. Good camouflage.

Raul had returned to Rachel and cut the line fastening her wrists to the canopy. Clay had to close his eyes to block out the sight of him running his hands over her breasts while he bent to fasten the harness around her. His blood made the razor blade slippery, and rotating it required his full attention.

In the meantime, the Grady-White was gradually slowing. Clay wasn't sure how far east they'd gone, but he couldn't see lights off the stern, and he figured Luscher had been aiming for a relatively isolated area. This part of Long Island was unfamiliar to him, a big chunk of expressway between the city and The Shack. However, he did know that Port Jefferson, home to a cross-Sound ferry service as well as a rail terminus, was located about mid-Island; so far they hadn't passed any lights indicating a town of that size. Just as he maneuvered the broken blade where he wanted it, firmly pressed by his thumb against his index and middle fingers, the engines were cut. A motor whirred as the anchor descended from the bow pulpit.

Luscher swiveled his chair around. His eyes ran over his prisoners' bonds and the bags of bricks. "Proceed," he ordered.

Seeing what was about to come, Clay began to hyperventilate, forcing air into his lungs. Raul grabbed his shoulders and dragged him a few feet closer to the stern, planting him next to a cleat on the wide starboard gunnel. The long line from his harness was fastened around the cleat. Amused by what he took for panic, Raul hoisted Clay's bag of bricks from the deck and raised it high above his lap, threatening to drop it directly on his groin. After a few rounds of his little ploy, he lowered it all the way, and none too gently. When he moved out of the way, Clay could see Rachel on the port gunnel, her bricks also resting on her lap.

"Is this what you're all about, Ryder?" Wil asked. Evidently, he'd just noticed Clay's big swallows of air, and was thoroughly amused. "Mr. Tough New York City Detective, losing it? What're you going to do when the real fun begins?"

Clay heard a gasp of pain, and then once again Rachel started to scream. Still sucking in and expelling as much oxygen as he could, he leaned to see around Wil. A raw, angry red rash ringed Rachel's mouth where the tape had been torn away a second time, but that didn't stop her from cursing nonstop. Wil brandished a fist, and she spat at him, damned him along with Luscher, and kept on ranting. Grabbing her hair, he whipped her head back until her face was parallel with the black sky; the next time, her spittle would land on her own face.

"Rachel, Rachel," he said with amusement, "you don't get it, do you? Yell all you want—no one is going to hear you!" He shook his head. "Quite a pair we've got here, Raul—she won't shut up, and he looks like he's about to faint."

For the first time since the tape came off, Rachel glanced Clay's way. Her brow furrowed at what Wil and Raul had taken for his desperation. From their time at the NYU pool, Clay knew she was a practiced swimmer, and he could only hope that at some point she'd learned about expanding her lungs via hyperventilation. With an exaggerated movement, he slipped his crossed wrists over his bricks, hugging the net bag to his stomach.

The Grady-White sat at anchor, its bobbing almost imperceptible. Luscher rose from his chair and leisurely walked to the stern. From the breast pocket of his safari jacket, he produced a cigarette and a book of matches. Cupping his hands around the flame, he lit up. Briefly, he stared up at the night sky—the light cloud cover still blotted out the stars—and he took a long, deep drag on the cigarette. Supremely unhurried, at ease . . . as if he were all alone out on the calm black water.

Clay eased off on the deep gulps of air.

It was evident that Luscher viewed his prisoners dispassionately, as if they were lab animals pinned to a board. If he could excise information from any physical part of them, he would slice it out deftly, with neither hesitation nor regret. Between puffs, when he lowered his right hand to his side, Clay noticed his right thumb working . . . was it stroking the hilt of a spectral dagger, like an amputee who still feels a lost limb?

Not until after he'd tossed away the smoked-down butt did Luscher address them. His low voice was not without a certain seductiveness.

"Since you are intent on withholding the location of the Van Gogh, we will withhold something from you." He paused for effect. "Air." After another brief silence, he continued, "You have compelled us to throw you overboard.

"As you can see, we have no way to gauge exactly how much pressure your lungs will be able to withstand. All we can do is guess. Only at our discretion, therefore, will you be brought to the surface. At that point, one of you will tell us where the painting is hidden. Should you choose not to cooperate, you will be submerged again . . . and again. Each time, we will keep you down longer. The first one to talk will live. Bear in mind that the bricks will counteract any natural buoyancy. I would advise you not to panic. Any struggling will be ignored."

"How will you know we're not drowning?" Clay asked.

"Ah. I wouldn't trouble myself so much about that."

Incredulous, Clay watched as his hand once again reached into the jacket. *Not another smoke, you sadistic cocksucker.*

With a small flourish, Luscher produced not another cigarette, but a long, narrow, black comb. "Drowning? This shall prove so much more . . . distressing." A flick of his finger and a metallic click demonstrated that what he was holding was not an ordinary black plastic Ace. In fact, it definitely wasn't a grooming device at all—unless you wanted to remove a broad, bloody swath of scalp from the top of your head. The top edge of the comb had thrust forward a six-inch steel weapon. It resembled an ice pick, but the way Luscher played the glint of the running lights off it left no doubt that it was honed as sharp as the old Himmler dagger.

The sight of the blade instantly brought back one of the last testimonies in Eli's dossier, given by a liberator of the SS headquarters at the rue de Saussaies. The man's utter revulsion had been unforgettable:

"As soon as you went below street level, the smell hit you—piss and sweat and vomit and shit and God knows what else. The Gestapo had cells with meat hooks in the walls, an ice bath chamber, a room reserved for electric shock . . . rooms with unimaginable devices. And the further down you went, the worse the stink got. That's where Luscher worked. Even at Saussaies, he stood out. He didn't need those rooms—not when he could inflict agony with that knife of his so efficiently. 'Meine Ehre heisst treu, in herzlicher Freundschaft, H. Himmler.' That was engraved on the blade . . . German words I will never get out of my head. Luscher carved it, word by word, into his victims. One poor bastard used his last breath to tell us how he'd used it to play one prisoner against the other, carving 'Meine' in the first, 'Ehre' in the second, back and forth, until one ratted. From what I saw—and still see in nightmares—he cut where he knew the most blood would flow. Perhaps the sight and the smell of it intoxicated him."

Clay pulled his eyes from the blade, and looked up. Luscher was shaking his head, as if Clay and Rachel, two dim, disobedient children who'd been scolded and warned countless times before, were sorely trying his patience. "Each time you persist in your stupid refusal to report the location of the Van Gogh, you will go down into the water again. And each time, you will go without a part of you." The ice blue eyes flickered. "I will pick the part."

Raul, whose English was obviously limited, nevertheless caught the gist of that, and laughed heartily.

Would he laugh if he knew that his *Découpeur* uncle was notorious for that same ghoulish method in the prisons of Paris? Clay's stomach churned, as it had when he read the very last of Eli's files, the damning words of an unnamed woman:

"He'd go from cell to cell, flashing that damn dagger. Sometimes he'd engrave something that had to do with Himmler across a prisoner's stomach, or breasts. That prisoner would be one of the lucky ones. The others, he'd slice off body parts—fingers, ears, testicles, nipples. Or an eye . . . he

could excise an eyeball in a second. Then he'd flick it on the floor and squash it under the heel of one of his shiny boots. Did I mention how well-groomed he was? Immaculate, in spite of all that blood. I'll never forget him holding that knife of his over the belly of a pregnant woman . . . he took his time driving it in, slow and steady. A monster is what he was! I saw prisoners die even when his mutilations or stab wounds weren't life-threatening. It was Luscher . . . when he pulled his blade out of them, he sucked out their will to live at the same time."

Luscher, Clay knew, was now back playing a role he'd played hundreds—perhaps thousands—of times before. His cool indifference was betrayed only by the impatient twitching of his right thumb as he gave his prisoners one last opportunity to contemplate the pain and peril ahead. "If you speak now," he added, "such losses can be avoided."

When neither Clay nor Rachel divulged the Trabuc's whereabouts, he said, "Both of you are far more foolish than I imagined." His tone was flat, yet full of menace. "The painting will be mine again, and your suffering will be in vain." He motioned to Wil and Raul.

Wil bent over Rachel. "Fuck you, Nazi boy!" she screamed at him.

"Hold on, Wil!" Clay yelled. "Maybe I do have something to tell you."

Wil's eyes darted to his father, who gave him a signal to hold off.

"A car followed us out. The driver was very discreet. Tailed us all the way from the studio to Lloyd Neck. I'd say that right about now, some unexpected company has dropped in on Benito."

Wil spun around, ready to strike. "You're full of shit!"

"Am I? You were the one who said I had to have help."

"Who?" Wil demanded, "who the hell is helping you?"

"Where's my incentive to tell you that, or anything about the Trabuc? Aren't you going to kill me anyway?"

The last thing Clay saw onboard the Grady-White was Raul's meathook hands grabbing for him. But he had already rolled out of reach, backward over the gunnel and into the sea.

CHAPTER

THIRTY-TWO

Clay held on to the razor blade for dear life. He gripped it as he hurtled through thin air in reverse, clutched it even harder during his crash through the surface. At the same time, he kept his bound arms wrapped tight around the bricks, pressing them to his stomach. Barely a second after the water closed over his head, the rope that attached him to the boat played itself out, and the hard jerk of the harness squeezed his shoulders, upper back, and chest like a metal vise. Bracing for the wrenching pull on his legs, he shoved the bag off to the side. A lightning bolt of pain shot up to his hips.

Immediately, he started on the first of the three tasks he'd set for himself: severing the harness rope. In the black water, he had to limit himself to small, tight movements of the razor blade, while exerting as much force as possible. Cutting a notch into the thick rope was proving more difficult than he'd estimated, considering the tautness of the line.

He had a pretty good idea of what had to be happening simultaneously on the Grady-White: disbelief, rage, then a rush to the spot where he'd sat just before he hit his personal Eject button.

His underwater carving finally produced a groove in the rope. At the same time, the line jiggled—no doubt Wil and Raul trying to lift the line away from the curved bulkhead, frantic to get enough of a grip on it to hoist him up—so *they* could throw him over the side. Finally, Clay was making an inroad; he felt a few strands breaking away, then several more. The longer they kept busy in their attempt to haul him up—he felt a jerk on the line above him—the longer Rachel would be temporarily ignored. A hard heave raised him about two feet, enough to put sufficient strain on the rope for him to progress more than halfway through. More concerted effort from above jacked him up into the half-dark of the ship's running lights. The added tension split the last intertwined strands apart. At the very instant the rope snapped, the sack plummeted, dragging him along. Because the bricks added so much acceleration, judging the depth was difficult, but he guessed he was on a plunge of more than forty feet. His mind flashed an image of Raul reaching for the rope—shoulders tensed to yank him up, arm over arm—and his bulky torso nearly pitching over the side as it went totally slack.

If the boys from Argentina thought Clay knew the Trabuc's location, they were about to scratch him off their list. Rachel was now their sole key to finding the Van Gogh. It was a good guess that Luscher would abort his proposed method of getting her to talk. Unfortunately, it was a better guess that he had a whole bagful of backups.

Clay landed on a smooth, sandy bottom. Down that far, the pressure of the water negated his body's buoyancy, so he could work without being forced toward the surface. He did a test pull of the rope twined around his ankles; his attempt to separate them when Raul tied him up had paid off. Chin on knees, arms looped over shins, he strained to keep his feet apart and the rope taut. Keeping his movement constant and rhythmic, he attacked one of the coils with the blade. In the total darkness, he sawed up, from bottom to top. He had to force his mind to focus on the simple job before him—not the pressure building in his lungs. The line was thinner than the harness rope, and he cut through it faster, but it was still twisted around his ankles. Trying to kick it loose only tightened it. Second objective not quite accomplished.

The line around his wrists was next, his biggest challenge: he'd have to transfer the blade to his outside hand. To drop it was to die. With his thumb, he pushed it up between the index and middle fingers of his left hand to those of his right. Never in his whole life had he ever held anything with such ferocity. The pressure was going from intense to excruciating. Panic was death; he pushed it down. At no time in the SEALs had he ever felt so completely cut off, so isolated.

Even if he'd been able to see what he was doing, slicing into his wrist was inevitable; his blind state only made it worse. Afraid of losing the blade, he had to duplicate what he'd done with the other lines, which meant applying pressure and channeling out a groove until the rope split, strand by strand. At the same time, he would also be hacking at his own flesh. Better just below the back of his hand, rather than the tender inside wrist, that preferred locus for suicides; better that the water provided a cooling—although by no means numbing—effect. At once, he struggled with both the boulder pressing him down and the explosive force gathering within his chest and inside his head, ready to burst—he was glass, about to shatter.

Fighting the running clock of his lungs, close to losing consciousness in the blackness of the night sea, he dug the blade into both the line and his skin. The pain was searing, but its intensity kept him alert, kept him slashing away with the razor. Rachel . . . what if that sadistic Nazi had in fact given the order to throw her overboard . . . would he have felt the reverberations of her splash this far down? And Jesus, which was going to happen first—passing out or hitting fucking bone? As if nothing had ever locked them together, his hands abruptly floated apart, granting him a revitalizing surge of freedom. With his left hand—he might not ever relinquish his grip on that blade—he snatched for the rope, plucking it by the tail end just before it drifted away—the last thing he wanted was any indication that he was still alive popping up under Luscher's running lights. Holding on to it, with his free fingers he probed the tangled line still attaching him to the brick bag. With no time left for another cut, he lunged out with his legs, thrashing in desperation, until the rope around his feet mercifully unspooled.

Immediately, he stopped kicking. Resisting the temptation to rush for the surface only added to his agony, but he slowed his ascent, using his last shred of will not to go past his own air bubbles.

Beams of light cut back and forth through the water, blinking and sporadic—was that a warning signal from his brain that it was on the verge of shutting down? Craning his head back, he made out the Grady-White's hull, a big dark spot in the middle of the flashes. To his relief, Rachel wasn't dangling over the side—not that she was much safer onboard. The glinting lights, he quickly realized, came from the boat: Luscher and company, fanning out methodically with high-intensity searchlights. They were bright enough for Clay to see the anchor line, which was close to the place he wanted to surface, under the point of the V-shaped bow. The bow pulpit lanced out slightly over the water, allowing him just enough space—if he positioned himself properly—to regulate his breathing, unobserved. No one on deck would be able to see him there, short of hanging off the wraparound bow rail by the heels. Hearing him was another story: Clay had to control his break of the surface and his heaving swallows of air.

Overhead, the Grady-White's fiberglass hull was molded into a series of progressively wider wedges, fanning out from the center. Besides enhancing stability and speed, the design also provided a superb fingerhold for anyone beneath it seeking something solid to cling to. Stuffing the rope in his pocket, his razor blade–talisman clamped between two fingers of his right hand, Clay gripped one of the wedges of the hull with his slashed, bleeding left hand. When he grabbed hold with the thumb and ring finger of his right hand and pulled up, he was literally kissing the bow. Most of his face was in the clear—in the air at last!—but the back of his head was underwater. He tightened his thighs against the downward swell of the hull, attaching himself like a barnacle. The sea, not distinguishing him from the boat, gently lapped up against them. He imagined he resembled a turned-about figurehead of an old sailing ship, one who stared nearsightedly at the bowsprit, instead of gazing out to sea.

Soundlessly, his mouth shaped "I frankly feel fucking fine, Fred!"

As his breathing became less labored, he picked up snatches of onboard conversation, all in Spanish. Luscher, tense and icy, was calling all the shots.

Raul, directly over Clay's head, spoke the words for water and minutes—

probably calculating how long Clay had been underwater. Luscher snapped at him dismissively. Wil also took some of his old man's heat. Calling him "Julian," he snarled something about a woman—possibly, a "hysterical woman!"

All along, Rachel spewed a stream of curses at them, a raging, unending aria. "You're really fucked now, aren't you?" she screeched out. "First you lose the war, then the painting, and now *I'm* all you have left! Come on! Hit me again, Hitler!"

Someone must have taken her up on that, because she grunted, then burst into a coughing fit. As soon as it subsided, she resumed her rant—her voice hoarser and thinner. She was doing the only thing she could to distract them from the search, still hopeful that he'd bob to the surface. "Please—throw me overboard!" she shrieked. "It's the only way to get away from your rotten Nazi stink!"

Maybe Luscher caught on to her, maybe he just lost all patience. "Julian! The woman!" A flurry of protest from Rachel was followed by a series of thumps—Julian-Wil forcing her down the stairs. A door slammed. Silence.

Clay pressed harder against the hull separating him from Rachel, as if he could transmit a message through the fiberglass: he was alive, and he'd get her to safety, even if it took the last breath in him. And there was more, so much more, that he still didn't fully understand himself.

Luscher ordered Raul to telephone his mother, then Benito in Lloyd Neck. It was obvious that neither answered. A flurry of overlapping flashlight beams played over the Grady-White's gunnels—a final search? One by one, they switched off, and the engine roared back on.

Clay slipped off the bow as the anchor began to retract. Weighted down by his clothes and still hampered by the harness, he quit the area as fast as he could, swimming underwater in the direction he reckoned to be east.

When he finally resurfaced, a wide swath of wake was spreading toward him. His pale face would be impossible to pick out in the boiling white foam, and before the water quieted, the Grady-White would be long gone. He twisted out of the harness without having to cut it. With regret, he kicked off his shoes—his favorite pair, Italian lace-ups comfortable from the first day, no breaking in necessary. He dug for his wallet in the back pocket of his slacks, until he remembered that it was still in his sports jacket back in the Meredith Studio office, draped over the chair by the safe. Using the razor blade yet again—dull by now, but still useful—he cut a long strip from his shirt and wrapped it tight around the gashes on his aching left wrist. He stripped down to his shorts, but not having his shield and ID—and especially not his gun—made him feel bare-ass naked. As the boat's lights faded from sight, he consigned the precious razor blade to the sea.

Not a single glimmer came from the south, Long Island's north coast. Any hope that he'd make it to shore and alert the police before Luscher returned to Lloyd Neck with Rachel evaporated. With a hell of a swim ahead of him, he struck out, grateful for two things: first, that his daily workout included laps at the Academy pool; second, that he wasn't bucking a current. As experience taught him in the SEALs, a strong drift can keep you swimming in place for hours.

Heading in what he guessed to be a southerly direction, he cursed himself for putting Rachel in Luscher's grasp. Julian—no, with all due respect for the dead photographer, he still thought of him as Wil—had been doing his damnedest to murder her, and Clay had all but delivered her into his hands. If only he'd refused to go to the studio, refused to try the safe . . .

In spite of the spunk she'd displayed on the Grady-White, he wondered how much longer she could hold out. To be sure, she still had her grandfather's painting to hang on to, but Udo Luscher and his son had invested years in destroying her emotional underpinnings. The two of them had chopped away rung after rung of the shaky ladder they'd forced her to climb, all the while pushing her higher and higher. Now all they had to do was stand back and watch it splinter out from under her.

Once again, he was overwhelmed by memories of his grandfather. Undeniably, they were two peas in a pod, old Udo and old Jonas. In the end, considering that Jonas Ryder didn't have the dubious advantage of practice as a Nazi war criminal, he'd done a damn professional job of crushing Clay's mother. In one sense, the old man was ahead on that score: he'd expertly pierced Betsy Ryder's soul, without spilling a drop of blood.

A major cloudbank was breaking up, giving him sporadic readings on the stars; they were enough to keep him on course. He swam without thinking about swimming, the way people take a long stroll without giving any thought to the act of walking. For a while, he distracted himself with a tally of all the charges that could be brought against Wil on the Meredith-related crimes alone.

Many times over, his thoughts returned to the gray sedan. Had one of Grauberger's lackeys been following Rachel, or was it the Mossad? After all, he'd called Aaron earlier in the week, requesting a few details before he contacted the authorities in Córdoba. Aaron was sharp enough to have seen where things were going. According to the Argentinean reports, everyone at the winery had perished in the fire. Eli, of course, had always appended a question mark to one of the names listed as deceased: Javier Delgado. Now there was no question that he and his only son, as well as the survivors of a certain Suarez family—Señoras Suarez and Delgado had the same maiden name—were very much alive. All had been part of Luscher's personal Bund, merrily stomping the grapes into wine until that small squad of Israelis arrived.

Whoever tailed them out to Lloyd Harbor had eventually crept down the long driveway. That unexpected monkey wrench of a housecall had to be why Benito wasn't answering back at the hacienda. Clay wondered if the BMW had been at the head of a long procession: the puzzling gray sedan, followed by Grauberger's Mercedes, the Japanese contingent in a Toyota, Rasenstein in a Peugeot, Deirdre Sands in a Jag . . . what the hell did Auntie Angelina drive?

Clay had no idea exactly how long he'd been at it. Two hours? He'd done ten- and fourteen-hour swims in the SEALs, in rougher, colder seas. True, now he was twelve years older, and no longer a mean machine, but he'd make it back to shore, easy. Revenge might be best served cold, but no one ever said it couldn't be a little wet, as well. All the Luschers. All the Graubergers. All the rest of the art crazies. Nail 'em and jail 'em. Long enough to keep the whole cursed lot of them away from Rachel for the rest of their godforsaken lives.

But that little dream just blew up in my face, didn't it? And I have no one to blame but myself. Rachel never talked me into anything—God, how I wanted in on that safe! Right from the moment Phil uttered that "how could I forget my mother's birthday?" remark! I had to prove how damn clever I was, how I could solve anything—after all, hadn't I traced the Trabuc to Rachel? Wind me up, and watch me unravel any mystery, from the phony Wil, to the safe combination, to the Preminger murders, I was going to do it all: save the girl, save the painting, cuff the perps, tie it all up in a neat little package with a bow on top. My one big mistake was thinking I could outwit Luscher. God, when I think about it, if I hadn't linked Rachel to the Trabuc, he would've sent me a fucking roadmap. I'm simply a jerk cop who overplayed his part. And the shit it got me into with Hickey is deeper than the deepest part of this fucking, unending Sound.

More and more frequently, he searched the eastern sky for the thinning gray of dawn. July . . . the night would start to slip away sometime after four-thirty. The last time he'd looked at his watch was after twelve, before Raul had bound his wrists. It was supposed to be water-resistant to 30 meters, but the face was a blank—well, no claims had been made about the seaworthiness of the battery. Where the hell was he, anyway, swimming so long without spotting a single light? Long Island, or Madagascar?

He tried to reconstruct all the exits along the expressway east of Huntington: a road to Northport, Route 4 to Commack—did he miss one in between?—the Sunken Meadow State Parkway, the next a blank. . . . *No, back up. Didn't a state park give that parkway its name? Some dinky little park wouldn't have its own parkway leading up to it. It would have wide stretches of beach . . . most important, it would be closed to the public at night. That was why Luscher had made it his destination. And that was why the coastline was so damn dark.*

A knot formed in his stomach. From the start, he'd counted on reaching a residential area, even a single house, where someone would call the police. Now he'd have to run God only knew how far before he made contact with anyone . . . more time lost before help could be dispatched to Rachel.

And he'd been wrong about the swim. Not such a piece of cake.

For at least fifteen minutes, the siren song of fatigue had been rippling across the water, and he couldn't block it out much longer. The urge to give in to that awful, improbable combination—feeling weightless and heavy-limbed, simultaneously—was irresistible. Then, just before he gave in and closed his eyes—to rest only for a few seconds, or forever—he saw them. They were tiny pinpricks at first, so small he had to blink to make sure they were really there, not flashpoints generated inside his exhausted eyes. Two lights, a little to the east. Then more, east of those.

Hardly any surf, stony beach, typical North Shore; Clay just kept on moving his arms and legs until his stomach scraped the bottom, like a car that keeps rolling after it runs out of gas. On his hands and knees, he crawled up onto the beach. Stretched out prone, he lay panting while the water advanced and retreated over his toes. Numb from exertion, he was already dreading the moment when his insensate muscles would howl back to life. He lifted his head and looked straight ahead. His beachhead was somebody's backyard.

At the center was a round umbrella table, umbrella closed, with four white resin chairs tilted forward onto it, so dew wouldn't collect on their seats. Jaunty, like a one-table sidewalk café. The light he'd been swimming toward was a two-headed anti-intruder light affixed to the corner of a white clapboard house. One light was aimed at the beach, the other at the driveway at the side of the house, where a red Chevy Blazer was parked; the lot had no room for a garage. The house was small, a bungalow, and the second story looked like an attic expansion, maybe one big bedroom. Clay crawled to the table and pulled himself to his feet. Still feeling the roll of the sea, he staggered toward the back door. The outer screen door was latched, too far from the inner door's glass panel to knock. He dragged himself around to the front.

Instead of a doorbell, the front door had a brass knocker, and, leaning on the doorframe to support himself, he struck it against the door three times. No one responded. Another unsuccessful try with the knocker, and he resorted to rapping on the door with his fist, hard as he could—not all that hard, but louder than the knocker.

"Who's that?" a man yelled down from a dark, screened window above his head. Not totally awake, but totally irritated.

Clay tried to call back up, but what came out sounded more like an old newspaper being crumpled than "Police! I need help!" He banged on the door again.

"What is this bullshit? Take off!"

Clay resumed pounding, and a light was switched on upstairs. A woman murmured something, then the man answered, "No—first I want to see the ass-hole who woke me up in the middle of the night!"

Clay stepped away from the door and into the half-moon of light cast from above.

"You're not going to believe this, Michelle! It's some pervert, parading around in his underwear!" At full throttle, he shouted, "Get off my property right now, you stoned-out piece of crap, or I'll call the police!"

To the right and the left and across the street, lights popped on.

"Go ahead," Clay croaked, "call them! Call the police!" He turned, and saw that the trash had been left out near the end of the bungalow's driveway, in a plastic barrel with lockdown handles. The next-door neighbors still had an old-fashioned metal garbage can. He lurched to it, tried to lift it. Blood seeped through the cloth of his wet wrist tourniquet. He couldn't believe how weak he was. After throwing off the lid, he hauled out the overstuffed plastic bag. Empty, the can was manageable. "Call the fucking police!" More lights. He half-dragged, half-carried the can across the miniature front lawn and hurled it at the side of the white house, barely missing a window. He recrossed the lawn, re-trieved the lid, and banged it against the metal mailbox. People were hanging out of windows, their outrage operatic.

In minutes, he was caught in the glare of a cruiser's high beams. He raised his hands. The officer inside was talking into his two-way; squawk acknowledged his transmission. When he climbed out, hand on the butt of his gun, Clay saw "Nissequogue Police" printed on the door. The cop was a wide-shouldered man, with just enough extra padding of his own to give the impression that he was wearing a bulletproof vest. With a salt-and-pepper mustache, semi-military brush cut graying at the temples, and a take-no-prisoners-take-no-shit attitude, he was just the kind of guy Clay wanted to see.

"Hello, Ringo. We've had half a dozen calls about you and that drum of yours."

"I'm a cop." His voice was strained, but it was working better. "Detective Clay Ryder, NYPD. Major Case."

"Yeah? You have that printed on your dick?"

"Listen, I just swam here from somewhere in the middle of the Sound," Clay protested. "I was dumped off a boat headed for Lloyd Harbor. There's another person still onboard, in serious trouble. I needed another cop to help me, so I banged on—"

"Lloyd Harbor?" The cop glanced around, then deftly handcuffed Clay, who resisted as the metal dug into his lacerated wrist. One bear paw clamped on Clay's shoulder, the other notched in the waistband of his shorts, and he was quick-marched toward the cruiser. A murmur of appreciation went up from the spectators. Clay's feet lost contact with the ground; he was suddenly facedown on the vinyl seat, still slightly sticky from a beer drinker whose one-too-many had recently graced it. Now the good people of Nissequogue were cheering their peace officer. Before his prisoner could right himself, he'd slammed the doors and peeled away, lights flashing. "Give me your name again, and your shield number!" The bantering had turned to urgency.

The officer called in a request for photo ID ASAP. He took a deep breath, then explained, "Just before the call on you came in, we received something about a . . . about Lloyd Harbor. But I've got to check you out first, you understand?"

"Sure . . . what do you have on Lloyd Harbor?"

"I think every cop in Suffolk County is headed there right now. No details yet. Headquarters is less than three miles from here." While the cruiser's lights washed over a series of neat, tranquil lanes, Clay asked, "Nissequogue—where the hell are we?"

"Between Smithtown and Stony Brook."

"Near Sunken Meadow State Park?"

"Near? By car, there's no bridge over the Nissequogue River, so you have to take 25A all around it. By water . . . at night . . . man, if that's where you started swimming, I don't know how the hell you did it." The cruiser pulled into a drive past a small, whitewashed town hall that had to be more than a century old. At the back, a gray shingled annex housed the local police.

They walked into the bright light of the police headquarters, Clay first. The officer working the desk took one look at him and jumped out of his chair.

"Holy shit! Stan, the guy's lips are blue! Other than that, he looks just like the guy in the fax!" He stuffed the paper in his colleague's hand and ran to an adjacent room. Stan had the cuffs off before he returned with a blanket, which he threw over Clay. "You've got a nasty gash on your cheek—you should have it looked at. And that rag on your hand is all bloody."

"I'll get around to all that. Thanks for the blanket. Please, right now what I need most is some water."

"Better." He went to a supply closet and pulled out a big bottle of apple juice. Just hearing the seal pop drove Clay half-crazy. "Drink it slow," he admonished Clay, making him feel like a runaway kid placated with milk and cookies.

While he drank, Stan pulled a first-aid kit off a shelf and made the hasty intros: "I'm Stan, he's Ron, and you're"—he held up the fax—"who you say you are." He handed Clay a bandage big enough to cover the worst cuts on his wrist.

"I couldn't tell you in the car, but the Suffolk County Police are swarming over Lloyd Harbor. Lots of guns, lots of bodies. A real mess. They've never seen anything like it before. You think that's where—?"

"I don't think. I know. I've got to get over there."

"I'll drive you," Stan volunteered. "Even let you sit up front. But hold on— I've got sweats and sneakers back in my locker." He bolted out of the room.

"Ron, please—one more favor." Clay picked up a pad and wrote down Cello's name and number. "Can you get directions from Little Neck, Queens, to the crime scene, and give them to Detective Martino? Ask him to meet me there."

As they fastened their seat belts, Stan asked, "You going to be up to this?"

"Me? Sure. But the other person forced onto that boat . . . if anything happens . . . it's tearing me apart."

"I hear you," Stan said softly, and Clay's thoughts returned to Rachel. He refused to believe she was one of the bodies at the end of Lloyd Neck. Luscher wouldn't let her die. Not until he had the painting.

All along, the Van Goghs had been Luscher's lifeline.

As Berlin fell, he'd rolled up the two Trabucs, concealed them in a hollow metal cane, and proceeded to murder his way into Switzerland. Selling Madame Trabuc had rescued a desperate Himmler's boy, saved him from the hangman's noose at Nuremberg and transported him to Argentina. Decades later, after the battle at the winery, the forger's copy of Monsieur had funded his escape from South America. For fifty-six years, Luscher had always managed to control the exact whereabouts of the genuine Monsieur Trabuc, the legacy he'd so fanatically schemed to hand down to Wil and his nephews . . . until the previous night, when Rachel spirited the portrait away, out of Luscher's reach at last.

THIRTY-THREE

Stan and Clay could see the floodlights long before they reached the Bara-nowski driveway. Off to the side of the road on a neighboring property, a car was being dusted for fingerprints. The vehicle was partially concealed by a stand of rhododendron bushes, and the entire area around it had been taped off. Clay was positive it was the sedan that had trailed him all the way from Twentieth Street.

"You're going to have to park it up here," a uniform at the mouth of the driveway told Stan when he rolled down his window. He was wearing a baseball cap embroidered with a flying seagull insignia and *Lloyd Harbor Police.* "No more room along the driveway."

"Nissequogue called ahead about the NYPD detective—I'm just dropping him off," Stan replied. Turning to Clay, he said, "Go on—I know you can't wait to get down there." He handed him the fax from Police Plaza. "Don't forget this. Proof you're the real deal."

"Stan . . . I . . . hey, thanks for everything. I'll get your stuff back to you."

Stan put out his hand, and they shook. "Not to worry. And Ryder—next time you visit Nissequogue, come by land."

A Lloyd Harbor Police sergeant who'd been observing the investigation around the sedan fell in step beside him on the driveway.

"What's the line on the car?" Clay asked.

"Nothing much, so far. Hertz rental, Midtown. Suffolk County's on the prints. I called it in before I even went down the driveway. There's no parking permitted on village roads."

"You were the first on the scene?"

"Neighbor to the north phoned in a complaint about the noise. Thought they were still celebrating the Fourth of July down there. Neighbors to the south are away."

"Was there a woman down there?"

"No one down there is alive."

Clay's breath caught in his throat. "A woman's . . . body?"

A long, single-file line of parked police cars stretched along the right side of the steep driveway. Half on, half off the narrow blacktop, their passenger sides jammed up against dense hydrangea bushes, crushing snowball clusters so white, they glowed like frosted light bulbs. Suffolk County blue-and-whites were closer to the top of the hill; Lloyd Harbor cars were further down. The last grainy, gray shreds of night faded, and color slowly seeped into a morning saturated by dew and a salt breeze.

"No woman that I saw. I secured the scene and called for backup. Suffolk County took over. We've never had anything like this here before."

"So I've heard." Clay pictured the officer finding the first body and calling in immediately. How thoroughly had he searched the rest of the house? He picked up his pace; he'd recouped some energy on the ride back with Stan.

Nearing the bottom, he saw a police emergency services truck next to the ambulance in front of the house. The sergeant stopped next to a Lloyd Harbor cruiser. "I've got to call in—you okay?"

Clay thanked him and continued on. The night before, he hadn't noticed that the garage was detached. It was off to the left, up the hill from the house; they were connected by a covered breezeway. The side of the garage farthest from the house gave minimal cover to the car parked parallel to it: Grauberger's black Mercedes. The once-handsome automobile was riddled with bullet holes, its windshield fractured and sagging. The new hood ornament was a short man in a pinstriped suit, who'd apparently been trying to escape into the narrow space between car and garage. He'd been stopped by multiple gunshots in the back. Med techs blocked the body, but the balloon head was all Clay needed to ID him as Grauberger. Dial-a-Picasso's number was permanently disconnected.

Just outside the front door, the German shepherd lay in a thickening puddle of blood.

Sweet birdsong broke out in the oak trees that towered above the garage, an incongruous accompaniment to the carnage. Not too far off, the dizzy gargle of a loon joined the chorus.

"Hold it right there! Who are you, and where the hell are you going?"

Clay explained, and the Suffolk County cop who'd challenged him conveyed the information into a walkie-talkie. After three repetitions, it filtered its way up through the chain of command. The officer pointed to the side of the house. "Everyone has to go that way, and in by the back. Ask for Cochran— Chief of Detectives. He's in charge."

"Who's he with—Suffolk County or Lloyd Harbor?" Clay asked.

The cop bristled. "Suffolk." He looked around. No flying seagulls in sight. "The two major crimes in Lloyd Harbor are speeding—that's exceeding thirty-five miles an hour—and cutting down trees without a permit."

"I could live with that," Clay called over his shoulder.

The front of the wide, ranch-style house completely blocked the water view. It was introduced on the side, through an arched trellis—the old-fashioned, wooden kind. Vines of blue flowers framed a narrow but perfect landscape: a slice of harbor and green, low hills rising on the far shore. As Clay passed through it, the rim of the sun pushed up into the pale sky above the hills. The slate path curved through a bloomed-out rose garden. With each step toward the rear, the view expanded.

By the time Clay reached the back, he was aware that the house sat on a point that provided a three-hundred-degree panorama. On the landside, the long driveway provided privacy; waterside, the thirty-foot elevation ensured that any approaching boat would be sighted at least ten minutes in advance of its arrival at the dock below.

The patio was crowded. First to notice Clay was a towheaded man whose freckles and jeans made him look far too young for the detective's shield hanging over the pocket of his polo shirt. He nudged the elbow of a man in his late forties, who was dressed in several shades of dull, greenish khaki. The color did nothing for his waxy complexion.

Turning his way, the older man asked, "You Ryder? I'm Cochran."

Clay made right for him. "Any sign of a woman here? Rachel Meredith? Rachel Preminger?"

"Hold on, Detective! Nissequogue told us you had a pretty rough night, and that's a nasty cut on your face, but if you don't mind, I'll ask the questions." Suddenly, the rising sun bathed Cochran, a gaunt man with thinning light brown hair, in a rosy copper light. For a scant few seconds, he looked robust, brimming with good health. He put up a hand against the glare, and left it there longer than necessary while he studied Clay's face. Whatever he saw there, the confrontation in his voice was gone when he finally answered. "No Rachel here—no woman at all. But we've got a hell of a lot of dead guys."

The chief of detectives pulled a pack of cigarettes out of his jacket and extended it toward Clay, who shook his head. "Shit. Should've figured. Anyone who swam halfway to Nissequogue doesn't smoke. Tell me," he asked as he lit up, "how do you fit in with all this, Ryder?"

Clay glanced down at his feet. Stan's spare sneakers, three sizes too big, might look like clown shoes, but the rest of him had to be pretty damn scary. Fixing Cochran with an eyeball-to-eyeball stare, he gave him a full rundown. When he finished, the chief coughed violently, ground out his butt, and took a step back, appraising him.

"If you weren't a cop . . . You're telling me that you and the Meredith woman were kidnapped?"

"Correct."

"By the guy she's married to, but who's a dead photographer? And he brings you to his father, who's a Nazi war criminal? In Lloyd Harbor, no less? Do I have that straight?"

Clay realized that everyone on the patio was absolutely still.

"That's right."

The crease between Cochran's eyes deepened, and he touched his fingertips to his temples, as if his brain were receiving alien signals. "Okay. Now for the easy part. Last night. You say that Hertz rental up on the top of the hill followed you here, and you figure the Benz tagged along somewhere behind it?" After Clay's nod, he continued, "And as far as you know, only one person was left behind in the house when you went for your midnight cruise? Plus the dog?"

"Right. One man was left, that I saw. He's on the Nazi side. The Nazi side and the Mercedes side . . . let's say they're working at cross-purposes. I assume you've traced the Mercedes to Gregor Grauberger, a Swiss art dealer doing business in Manhattan. That's Gregor himself, hugging the hood. I have a feeling I'll know some of the others."

" 'Come into my parlor,' said the spider to the fly." Cochran pointed a bony finger toward the living room. "You, too, Bernie," he said to the freckled detective, who was introduced as Bernard Ross on the way in.

Even with the slider doors wide open, the stench was overpowering. The first thing Clay saw was a man sitting on a chair that hadn't been in the room the night before—a straight-backed, chrome-legged Sixties kitchen chair. An extension cord was wrapped around his chest, a restraint that now kept him from slumping. His head was tipped forward on his chest, and Clay had to bend to look up at his face. Someone's fist had pushed the nose off-center, blackened an eye, pushed in the front teeth. Multiple bullet holes in his chest indicated he'd been caught in the crossfire when the shoot-out began. "This is Luscher's nephew, Benito. He liked to play doctor." He acknowledged Cochran's puzzled glance. "I'll explain that some other time." The other, elusive connection which had jogged Clay's memory the night before was still out of reach. "He was the man left behind."

Cochran pointed to the next victim. An XXL-size man in a cheap suit, he'd fallen backward, away from Benito. The wooden coffee table that had taken the full impact of his torso was in splinters. Clay angled around to get a look at his face. "Okay, that's Lothar."

Cochran was impressed. "Like from *Mandrake the Magician*?"

"Yup. Swiss passport. Lived on the West Side. Grauberger's bodyguard."

"Ready to take the bullet for the boss?"

"Not exactly a candidate for the Secret Service. Just big."

"He was probably busy pounding Benito's face into a pulp when they came in shooting," Ross observed.

"Looks that way," Clay agreed. Lothar's own face looked as if it had taken an entire clip from Raul's Uzi, a true Swiss cheese. "He was under investigation, but nothing stuck enough to bring him in. He was in bad company, though."

"The art dealer was dirty?" Cochran asked. "You didn't say."

"World-class garbage." *But even Grauberger isn't in Luscher's league.*

Clay glanced around. The living room walls were pockmarked with bullet holes. Shards of ocher ceramic lamps, their end tables overturned, protruded from the shag carpet. *Where the hell are they—Rachel, Luscher, Wil, Raul?*

"That's three down, two to go," said Cochran. "Another one's right behind the sofa. This was like the gunfight at the O.K. Corral."

Clay moved around the large sectional. Arms and legs apart, the fourth dead man lay on the floor, a big X. He'd taken a lot of automatic fire, mostly in the chest, and his clothes were soaked with blood. "Florian Koors, Austrian. Grauberger, Lothar, and him: The Three Stooges. But this guy was the scariest by far." Koors's black reptilian eyes, open just a slit, confirmed his opinion. Beyond one outstretched arm, a crooked track of blood wove out of the living room, in the direction of the front door. Either the dog or Grauberger, not much difference between the two.

"Chief Cochran!" A uniformed cop was making his way toward them. "We've got everything in the cellar packed up and ready to go."

"Anything more turn up?" Cochran asked.

"More? Enough for this whole damn house to make a moon landing."

Clay's mind, feeling like an overstuffed Rolodex file, twirled backward. It stopped at the emergency services truck parked outside. "You're a bomb tech?"

Instead of answering, the cop shot Cochran a questioning look.

"He's okay," Cochran told him. "NYPD." He shrugged, as if that explained the beast in the scruffy sweat suit and sneaker canoes.

"Did you find C4 down there?" Clay asked. "Maybe a couple of remote control detonators?"

"How'd you know that?" the tech asked suspiciously.

"The bomb at the Gay Pride parade." *A meticulous plan: As she did every year, Rachel would go to the parade. A couple of mouse clicks, and the Staten Island homophobes' Web site provided the perfect cover. Inviting Clay would eliminate a nosy cop—him and Rachel, a two-for-one vaporization. But Wil had retreated so far back into the Cosmetics Plus before detonating the bomb, he couldn't see that the two transvestites had wedged themselves next to the trash basket, creating the human barrier that protected his real targets. After the blast, to better play the widower wannabe, he'd scratched his face and hands with broken glass.* "I think—I know— you'll find a connection." Bitterly, he added, "All brought to you by the same killer behind this mess and a significant portion of the Holocaust."

Cochran pointed to the front hall. "Come on, time to take a look at number five. He's the only one we were able to figure out."

The *he* was a small consolation—where the hell was Rachel?

A tech carrying a plastic tray of baggies and vials bustled out of a door at the opposite end of the entrance hall. The sickroom smell from the night before intensified as they entered a bedroom that was large, but cramped by a massive, matching furniture set: bureau, high chest, dressing table, night tables. Only the headboard and bed frame were missing, replaced by a hospital bed. Another tech was dusting the orderly groupings of prescription bottles, medical supplies, and toiletries on the bureau for prints. An oxygen tank in one corner was hooked up to the breathing apparatus of the old man propped up in bed, but he wasn't doing much breathing.

"A guess—am I looking at Anton Baranowski?" Clay asked.

"The homeowner himself," Cochran replied.

Every sign indicated that Baranowski's care was fastidious: his frail body was dressed in bright paisley pajamas, and a shawl was still neatly draped over his shoulders. What hair he had was perfectly parted and combed, and he was clean-shaven. The only thing that wasn't neat as it could be was the off-center bullet hole in the middle of his forehead.

"Using what you've told me," said the chief of detectives, "the Nazi was posing as what Baranowski's daughter calls her father's 'caregiver.'"

"Daughter?"

"He has a son, too, but he lives in L.A.—she's over in Connecticut. On her way, but it's a long drive from Westport. Ross spoke to her."

"When I told her there was an accident," said Ross, "first thing she asked was why the police were calling, instead of Jozef. Turns out one Jozef Kelski's been taking care of Baranowski for about three years. She sounded just as worried about him as about her father." He paused. "Ryder, were there Polish Nazis?"

"Why?"

Ross pointed to the armchair positioned near the bed. A foreign-language book was on its seat, a bookmark protruding about three-quarters to the end. "Looks like he read to the old guy in Polish. The daughter said the two of them were always talking about the old country. He brought in a Latina housekeeper and taught her how to cook Polish meals. All that heartwarming crap."

"Yeah, that fits. Luscher spent enough time killing Poles to have a real knack for the language. What do you have on Baranowski?"

"Immigrated in the Thirties," Ross replied. "Worked in a Polish butcher shop in Queens. Bought out the owner when he retired. Branched out into Nassau, then Suffolk. Became the kielbasa king. Actually, he called himself the Sausage Baron. *Baran*-owski, get it? Bought this property in 1956, built the house a few years later. His wife died in '69."

"And he didn't change a thing."

"A real museum," Ross agreed. "I'm afraid if I turn on the TV, *Gunsmoke* will come on." He inclined his chin toward the corpse. "So what do you think? Any way Baranowski's involved in this mess?"

"I don't see it."

"Then why'd they kill him? Sick old guy . . . bedridden . . . on oxygen."

"He knew the whole cast of characters. Luscher played nurse-companion and his sister-in-law played cook-housekeeper. Did the daughter mention a handyman? Maybe a gardener?"

"No," Ross replied, "but the house and property—three acres— everything's really well-kept. And sitting right on the water—that's rough on a house. Do it right, maintenance can be a full-time job."

"That's got to be Benito's role—the one back there in the chair. Last night, he was in charge of the dog, like he spent a lot of time here. But why *here*?"

"The end of the Neck, the end of the road, the long driveway," Cochran answered, "close to the city, but tucked out of sight. And let us not forget the en- trancing waterview. Okay, Ryder, now that we know who's dead . . . who's miss- ing? Aside from the Nazi and his son and the Meredith woman?"

"Raul, Luscher's other nephew—about a head taller than his brother Ben- ito."

"Jesus!" Cochran exclaimed. "Ross, get me a fucking scorecard!"

"The waterview . . . damn! What about the boat?" Clay shouted.

"Yeah, the boat. That's a problem." Cochran tapped out another cigarette from his pack. "Come on out back again."

When they returned to the patio, the crime scene people had thinned out, and he could see the bloodstains that ran from the slider doors to the dock stairs. Clay made straight for the edge and peered down. Blood streaked nearly every step. The Grady-White was gone. The breeze had picked up, and he could hear the water slapping against the pylons. He scanned the harbor, but the boat was nowhere in sight.

"With that blood going all the way down to the dock," Cochran explained, "we figured that had to be the way the shooters took off."

"Have you called Motor Vehicles?"

Ross answered. "Sure, first thing. But no boat is registered under Bara- nowski's name. We questioned the neighbors, and they don't remember a boat tied up at his dock in the eight years they've lived here. Not a clue as far as telling the Coast Guard what the hell to look for."

"Get them out after a Grady-White! A twenty-seven or twenty-eight footer, with twin Merc two-twenty-five screws!"

Ross started punching numbers into his cell phone.

"Raul could've lived on a boat that size!" Clay exclaimed. "The boat was Luscher's escape hatch! Plenty of marinas close by, right?"

"Sure," said Cochran, "over in Huntington." He pointed past the lighthouse, toward the inner harbor Clay had noticed. "Electric hookup, fresh water, shopping, restaurants, the works. Ten, fifteen-minute trip from here."

Ross held up a hand for quiet. "Commander—Detective Ross again." He rattled off the specifics to the officer on the other end as fast as Clay gave them to him, then stood listening, frowning. "Yes, I understand it's a Friday in July, and a zillion boats are out on the water. But this has turned into a kidnapping. . . . Well, we just found out ourselves. Four onboard. One is the kidnapping victim—the only woman onboard. No, but the detective right next to me can. Hold on." Ross handed the phone to Clay. "He needs descriptions."

Clay went through the men first. When he got to Rachel, he was able to describe the clothes she was wearing, her height and weight. "Auburn hair, down to her shoulders . . ." His voice broke. "Hazel eyes. Fair skin, no marks." A tear burned the welt on his cheek. "No . . . that's wrong. She's been roughed up, one eye swollen closed . . . bruises on both cheeks . . . abraded skin around her mouth. But other than that, she's very . . . she's . . ." Shaking his head, he returned the phone to Ross.

The detective ended the call and clicked his phone shut. He and Cochran averted their eyes.

Clay took a minute to collect himself. "Look, I don't want to contaminate the scene, Chief, but I need to check out the dock."

Ross pointed left, to a sloping wooded area. "Over there, see? That's another way down to the beach. But the tide's in."

"After last night, you think wet feet are going to bother me?"

Cochran and Ross watched him from the patio as he waded around, sneakers in hand. Looking up, he saw that the door to the shed under the stairs was open.

Back up on the patio again, Clay reported, "Bad news. That shed was packed with five-gallon gas tanks, and not one is left."

"So they take you out near Sunken Meadow Park where no one could hear the head Nazi torturing you and the woman," Cochran summarized. "You drown and Benito isn't answering the phone, so they hightail it back to Lloyd Neck. They probably cut the engine, drift in, sneak up from the dock, and see uninvited visitors beating the shit out of Benito. They whip out the Uzi and wipe out the Mercedes gang. One or more of them gets hit—the blood on the steps. It's a coin toss which set of miserable pricks shot Baranowski. But with their cover here totally blown, the Nazis take off by boat again."

"And with all those gas tanks," Clay added, "wherever they're headed, it's not local."

"I'm looking for Detective Ryder, NYPD," a voice boomed out. A wide-bodied man squeezed his way in between the two Suffolk detectives. "They said he was back here, but . . . My God! I didn't recognize you! For Christ's sake, Ryder! You looked better when you were in the hospital!"

Clay had never been so happy to see Marcello Martino in his life.

Cochran was reluctant to let Clay go, even with all his contact numbers in hand. While they wrapped up, Cello took a quick tour of the massacre. His face was ashen when he rejoined Clay.

"Holy shit," he rasped, as they started back up the hill, "it looks like they started World War Three in there."

"No," Clay corrected him, "at least one of them is still fighting World War Two."

"What a waste," Cello said, flipping his thumb at the Mercedes.

"Grauberger? The guy was total scum."

"Not him. The Benz. One thing you have to give the Krauts, they make a damn nice car."

Clay froze in his tracks. "Cello . . . the BMW!"

"Yeah, that's nice, too."

"Wil's BMW! It's not here!"

CHAPTER THIRTY-FOUR

"Move it, Cello—the son of a bitch is already hours ahead of us! And he's the only one who knows where Luscher's taking Rachel!"

Neither the Suffolk Police nor the Lloyd Harbor sergeant first on the scene had seen a BMW—both had checked the garage, to find only Baranowski's Jeep and Volvo inside.

Clay had grabbed Cello by the arm and was practically pulling him up the steep driveway toward his car. "Wil thinks I'm dead—that no one else knows who he really is, or what he's done. That's why he's gone back to the city, to search for the painting. Why not? Who is there to connect him with the slaughter at the bottom of this hill, except one drowned cop?"

"It'll be rush hour by the time we hit the expressway," Cello panted, as they slammed the car doors. "Traffic'll be pure hell." Losing no time, he backed into a neighboring drive; pebbles flew as he roared off in the direction of Lloyd Neck's single main road, red light flashing. "You know how much that fancy white gravel costs at Home Depot?" he asked, with a glance at his rearview mirror. "That's gotta be at least $29.99, sprayed all over the street! I'd be running out with a hand broom, to sweep it back in!" He leveled a look at Clay. "Understand, my friend, I have no idea what the fuck you're talking about. For all I know, you could have some kind of condition, like sunstroke, but from water. Like maybe your brain has to dry out a little longer before it can work right again."

"Believe me, Cello, it's working fine. I've got something for you that'll make this trip worthwhile—guaranteed. But first, I have to call in."

Shaking his head, Cello handed him his phone. Bloomie picked up. It was good to hear her, tough as ever. The Deputy Inspector clicked on immediately. Clay asked, "Sir, you remember the Meredith case? The Van Gogh?"

After a sharp intake of breath, Hickey snapped, "Why did I know it had to be you, Ryder? Every other cop understands that a closed case means you don't keep sticking your nose back in. Now what?"

"The husband. I need surveillance on him. Immediately."

"You don't say? Then we have quite a coincidence on our hands. Detective Brewster of the Sixth has been trying to track you down for hours. Half of his precinct is at the Meredith residence. A response to the husband's 911 call."

"What for?"

"He came home to find the maid murdered, the wife missing, and no Van Gogh." He hit the 'no' and the 'Gogh' hard, to make them rhyme. "You still want that surveillance, Ryder?"

Clay worked to organize his thoughts, to get a grip.

"Where the hell are you, anyway? And why did the Nissequogue Police need to confirm your identity? All this art crap—all you do is keep painting yourself into corners!"

"Sir, I'm on my way in with Martino. It's a long story, but please hear me out."

They were long out of Lloyd Harbor, easing onto the Long Island Expressway by the time Clay finished. Hickey murmured, "Sweet Mother of God! Shit! Hold on." His voice was muffled for a moment, hand over the mouthpiece. "Brewster's on the other line. I can't figure out these damn phones. Bloomie is going to patch us all together."

While they waited, Cello asked, "You said the Nazi started planning *when*?"

"He already had the cleaning lady—his sister-in-law—in place seven, eight years ago. So it had to be at least a few years before that. But he had no other option for selling the painting on the open market, where the Trabuc would get the highest price."

After beeps and vocal confirmations, Clay blurted out, "Brewster! Oh, man, am I glad you're on this one! Listen, you've got to keep Meredith there until I—you *what*?"

Even Hickey groaned at Brewster's reply.

"I said," repeated Brewster, "I let him go. He asked to go to his studio, and there was no reason to detain him any longer." Clay tried to interrupt, but Brewster plowed ahead. "Ryder, the doorman who was on between four and midnight says the maid—Meredith gave her name as Angelina Chavez—left around seven. Dr. Meredith went out eightish. He's not positive when Chavez came back, but when she did, she was with another maid from the neighborhood, who was looking for her earlier. He figured they ran into one another. She was helping the Meredith maid with some bundles."

"Another maid?"

"Latina, around fifty, medium everything, round-shouldered, glasses. They were both speaking Spanish. Couple of hours after they went upstairs together, the friend comes down alone. The doorman on the next shift lets Meredith in around three-thirty A.M. In no time, cops are rushing in, responding to

Meredith's 911. He has no idea where his wife is, Chavez is dead, and the Van Gogh is gone. Got all that?"

"So far."

"Well, maybe *you're* happy I'm here, but I sure the hell am not. I was tapped because the cat burglar murder is still open. They got me out of a deep sleep—my wife and I went out for our anniversary last night, and you can figure out the rest—and before I even walk in the door here, Meredith's already yakking nonstop, blaming the whole Department, like *we're* the perps. I took his statement, corroborated with both doormen, and practically shoved him out the door. Keep him here? I couldn't wait for the belligerent bastard to leave!"

"What was his reason for wanting to go to the studio?"

"Reason? You haven't seen this place. The entire apartment's been tossed. No, that doesn't say it. Ripped apart, uninhabitable."

"Marcus, what was the murder weapon?"

"Would you believe a twelve-inch cast-iron skillet? The corpse looks like— well, the politically incorrect phrase is, 'Mama done whacked that girl upside her head.'" Damn thing weighs over seven pounds. Not a print on it."

"M.E.'s time?"

"Give or take nine last night." After a pause, he added, "Both women— nothing's coming up on either of them. Probably some green card thing, but Chavez had been working for Dr. Meredith forever. As for her buddy, no one seems to place her earlier than a month or so ago."

Clay considered the time of death, and the Luscher crew's frantic attempts to contact the apartment. Getting past Angelina was Grauberger's last hope of gaining entry. "That figures. Angelina's girlfriend had to be on the same payroll as Lothar, Koors, and St. Charles."

Brewster perked up. "You have a Grauberger–St. Charles connection?"

"As far as absolutely proving it, we've hit a dead end. Grauberger and his buddies are being zipped into body bags as we speak."

Brewster started firing questions, but Clay stopped the barrage. "Hold on, Marcus. I'm going to give you plenty of good reasons to make Wil Meredith the headliner on your personal Most Wanted list. Killing the old lady is the only thing he *didn't* do."

"Meredith? You're kidding! What do you have?"

"At least three counts of murder," Hickey broke in, "attempted murder, conspiracy in the Gay Pride Day bombing, and kidnapping. I couldn't write it down fast enough. And that's just scratching the surface."

"And this garbage is badmouthing us cops? He's got a—"

"Marcus," Clay interrupted, "the kidnap victim—she's Rachel Meredith."

"His *wife*? How do you kidnap your wife?"

Clay explained quickly as he could, while Brewster swore under his breath.

"So only she knows where the Trabuc is—and that's keeping her alive?"

"That's the gist of it. But what scares the shit out of me is the possibility that she wrapped it up and left it with a friend. I think that's why Meredith didn't waste any time calling 911. It's a juicy story for the press. Maybe he's counting on the friend contacting him direct, right after the news about the maid's murder hits the air. The minute he gets his hands on that painting, Rachel Meredith's execution is a phone call away."

Hickey took charge. "Look, I want this kept small and tight. Ryder, where are you and Martino right now?"

"L.I.E. Just crossing into Queens."

"Okay. From what you've told me, you know your way around the studio on Twentieth Street. Detective Brewster, you're currently the only one we've got in Manhattan who can positively ID Meredith."

"Me and my partner, Sal Vernier. Meredith's been giving us both grief."

"Okay. I'm adding two more detectives, Merriweather and Sparks."

Clay was relieved; Hickey couldn't have picked better. Freddie Merriweather—"Hula"—was relatively new to Major Case, the only Hawaiian Clay knew in New York, and the widest Hawaiian he'd ever met. A scant hundred pounds more, and he might be mistaken for a sumo wrestler. Richard Sparks was Big Black Dick, a veteran known for his thoroughness and unflappable cool. Hula was too new to be into office politics, and Sparks was above them.

"They have to get a search warrant and a warrant for Meredith's arrest," Hickey continued. "Brewster, in the meantime, you and your partner plant yourselves outside the studio. If Meredith comes out, detain him. Dream up something to hold him until Sparks and Merriweather get there with those warrants. I figure Ryder and Martino should get there around the same time. If Meredith stays put, all of you go up together and get him."

"Marcus, he's armed," Clay warned. "And he's Daddy's little boy."

Clay shut off the phone and stretched impatiently, straining against his seat belt. Some detail had been overlooked, and it was gnawing at him.

"What about the Swiss dealer?" Cello was asking, "How did he fit in?"

"Grauberger? Right after the war—" Cello passed a restaurant supply truck. Chinese characters were printed in between its English name and an address on Canal Street. His fingers couldn't move over the phone fast enough.

Bloomie picked up. "Hula and Big Black Dick just left. Should I try to—?"

"No, look in my case file for the home phone number of Phil Chang."

Chang's answering machine switched on. "Phil! C'mon!" Clay pleaded. "Phil, it's Ryder! NYPD! I've got to—"

A frightened woman answered in Chinese, her speech a series of tiny explosions, like the minifirecrackers on a string that sizzle and fizzle in the China-town streets every Chinese New Year. All was lost on Clay, until she asked, "Yoooo say NYPD?"

"Yes. Detective Ryder."

The phone clattered onto a hard surface, and, after a one sided harangue conducted by the woman in another room, Phil came on the line.

"Phil, were you planning on going to work today?"

"I was, until Wil called me. He told me to take the day off."

"Really?" It was tough keeping his voice level. "When did he call?"

"Maybe half an hour ago, when I sat down to breakfast. After that, I took my time, read the paper. My mom just got me out of the shower. I told Wil I only had a couple of backup shots from yesterday, but he told me not to bother."

"Was that unusual?"

"Hell, yes!"

"Phil, I . . . Don't go to work, man."

"What's going on?" he asked, over the one-woman dirge in the back-ground. "Hold on, my mother thinks I'm about to be arrested." After a volley of respectful but rapid-fire Chinese, the lamentation ceased.

"Phil, did Meredith ever mention a boat? Going anyplace on a boat?"

"No, not that I remember."

Clay could see the Lloyd Neck shed filled with the red gas tanks, then the shed stripped bare. "How about weekend trips? Calls to places along the coast, north or south? Maine? Jersey? Connecticut? Delaware? Any of that ring a bell?"

"No, but he sure could use a vacation. He's been like, ultra tense. As far as a boat goes, he's pretty much a city person. He doesn't even own a car."

Clay sighed. "Right." He gave Chang Cello's number. "You remember anything along those lines, call me."

"He did ask me something strange, right before he hung up."

"Like what?"

"He wondered if Rachel gave me anything to hold for her. I told him I haven't seen her for at least two or three weeks."

"Okay. Good. Phil, listen to me. Unless you really want to give your mother something to cry about, don't even go near that studio until you hear from me again. I can't explain now, except that it has nothing to do with you and everything to do with your safety."

Clay exhaled a long sigh of relief. "Good news, Cello. Wil was still trying to find the painting half an hour ago." He sat back and looked out the wind-shield. "Nice trick. A single complaint from you about getting stuck in rush hour, and the traffic doesn't dare to materialize." As they whizzed past Little Neck, he pointed at the large green exit sign. "My best friend lives there."

"And all along, I thought it was the barbecued pinwheels."

"Frosting on the cake. And right about now, you're thinking, 'Didn't Ryder say there was something in this for me?' "

"About two counties back. Yeah, it's crossed my mind. But then you started talking about the Nazi getting the Van Gogh onto the open market. Keep going."

"Right. His version of legitimizing it. Which is supposed to end with his son burying the legal heir and cashing it in. After the war—up to maybe as recently as thirty years ago—such an elaborate scheme wouldn't have been necessary. But he was lying low in the Seventies. The timing wasn't right.

"It's a totally different world today: looted art's listed on the Internet, the Holocaust is a high school elective, and Jews took on the Swiss banks and won. In the interim, stolen artworks have turned up in museums all over the world, creating all sorts of accusations."

"But the museums, the collectors—don't they all keep records?"

"You'd need a Solomon to figure out all the claims and counterclaims, Cello. Lies about ownership go back sixty years. Records were lost, altered, or destroyed. Plus, a lot of the stolen art has been sold and resold many times over—some actually wound up in the homes of decent, honest people."

"So if an heir with hard proof comes along, there's no one around to give the current owners a refund—even if they bought in good faith?"

"Exactly. All the way back along the line, everyone claims innocence. Cello, you know I worked at Esterbrook-Grennell. They had a cutoff period for what they called 'challenges.' In other words, they'd stand behind what they sold for one year. Past that, they washed their hands of responsibility."

"Let's say the relative of a person who died at Auschwitz picks up a catalogue a year and a day after a sale . . ."

"That's the concept. The buyer finds himself in a legal no-man's-land. And Esterbrook-Grennell is by no means the only auction house with a cutoff date. As for museums, here in America they've only recently agreed to check all the art added to their collections since the Nazis took power, and that—"

"Oh shit!" Cello hit the brakes. He'd come hood-to-tail with the inevitable L.I.E. parking lot just east of the '64–'65 World's Fair site. Pounding the steering wheel, he stared at the left shoulder and the low concrete barrier that separated west and eastbound traffic. A devilish grin swept over his face as he swerved left onto the shoulder. "Let's hope nobody changed a tire recently." Cans, bottles, weeds the size of saplings, and curling shreds of rubber crunched beneath his wheels as he zipped by the creeping traffic. "So nowadays," Cello summarized, "your basic Nazi plunderer is screwed."

"No poet could have put it better. You drive this lane often?"

"Only when I'm really late."

Clay checked the tension on his seat belt and continued. "From what I've pieced together, Grauberger's late father fucked Luscher right after the war. Udo had just murdered his way into Switzerland, and Grauberger Senior's art gallery was the first stop for war criminals with paintings rolled up under their arms. A place to trade stolen art for a Get Out of Europe Quick pass. My guess is Luscher offered him Madame Trabuc, and Grauberger paid peanuts for it. Luscher didn't have much of a choice, but what Grauberger didn't know was that Luscher was the last person you'd ever squeeze by the balls. Not if you wanted to keep your own.

"Sometime in the early Seventies, Luscher retaliated—by screwing Grauberger with a fake Monsieur Trabuc. Because it was an exceptionally expert forgery, and because it came from the same source as Madame Trabuc, Grauberger was primed to believe it was genuine. He put it up for sale in a private black-market auction, and—not surprisingly—the high bidder was the same customer who'd bought Madame earlier. Everything was fine, until Rachel's original turned up last year. Suddenly, the Graubergers were knee-deep in shit with the black-market guy."

"What goes around comes around."

"Never truer. Anyhow, at some point, Luscher brought the authentic Van Gogh into this country from Argentina. The last few years, he hid out at the end of Lloyd Neck, pulling all the strings. He narrowed it down so that the only person left to kill is Rachel. That done, ta-da! His son Wil legally inherits the painting."

"Not if we catch up with Udo and his U-boat! But where the hell are they?"

"Wherever he lived in the years between South America and Baranowski's house—that's got to be where he's headed."

Cello stayed on the shoulder as long as he could. They were forced to slow down for a stretch, but once they cut onto the Midtown Tunnel's express bus ramp, they had wings. Across the river, Manhattan's towers rose up like the grand finale pages in a kid's pop-up book. A shiver passed through Clay as he tallied how many had died in the brief hours since his last look at the skyline from the BMW's mirror, all because of the Trabuc.

"Hold on!" Cello yelled. "Didn't you say Luscher smuggled the painting into the States? Why sneak it out and ship it back here again?"

"We're talking lies, illusions. In this case, the main illusion is that the Nazi who stole the painting was dead as a doornail—as the letter from the old lady in South America stated. Luscher knew he'd be connected to the painting, but it was essential that he be considered long gone."

They sped past the tollbooths and into the netherworld of the tunnel. Signs warned that changing lanes was prohibited. Cello switched back and forth with a frequency that would have earned a civilian motorist triple the points necessary to kiss his license good-bye forever.

After calling in their position, Clay continued, "As for the package from South America, Luscher knew where it'd be every mile along the way—almost to the minute."

They emerged into dazzling July sunshine. Red light flashing, Cello threaded through the trucks and taxis clotting the tunnel exit. As he turned onto Thirty-fourth Street, he announced his game plan: "Thirty-fourth west to Fifth; south on Fifth to Twentieth."

"You can't turn onto Fifth at Thirty-fourth!"

"*I* fucking can!" A jaywalker in Cello's path flung himself back onto the curb. "What are you telling me about the damn package? What am I missing here? Of course he can track the painting! The old lady shipped it UPS!"

"I said the package, not the painting! Luscher wouldn't let Trabuc out of his sight for fifty-five years! He was obsessed by what could have happened if he shipped it anywhere! What if it was damaged, or lost? No, he sent his sister-in-law to Argentina to mail two worthless sheets of cardboard!" Clay paused. "But at the same time, he knew the route of the UPS truck that delivers to the Metropolitan like the back of his hand. In fact, he knew the routes of many overnight delivery trucks." They crossed Third Avenue.

"What the hell are you saying? That there's a connection with the holdups?"

"Strange as it sounds, the holdup was Luscher's insurance policy—the only way he could absolutely guarantee that the Trabuc would make it to the Met intact, without even a hint of a threat, for the few hours he had to let go of it."

"That devious, evil bastard!" Cello started slapping the steering wheel as he rolled past Park Avenue. "I'm starting to see it—yes!"

"Luscher's late nephew Benito—Mr. Crossfire, the guy tied to the chair with the medium height and build and the dark olive skin—he was the UPS shooter. Because of the sunglasses and the stick-on mustache he wore on the Eighty-first Street job, I didn't make him when we were face-to-face last night. But he was the one who hopped on that truck, knocked out the driver, slit open the package his mama sent, slipped in the Van Gogh. The wrapping was a shiny tan paper. It would've stood out—but not too much—among all the dull brown boxes. Benito had the same tape his mother used in Argentina. He resealed it. Put it back where he found it." Madison was behind them.

"So when you responded to Eighty-first Street, the Van Gogh was tucked in the van," Cello concluded for him. "Beating and robbing the driver cleverly ensured that UPS would guard every package on that truck like a hawk until the last one was delivered, nice and safe."

"From that point on," said Clay, "Luscher didn't have a worry in the world—his plan was rolling ahead."

"It all fits, Ryder, right down to the getaway car! Of course, when you interrupted their fine-tuned little game plan, Benito lost his cool."

"Not enough to stop him from emptying his .45 at three cops."

"And if all that wasn't enough, he completely controlled the investigation's focus—those two previous holdups made it look like a pattern crime," Cello snarled. "By the fourth one, he had us in knots—totally diverted. The painting was incidental by then."

"Precisely. And the same fastidious planning went into Gay Pride Day. One bomb, just where Rachel and I happened to be, would have raised questions. But two bombs were planted, at Tenth and Sixteenth, same as the charter date of S.T.R.A.I.G.H.T.—deflecting the blame again. Luscher is meticulous, Cello . . . and very, very smart."

"All the time we wasted patrolling uptown . . . then that chase up Amsterdam, and the way those heartless motherfuckers whacked that lady!" Brakes screeched and horns protested as Cello turned south on Fifth. "You don't know how good it feels, getting those robberies off my back!" He skidded to a stop along yellow curb just north of Twentieth Street. They flung open their doors and raced toward the corner.

As soon as they rounded Twentieth Street, Hula and Big Black Dick jumped out of their car, which was positioned about ten feet behind the Meredith Studio building, on the opposite side of the street. A woman in wrinkled black linen exited from the backseat, a file folder tucked under her arm. In her flat-heeled shoes, she was the same six-one as Big Black Dick. Clay was glad to see her: R. Gold, the toughest assistant district attorney he'd ever met. Few knew the R. stood for Rainbow, which smacked of parents who'd conceived her in full body paint at Woodstock, but R.'s no-nonsense style belied any hippie forebears.

Looking back over his shoulder, Hula nodded to a car parked another twenty feet or so behind theirs. As the three of them crossed the street, walking toward Clay and Cello at a brisk pace, Brewster and his partner left the other vehicle. Sal was a gal; Vernier looked half the size of Gold, but walked as if she owned the whole sidewalk.

"The warrants?" Clay called out to Gold. She patted the file with an expression that was as close as she would ever come to a smile. By this time, Sparks, Merriweather, and Gold had the Meredith Studio building behind them. Brewster and partner stepped up onto the curb a good distance west of the door. A couple in shorts and a woman walking two small dogs were the only other pedestrians nearby.

At that very moment, Udo Luscher's son walked out of the building.

Even from where he was, Clay could see the dark circles under Wil's blue eyes. As he cleared the door, he glanced down at a handful of change he'd just pulled out of his slacks. When he looked straight ahead, he saw Clay. All color drained from his face, turning it the same ghastly, ghostly white Clay's would've been, had that bag of bricks still anchored him to the ocean floor. For a split second, Wil was immobilized. He hadn't even seen Brewster and his partner, who were actually closer to him than Clay.

"Freeze!" Clay shouted. He charged at Wil, spinning Gold around.

With a jerk, Wil snapped to and backed into the building.

Behind him, Cello was yelling at the pedestrians, "Police—get down!"

Clay, Brewster, and Vernier, converging all at once, almost crashed into one another. They rushed inside, just in time to see the elevator door slide closed. Seconds later, Cello and the group from Police Plaza burst in.

"He's going to four," Clay said through clenched teeth. "Then he'll lock the elevator."

Brewster's partner pulled out a phone. "I'm calling for backup!"

"This is a kidnapping!" Clay warned her. "Meredith's our only link to the victim. We can't take a chance on someone getting trigger-happy."

Cello leaned on the up-down buttons. The floor indicator slowly rose from two to three. With a distant clang, the cranky elevator stopped at four. Something strained in the cable, but it stayed where it was.

"I know there's a fire escape outside the back windows," Clay told the others. "If we can get in on one of the other floors, maybe we can get into the studio from the fire escape. Or even get into the elevator from an upper floor. Problem is, except for the studio, the building's all residential—God only knows if anyone's at home. Hula, you're the only one of us with a shot at breaking down the studio's fire door."

Hula immediately headed for the stairway.

Pointing at the wall mailbox unit, Clay turned to the DA. "Gold, start ringing everybody's doorbell. Martino and I will run up to five, to try—"

"Rest of us'll each take a floor," Brewster called after them.

Clay and Cello hustled up the stairs. Cello was panting, and Clay went on ahead. He heard bells ringing, fists pounding on metal. As he passed four, Hula was alternating kicks and shoves against the metal door, with nothing but dents for his effort. He rapped on the fifth floor's fire door. No answer. "Cello," he called down the stairwell, "you take six, I'll run up to seven."

Two flights up, the loft's bell was piercing, audible even through steel. So was a crying baby.

"Police!" Clay shouted at the door. "Open up! We need access through this apartment! I hear the baby—I know you're in there. Open the door!"

As if it were being rocked, the baby calmed down a little. Hearing that Clay had made contact, Cello sent the message down, then headed up after him.

"A kidnapping victim is going to be killed," Clay implored, "unless we get into your apartment now!"

"I'm only the baby-sitter," came the faint reply. "I'm not supposed to let anyone in. Ever."

The doorbell sounded again, startling the baby into another crying jag. Cello, out of breath, was at Clay's side.

"That's the district attorney ringing your doorbell," Clay yelled over the wails. "That means nobody else is answering, no one else is home. You'll be the one on the six-o'clock news."

A dead bolt clicked. They rushed in past a teenager cradling a wriggling infant.

Cello stared at the padlocked gates barricading the oversize windows "Where're the keys?" he demanded.

The girl pointed under the sill. Dangling from a plastic hook glued just out of sight was a key. Cello grabbed it, bent to open the lower padlock, and passed it up to Clay. The accordion gate was stiff; it probably hadn't been opened in years. Pushing hard, they half-crushed, half-folded it aside. Cello banged at the window sash and crossbar while Clay pushed up, but countless layers of paint had the frame glued shut.

Cello wheeled around, grabbed a retro bronze torch lamp, and yelled, "Get back—all the way back!" at the terrified baby-sitter. Wielding it with two hands, he rammed the heavy base through the pane, smashing it several times more to make an adequate opening

"There he is!" Leaning forward through the window frame, Cello was the first to spot Wil. He was scrambling onto the fire escape of the building directly to the rear, which faced onto Twenty-first Street. A narrow gap separated the two buildings, eight feet at most. Linking the two fire escapes was a board that looked like the top of the sawhorse-table used for photo shoots. Wil spun around, lifted it, and shoved it over the railing. As it crash-landed on the thin strip of concrete below with a resounding crack, he took off for the third-floor landing, a gun in his hand.

Clay pushed past Cello, out onto the seventh-floor fire escape. Behind them, a commotion was building. Both baby-sitter and baby were wailing; Marcus and Sal were racing breakneck into the loft; Sparks was calling down to Hula to stop banging and get upstairs; below, Gold was still ringing bells. And Cello, one leg through the frame, was screaming, "Ryder, what the hell are you thinking?"

Clay had already concluded, after a lightning survey of body types (from Sal Vernier, who'd literally fall short, to Hula, who'd rip the fire escape from its supports), that no one else had a chance. He was balanced on the railing, flexing his knees.

"Who do you think you are, fucking Tarzan?"

He had to do it before Cello yanked him back. From the corner of his eye, he saw Wil descending from three to two. Fixing Rachel's face in his mind, arms stretched forward, he made the leap.

His aim had been to grab the vertical supports of the landing with both hands. Instead, only his right hand made contact with the fire escape, and he'd caught it much lower down, on the sloping railing. While his left hand clawed at air, he immediately began sliding down. Worse, the impact had swung him out, so he was sliding backward . . . fast. He held on to the weather-pocked railing with all his might, the crack of the board when it hit bottom still ringing in his ears. Mercifully, the sixth-floor landing ended the ride. As he clambered over the railing, he saw Martino out on the fire escape, calling something down to him, but the blood pounding in his ears blotted out most of it. Then he saw the gun he was holding out toward him. Clay put out his hands and Cello's Glock smacked into them. When he looked down again, Wil was out of sight.

No building stood east of the Twenty-first Street building; the empty space was filled by an open parking lot. Because the adjoining buildings didn't conform to the same width or length, the rear of the crowded lot formed an L-shape. It extended nearly halfway behind the building Clay was racing down. The fire escape ended in a metal walkway on the second floor. Below the walkway, a wooden fence blocked off the end of the parking lot. It was typical of the hodgepodge of lumber used to shore up demolition sites, and evidently had been left in place when the structure that once filled the lot was torn down. A nasty bramble bush of concertina wire sprouted beneath and all around the sides of the walkway, between it and the ragtag fence. If the intention was to deter anyone from breaking in by gaining access to the walkway, it had to be effective. Breaking out, however, was another story. A jump onto the fencetop followed by a leap *over* the razor wire wasn't out of the question.

When Clay hit the walkway, the only trace of Wil was a shred of his light blue shirtsleeve, snagged on the very edge of the concertina wire.

"East!" Cello was yelling.

Clay landed with two feet on the narrow fencetop, and never stopped moving: he jumped to the roof of a van, the hood of a sedan, and exited the lot in time to see Wil dash across Fifth as the light turned red.

The block between Fifth and Broadway was short, making it easy to track Wil's progress. Unable to stand still and watch Wil's head start of fifty yards lengthen, Clay darted out across the path of southbound traffic. Only a long leap onto the far curb saved him from a slow-moving van that suddenly sped up to run the light.

Up ahead, at Broadway, it was Wil's turn to be slowed by the stoplight, to dodge and duck and thread his way to the other side. The click to green when Clay reached the intersection was a real break; even in his oversize sneakers, he was able to keep up his momentum and have a shot at closing the gap. The next block, which ran to Park Avenue South, was exceptionally long: a dark, narrow stretch of motley commercial buildings, only occasionally brightened by a storefront or coffee shop. Little was revealed about the businesses behind the grim facades, nor did the boxes being loaded on and off trucks provide a clue.

Like many men well over six feet, Wil was more a loper than a runner. Also, he tended to zigzag every time he looked back over his left shoulder at

Clay, something he was doing with increasing frequency. He never saw the tall black woman who'd just worked herself out of a low-slung Corvette; he rammed into her so hard, she hit the pavement, headfirst. After a half-stumble forward, he spun around and fired a burst at Clay. A pile of cartons sat on the edge of the sidewalk, and Clay dove behind them. He wound up in the gutter, along with the two truckers who'd just off-loaded them. Seeing his gun, they plastered themselves to the ground, hands shielding their heads. As soon as the shots stopped, Clay sprang up onto the truck's mechanical lift. He poked his head out for a quick look over the stacked-up boxes. Luscher Jr. was once again running east. Clay hopped down and took off after him.

He had no choice but to jump over the Corvette lady, sprawled bleeding and dazed across the sidewalk. A few feet away, a woman who'd taken cover behind a mound of trash bags was weeping and holding out a trembling hand toward her, too terrified to venture out and render aid.

In the distance, the mosquito-whine of police sirens grew. With dread, Clay imagined the flash of a fellow officer's gun, and the path of the bullet that would simultaneously finish Wil and sever the only link he had to Rachel.

Running with his gun in full sight, Wil had Twenty-first Street's pedestrians huddled in doorways, pressed behind columns, wedged between cars. Literally no one stood between him and Park Avenue South. Even with the sirens drawing close, he didn't hesitate when he reached the corner. He barged right across the broad, busy thoroughfare.

In the wake of his crossing, brakes screeched—a thousand fingernails on a thousand blackboards. Metal struck metal with a grinding crunch. Like a CD gone haywire, the terrible sounds repeated over and over again. Before Clay reached the avenue, he knew that Wil's mad dash had set off a monstrous chain reaction. The first thing he saw was a crumpled station wagon straddling one of the giant concrete planters that lined Park Avenue South's center divider. To his left, on the avenue's west sidewalk, steam was escaping from the hood of a mangled taxi, and a three-car pileup had traffic on the east roadway totally snarled. People were screaming, and smoke and burning rubber fouled the air. Clay spotted Wil moving uptown at a steady pace toward Twenty-second Street. He seemed to be veering toward the corner subway entrance.

Only local trains stopped at the Twenty-third Street station—the Lexington Avenue IRT number 6. If you wanted to go uptown, you entered on the east side of Park; downtown passengers, on the west. Number 4 express trains roared along the middle two tracks as if Twenty-third Street didn't exist.

Because traffic was at a dead standstill, Clay could race right across the avenue, but he instinctively turned to look both ways. Two unmarked cars with flashing red lights had been trapped in the backup from the multiple crashes while negotiating the turn north onto Park from Twentieth Street. Hula was the first to emerge, tall enough to catch sight of Clay as he sprinted across Park Avenue South. On the opposite side, Wil was melding into the darkness just inside the gaping mouth of the subway stairs.

Half in the sun, half in the subway gloom, at first Clay couldn't make out exactly what was lying across the middle of the worn stone steps. As his eyes adjusted, he saw two girls, barely in their teens. One was sprawled over the stairs, while the other was desperately urging her to get to her feet, frantically trying to pull her up. Female adolescent gear—books and hairbrushes and pencils and lipsticks—were scattered all around them. Foreheads practically touching, each wailed directly into the other's face. In his breakneck run down the stairs, Clay tried to avoid them and any paraphernalia that could send him skidding headfirst toward the turnstiles.

A few steps below them, where the token booth came into view, he made a grab for the banister, flattening against the stairwell wall. The glass part of the booth was splattered with red. In front of the base, a transit cop was slumped on the floor. One leg was stretched out straight, while the other, bent at the knee, pointed right. Her hat had fallen forward onto her lap. Except for the blood, she looked like a broken police doll, waiting to be fixed. Hugging the wall, Clay cautiously crept down the remaining stairs. Although the booth operator had crouched out of sight, Clay heard his frantic shouts for help filtering through the bulletproof glass via the microphone above his head.

On the other side of the turnstiles, Wil had taken control of the platform. Brandishing his gun, he rotated slowly, readying for his next move. People were stretched out prone on the platform. As Wil came full circle, he caught sight of Clay. Two shots pinged off the bulletproof glass of the token booth just as Clay hit the deck. On his stomach and elbows, he wriggled under a turnstile. The bullets had touched off a chorus of moans and panicky cries from the people cowering on the floor. Clay cleared the turnstile and lifted his head. Once again, Wil had vanished.

With a rumble, the number 6 downtown lumbered into the station on the opposite track. Clay quickly rose to one knee. Not too far from the track, a line of white-tiled columns, all bearing black 23s, ran the length of the station. Wil could be lurking behind any one of them. Keeping low, Clay made a dash for the closest pillar and peered out. On the left, Wil was running downtown. No target could have been more tempting—if not for the threat to Rachel. Using the row of columns to provide cover like a straight stand of trees, Clay sprinted along to their right, near the platform's edge. In between, he caught glimpses of Wil, looking back over his left shoulder.

Ahead, a low red gate with a DO NOT ENTER OR CROSS TRACKS sign blocked off the downtown end of the platform, a clear-cut line of demarcation between passengers and authorized transit personnel. Often a station's platform extended into the tunnel for a little way, ending in a short flight of stairs for tunnelworkers that led down to the tracks. As Clay made up the distance between them, Wil cut in front of the southernmost pillar, heading for the red gate. He had to stop to bend forward to unlatch it, and in that brief pause, he must have sensed Clay coming up behind him. Only half-straightened, Wil whirled around to the right, his right arm following up and through in an arc. Before the gun in his hand—a Glock, probably Clay's own—came down into firing position, Clay made a running grab for his wrist. Wil's slightly off-balance stance, combined with the impact of Clay's lunge against him, forced them both off the platform. The grating thunder of the downtown local pulling out reverberated through the station as they hurtled down onto the tracks.

The fall of about five feet felt like twenty when Clay's back hit the steel rail with Wil right on top of him. The impact sent Cello's gun flying out of his right hand. Pain short-circuited through every bone in his back; it relayed back and forth on a chaotic course, deranged and jangling as a pinball machine. Mercifully, they kept on rolling toward the center of the tracks, relieving him of Wil's full weight. Clay's left hand hadn't relinquished its viselike lock around Wil's wrist; his right hand, now free, rammed Wil's finger up against the trigger.

The Glock's clip held sixteen shots, several already expended. The remainder began spraying everywhere, ricocheting off the tracks, steel beams, tiles, concrete. Even the departing downtown train couldn't drown out the tinny echo of the bullets, and they set off another round of despairing screams from the uptown-bound platform.

With Wil still grappling for the gun even after the clip was spent, they continued to roll until they settled—with Wil on the bottom—into a trench in the middle of the track bed. The centers of several wood ties had been sawed away to create the crude drainage channel, which was about nine inches deep. Only a sluggish trickle of muddy water moved through the trench, but Wil dropped the gun as soon as he began to sink into it, struggling against the suck of the filthy ooze. Clay seized his chance, immediately pinning Wil with his left arm, preventing him from fighting back with his right.

"You think I'd let you drown in this little rat shit puddle?" he asked, as he began to pummel Wil's face. "Drowning's too easy for you." Relentlessly, he pounded Wil's left eye and nose. "I should know, right?"

Wil was bleeding profusely. "I can't shoot you, though. I can't shoot you. I can't shoot you," he repeated with every subsequent blow, whacking away like a madman. Beneath him, Wil's resistance weakened.

"Tell me if you've had enough, cocksucker," he yelled into Wil's ear.

Something gargled through splintered bone and broken teeth and blood.

"Was that Nazi for 'Enough'?" Clay asked politely. He paused, holding his fist aloft—not that Wil's left eye could see it, or might ever see anything again.

The reply was another clotted gag.

"You said it too soon!" Clay delivered one more shot to Wil's head. Then, grabbing him by the shirt with both hands, he strained to lift them both to their feet.

An explosive, high-pitched blare suddenly sounded from the south.

Back in the tunnel, the rails turned to silver ribbons. A gleaming blue-white, they unfurled rapidly, rushing at them out of the darkness. Blinding light streamed over the station's white tiles. Squinting, Clay stared into the headlights of the uptown local. Before he realized he'd relaxed his grasp on Wil's shirt, a knee slammed into his groin. Writhing in pain, Clay began to double over, but Wil pushed him backward, even closer to the oncoming train. Staggering in reverse, Clay stumbled over the rail. The back of his head struck the edge of the platform.

The shrill screech of airbrakes tore through the station. It spiked through his throbbing head, through his eardrums, through every nerve in his teeth. A metallic grinding followed the screech. The train was trying to stop, but the grinding kept on going. It was audible through the next warning blast of the horn.

Clay struggled to raise himself out of the track bed by angling his elbow onto the platform, but he could barely maintain his balance. In the blaze of the onrushing headlights, he saw Wil leap over the third rail, toward the steel pillars that separated the local from the express tracks.

The bastard was getting away, and he was going to die. Rachel was going to die.

For all their noise, the brakes had done little: from his perspective down in the track pit, the bigger the train grew, the faster it seemed to be coming at him. He could see the motorman's face, panic-twisted.

At the last possible second, a hand closed around his elbow; the crook of an arm came around his neck, and strong fingers grabbed him by the elasticized waist of his pants. While all these disembodied, snatching hands hoisted him up, something whooshed by underneath him. He knew it was nothing more than a rush of wind filling the space he'd been helped to vacate so abruptly, but he'd never felt anything so cold in his entire life.

The next thing he knew, he was on the platform, gasping from the temporary pressure that had been exerted on his windpipe. He watched as the number 6 uptown local shuddered to a stop, two and a half cars into the station. Hula, who had not yet let up his grip on the sweatpants' waistband, had leaned Clay's back and head against his massive torso for support. Big Black Dick, his other savior, bent beside him, asking if he was okay. Really okay. No shit okay.

Right in front of them, the local had shuddered to a complete standstill, but the harsh shriek of airbrakes still hadn't stopped. Hula straightened up, raising Clay with him. The high-pitched rasp was coming from the express tracks. Through the windows of the uptown local, they could see the uptown express, bucking to a stop a few car lengths beyond where he'd last seen Wil. Seconds later, except for a few metallic pings, the station fell silent.

Directly in front of them, people in the local began picking themselves up off the floor.

Arms pumping, Marcus Brewster was running toward them from the Twenty-third Street entrance.

From the other side of the station, a familiar voice called out, "Ryder—you okay?"

"I'm okay, Cello!"

His voice was weak, so Sparks shouted back, "He's okay, Cello!"

"Tell him not to get pissed off, thinking anyone shot Wil. No cop is going to waste bullets on roadkill."

"No, Inspector, I don't think he could hear it coming," Cello reported into his cell phone. "The airbrakes from the local were definitely loud enough to drown out the express." Cello briefly weighed his words before he answered Hickey's next question: "See it? No, Sir, it seems his left eye was swollen shut." Again he listened, then summed it up: "Let me put it this way, Inspector. I'll never eat chunky salsa again."

Like half of Manhattan, both at and below street level, Hickey was caught in traffic. Glancing at Clay, Martino whispered surreptitiously into his phone, "To be honest, I've never seen anyone so disgustingly filthy, so it's hard to tell if he's—"

"Damn it, I'm okay!" Clay protested. Still shaky, he forced himself up into a standing position, waving off Hula's assistance.

"She did? Great! We'll head right back there. Sure. I'll put him on."

Hoping he looked more exasperated than exhausted, Clay leaned back against one of the white tile "23" columns and reached his hand out for the phone.

"Not you. Big Black Dick." Cello passed the phone to Sparks.

Martino leaned against the column next to Clay's. He put his hands in his pockets, just another guy waiting for a train, even though two were already in the station. "Hickey wants you and me out of here before the mayor and the megabrass show up. The last thing we need is to get bogged down in this investigation. If you're up to it, the plan is for us to get back to the Meredith studio ASAP. Thanks to a little help from the Thirteenth Precinct, Gold got in."

"Yes, Sir," Sparks was saying, "uniforms came down right after us. The area's secured." He turned north, in the direction of the token booth. "No—she never had a chance. Yes. Yes, we will. Right, I'll put him on."

Again, Clay held his hand out.

"Detective Brewster!" After Sparks passed the phone to Brewster, he turned to Clay. "For now, Brewster and Vernier are in charge of the mess down here. A transition team's being assembled—Hickey wants Hula and me to hang in until they show up. And don't worry, we'll make sure the tracks are searched for two Glocks—or what's left of them—soon as the trains move out. Anyway, the DI and the commanders of the Thirteenth and Transit District 2 will meet right here in the station. Then we'll regroup downtown. And Ryder, you're gonna love the official phrase of the day: 'The train victim cannot be identified.' "

"Hey, it plays both ways," Vernier agreed. "Either 'We're keeping a lid on,' or 'No one knows who the instant Spam on the tracks is.' Or was."

Finally, Brewster handed the phone to Clay.

"Ryder," Hickey began, "you're either the best damn detective I've ever had in my squad, or the luckiest."

After experiencing visual hallucinations back in the Sound, Clay wondered if his hearing was being affected the same way. "How's that, Sir?" he asked tentatively.

"Preliminary results on the explosives that turned up in Lloyd Neck are pointing to a link with the Gay Pride bombing. Plus, Ballistics is optimistic that a gun found out there will be the cannon the UPS shooter used up on Eighty first Street. Assuming both those possibilities pan out, we'll have two more closed—get it, *closed*—cases. I kept you hanging because a fax was coming in at the office. That Suffolk chief, Cochran, sent it. You know anything about blood they collected from stairs leading to a boat dock?"

"What've they got?"

"Cochran wanted you to know the bleeder was a male."

"That's got to be the best news of all."

"Good job," said Hickey. He abruptly clicked off.

"Sir," Clay said into the phone, as if the DI were still there, "does that mean you've forgiven my sins against your Crown Vic?"

"How did you get here from there—from Fifth?" Turning his face so Cello wouldn't see him grimace at the pain in his back, Clay lowered himself into the car. It was parked at the corner of Twenty-second and Park.

"I guess this is my bad-boy day," Martino confessed. "A U on Fifth."

Clay shook his head. "Why didn't you just throw it into reverse?' "

"I'll save that for next time. Besides, I only went uptown for two blocks." Since he'd parked north of the accident site, Cello had no trouble getting out of the area. Following a more conventional route back to the studio, he doubleparked under the care of the uniforms posted outside.

Gold's serious face, usually grim and pale, was grim and flushed when she greeted them at the studio. "I'm beat. We've been searching everywhere— nothing's turned up. Not a scrap. Meredith—or whoever he is—dumped it all."

"What you want is in the safe," Clay insisted. "Everything he—"

"That safe?" Gold stepped back so that Clay and Cello could precede her into the small office. The combination door was wide open. All the cameras were lined up, but the lower shelf was bare. She pointed to a shredder. "All we picked out of that was minuscule fragments of photographs. Nothing usable. I checked with the Department of Sanitation. Sure enough, the trash is picked up early— more than two hours before we showed up. Meredith had plenty of time to shred everything, then stand back and watch it get churned in with the rest of the garbage in one of the fragrant white trucks."

Clay stared at the shredder, remembering Rachel's agony over the shots of her brother and mother. "Rachel knocked some pictures out of my hands. Maybe they're . . ." He dropped to his hands and knees, but nothing was visible on the floor. Suddenly, he sprang up and groped along the back of a file cabinet. "Those negatives!" They'd slipped out of sight, but he found them wedged in the narrow space between cabinet and wall. "Gold, can you get these printed?"

"Ryder, this is a photo studio—millions of negatives are lying around!"

"But these are from the safe! I put them up there, and . . ." All of a sudden, Clay whirled around. "My jacket—it was on that chair! My wallet was in it! My shield! And Meredith put my .38 in the safe!"

"Same white truck," Cello said. "Anything connected to a dead cop—you better believe that was the first thing he dumped."

"Pretend you were mugged," Gold cut in. "But from the way you look, Detective, you don't have to do much pretending, do you?"

Sitting down hard on the office chair, Clay put his head between his hands. "How the hell do we find Rachel now?"

"Find the painting first," said Gold, "and start negotiating."

"I wish to God I knew where she hid it! It took her an hour and a half to meet me here—it could be anywhere! Luscher is going to pry it out of her eventually . . . I don't even want to think how. Right now, all I know is that he has a place to lay low that's accessible by boat. He's probably there already. Once he gets Rachel to talk, he gets in touch with Wil. As soon as Wil confirms that the painting's back in the Luscher fold, Rachel's dead. Or that *was* the plan, before Wil beat her to it. To being dead."

When Clay glanced up, Gold's cheeks had drained to their customary pallor, and then some. "We've checked the answering machine here. No messages. Not yet, anyway. I've already requested records for the phones here, at the Ninth Street apartment, and Lloyd Harbor. The last three billing cycles were emailed here. The rest will take a little longer. Nothing but local calls so far."

Cello beat Clay to the computer and scrolled down. "Look how careful they were—not a single call between the Lloyd Harbor number and the city, or vice versa. What about a cell phone, Gold?"

"Nothing turned up, under either Meredith, Kelski, or Baranowski."

"What if it's the other way around?" asked Cello. "What if Wil was supposed to call in to Pa Hitler every couple hours or so . . . by pay phone? Remember when he walked out of here? Looked like he was checking his change."

"Sure," agreed Clay, "that has to be the way they stayed in touch!"

"Yeah. Great theory," said Cello. "But where's it go? It only backs us up closer to the wall."

"I'm going back downtown," Gold said wearily.

"I'd give you a lift, but Ryder here has to go back to his apartment."

"I do?" Clay asked.

"You ever read about those people who live in the train tunnels? Ever wonder how they smell? I no longer have to use my imagination."

"Damn! My keys! They were in my jacket along with everything else!" Heat rolled off the hood of Cello's car as Clay came around to face his brownstone. He was desperate for a shower, if only to clear his head.

Cello stared up at the building. "Isn't there a super?"

"Just a guy who lives down the block and takes care of five or six buildings. Good luck finding him. And he doesn't have my apartment key, anyway."

"Maybe you don't need a key," said Cello, one step ahead. "Take a look."

Hardly perceptible to a passerby, the gate was ajar. After pulling his backup gun from his ankle holster, Cello gave the metal grillwork a little push. Pressed up flat against the wall of the hallway, they both advanced on Clay's apartment. Yellowish electric light escaped through the partially open door. Cello was closest to it, and he listened hard, barely breathing, for a long time. With the tip of his shoe, he nudged the door open. Except for the ancient refrigerator's overworked motor, all was quiet. Once they slipped through the doorway, however, they saw it would be impossible to maintain their silence: the living room–kitchen had been thoroughly ransacked, and every step would crunch noisily over the flotsam and jetsam of Clay's years there. Abandoning any attempt at stealth, the two of them rushed the bedroom. Something moved, and Cello almost fired, but the orange cat scampered out the open garden door on one of its nine lives. Clay pointed to himself, then to the bathroom; Cello took the closet.

"Long gone," said Cello, when they regrouped in the wreck of the living room.

Looking around, Clay saw that they'd charged right over the shattered remains of the *Shelter Island*. In the work area, only the smokestack, a blue-and-white striped shred of flag, and a bottle of stain were identifiable. The rest, scattered splinters, was all that remained of his harrowing postmortem relationship with Lauren. Instead of anger or frustration, a profound sense of sorrow settled over him. To feel sad, and only sad . . . perhaps that was the most therapeutic result he could have wished for.

"You think Meredith did this, looking for the painting?" asked Cello.

"Wil this morning, Grauberger's boys last night—it doesn't matter anymore." As Clay crossed back toward the bedroom to rebolt the garden door, he noticed the band of perspiration that had broken out across Cello's forehead. "Martino, are you sick?"

"Yeah, just a little indigestion. The heat. I have to lose a couple of pounds."

Bending here and there, Clay assembled a change of clothes and found shoes that matched. "I'm taking a shower."

"Good. Wash at least twice."

"Grady-White!" Dripping wet, Clay bounded across the debris-strewn apartment. The phone in the bedroom was irretrievably buried, but the one in the kitchen was wall-mounted. "Grady-White!" he repeated to 800 information. "Boats! They make boats!"

"This might sound crazy," Clay said when he reached the Grady-White switchboard operator, "but I need to speak with someone who knows every model your company's made for the past ten years. Right away."

As if callers with great desperation in their voices made such requests regularly, Clay was put through instantly. After explaining who he was and describing the boat, he blurted out, "The range is what I'm looking for. An estimate of how far the boat can go on a tank of gas. I know you're going to ask me for the model or the year. And I have absolutely no idea."

The Grady-White man was a Southerner, as congenial as Clay was impatient. "Oh, we'll find it, Detective! I like a challenge! Besides, we've got twenty-seven or twenty-eight feet and twin Merc two-twenty-fives to go on. My guess is . . . right! Just wanted to confirm. Okay, we can pin it down to a Sailfish. '95 or later. Twenty-eight footer. Did she look five years old?"

"She looked perfect. The engine sounded well tuned."

"Music to my ears. I'm pretty sure we're looking at a two-zero-two . . . yessir, that's it! A two-hundred-and-two-gallon tank. Rounded off, she'll take you about three hundred miles at cruising speed. Up in your neck of the woods, they call her a 'canyon runner'—leave the dock at dawn, come back late at night, nary a worry . . . a nice, easy ride."

Imagining Rachel, bruised and bound, Clay couldn't agree with the nice, easy part. "Cruising is what—about thirty-five an hour?"

"Correct. Wide open, fifty-plus. Give or take, you'd go from one point five miles per gallon cruising, to around one wide open."

"Cruising, about seven hours to go three hundred nautical miles?"

"Give or take." After Clay thanked him, he politely asked, "Would you like me to send you some literature on this year's models?"

"A Grady-White? *Me?*" The guy had been a big help, and he didn't want him to waste his time. "Thanks for the offer, but I'm a little short of cash right now—my wallet's been stolen."

Tracing a mental map of the East Coast, Clay headed back into his bedless bedroom to dress. Three hundred miles . . . Would that get him as far north as Maine? Or as far south as Virginia? He rummaged on the floor until he found a tie. "I'm ready, Cello. For what, I'm not quite sure."

Back at Police Plaza, Gold had more phone records, but they yielded nothing. The negatives were still being developed. Miss Vanilla smiled as he passed her, and not one, but two other detectives mumbled, "How you doing, Ryder?" A message to call Detective Ross out in Suffolk County was on Clay's desk.

"We started checking out the Huntington marinas, but we also ran another check with Motor Vehicles—by address," Ross told him. "Sure enough, we got a match at the Lloyd Neck house. That dead handyman had it registered in his name. Just like you called it, a twenty-eight-foot Grady-White. A '95 model, bought used in '98. I've been trying to reach you for two hours—where've you been?"

"Thought I was going to be stuck in the subway forever."

"Anyway, I wanted you to know the Coast Guard has the registration number. But they didn't get it until around ten. God only knows how many miles the Nazi had behind him by then."

"Ross, your contact at the Coast Guard—I need that number."

Ten minutes later, using a dog-eared 1991 Road Atlas Cello had scrounged up, Clay figured where three hundred and fifty nautical miles could take Luscher from Lloyd Neck. (Assuming the Grady-White had a topped-off gas tank before it went back and forth from Sunken Meadow State Park, then took on all those five-gallon tanks stacked in the shed, he could eke out another fifty-plus miles.)

To the north, his destination could have been anywhere in the stretch between Connecticut, Rhode Island, Massachusetts, New Hampshire, and the lower half of Maine. (Considerably farther north in Maine, the Coast Guard officer had explained, if he chose to cut through the Cape Cod Canal. But Clay's gut told him Luscher would never put himself in a position to be pinned in like that. Rather than risk being bottled up inside a narrow canal, he'd opt for the longer run in open water around the Cape.)

As for a route south, the same concept would hold true if he headed for Manhattan—the Grady-White couldn't exactly sneak down the East River. Heading east, all around Long Island, would waste a good portion of his gas in a place he didn't want to be—New York waters. At best, he wouldn't wind up too far south of New Jersey, probably along the Delaware part of the Delmarva Peninsula.

"There were two cars in that garage," Cello said. "If I had a hideaway in New Jersey or Delaware, I'd take a car." With a stubby finger, he traced the major roadways: "L.I.E., Belt, Verrazano Narrows—a snap! Leave at two A.M., you're sailing down the Jersey Turnpike a little after three. Detour over to Atlantic City to play the slots? No? Then in seven hours, you could be so far south, you wouldn't be able to order breakfast without getting grits on the side." He looked up at Clay. "No. He's going north. And of course he's going the max."

"That's where I'm at—otherwise, why spend the time and effort taking those extra tanks? Plus, he's got all those navigational gadgets. No, he's not just scooting out East or across the Sound to Connecticut."

"North it is." As soon as Cello got to the map of Maine, he groaned. "Oh boy—look at all these little fingery things! Every one's an inlet or a harbor . . . that gives *der Führer* about a zillion miles of coast to hide in. Talk about finding a swastika in a haystack."

Pacing back and forth, Clay tried to picture anything on the boat that would provide some sort of clue. "He's not going someplace new. He's going back to a place he's been to on that boat before."

In his mind, he scanned the Grady-White's console: the radar, depth finder, and GPS screens. Autopilot controls, compass, radio . . . what else? Side window—a Coast Guard courtesy inspection sticker. With that prominently displayed, unless you were doing something outrageously stupid, you wouldn't be boarded and written up for not having enough flares. Clay remembered another decal on the side window, right next to it—definitely something familiar. Yellow and black. But he was dead-tired and banged up, and a thick fog was creeping into every corner of his head. What the hell was that second sticker? Something to do with water. Marine . . . surf . . . ocean . . . wave . . . sea . . . ? "Sea-Tow!" he whooped, startling Cello. "The second sticker! Luscher's a detail man. He won't leave anything to chance!"

Already grabbing for the phone, Clay told a puzzled Cello, "It's a towing service for boats. You know, like an auto club, annual fee. But instead of rescuing people stuck on the road, it's for anyone stuck on the water. No matter what—whether your engine breaks down, or you run out of gas, or you hit a buoy, or start to take on water—they'll get you back to the closest port. If Luscher ever had a problem on the water, he would've called them."

Cello whistled. "Long shot."

"Only shot." While Clay scrambled to get the number of Sea-Tow's headquarters, Hickey returned. Head down, the DI made a beeline for his office.

"Every rescue is logged in a computer file," the Sea-Tow lady assured Clay. "But the system isn't centralized. Records are maintained by the local captains."

"You mean I have to call every location?" Clay groaned.

"I'm afraid so. But as soon as you lock in the spot, they'll have no trouble tracking the incident. We have two in Maine, four in Massachusetts, and so on. I'll fax you a listing of all the phone numbers up and down the East Coast."

They planned to work their way south: Clay took Maine, Cello, Massachusetts, and Bloomie, who complained that it was a slow, boring day, volunteered for Rhode Island. Sea-Tow Mid Coast Maine was the farthest north, and Clay called there first. It didn't take the captain long to find the entry. "Here it is. Member since '98. One assist up here, back in '98. Hold on, I'll have the details in a second."

Clay swiveled his chair around and made a swipe across his throat, for Cello to cut the search. As Cello signaled Bloomie to stop, Hickey's door opened.

"Ran out of gas," the captain resumed. "That'll happen, till folks get used to boating or the hang of a new boat, you know? We gave him twenty gallons in Muscongus Bay."

"Do you have any idea where he was going?"

"Afraid it wasn't me delivering the gas. The man you're looking for became a one hundred per cent landlubber last year. Went into the construction business. Lives over Spruce Head way, and I'm sure he'd have no objection if I give you his number. But it's a beautiful day up here, and it's a good guess he's out on a job."

"Ryder, the inspector wants us in his office."

Clay started to dial the number. "Go ahead, Cello—I'll be right in. Two years ago, the Grady-White took on extra gas in Muscongus Bay."

"Muscongus? Sounds like something you get between your toes."

After several rings, a machine answered: "Hi, Ed T. Saunders, Saunders Construction. Please leave your name and number, and I'll get back to you soon. If you want, leave word what needs fixing or building."

With an eye on Hickey's doorway, Clay left his number and Martino's cell phone number—his own phone had been yet another casualty of his trashed jacket. "It's extremely important, Mr. Saunders. Police business. Please call as soon as possible."

Sparks, Merriweather, and Cello made room for him in the Deputy Inspector's office. "Luscher's taken her to Maine," Clay blurted out.

"Martino just explained that things are pointing that way," Hickey replied. He was standing behind his desk, looking at the four of them as if they'd all been expelled from Sunday school. Slowly, he turned and walked to the window, hands clasped behind his back. The trip to the Twenty-third Street IRT station had warranted an appearance in uniform, and he still hadn't removed the jacket.

In ordinary shirtsleeves, his shoulders hunched forward, a little more every year. In the uniform, they couldn't have looked more squared-off or confrontational.

Clay, unable to see his boss's face, had to settle for the sun glinting off his gold leaves. No one spoke. Hickey's office might have been a ten-by-fifteen space capsule, so totally disconnected was it from all the activity out in the squad room.

Still facing the window, Hickey asked, "Ryder . . . you want to take a trip to Maine?"

"Inspector . . . you know I do." He wanted to twirl Hickey around and hug the son of a bitch.

Before he had a chance, the Deputy Inspector turned around on his own. "Nobody fucks with my men the way they fucked with you."

"Yes! Yes!" Martino shouted, slapping Clay on the back.

Hula pumped Clay's hand as if they were old friends meeting after a ten-year separation. Sparks, putting an arm around his shoulder, said into his ear, "Hang tough, Ryder, we'll get through this. And with a little luck, so will the lady."

Clay choked down a tangle of emotions. "I appreciate that, I really do. The problem is, we'll need *lots* of luck. I don't know exactly where in Maine . . . it's a big state." While he brought them up to date, Cello hurried out and charged back in with the atlas.

"Should be around here." Cello swept midcoast Maine with a pencil eraser.

"In a way, that's good . . . not knowing the precise location," Hickey mused. "It gets me off one hook—contacting Maine law enforcement. Don't know the town, don't know the county. Probably won't even know it's the right goddamn state, until you get there."

"Are we flying up, Inspector?" Hula asked.

"Forget it. For starters, consider the problems with firearms. Getting hold of a plane is a red tape nightmare. I've been through it, in-state, on ground not half as shaky. Damn paperwork took forever. Besides, you'll still need cars when you get up there."

"So if we drive up, as private citizens . . ." Sparks ventured.

"Absolutely! Driving is the way." Fixing a reproachful eye on Cello, Hickey warned, "But without flashing lights, sirens, speeding, or unorthodox maneuvers. I'll be in enough hot water without shit like that. I'll get you two unmarked cars."

"Two?" Clay questioned.

"The way those bastards have been blasting away, I want to add some firepower. A couple of guys from Emergency Services."

"Inspector—the problem with their Glocks?" Sparks reminded him.

"Oh, yes. Your gun was pretty much destroyed, Martino. Ryder, yours was recovered in good shape, but it's with Ballistics. Before you leave, both of you have to get loaners. Bloomie'll help you with the forms. Just make sure you get some sleep on the way up. I'm talking to you, too, Martino. Sparks and Merriweather, I'll expect you to call in regularly."

"Will do."

"If you can't get in touch with this ex–Sea-Tow captain, or if he can't provide any leads, the next step is to notify local water patrols in the Muscongus Bay
area. Even if the Coast Guard is on the alert for the Grady-White, we can't assume every bay constable in the area is in on the search. KISS still applies."

The context didn't quite fit Hickey's most oft-repeated maxim, *Keep It
Simple, Stupid.* But Hickey quickly amended it: "Keep It *Small.* The most important consideration is Rachel Meredith's—no, Rachel *Preminger's,* safe return.
As for the Nazi and whoever's with him . . ." Hickey trailed off. "Just keep me
informed."

"Thank you, Inspector," Clay said. Contrition for every bad thought he'd
ever entertained about his boss swept over him.

When he walked out of Hickey's office, he walked right into Gold, who
was holding the developed photo contact sheets and a magnifying glass. Heads
together, they leaned over his desk while he explained their significance.

"Damn!" Gold flipped back through the photos. "There's only one bad
thing about Julian Luscher being dead, and saving taxpayer money on the trial.
That's missing out on the pure pleasure of prosecuting the bastard!"

"Don't give up. We still have a shot at the old man. And there's something
else . . ." He thumbed through the series with palm trees. "The car that ran
down Rachel's mother in Miami. Wil singled it out because it was so flashy, figuring the cops would trace it in no time. Maybe the Cuban punk it belongs to
should be doing time for other shit, but not for manslaughter. His attorney's
number is in my file. Could you . . ."

" 'And justice for all.' Sure, I'll get right to it. Damn, it would've been one
hell of a trial!"

chapter THIRTY-SIX

Night had fallen by the time they reached the far side of Portland, Maine. Somehow, Hickey had scavenged up two SUVs with backseats that folded down flat, and Clay was able to curl up in the cargo area. More passed out than asleep, he didn't even last as far as the FDR Drive. Noonan and Lutzer, the E.S. team, were the drivers for the first half of the trek up I-95.

Clay incorporated the tapping on his shoulder into his dream, and tried to fend it off. From behind the wheel, Sparks yelled, "Ryder, wake up and take the damn phone—it's that guy Saunders!"

"God—it's dark out!" Not fully awake, Clay reached for the phone.

"Sorry to take so long getting back to you," Saunders apologized, "but I was finishing up some odds and ends before the weekend, and I had a good forty-minute drive back from the site. How can I help you?"

Clay asked about the Grady-White assist back in '98.

"Nice boat, that Sailfish. Not surprising, running out of gas, coming all the way from New York . . . plus the fact that there was rough weather from here to the Cape that day. Hell, I not only remember the incident, I know the guy who was onboard."

Clay hardly dared to breathe. "Who might that be?"

"Don't recall his name, but he used to work just outside Thomaston. Real big guy, the kind it's hard *not* to remember, you know? Worked at the Mobil station—his brother's managed it for years."

"So the man on the Grady-White . . . you know his brother, too?"

"Just that he's a dang good mechanic. Marty Olivera. Quiet guy, has an accent. Sort of Spanish accent, I guess."

"Where exactly is the station?" Clay did his best to stay cool, while he tried to figure out this Marty.

"Route 1, few miles south of Thomaston. Owner has a string of stations. Marty must be working in that same one . . . oh, at least twenty-five years. Vietnam vet."

"Vietnam? You're sure?"

"That's what Marty said. Showed up after the war, all crippled and burned—Marty ain't a pretty picture. But he's a dang—"

"—good mechanic," Clay finished.

The burns and the twenty-five plus years in Maine clinched it: Marty Olivera had to be the older Suarez brother, the one wounded in the Israeli attack. Angelina, returning to the winery, had scrambled to get a doctor for her burned and wounded son and brother-in-law Udo, the only survivors. "You have any idea where Marty lives?"

"Nope."

"The Grady-White—anyone else onboard?"

"Marty's brother was the only person I saw. And you know, that struck me funny, him coming up all alone such a long way."

Clay called Hickey about Marty and Thomaston, while Noonan checked the map. The town was about an hour away.

"The guy at the gas station . . . he's the big Nazi we're after?" Noonan asked.

"Not him." Clay explained, "It's his uncle, Udo Luscher." Awake, but stiff and sore, he crawled around the back of the SUV, struggling with unfamiliar handles and releases in the strobing flashes of other cars' headlights. After he finally pushed the backseat into place and settled in a sitting position, he added, "Luscher was awarded one of the rarest of all German medals. Himmler himself pinned it on."

"War hero?"

"More like the fanatic who saved face for Himmler, big time."

Up ahead, Sparks's head nodded up and down, confirming that was the way it usually went.

"What was it for? D-day? Battle of the Bulge?" Noonan persisted.

"The Warsaw Ghetto Uprising. Which started when Himmler gave the order to send every last Jew left in Warsaw to the death camps. An empty ghetto was his idea of the perfect birthday present for Hitler."

Noonan twisted his torso all the way around to look at him. "You're shitting me, right?"

"It's in the history books," said Clay, even though no account could be more compelling than that of one of Eli's witnesses, an SS Mann under Obersturmführer Luscher's command. "In April of 1943," Clay explained, "two thousand SS troops marched into the ghetto to round up the Jews. By then, the Germans had the ghetto squeezed down to what would be just a few blocks back in Manhattan, but the Jews had turned it into a fortress: roofs, cellars, alleys, sewers—all interconnected. Anyway, once the SS soldiers were inside, there was a huge explosion, then machine-gun fire. Wounded SS came running out, screaming, 'The Jews have weapons!' That was unheard of."

"What kind of weapons?" Noonan shot back.

"Small arms, Molotov cocktails, grenades, rifles, machine guns. The commanding officer, General Stroop, went nuts. Jews daring to fight back! Jews kicking German ass! Total humiliation! He countered with a tank assault, but the Jews kept on fighting. Then he switched to aerial bombing, to fire, to flooding and smoke-bombing the sewers—but the Jews still kept fighting. After two weeks, the SS didn't have a clue how they were organized, or where their headquarters was. Stroop's last resort was to flatten the ghetto completely. He gave the order to dynamite it, district by district. Under that directive, Luscher was one of the officers leading a squad into the ghetto."

Clay paused for a moment, considering the evolution of the Udo Luscher shot by the young Jewish smuggler on the road to Krakow into the Udo Luscher observed by the SS Mann that day in Warsaw.

"They were following a medium tank. Their objective was a small square, and engineers were waiting to blow up the houses around the square's perimeter. The houses were nothing more than shells, but Jewish snipers still held positions behind the facades—narrow footholds. Luscher's squad waited in a side street while the tank moved into the square—it had to crawl over tons of smashed brick and concrete from the bombings and all. When it reached the middle, Molotov cocktails hit it. The tank crew climbed out and ran, but they were all shot by the snipers. The squad returned fire, but the Jews kept on the move. A shot from their rear killed the SS Mann standing right next to Luscher."

"So they were pretty much boxed in?" Sparks asked.

"Totally. All of a sudden, Luscher took off, running. Bullets went whizzing by him, but he zigzagged to the Panzer and jumped up onto its treads, just making it over a low fire in the rubble. He ducked behind the turret for cover. From there, the machine gun mounted on the turret had to be all he could see. Another Molotov cocktail exploded, and Luscher grabbed the gun—which had to be hot as hell—to keep from being knocked off. Up there, his only cover from the snipers was a screen of smoke—very thick, almost oily. He started to fire up at the attics and rooftops, raking back and forth. He took a hit in the left shoulder, but he didn't let up. His men were able to advance, and they started launching grenades at the facades. Another Molotov cocktail started a fire at the bow of the Panzer, but Luscher didn't stop until the gun either jammed or ran out of ammo. When the fire was about to hit him full in the face, he hurled himself off the tank. A second later, the ammo inside the Panzer blew. Lifted it right off the ground, and it collapsed coming down."

"Jesus," Noonan whispered. "I'm thinking *The Terminator*."

No, scarier. Le Découpeur is about to be activated. "When his men reached him, Luscher didn't want a medic, just help getting up. His uniform was literally shredded. He was shot up, badly burned—his face was totally black, except for his eyes. By then, his squad had three Jews, all in their teens, at gunpoint. Luscher gave the order for them to be taken to Gestapo headquarters. All during the siege, not one of the Jews interrogated there had given up their leaders' identities or locations."

Sparks whispered, "Don't take us there, Ryder. Keep your nightmares to yourself."

"No, I want you to know what kind of psycho we're up against." Clay took a deep breath, and plowed ahead. "Luscher had the three kids strapped to chairs around a table in the smallest of the interrogation rooms. He ordered a guard to spread the tallest prisoner's right hand flat on the table. Luscher's own right hand was wrapped in a filthy handkerchief, and the soldier who'd helped him limp there from the square saw it go to the sheath of his knife—a weapon he'd never seen him use before. Luscher ordered the soldier to wait out in the corridor, and the guard kicked the door closed. Right away, terrible screaming started. The soldier could barely hear Luscher over it: 'Do you have something to tell me? Am I wasting my time with fingers? Shall we try something new? Who are your leaders? Where are your headquarters?' The screaming got even worse. 'Do you have something to tell me about your leaders now? No? Then you don't need this anymore, do you?' Over and over, relentless. Before it ended, the soldier felt something sticky under his boots. There was so much blood, it was running out from under the door."

Clay paused. The only sound came from the car's engine, as it rushed them forward into the Maine night.

"The next morning, SS troops surrounded a building on Mila Street. Two hundred civilians came out. The leaders and fighters refused to surrender. After the entry points were demolished with grenades, gas was injected into the bunker. Then it was blown up. The resistance was crushed."

"But at least nobody marched them off to any fucking death camp," Noonan observed. "And Hitler didn't get to blow out the candles on his cake."

"What about Luscher?" Sparks asked. "Was he discharged?"

"Unfortunately, his career was far from over. He was shipped back to a hospital in Germany. Had his picture taken with Himmler, receiving a flashy medal and a fancy knife. Udo's big moment. His reward for ending the Third Reich's embarrassment over the Warsaw Ghetto Uprising. When he recovered, they sent him to Paris—and there . . . you have no idea." Clay groaned as he shifted to stretch his back muscles. "You know what I can't figure out, what drives me nuts? What Luscher's honors were really for. For hanging on to that tank's machine gun in the middle of a pile of rubble? Or for hacking up kids until they talked in Gestapo headquarters?"

"God, I don't want to know," said Richard Sparks.

Noonan cleared his throat. "That's the exit."

As they turned off, Clay was haunted by another unanswerable question: Had Luscher read more meaning into Himmler's dagger than even Himmler had intended? All that Nazi glitz—eagles and tassels and swastikas and lightning bolts—had it persuaded him that the tip of the blade pointed to a continuation of what he'd started in that Warsaw interrogation room? Was the directive all in Udo's head, or was it really one madman sending another madman off on a twisted mission?

"Hey, is Marty around?" Sparks asked. Roughly an hour after the call from Saunders, they'd pulled up at the gas station outside Thomaston.

The man who walked up to the car gave the New York plates a long look. "Marty only works days."

"You know where he is?" The attendant eyed Big Black Dick even more suspiciously. "Hey, we're army buddies. Surprise reunion." Clay and Noonan turned their faces away, not giving the man a chance to guess they were riding tricycles when the war was raging.

"Can't rightly tell you. Marty didn't come to work today."

"I hope he's not sick."

"Dunno. Can't recall him ever not showing up before."

"Can you tell me how to get to his house?"

"Nope. Don't know where he lives, except that it's somewhere down Cushing way. Yup, that was unusual, him not coming in today."

"How about a phone number?" Before the night attendant could think of an objection, Big Black Dick shoved a pad and pen into his hands.

After the man wrote it down, he pointed toward one of the cars locked inside the glass-fronted triple bay repair area. "Truth is, that Ford's owner called a while ago. Said Marty had to order a part, and he wanted to know if it came in. I called Marty, but there was no answer. Two other cars seem to be done, but he never got to writing up the bills. He's a darn good mechanic, but folks do get annoyed, especially on a weekend."

Concern in his voice, Sparks asked, "You think the Cushing police could tell me where he lives?"

"None such. It's the Thomaston police cover the area. Just keep heading the way you came."

Just as he had after speaking with Saunders, Clay called in to Deputy Inspector Hickey. "I think we hit a break. The target town is Cushing, south of here. Thomaston Police has jurisdiction over the whole area. You see it on your map, Inspector?"

"Right where the St. George River empties into Muscongus Bay. Go for it."

Once the two SUVs were parked outside the Thomaston Police headquarters, Cello observed, "There might be more of us than of them. Maybe just you and I should go in for now, Ryder."

Sure enough, there were only two officers in the station house: the chief of police and a sergeant. Their nametags read Creegan and Stafford, respectively. Cello displayed his shield, gave them a business card, and Clay began to explain the reason they were in Thomaston.

"Let me stop you there. Seems odd that two of you would drive all the way up here like—"

"Not two, Chief Creegan," Cello interrupted, "six. The other four are parked outside."

"Better that we call NYPD to confirm," the chief said. His words were noncommittal, but his tone and body language were distinctly uneasy. "Go ahead, Stafford, make the call." The sergeant picked up Cello's card. "No. Go through ordinary information."

The sergeant was put through to Hickey immediately.

"Okay, they check out—names, license plates, et cetera." Pointing at Clay, he said, "Detective Ryder's been working the case from the start."

After listening in stony silence to the chain of events that brought them to Maine, the chief's only comment was, "A kidnapping. And you're dumping it in *our* laps?"

"*Dumping?*" Clay tried to keep his incredulity down. "Sorry, but no one at NYPD sees it that way. We're not even convinced the victim is in your area, Chief Creegan. The only way we can ascertain that is by finding the Grady-White. We're asking you to help us locate it." He took in the small room. "How many men on duty tonight?"

"Our entire force is four. We have two patrolmen out on the road—one in a plain wrapper, one in a squad car. Summer weekends, we're all on. Usually we hang in until an hour after the bars close." Reluctantly, the chief walked up to a large cardboard-mounted map. "I know Marty Olivera. I should say, I know where he lives. We patrol every road in our jurisdiction regularly."

Sergeant Stafford cleared his throat. "I grew up in Cushing. I do a bit of sailing, so I'm familiar with most of the riverbank in the area. That property . . . there's an old boathouse on it."

"Well, can we go take a look?" asked Cello.

"No way!" the chief snapped, as he wheeled around. "Not until we get

Knox County police to back us up. I was with the Portland Police for fifteen years, and they called County for a lot less than this!"

Cello was trying hard not to yell in Creegan's face. "We want to avoid an entire army bivouacking down there before we even eyeball the boat."

"That's a fairly isolated house, Detective. It's not a small house, either. We respect people's privacy around here."

"What exactly are you saying, Chief?" Clay asked.

"That I don't know how many people are there—in the Olivera house."

"All together, we're ten! Do you seriously believe they have us outnumbered? Besides, two of the men who drove up with us are Emergency Services!"

"Really? And what kind of weapons did they transport over state lines?" the chief countered. "Who the hell do you think you are?"

"Someone who's willing to put his ass on the line!" Clay yelled.

"All my men have families! You drive up from New York like a tourist, and you expect us to risk all on your hotshot say-so?"

"Sure, you have families, Chief. So did the lady who was kidnapped. Before her mother and brother were murdered."

Out of nowhere, a loud mix of taunts, laughter, rock music, and beeping horns exploded outside. Two convertibles full of kids flew by, not so stoned or drunk that they couldn't figure out that the patrol cars were somewhere else, and that two out-of-state cars were keeping the cops inside busy. Clay read it all in the chief's face: wise-ass kids, lost tourists, drunk and disorderlies, cars wrapped around trees, deer wrapped around cars, hash grown in garden plots. An endless cycle of busy, understaffed summers and dead winters. Hanging his head, he said, "I'm sorry. All this trouble is my fault. I got her—the hostage—into it. Now I have to get her out. I have to."

Everyone was looking down. Martino broke the silence. "Chief Creegan, can we maybe go in your office and talk?"

A few minutes later, as they both emerged, Creegan said, "Okay, Ryder, we'll take a look to see if the boat's there. But let's make no mistake: the Thomaston Police Department is running this operation."

Clay could only nod in stunned agreement.

After Stafford radioed in the two officers who were out cruising, he worked up a map of the area around the Olivera property. Within fifteen minutes, all ten men were crowded into the police station. Once it was clear what everyone had to do, the four cars left for Cushing.

On the way, Clay asked Cello, "How did you get the chief to change his mind?"

"Something about Rachel Preminger, something about you."

"Like what?"

"Something borrowed, something blue. I told him you were going to ask her to marry you." Cello cocked an eyebrow at him. "She became a widow about twelve hours ago. Got to catch the good ones fast, while they're single."

Not many miles south, Cushing was a quick heartbeat of a town: four structures that served as school, firehouse, post office, and general store—the latter with gas pumps out front.

Hula was in the first car of the procession, the plain wrapper, which was driven by one Patrolman Marsham. The marked police cruiser followed, with Scoggins—the other patrolman—and Chief Creegan. Third was the SUV with Clay, Cello, and Lutzer. Taking up the rear in the other SUV were Sparks, Noonan, and Sergeant Stafford.

In the backseat of Clay's vehicle, Lutzer removed his weapon from its case.

"What've you got back there?" Cello's head swiveled back from the driver's seat. "And does your mother know you're playing with it?"

"It's an SSG, Steyr-Mannlicher Sharpshooter. Because of its color"— briefly, he brought the plastic stock into the light from the dash—"known as the Mean Green Gun. Holds .308 Winchesters." Lutzer removed the scope's cover. "This one's fitted with a Kahles 10-power. It's an exceptionally accurate weapon."

"So, you're like . . . our sniper?"

"I'm qualified with this weapon, Detective Martino."

"And what's Noonan got, the A-bomb?"

"Heckler & Koch MP5—a submachine gun. Extremely controllable. Also known for its accuracy."

The talk about weapons brought back Wil's account of the attack on Córdoba, and how Luscher's lookout had night vision. Clay hoped that there was no night vision capability in Cushing . . . nor even reason for Luscher to expect any visitors. Even more, he hoped that Rachel still had the strength and the will to resist telling Luscher where she'd hid the Trabuc.

"There they go." Clay pointed through the windshield. Up ahead, the Thomaston Police vehicles had just turned left off the two-lane blacktop, onto a considerably narrower road. Just as in Stafford's sketch, after a quarter mile they passed a lane on the left. About a hundred yards after that, they came to a short wooden bridge wide enough to accommodate one car at a time. The sergeant had drawn it as a gangplank of sorts; it connected land cut by a thin offshoot of a tidal creek that meandered inland about five hundred feet. The main creek, considerably broader, ran along the right side of the road the rest of the way. The bridge groaned as they crossed over; it sounded flimsy, even though concrete pylons supported it at each corner.

From there, only about a mile lay between them and the Olivera property . . . the Luscher property. Just past the bridge, the road curved sharply left. As the headlights swept around, Clay caught the glint of wet riprap below them on the right; the creek evidently ran deep enough at high tide to pose an erosion threat to the bluff supporting the road. After half a mile, the Thomaston cars shut their lights off, and the SUVs followed suit. On the left, they passed ten or twelve houses in a row, spaced at a comfortable distance apart. From their living rooms, the owners would all share a view of the creek as it widened to join the St. George River. A short way past the last house, the road ended, and a dirt and gravel private driveway—Luscher's—began. It curved in an S, preventing a direct sightline to the house from the road. Most of the property, according to Stafford's sketch, occupied a point; the vista stretched both upriver and down, all the way to the bay. Like the Baranowski house back in Lloyd Neck, it was past its prime, a very private redoubt, and had a dock of its own.

The first car in their procession, the unmarked sedan with Hula and Officer Marsham, turned into the drive of the last home on the paved road and parked in front of its garage. It was the only creek-facing house with a dock, owing to a curve of the river. Every window was dark. According to the chief, the owners ran a bar-restaurant in Friendship, the next town south, and never returned home until the early-morning hours, well after their dining room closed.

Beyond their driveway, Scoggins maneuvered his patrol car until it diagonally straddled the last few feet of hardtop, blocking the dirt drive. The two SUVs parked behind it, one after the other, on the creekside shoulder.

Patrolman Marsham had a point-to-point radio set to communicate with Chief Creegan. A short flash of interior light indicated that he and Merriweather had left their car. The other eight men waited while the tall, thin Marsham and the humongous Hula ran along the thickly wooded area separating the two properties, headed for the dock at the rear of the house. From there, they had to make a dash to Luscher's boathouse, a distance Stafford estimated at no more than two hundred feet.

Finally, a transmission came in. It was Hula. "The Grady-White's here, all right, under a tarp. There's also a seventeen-foot Boston Whaler. Marsham's disabling both boats."

"Copy," Creegan replied. Clay couldn't read what was in his voice, excitement or dread. Marsham and Hula were to remain at the boathouse, to counter any escape attempt by water.

Stafford's knowledge of the house was limited—he knew it was an expanded cape with three dormers angled to face the bay, and a large screened porch on one side facing straight across the river. The two-car garage was on the opposite side, only a corner of it visible from the road's end. (The treeline between the two houses extended all the way to the dirt drive and continued on the other side, right up to the creek.) Except for a large, raised oval directly in front, the house was surrounded by open lawn. The oval was filled with big, craggy rocks and a few specimen plants. From the edge of the winding driveway, the house appeared dark, with no sign of activity inside, although Stafford was sure he'd seen a light through the trees when they first moved onto the property.

The plan of attack called for the E.S. team, Lutzer and Noonan, to go first. They ran along the narrow band of creekside trees and crossed the lawn to the imperfect concealment of the oval. After positioning themselves to cover the front of the house, they signaled by radio for Stafford and Cello to join them, following along the same path. Once they reached the oval, Stafford and Cello would make another run, this one to the screened porch, which presented a chance for entry into the house.

The same radio signal simultaneously launched Clay, Chief Creegan, and Sparks on the other side of driveway. Their immediate objective was the garage, another possible point of entry. Patrolman Scoggins was to remain in the patrol car as communications center and coordinator for each team's point-to-point radios.

Just about the time when Cello and Stafford had broken away from the oval and Clay's team was halfway to the garage, everyone on the property heard the roar of an auto ignition. The three advancing on the garage all froze.

From out of the quiet night, all hell broke loose.

An explosion of nonstop automatic fire ripped from the middle dormer window, methodically raking the area.

At the very same moment, the garage doors—the old-fashioned wood swing-out type—crashed apart. An immense tow truck burst out, its brights on. Brilliant blue and yellow flasher lights fractured the darkness, their rapid flicker dazzling and disorienting. A furious, blinking beast, it charged straight toward Clay, Creegan, and Sparks. Blinded by the lights, they lunged for the trees. Crunching and spraying gravel, the tires, wide as tank treads, missed them by inches.

As the truck zipped by, Clay caught a glimpse of the man in the passenger seat: Luscher, back straight, staring directly ahead.

From his prone position, Clay could see down to the end of driveway; it was well illuminated by the speeding truck.

Scoggins, alarmed by the commotion, jumped out of the patrol car blockading the road and started to run toward the house. As soon as his head registered that his feet were propelling him into a head-on collision with a monster of a tow truck, he made a flying, horizontal dive for the side of the road. Unable to check his momentum, he kept rolling and tumbling over the side of the creek, onto the jagged riprap.

Careening around the driveway's final curve, the tow truck hit the squad car broadside like a battering ram, pushing it into the first SUV with such force that both vehicles skidded off the road and down the riprap embankment. With no more obstacles remaining in his path, the driver pulled alongside the remaining SUV and fired a burst from an automatic pistol directly into its hood.

Meanwhile, the shooter in the dormer was raking fire in a broad semicircle, side to side, across the front of the house. Noonan returned the fire with the MP5. Lutzer, unable to get a clear shot, had temporarily abandoned the SSG for his Glock, and was spraying bursts at the dormer. The surge of retaliatory firepower shattered the window and ruptured the frame, driving the shooter to take cover in the corner of the dormer.

Clay took advantage of the temporary halt in the attack. Before his area was hit again, he raced for the smashed-out garage doors. The gunman jumped back; bullets flew around Clay, hitting trees, snapping off branches. He could hear Creegan and Sparks running right behind him. Charging forward recklessly, he rushed through the garage and up a short flight of stairs. As he blindly groped his way through darkness, he strained to hear under the spurts of automatic fire. Sensing no movement, he worked his way to a stairway leading to the second floor. Once again abandoning all caution, he raced up, headed for the middle dormer front. Without stopping, he hurtled against its door with such force, the hinges and doorlock ripped away. The door slammed forward into the room. Clay fell with it, winding up sprawled on top of it on the floor.

In the dark void before him, he saw one patch infinitesimally paler than the rest—the charcoal blur that was the sky outside the window. Against it, he made out the barrel of a gun. As the barrel began to swing around toward him, he emptied his entire clip into the black mass that was the shooter's body.

His own clip was spent, but the firing continued. Creegan was firing relentlessly from the open doorway behind him. As the gunman staggered back, exposing his body in the frame of the window, Noonan's MP5 caught him, spun him around, and propelled him deep into the room. His body thudded on the floor, inches from Clay.

In the ensuing moments, the only sounds that could be heard were a series of clicks: spent clips ejected, new clips loaded, muzzles being pulled back to propel new bullets into chambers.

After a brief wait, Creegan said to Clay, "I'm turning on lights."

When the light switched on, Clay jerked back. Raul's shirtless, hulking body seemed to fill the entire room. Two thick gauze patches on his chest—no doubt taped on in haste after the Lloyd Neck massacre—were saturated with blood. All the gauze pads in Maine couldn't have done a thing for the twenty new bullet holes in his torso. On the floor near his neck were blood-smeared binoculars—night vision, judging by the camouflage pattern and boxy shape. *But what the hell had alerted them in the first place?* Besides the Kalashnikov next to Raul's hand, two more were propped up on the wall near the window, next to a huge mound of clips. Raul, left behind to prevent any pursuit of Luscher, could have kept a small army at bay for a long, long time.

Without a word, Clay and Creegan split up; they began a check of the other rooms on the top floor. Downstairs, Sparks, joined by Hula and Patrolman Marsham, could be heard searching the first floor.

"Ground sensors! All over the perimeter!" Creegan exclaimed when they met in the hall. "There's an alarm system in the last bedroom sophisticated enough for the damn Mint! Those bastards knew which way we were coming before we knew which way we were going!" Once again, Udo Luscher had kept up with the newest technology.

Sparks shouted up, "Clear downstairs!"

Creegan answered, "Clear up here!"

"Any sign of Rachel Preminger?" Clay called out, as he and Creegan raced down the stairs.

"Negative," Sparks responded.

Clay looked around. Noonan and Lutzer would've remained outside, still covering the front, but a team was missing. "Martino and Stafford, where are—?"

"What the hell is that?" Marsham broke in, cocking his head.

Aware how far sound can travel at night, especially over water, they all stood in place, their breathing stilled. After the tail end of the first sound, the shrill screech of brakes, came the thud of metal on metal. A pause, then the *pop-pop-pop* of small arms fire.

Staring at Clay, the ashen-faced chief asked, "Do you have anyone else out there?"

"Hell no!"

Marsham and Creegan were closest to the front door, and they ran out first, Clay and Sparks and Hula right behind them. Noonan was still at the oval with his MP5. He pointed toward the screened porch at the side of the house. With nearly every light inside turned on, they could see Lutzer, his Mean Green Gun in hand, kneeling between two figures lying on the grass.

"They're both hit," Lutzer called out. "I heard it, too—whatever the hell happened down the road. Go for it. There's nothing you can do here right now."

Limping and cradling his wrist, Patrolman Scoggins was moving up the driveway. "Chief," he yelled, "only one drivable car is left—the plain wrapper back in the neighbor's driveway!" Creegan gave him an order to assist Noonan in securing the area, and the rest of them sprinted to the neighbor's property. While they jammed into the car, Creegan called for an ambulance. He also alerted the county police to be on the lookout for the tow truck and advised them to secure the Mobil station immediately, in case it stopped there and a vehicle-switch was attempted.

Meanwhile, Marsham turned on the siren and the flashers hidden in the unmarked car's grill and peeled out of the driveway. As they sped past the row of houses overlooking the creek, lights were switching on; a few people were running down their driveways, shouting after the police car.

As soon as they came around the bend that ended at the bridge, they screeched to a halt. The tow truck hadn't made it over the bridge, but they couldn't yet tell what had stopped its flight. It stood absolutely still, except for the flashing lights mounted on the cab roof; lazy swirls of smoke twirled through and above them. The smell of discharged ammo, gasoline, and burnt rubber overwhelmed the scent of pine and salt marsh. Guns drawn, they scrambled out of their vehicle.

The truck's bumper was embedded in a sedan that had blocked the end of the bridge, much the same way the Thomaston cruiser had been angled across the end of the hardtop. However, since the sedan's front passenger side was butted up against one of the bridge's concrete corner supports, it had not been so easily disposed of. Instead of being deflected into the creek, its frame was half-wrapped around the sturdy pylon.

Both doors of the tow truck were wide open. Clay, Sparks, and the chief approached on the left, Hula and Marsham on the right, until they stared at one another across the empty cab.

Marsham obviously caught sight of something in the blinking lights. Pulling the flashlight off his utility belt, he hurried toward the edge of the embankment. He'd spotted a shoe.

"That was Marty," Creegan said, when they were all staring down at the man lying spread-eagle on the riprap. The back of his head was half-submerged in the oozy, low tide mud. A chunk of his neck had been shot away, and one eye socket was a black hole.

"Where the hell is Luscher?" Clay exploded. "He was in the passenger seat when they busted out of the garage! Damn it, what's that maniac done with Rachel?"

All of them moved on to the wreckage of the mystery sedan. Marsham played his flashlight over the interior. Empty.

Suddenly, his light caught something on the far side of the bridge, propped up against another of the concrete supports. It was a body, still and limp. Shreds of rope and duct tape were scattered around it. To get to it, Clay had to climb over the smashed trunk of the car.

Sparks was right behind him. "Is that . . . ?" he was yelling.

Rachel was flexing the fingers of one hand toward him as he ran to her. Reaching out, he lightly clasped it between both of his. The skin was shockingly cold, without the slightest twinge of response. Had her fingers moved at all, or had it only been an illusion in the flicker of the truck's lights?

Clay kneeled down next to her, forced himself to look at what Luscher had done. She'd been cut, bruised, broken . . . far beyond what she'd suffered the night before. If the past twenty-four hours had been hell for him, he couldn't begin to imagine what they'd been for her.

Everything that he'd learned about accident victims ran through his head, all the stern warnings about how moving a gravely injured person could only cause additional trauma.

Fearing that no more harm could be inflicted, he gently lifted Rachel and cradled her in his arms.

CHAPTER THIRTY-SEVEN

Martino's cell phone rang. "Everyone's still in surgery, Inspector," Clay answered.

"This isn't New York," an exhausted voice answered, "it's Aaron." Stripped of his irony, the Mossad agent sounded like a stranger.

"Do you have him, or did he vanish into thin air for another thirty years?" Clay demanded. "And if you do have him, what the hell were you thinking, snatching him like that? We were out on enough of a limb, without you—"

Aaron hit back, equally raw and accusatory: "Your objective was the woman. You have the woman. If we hadn't been at that fucking bridge, let's not even think where she might be right now!" His venting done, he asked, "She is going to pull through, isn't she?"

"No one's giving odds."

After a long pause, Aaron replied, "God, I didn't realize . . . Ryder, I'm sorry. Truly sorry. With all the blood on his hands, I don't want her to be his last victim. Not her."

"Where is he, Aaron? Where the hell is Luscher?" When the Israeli didn't reply, he hit him with the questions that had dogged him ever since he found Rachel at the bridge: "How did you get to Maine? No, how did you even know we were here?"

"We're an intelligence agency, Ryder, and the people who work for us are exceptional. We were able to hop a plane from New York. Not exactly El Al, but we were in Maine long before you. Had no luck finding that guy Saunders, but we had a chance to familiarize ourselves with the area while we waited for you."

"Then you tailed us to the police station, and out to Cushing?"

"We were behind you, yes. Then, nothing fancy, just one of our agents sprinting after you on foot once you crossed the bridge. Didn't catch up until they started shooting and that tow truck ripped the garage doors off. He radioed back to us, and we had less than a minute to get into position. He thought all your vehicles were out of commission and couldn't pursue."

"No, one car was left. What did you have besides that sedan?"

"We pulled a van onto the bridge just as the tow truck came around the bend. Last second, we put on the high beams. Blinded the driver. He crashed into the sedan, then came out shooting."

"What if we got there before you left?"

"You didn't. Leave it at that."

"I can't."

"Ryder, let's just say our contingency plan had a contingency plan. No matter what, if Luscher was alive, he was ours."

"Bring him back, Aaron. It's not 1960, and he's not Eichmann."

"Luscher sat in that truck like a king on a throne. Waited for us to open the door. He stepped out like . . . You've seen him. You know."

"Taking him out of the country—that's a big mistake."

"He didn't say a word, didn't even care who we were. We were dirt—just like the Preminger woman. She was trussed up and stowed under his feet like a sack of garbage. I think the worst part for him was when we cuffed him and patted him down—Jews, daring to touch him."

"Aaron, if we put him on trial in New York, we expose—"

"Cut it, Ryder!" Anger flared up through the Israeli's fatigue. "Listen to me! An old man, almost eighty—but he still made me want to rip him apart! I wanted to get at that thing inside him—whatever it is, that's so fucking strong! Like a cancer in reverse, that could keep him alive!"

Somewhere in Aaron's vicinity, an engine revved.

"On our way out of there, I started interrogating him, trying to get something down on tape. Nothing. I expected that. I tried Poland, I tried Paris . . . babies, children, old people. I'm not a particularly religious man, but I tried to make him feel the weight of all those souls. And all he said . . ." Aaron faltered briefly. "All he said was, 'It ended too soon. Those were far too few.'"

The engine sounded like a small plane, taxiing.

"I told him all three of his nephews were dead. His sister-in-law, too. I was sure he'd snap when I came to his son—the blue-eyed boy he'd trained so well. I told him his son was mixed with rat shit in a subway sewer. Hardly a flicker, Ryder, hardly a flicker." Aaron took a deep breath. "Then I pointed out how all his years of planning and scheming and killing to get the painting were down the toilet, along with the bedpans he'd emptied for that old man out on Long Island."

"You know about that, too?"

"Hold on." Aaron covered the mouthpiece to answer someone, but whatever he was shouting over the noise was in Hebrew. "By that time," he resumed, "we'd been driving about an hour. Out of nowhere, Luscher asks, 'How much farther?' I tell him nearly fifty miles. We're on secondary roads, not exceeding the limit. Luscher says, 'Stop the car—now. I must relieve myself.'"

"Still calling the shots? I hope you told him to stuff it," Clay said.

"More or less. We went a little farther, and he told us he'd do it in the car if we didn't stop. The man's eighty, right? So we pull over on a deserted stretch. Three of us surround him, remove the cuffs. He takes a leak. Then he takes a comb out of his pocket. Before we had a clue to what was happening, he falls forward. We thought he was having a heart attack. But it was *Le Découpeur*, right to the end."

Clay could see Luscher on the Grady-White, the glint of the blade as it caught the boat's lights.

"The comb was a spring-loaded stiletto. I've never seen anything like it. You press two of the teeth, and a six-inch blade springs out of the top. Luscher shoved all of it into his gut, right to the hilt. In and up. Tore himself apart. I don't know where he got the strength. So, my friend, he's not going back to New York or to Israel or anywhere . . . unless there really is a hell."

Aaron paused; Clay said nothing, waiting for him to resume.

"He's weighted down with rocks, at the bottom of a lake. I don't even know its name. No grave, no marker . . . just like all his victims. But even in the end, the bastard beat us. He controlled his own death."

"Eli wanted him for more than closure, didn't he?"

"Can you blame him?"

Clay thought of all that Luscher had done to Rachel. "No. I wanted a piece of him myself."

THIRTY-EIGHT

Even the two bullet riddled cops had fared better than Rachel.

Because an ambulance couldn't get around the bridge, Stafford and Cello had been airlifted to the closest hospital, in Rockport. Sergeant Stafford spent seven hours in surgery, but a full recovery was expected. Martino took two bullets. Like everyone else, Deputy Inspector Hickey laughed when he heard where Cello was hit —his left buttock. But the DI sobered up right away when Clay relayed the surgeon's findings: if one of the slugs had come a hairbreadth closer to Cello's sciatic nerve, it would have paralyzed him for life.

Patrolman Scoggins and Chief Creegan found Clay in Rachel's room. Still heavily sedated, she couldn't be moved back to New York for several days. Clay was splitting his time between her and Cello, camping out at their bedsides.

"How's she doing?" Scoggins asked from the hall.

"I wish I knew." Clay walked to the doorway, and, because Scoggin's arm was in a sling, placed a hand on the young cop's shoulder. Then he extended his hand to Creegan. "Until I heard Stafford was going to be okay, I didn't think I'd ever be able to look you in the eye, Chief. You didn't have to help us, but man, did you ever come through. Thank you."

During the awkward silence which followed, Clay considered how many cops felt truly comfortable with their line of work, and how much of an aberration he himself was.

Taking his hand, Creegan said, "We did our duty, Ryder." He paused, then added, "You forced us to." His eyes crinkled up, and he was almost smiling. "You know, I'm of a mind to deputize you and confine you to Thomaston town limits until Labor Day, no pay. Look at Scoggins here—thanks to you, our entire force is cut in half."

"What about the county police?" Clay ventured. "Won't they help out? Or am I responsible for a major rift in the State of Maine's law enforcement structure?"

"My take is that they're more ticked off about being left out of the showdown than anything else." Creegan held up a thin newspaper he'd tucked under his arm. "You'll love what the powers that be fed to our local editor. The tale of a certain Vietnam vet who finally snapped. It starts out with County receiving an anonymous call about gunfire out on the point. Actually, that's a fact—by then, no one was left at our headquarters to respond, and the call was kicked over."

"Making them the guys in the white hats?"

"That's how the story goes. Oh, and by sheer coincidence, a group from the NYPD was in the area on a fishing trip, and when the war veteran flipped out, their vehicles were damaged and one of their party injured. To sum it all up? You look like tourists, we look understaffed—fine with me—and County looks like Delta Force." Unfurling the paper, he read the headline: "'County Police Put Brakes on Mechanic's Deadly Breakdown.'"

"I like that," Clay grinned. "It keeps our so-called fishing party out of hot water."

"Oh, don't think it's for you," said Scoggins. "Before you drove up here, Cushing's only claim to fame was the old Olson house. They plan to keep it that way." He addressed the questioning look on Clay's face. "Christina Olson. *Christina's World.* You know, the Wyeth painting?"

Hitting his hand to his forehead, Clay exclaimed, "That town in Maine is *Cushing*? I never made the connection! Wyeth—didn't he have a studio in that house in the picture?"

"Sure, upper floor. Used it about thirty years. They give tours there now, during tourist season."

Creegan leaned in close and whispered, "The town's doing everything it can to keep a lid on this. Otherwise, the headline would read, 'Police Expose Nazi War Criminal's Secret Lair!' And then there's the problem of explaining how that Nazi so conveniently disappeared." He shook his head. "No, we'll content ourselves with being identified with a famous painting."

A doctor hurried by, and when Scoggins asked if they could visit Stafford, he gave them a thumbs-up. Before they headed off, Creegan, voice still low, asked, "Haven't had a chance to ask her yet, have you?"

"Ask her . . . ?" With the talk of the Wyeth, for a moment he thought the chief meant Rachel's hiding place for the Trabuc.

"Come on—Detective Martino told me! Ask her to marry you, of course! That gal in there has a hell of a long road back, but I better get an invitation when you two set the date!"

Clay returned to Rachel's bedside. She was still heavily sedated. Gently, he arranged her matted hair up and away from her temples, seeing past her battered face to her radiance at the Met opening.

Wil's deception had been so artful, so horribly far-reaching in its scope, that she'd bought it completely. Yet, at the same time, she could still be the sharp-eyed woman who'd refused to be seduced by the art world's hyped-up, Holocaust-as-window-dressing bullshit. What had she said that night, about her grandfather not being a hero, nor she a heroine? Well, now she was, big-time. Anyone capable of surviving Udo Luscher and crew deserved to be.

CHAPTER
THIRTY-NINE

The brochure described the suburban rehabilitation hospital as "surrounded by twenty rolling acres, a serene mix of natural woodland and manicured gardens." After several glossy color pages extolling the staff and equipment and cuisine, it concluded, "No other facility so close to the Greater Metro Area provides a setting more conducive to recovery—which translates into an unequaled 95 percent success rate."

If success meant a return to normal life, Clay wasn't sure anyone could guess what that might be for Rachel . . . not even Rachel herself. Not after so many years of Luscher pulling all the strings.

As for her physical recovery, the long road Creegan described had begun in Maine: After treatment of injuries that included fractures of the skull, jaw, and collarbone, as well as multiple lacerations and contusions, her nose was recentered and her loosened teeth were splinted—the oral surgeon was hopeful they'd reattach. By the time she was deemed ready for transport to the rehab center, she'd been thoroughly braced, bolted, wired, plastered, and stitched together. The good news about her face was that once the swelling and discoloration faded, she would need only minor plastic surgery. The other good news was that the man who'd raped her so brutally was not HIV-positive.

Clay had to wait more than a week before his first visit was permitted . . . after the end of the "evaluation period," as they called it.

It was a hot, blue-sky day in the middle of August, and when the heavyset nurse came to fetch him from the reception area, perspiration was beading on her brow. "Rachel's in the shade garden," she explained. "It's a perfect spot for a day like today." She hurried him down a long, wide corridor, unlit because so much daylight poured in through the French doors at the rear. In its glare, the shiny floor tiles resembled a wet city street, and the woman waiting at the end was a silhouette. The nurse introduced her as Dr. Brickman.

They shielded their eyes from the sun as they moved out onto a broad, level lawn. Assisted by staff members, patients in wheelchairs or supported by walkers made their way over the flat expanse slowly and cautiously. The nurse quickly excused herself—an aide was temporarily watching Rachel—and strode off toward a distant copse of trees.

"Please, may I have a moment before you see her?" the doctor asked.

For the first time, Clay could see her face. Halfway between plain and pretty, no makeup over her pale freckles.

"We're weaning Rachel off painkillers," Brickman began. "Actually, it's been quite successful." Her dark blonde hair was cut into short layers. Overall, she was nice and fresh, except for the wilted daisy poking out of the pocket of her blouse. When she saw Clay's eyes on it, she touched it lightly. "My three-year-old picked it for me this morning, and made me promise to wear it all day. I haven't decided if I should switch it for a fresh flower before I get home, or give him his first teaspoon of reality."

Clay looked at her, then up at the brilliant sky, impatient.

"Okay, I'm dancing around. The problem is, Detective, we very seldom encounter a person quite so alone in the world as Rachel. Oh, you'd never know it—since she arrived, she's been swamped with cards, flowers, balloons. But it's all from her *outer* circle, if you will—neighbors, NYU colleagues, students, even the head of the Metropolitan Museum. I'm in need of the sort of background usually provided by family members. In fact, I'm desperate for information, and I have a feeling you can help . . . at least with the source of some of her anxieties."

"Anxieties," he repeated, not liking the sound of it at all.

"Considering the sexual abuse, her current fear of men isn't surprising. Please take care to avoid any physical contact. Maintain a comfortable distance—comfortable for her, that is." She took a deep breath. "Now that that's out of the way, perhaps you can explain why addressing her as 'Meredith'—Rachel or Dr. or Mrs.—upsets her so. She vehemently denies that Meredith is her real name."

"She's right. Her name is Rachel Preminger."

Dr. Brickman gave him a skeptical look. "Her health insurance is in that name, and when we checked with her employer, the university, they . . ."

Clay kept on shaking his head, so she proceeded to what was evidently a thornier issue. "Can you enlighten me on this 'Loser' who terrifies her so? At first, she claimed she saw him—he was quite real to her. When we asked her to point him out, she told us he was *everywhere.* Now that she's increasingly lucid, the delusion of his physical presence is receding, but the fear persists. She seeks constant reassurance that she's safe. Questions like, 'Does Loser know I'm here?' Or, 'When is Loser coming back?'"

"'Loser' isn't what Rachel's saying, Doctor. Look, I'll do anything I can to help, but not until I see her."

A small fountain made the shade garden damp as well as cool. Thin jets of water played over an oxidized elfin girl balanced on one tiptoed leg, head tilted back to extend the slight arch of her back. Her fingertips held the corners of her skirt, permitting a peek of a knee raised up in dance. Moss clung to the rocks surrounding the fountain's base, ferns grew around the rocks, and striped hostas encircled the ferns. With her back to him, Rachel sat in a wheelchair, facing the statue. The nurse's heft occupied most of a small stone bench close by.

Clay moved around the chair, expecting the worst, even though he'd seen her at the bridge and watched over her in Rockport. The woman inside the abused body was still there . . . barely.

As soon as she caught sight of him, she recoiled, pressing against the chairback. He kept his distance. When Dr. Brickman stepped beside him, Rachel became less rigid, although she was clearly still agitated.

"Do you know me?" he asked.

A minute passed before she raised a thumb, which he took for a yes.

"Okay if I come closer?" A down, then a reversal to an up. Without touching her, he knelt by the chair. Her fear was palpable, and she kept looking to her doctor for reassurance. "Rachel," he said softly, "no one is going to hurt you. You're safe. *Safe*. Luscher is *dead*. They're *all* dead—Wil, Raul, all of them. Do you understand? They can't harm you anymore."

Through clenched teeth and wired jaw, she gritted out, "Luscher sent you." The doctor hadn't exaggerated: "Loser" was exactly how it sounded. "Luscher's . . . everywhere! Everyone . . . works . . . for him!"

Struggling to keep calm, he whispered, "Rachel, he's dead! It's over!"

"Never tell! I'll never tell!" she cried, repeating it over and over.

For Clay, the second visit was far more alarming.

Once again, the day was fair, and he picked her out by her auburn hair, sitting in the shade of a giant red maple that nearly matched it, at the far edge of the lawn. The same nurse was with her, and as he grew nearer, he could see the stocky woman point him out and wave. When he was less than ten feet away, Rachel rested her head against the back of her chair and closed her eyes. As he approached, he called out to her, but she didn't respond. The nurse urged her to say hello, enjoy her friend's visit, but Rachel was asleep.

Or pretending to be.

He pulled a lawn chair over and started to talk, the way he had with his mother. He talked until his throat ached.

"Rachel," he said at last, "I know you're hiding from Luscher. But there's no one to hide from anymore. I told you the last time, he's dead. I know you've run out of trust for people, but you've got to trust me."

Her eyes were closed, her breathing steady and deep.

"I knew a lady who hid like this . . . by sleeping. There was a man who used her, who hurt her terribly. . . . I can't imagine anyone doing worse than what Luscher did to you, but this man did everything he could to manipulate her and isolate her. He tried to do it to me, too." Clay felt the nurse's eyes on him, inquisitive. "I resisted . . . I eventually blocked him out, but the way that works is you can't be as selective as you want to be. You block things going out, too. You lock too much inside yourself. Suffocation—that's how it feels, when you're under that kind of extreme control. That lady, she'd sleep to escape . . . to *breathe.*

"Rachel, you know what's wrong with the story about Sleeping Beauty? The problem is, no prince comes along and wakes you with a kiss—you have to do it on your own. But this lady I knew . . . she slept so long, she forgot how to wake herself up. And then she . . . she died.

"You know what the saddest part is, Rachel? She died without knowing whether or not the bastard who'd caused her so much misery was still alive. He was an old man, too, like Luscher. She died without *knowing.* By staying asleep, she gave him control so great, he could win *either* way—dead or alive. She let his power over her last for eternity.

"That woman was my mother. I couldn't rescue her. I can't rescue you." Clay had leaned closer and closer, until his face was inches from hers. "But you rescued *me,* Rachel, and the proof is that I can tell you . . . how much I care about you." High above them, a sudden breeze rustled through the mahogany leaves, but it didn't even ruffle her hair. "Please don't do this, Rachel. I can't stand by and watch it all over again. I know your body hurts, and I know how he tried to degrade you, but you've won. I doubt you can see it as winning right now, but if you make yourself wake up, then Luscher didn't beat you. If you wake up, he lost."

Despite his front of encouragement, Clay was overwhelmed by Rachel's wretched condition; he was responsible for it, no less than Luscher and Wil and Raul.

Although he accepted the possibility that she might not ever return to Ninth Street—either due to physical problems or because she'd lived there with Wil—he knew a big factor in any recovery was having a place to call home. Fixing up her apartment became his mission. Even if she never set foot in it again, he rationalized, it would still have to be made presentable enough to be sold.

Using his own trashed apartment as a test site, he hired a team of moonlighting cop and firemen cousins who plastered, painted, and refinished floors. Pleased with the results, he put them to work in Rachel's co-op, after personally removing everything that was either damaged or could remind her of Wil, and that didn't leave much. When her place was finished, he bought a bean-bag chair at Kmart, plopped it down in the middle of the immaculate and otherwise empty Preminger living room, and sat in the dark several nights running, trying to guess where Paul Bergère's granddaughter hid the Trabuc.

Seeing the painting, he was convinced, would aid her recovery. After all the suffering she'd gone through to keep it, losing it to accident or theft was unthinkable. Now that there was no spouse to claim possession, Clay was determined to get it to the Met for safekeeping as soon as possible.

But he had to find it first.

Clear as if it had been just the previous evening, he replayed Wil Meredith's black BMW driving out of the parking garage at ten to seven that Thursday night in July. Immediately afterward, he'd called Rachel. An hour and a half later, she'd arrived at the studio by cab.

That gave her fifteen minutes or so to feign the printer problem and get rid of Angelina with a long list of errands; later, approximately ten minutes to go downstairs, get a cab, and ride the eleven blocks uptown . . . leaving roughly an hour in between.

When Clay had started hauling out the rubble, the rather grand frame the Metropolitan had chosen for the Trabuc was still lying on the living room floor, relatively unscathed. The rear was pitted with minute holes left by dozens of tiny nails, similar to the ones St. Charles had pried out of Randall Broyce's Hals portrait. He purchased a box of the same nails at the closest art supply store, pounded them in with a small hammer, and pried every one out again. Careful removal took him nearly twenty minutes. That left approximately forty minutes, hardly time for a round trip to Brooklyn or uptown. The first place he'd searched and ruled out was Rachel's NYU office, only a short walk away.

What had she done during those extra forty minutes?

In the dark, Clay held the photo of Paul Bergère, Castelblanco's gift. His finger rolled over the silver frame's ornate embossing. What if she . . . ? He jumped up and paced the empty room. Rachel knew how her grandfather had safeguarded the Trabucs behind Cécilie and Léonore's drawings. Had she copied her grandfather's method?

Bergère, not yet aware of Udo Luscher's existence, had left the camouflaged paintings with neighbor Delamarche. But Rachel had heeded Clay's advice and kept her own friendly upstairs neighbor out of harm's way; she'd revealed nothing to Renny Corelli about her predicament. The police had already interviewed every person in the building, and Clay did it all over again, getting nowhere. Then something else she'd told him floated back, about buying stuff in a store that wasn't open over the summer weekend—evidently, stuff for the concealment of Monsieur Trabuc. Something to consider, but it was after one A.M.

By now, the hallway was familiar to him, and while he waited for the elevator, he paid no attention to the bland wallpaper or to the painted table with its dusty arrangement of dried flowers.

The elevator door opened and closed without him as he gaped with new-found interest at the Cézanne still life hanging above the flowers. It was a poor reproduction, and one of the greenish lemons was partially obscured by a stray eucalyptus branch. The dimensions, however, were perfect. Looking around to confirm he was alone, he lifted it off the wall. The frame consisted of four narrow strips of brushed aluminum, fastened together at the back with corner locks. They firmly enclosed a black cardboard backing. Only a special tool would unlock the metal strips; anything else would damage whatever was wedged in between the backing and the Cézanne. At the store where Clay bought the nails, similar frames had been on display.

After a sleepless night, he paced the sidewalk outside the art supply store until it opened the next morning. Yes, he was told, they closed on weekends during July and August. Minutes later, he was back in Rachel's building, a newly purchased Allen wrench in his pocket. It had folding parts, like a Swiss Army knife, except they weren't the usual life-saving necessities, like a corkscrew or a nail file. Fanning out its components, he found the appropriate match through trial and error. Loosening the two screw nuts that held the top section of the Cézanne's frame wasn't as easy as he thought, not until he got the hang of it. As the print and the cardboard backing finally slid out, he held his breath, but nothing more than ordinary corrugated cardboard was wedged between them. Cursing, feeling as if he'd let Rachel down all over again, Clay reversed the procedure, replaced the Cézanne, and trooped off to work.

"How's Martino doing?" asked Deputy Inspector Hickey.

"Getting better. Getting thinner, too."

"You think he'll make it, Ryder?"

The DI wasn't referring to Cello's survival. Three doctors up in Maine had lectured him nonstop about his cholesterol, his weight, and his heart—something his wife, Rhonda, had been doing for years. The discomfort of spending all his time on his stomach (not flat on his stomach, because Jello's abdomen was far from flat) was enough incentive for him to go on a diet once and for all. The day he started, he vowed to drop a total of thirty pounds by the time he returned to work, creating an office pool that eclipsed even the pennant race.

"He's really motivated, Sir," Clay replied. "I think there's a chance."

In the month that had passed since Maine, Hickey had taken a lot of shit, including a departmental reprimand—his first ever—for unilaterally sanctioning the out-of-state trip. The reproach didn't seem to bother him at all. "Saving a kidnap victim's life—if they dare equate that to a temporary medical leave, some overtime, and a couple of SUVs, I'll personally knock out all their miserable, piss-stained teeth!"

Not once had Hickey brought up the long-distance conversation he'd had with Clay immediately after Aaron's call about Luscher's suicide:

"The Mossad was waiting at the bridge? Took the Nazi and left the woman? How they hell did they even know you were in Maine?"

Clay had explained how information supplied by the Mossad helped lead to his discovery of Wil's true identity, and, eventually, to cracking the safe.

"But as for Maine—I have no idea, Sir. My last contact with them was a few days before I went to Meredith's studio. And we worked out the trip north right in your office."

Then he repeated, *"Right in your office."*

Snatches of past conversations flashed through Clay's head. Chance meetings. Too damn many coincidences. Aaron was good, but not that good.

"Inspector . . . are you thinking what I'm thinking? That someone in the office tipped off the Mossad?"

"You bet I am. Not a word, you hear? I'll look into it."

After their talk about Cello's weight, Clay lowered his voice. "Any progress?" They were standing just inside Hickey's office, and the DI, after drawing him in further, closed the door. "Ryder, how the hell do you think I got here? You think I wasn't a detective myself once?" Hickey's bushy eyebrows converged into a single storm cloud. "This wasn't the first time I've suspected a mole. But both persons I had my eye on transferred out. The upside was that in the related cases, no one was hurt, and the net-net was that we put away some serious trash very neat and tidy. I wasn't about to blow any whistles."

"And now?"

"Let's say I now know who it is . . . and, consequently, who it *was,* all along. And yes, I'm doing—I've done—something about it. And absolutely no, I'm not going to tell you or anyone. Case closed. If anybody knows my philosophy on closed cases, it's you." He moved around behind his desk and looked out the window for a while. Calmer, he asked, "How is she? The Preminger woman?"

"We're able to talk a little."

"I thought she had her teeth all glued together."

"They're rerooting."

"What is she, a plant? God, what these dentists can do today! Okay, Ryder, get out. And what we talked about—you breathe a word of it, no dentist will be able to fix your smile."

After consulting with Dr. Brickman, who thought it was a very good idea,

Clay began to bring Rachel videos of films she'd written about. She was ambulatory, and they'd stroll around the grounds if it was a pleasant day, watch the movie, then talk—a little more each time. Like a crack of light sneaking under a closed door, phrases squeezed through her clenched teeth.

Nearly two months into her stay at the rehabilitation hospital, Rachel began to talk about Wil. "Dr. Brickman made me see . . . I was in love with a person who didn't exist . . . someone who'd been prepackaged . . . sort of like a movie star's PR image . . . but tailored exclusively for me."

He nodded in agreement. "Did seeing that help?"

"To understand . . . yes. But it was very hard to accept . . . how easy it was . . . for them . . . to play me. I thought I was a lot . . . smarter than that."

"A lot of time and study went into it. It was in the works so long, they could've earned a Rachel Preminger Equivalency Degree."

"I couldn't decide who to hate more . . . Wil or Luscher."

She was silent for a while, and Clay contemplated how happy Grandpa Jonas would have been with a son or grandson like Wil. Another clone, just like his half-brother, Scott.

"Then . . . on the boat . . . on the way back to Lloyd Neck . . . when Raul raped me . . . Wil watched."

Unable to look at her, he put his head in his hands.

"Nothing else they did to me came close . . . even when Raul raped me again, in Maine . . . nothing was as terrible as my husband . . . watching . . . smiling."

For the first time since he'd pushed back her hair in her hospital room, Clay touched her. He took her hand in his, and she made no move to withdraw it.

"Luscher and Wil . . . how could I . . . hate one more than the other? They were the same person."

On a subsequent visit, she asked about Angelina. When Clay told her about the part she'd played in Luscher's scheme, she said nothing for a long while. "My mother hired her . . . sometime around 1992. . . . Write this down." She waited while Clay took out a notepad. "Maria Emilia Paz," she pronounced with great care. "Sweet lady . . . came on the D train from Brooklyn. . . . She was the cleaning lady . . . Angelina replaced . . . never gave notice . . . Maybe she never had a chance."

Clay thought of the Miami gang punk who'd done time for the hit-and-run of Rachel's mother. Maybe another poor bastard was rotting in jail for another crime hatched by Luscher. "I'll check it out. I promise."

"And what about Lulu . . . did Angelina . . . ?"

"No, the poison and the break-in were Grauberger's deal. And no need to worry about him. He's the Swiss no one will miss. But let me leave on a good note. Phil Chang."

"You spoke to him?" Rachel asked expectantly.

"He's the happiest guy in New York. Thanked you for ten solid minutes, once the realization that he could carry on in the studio had a chance to sink in. As long as he keeps on paying the rent, they can't kick him out. Doesn't know what to do for you first. I suggested taking you out to dinner as soon as you can eat real food again. A Chinese banquet—twenty courses at least."

Considering the condition of her jaw, she came close to a smile.

After savoring the moment, he asked her, "Rachel, where did you put Monsieur Trabuc?"

"You know I can't tell you that. Not if I want to stay alive."

CHAPTER
FORTY

"Where's Hickey?" Clay asked Bloomie.

"City Hall. Some big cheese organizational meeting." With her back to him, she was jamming folders into a file cabinet.

"When's he coming back to the office?"

"He's not." She glanced down at her tiny gold Benrus. "The meeting's just starting. It won't be over until six or seven."

"Good." With a hard shove, he pushed in the file drawer. Before it could even click closed, his hand was firmly under her elbow, propelling her into Hickey's office. He closed the door with his foot. "If not for you and Aaron, Luscher would've kept right on going. Nothing would've stopped him, as long as he believed he and his son were just one victim away from getting back the Trabuc. No matter how many rules you've broken, Bloomie, you're the only reason Rachel Preminger is alive today."

"I don't know what you're talking about," she huffed, trying to push past him.

"You were the key. The Mossad knew about Maine before Hickey did—right down to the name of the Sea-Tow captain and where he lived. Every time we contacted Hickey, you stayed on the line. You were better than a GPS tracking device. All my research on Luscher, from Paris to South America—you passed along to the Mossad. Maybe the only thing I've kept secret is the checking I've done on you."

"There's nothing to check on!" Flustered, she moved a shaky hand up to the bobby pins fastening her white hair.

"Humor me. I'm a detective. Knowing who without knowing why is hard for me to handle. The personnel files say Penelope Bloomberger is a naturalized U.S. citizen, born in Hungary in 1938. Arrived in America at the age of eight, part of a group of children sponsored by an orphan rescue organization."

"Since when is being an orphan a crime?" She was evading eye contact, but didn't know where to look.

"You've been with the NYPD over forty years. Single. You give blood twice a year and you rarely take a sick day. You've been to Israel five times. Every year, you donate a sizable chunk of your income to Holocaust causes. You recently handed in a thirty-day notice of your retirement."

"Don't you have anything better to do than snoop into my life?"

"You've compromised a hell of a lot to help the Mossad trap Luscher. And no one knows how many times you've helped them in the past."

"They may not print it on the front page of the *New York Times,* but the NYPD has exchanged information with the Mossad for years." Her hands had clenched into small, determined fists. "I'm just a civilian worker."

"No, you're a wonderful, brave lady. If more people were half as dedicated and principled as you—damn it, Bloomie, I'll miss you!"

He put his arms around her and gave her a hug. She was crying hard, trembling, but hardly making a sound—maybe tears weren't tolerated among war orphans. Gently, he lowered her onto one of the two visitor's chairs, then brought her the box of Kleenex Hickey kept on the ledge behind his desk. He sat next to her, held her hand, and waited.

"The Germans . . ." she finally began, "it was crazy—the way they put so much effort into rounding us up when they were losing the war on every front. We were shoved onto a train that was already full of Jews from another part of the country." Pausing, she took off her glasses and wiped them with a tissue, as if they'd been crying, too.

"The cattle car we were on had one window . . . a small hole with bars. There was no toilet, no water, no food. That hole was our only ventilation. It was our only reminder that a world with trees and light was outside, that we weren't in hell. Men tried to pull the wood away with their bare hands, to make the opening bigger. They worked until their fingers bled. One bar came loose." Still rubbing her glasses, she closed her eyes. "Oh, how I wanted to get out of that train! The dark, the smells, the crush. I prayed to God to help me get off the train.

"I was six, very small for my age. The men were waiting for the engine to slow on a curve. My father ripped me away from my mother and passed me to them. They threw me and two boys out the hole in the siding. I was the only one who survived—I fell in a ditch of water. I climbed out, and started to walk. No one wanted to keep me, but no one turned me in, either. I was given a little food, and passed along. Passed along. Passed along so many times, that the war was over before the Germans could catch me. It took me years to understand how much my father loved me."

Bloomie blew her nose and replaced her glasses. "I'm the voice of all the people on that train. I do what I can. Udo Luscher had nothing to do with me . . . and everything to do with me."

During the weeks before Bloomie's retirement, Clay continued his investigation of Grauberger's criminal sidelines. Odious as Gregor Junior was, the detective in Clay regretted that he'd lost the opportunity to put the screws on him in an interrogation room. Two invaluable lists had been stored inside that pumpkin head: the identities of his amoral private buyers, as well as the names of the world's most audacious art thieves.

Six stolen paintings on the Art Loss Register's Web site had Galleries Grauberger in their provenances, including the Rubens and the Ingres in Toshio Hashimoto's secret museum. Anxious as he was to make a move, Clay was still waiting for word of the safe passage of Aaron's operative out of Japan. Premature whistle blowing on that affair could cost a life . . . and push Madame Trabuc spiraling out of reach forever.

Lieutenant Malenkov had contacted him shortly after Maine. "You're not the only one who wanted a nice cozy chat with little Gregor. Ever since we got back the Hals, Broyce keeps thinking his fucking El Greco is right around the corner."

"Tell him he has as much a chance of that showing up as his wife. Make that his wife wearing her diamond necklace."

"I don't know, Ryder. I'm still not one hundred percent that Grauberger ran Dial-a-Picasso on his own. Not with all the other dirty dealers he could've been partners with. You know, like a cartel. Anything turn up on that Rasenstein character?"

"A couple of paintings with the Rasenstein name in their provenance are listed as stolen, but I still can't find a real connection. If the slimy bastard loses his lawsuit in France, what little credibility he has left slides right down the tubes. If he was a partner, he's pretty much out of the game."

"What about The Most Powerful Woman in the Art World?"

"Lieu, do you know how long Esterbrook-Grennell has been in business?"

"Maybe two hundred years?"

"A lot more. But it's still less than the jail time old Deirdre Sands is looking at. I heard that when the Feds walked into her office, she literally threw stuff at them. Did the whole cursing, screaming, foaming-at-the-mouth routine. Totally outraged that collusion and price fixing are actually classified as real life crimes."

"She'll never serve a day, you know that."

"Sure," Clay sighed. "As soon as she realized you can't throw things at people with subpoenas, she offered to testify against anyone they named in the big three auction houses, living or dead."

Malenkov chuckled. "Rasenstein's not the only one who's run out of customers. Who'll want to do business with little Miss I've-Got-a-Secret after she takes the stand?"

Cello returned to Police Plaza the morning of Bloomie's last day on the job. He weighed in thirty-one pounds lighter. To mark his return, Sparks and his son scanned Martino's face onto the body of the woman crawling toward the Olson house in *Christina's World*. "Welcome Back, Half-Ass!" was printed across the bottom.

Later that day, Hickey announced that Detectives Sparks, Merriweather, and Martino had been upped from threes to twos. Clay went from Detective third to first. Several of the Major Case detectives stepped forward and congratulated him. Those who wouldn't shake his hand—well, that was their problem, not Clay's. Hickey also passed along the news that Marcus Brewster had moved up a grade to first, and that his partner, Sal Vernier, had received a commendation.

At five, there was a big cake and champagne for Bloomie. After the toasts, she received a plaque from the Department. Hickey presented her with a silver bowl engraved with the names of all the men and women she'd worked with over the years, so many names that the engraving cost a lot more than the bowl, but everybody was happy to kick in. She burst into tears, holding nothing back.

A few days later, Hickey tapped Clay to work with the District Attorney's office on a new investigation: a number of art-loving Manhattan CEOs were suspected of bilking the city out of huge amounts of sales tax every year. After paying millions for paintings, they shipped them to another state, had the truck do a quick U-turn, and then drove back to a Fifth or Park Avenue address to make the real delivery. Although the dealers brokering the sales weren't required to collect tax if the merchandise was shipped out of state, collusion wasn't being ruled out.

"I suggested you as the best man for the job," said Hickey. In the same breath, he added, "And don't forget you're mine the minute that art crap gets flushed."

Returning to his desk, Clay dialed his contact at the DA's office, and they arranged to meet later in the day. The second he put the phone down, it rang. His brother Scott's wife was the caller.

"I'm here at your grandfather's house," she said, "getting ready for the closing."

"What closing?"

"Actually, there are two—his house and ours. I've made up a small carton of Betsy's stuff. There wasn't very much—photos of you and your mother, some clothes, books, things that might have sentimental value. I thought you'd like to have them. I didn't know if I should send the box to your apartment or your office, and I don't have either address. Grandpa Jonas locked the door to her room after she died—that's why I'm just getting to them now."

"You're *both* moving? First I've heard of it."

"You haven't heard about the business?" How put upon she sounded. Kicking herself for having taken the trouble to call when she should've just chucked out all his junk and been done with it. "It was in the *Wall Street Journal*," she sniffed.

"Sorry, but I still have no idea what you're talking about."

"Last summer, Scott and the rest of the board of directors suggested . . . well, your grandfather retired."

"Retired? No way. They would've had to carry him out."

Her silence was a confirmation of just that. Scott had eaten the old man whole. Scott, the new King of the Kooler. Not so amazing, considering how well he'd been taught.

"And after his alleged retirement, then what? Did they put my grandfather under house arrest?"

"That's not funny, Clay. But actually, he's been in an assisted living facility for several months. He had a stroke shortly after Scott sold the company."

"Scott sold the company," he echoed. *Yeah, that would have given him a stroke.* "That happened fast."

"Yes. Excuse me." She told someone, "That goes with the thrift shop things." Returning to Clay, she continued, "We're moving to Florida. My folks live there."

Honey, even in Florida, you'll never get away from the cold—you're married to it. "The old man—how bad was the stroke?"

"Not too bad. He can walk again. Theoretically, he can talk again, too, but his words are slurred. All he does is rant and curse, anyway. All the doctors agreed he couldn't be on his own, so we decided to sell the house before we left the area for good." The last phrase was succinct, final, and tinged with relief.

As insistent as a car alarm, *Does Scotty know?* kept ringing in Clay's head. For years, he'd fought the temptation to tell Scott who'd fathered him. Turn his little brother against Jonas before Jonas turned the kid into a carbon copy of himself. But even as a child, Clay had intuited that the one act that could have empowered him against his grandfather would have been a betrayal of his mother.

Does Scotty know? He considered Scott's actions of the last several months. Loathing definitely trumped love. Blurting out the truth could hardly make a difference anymore. Jonas Ryder was locked away, just as he'd locked away Clay's mom. He was the one standing between the chair and the fireplace now, powerless, without any means of escape. *Not even sleep,* Clay hoped, *not even sleep.* And that was the end of it. Now he was part of . . . yes, Clay's own private closed case. So closed, it would've made Hickey proud.

"Why do I think there's a reason I'm just hearing about this now?" he finally asked. "Was your husband afraid I'd try to stake a claim during negotiations? Listen, even if I read the *Journal* front to back every day, he could've rested easy. My grandfather took every legal precaution possible to cut me out. But the truth is, I never wanted a penny that had passed through his fingers."

She mumbled something, a small protest.

Cutting her off, he said, "Thanks. I appreciate your call. . . . Listen, is there an old blue suitcase in my mother's room? Maybe under the bed?"

After a moment, she replied that it was there.

"My mom's things . . . don't use a carton . . . send them in that suitcase."

One afternoon in late October, Desmond, who'd replaced Bloomie, called out, "Detective Ryder, your lunch beat you back. It's been on your desk for ten minutes."

"I didn't order lunch." Clay started to peel off his wet raincoat.

"If you don't want it," Desmond offered, "I'll eat it. Smells so good, it's driving me crazy."

A bag from Second Avenue Deli was in the middle of Clay's desk. "Who brought it?" Clay asked.

"Big hairy guy in shorts. Twenty, twenty-one, thick glasses. If Yeshiva University has a basketball team, he's their center. Didn't hang around for a tip."

At first, Clay mistook the two papers folded inside for napkins. When he smoothed one out, he saw it was a fax with the origination info scissored off. It was a copy of a Japanese newspaper's lead article, featuring a photo of a Degas ballerina. The second sheet was a translation of the article, *Shameful Secret Museum of Stolen Art*, dated that same day. A subhead expanded the story: *Horde of Missing Paintings Recovered from Hashimoto Residence.*

Clay unwrapped the pastrami sandwich, took a bite of the sour pickle, and slathered mustard over the seeded rye. Like a man who wants for nothing, he tilted his chair as far back as it could go and planted his heels on his desk. He took a big bite of the best pastrami in New York City, popped open the can of Coke that had thoughtfully been included, and lifted it high. Silently, he toasted Aaron, Eli, and Bloomie. The sandwich was as delicious as the story.

That evening, Clay visited Rachel. A week before, her jaw and her teeth had been deemed ready for the first step beyond nutritional supplements sucked through a straw. Already up to pasta and steamed vegetables, her skin glowed from the change in her diet.

"I told Dr. Brickman I'm ready to go home next week," she said. "She thinks it's a good idea."

"Home. That's great. It's clean as a whistle . . . but it's pretty empty."

"That's exactly what I need, to start off fresh . . . in my parents' home. What you did was so kind—I can't wait to see it!"

"There's no place to sleep."

"I know. I have an invitation to sleep on Renny's sofa until I get a bed delivered and all. I'll be fine." She raised her eyebrows. "No video tonight?"

"No, I brought something I think you'll find more interesting."

He handed her the fax. She skimmed it quickly; near the end, she looked up and smiled at him, her eyes blinking away tears. "Madame Trabuc! Everyone thought she was lost forever! Clay, I want to shout, 'Madame Trabuc *lives*!' "

"Then go ahead. Loud as you want."

"Okay." She took a deep breath, and yelled out, "Madame Trabuc *lives*!" After a burst of laughter, she said softly, "You rescued her, too. You do a lot more rescuing than you give yourself credit for." She bent forward, and her lips brushed over his cheek. "It's wonderful, wonderful!" Straightening, she said through a smile, "But you know, of course, that I don't want her."

"What?"

"I mean, not at home. I want her in a museum. She belongs in the Met. On permanent loan. Right alongside Monsieur."

"Ah. That's a problem. You won't tell me where he is."

He told her about his unsuccessful attempts to find the Trabuc. "I even went out into your hallway and pried apart the Cézanne print near the elevator."

"Pried it apart?"

"Not literally. I had to buy a special tool."

"Sometimes even the best detective can overlook the most obvious clue. Try again. And bring your Allen wrench."

That evening, he stopped the elevator on every floor. Every one had the same wallpaper and carpet, the same painted table bearing dried flowers. The flowers differed; so did the framed reproduction just above them. Most were by Impressionists or their successors, stretching into the twentieth century. He hesitated when he came to the Chagall on the sixth floor, but the Van Gogh *Sunflowers* a few stories up had to be what Rachel meant as "the most obvious clue."

Almost tearing the picture hook off the wall, he grabbed it, ready to run for the fire doors. But his fingers closed over the same thick black cardboard backing used on all the other prints. A thick layer of dust along the top dispersed, and Clay couldn't suppress a sneeze. He couldn't get it back on the wall fast enough.

Only one floor remained before Renny's penthouse. When the elevator opened, and he saw the reproduction, Clay was transfixed. The doors began to close automatically, and he lunged forward, elbowing them apart as he prepared to pounce on the lady in the sarong. "Brilliant, Rachel, brilliant!" he whispered over and over, as he lifted Gauguin's portrait of his Tahitian mistress from the wall. Sure enough, the black backing wasn't half as thick. He raced down the fire stairs two at a time.

Van Gogh's attempt at friendship with Gauguin, his invitation to join him in Arles and begin an atelier, had turned into a disaster: the two artists quarreled violently. Finally, Vincent—spurned, bereft, gripped by depression—threatened Gauguin with an open razor. Later, he turned it on himself, mutilating his ear. It was that sad, doomed relationship which brought him to Saint-Rémy . . . and to the head attendant at the asylum, Monsieur Trabuc.

Back in Rachel's apartment, Clay unlocked the frame's corners with unsteady fingers. No cardboard was wedged beneath the thin backing. Instead, there was a canvas, with a single marking: *Léonore*. Holding his breath, he turned it over.

Monsieur Trabuc, his suspicious gaze unrelenting as ever, glared up at him. "Those Bergères! Like grandfather, like granddaughter," he whispered. "Stuffed you away again, didn't they?"

"Don't you want to take your coat off?" asked Rachel. "I know you said you were only stopping by for a minute to see the new living room furniture, but it's so cold, how about a cup of coffee?" She jumped back. "What the hell was that?"

"What?" He looked really concerned, as if she were hallucinating.

"Your coat! It just moved!"

He looked down. "My coat? Moved? What were you watching tonight, *Alien*?" Unmistakably, there was movement in his chest area. He opened the top button of his coat. A long-eared, silver gray head popped out. Cornflower blue eyes blinked at Rachel. "Now how the hell did that get in my coat?"

Rachel put out her hands. "For me?" She didn't wait for an answer. She took the puppy and hugged it against her chest. Clay backed out toward the door. "Aren't you going to stay?" she called after him.

"Maybe someday," he answered, as he let himself out.

EPILOGUE

Oliver Plumworth, hearing from his friend that *Madame Trabuc* was not the only painting sent to Rachel Preminger from Japan, suggested floating the possibility that she might consider the sale of the forgery of *Monsieur Trabuc* as such. Immediately, the three major auction houses clawed and clamored for the right to sell the faux *Trabuc*—and all vowed not to charge Dr. Preminger a penny in commissions. To everyone's astonishment, the phony *Trabuc* was hammered down in a frenzy of bids at $505,000—the highest price ever paid at auction for a known forgery. At Dr. Preminger's behest, the proceeds, in addition to those from the sale of the house and boats in Cushing, Maine, were divided among the survivors of Udo Luscher's victims in his failed quest to gain legitimate ownership of *Portrait of Monsieur Trabuc*.

ABOUT THE AUTHORS

Al and Jean Zerries, husband and wife, coauthor as A. J. Zerries. They previously worked together as a creative team at several New York advertising agencies. They now live on Long Island.